DECEPTION
BAY

N.N. PARKER

Published by BookPublishingWorld in 2023

Cover design by Youness Elh

ISBN: 978-1-915351-23-4

Published by
BookPublishingWorld
An imprint of
www.dolmanscott.com

For Jemma, Emilio and Audrey

CONTENTS

PROLOGUE

Lacey wore new gloves the day her mother was hung. They were supposed to be a birthday present, but her birthday had fallen between the days her mother was charged and executed and had as such been forgotten. So the morning of the hanging, after finding them, her father had ordered her to put them on. They fit very well. Being the younger sister, and wearing only hand me downs, they were the newest thing Lacey had ever worn. She felt an almost repulsive rush of pleasure at feeling how soft they were against her small fingers.

In lieu of gallows, (the town of Lower Lynch being so small executions were all but unheard of) the councilmen had ordered the hanging take place from the Old Oak Tree at the bottom of Main Street. A cart was brought down to carry the body to Deception Bay where it would then be taken by boat to The Island. As she had been sentenced for witchcraft Alice Emerson had forfeited her right to be buried on the mainland.

Being only seven Lacey understood little of this. She walked down to the Old Oak Tree between her sister Bella and her father, with her hands clasped in front of her, staring down at them as though they were not a part of her body. Her scalp ached from her hair being plaited too tight, but still a few black and white strands managed to escape and fly across her face in rebellion. Bella's in comparison stuck obediently to her head like a cap.

A crowd had already gathered, and when her mother was bought forward with her hands tied they began to boo. Lacey glanced around at her neighbours' faces full of hate. Though it was August the weather had turned unseasonably cold, the chill intensified by a wind coming in from the coast. The noose wriggled and whipped, finally having to be held steady by one of the villagers while the Mayor read Alice her last rites.

Lacey began to cry when the hood was placed over her mother's head, her little body vibrating with fear. Her father's arms wrapped around her, his mouth against the side of her head, shushing her. She felt his tears wet against her face, mixing with her own. Bella silently squeezed her hand in comfort. Alice called out her daughters' names, her hooded head twisting wildly, desperately trying to find them. She attempted to run, but a swift jerk of the rope around her wrists brought her to her knees.

Still, her cries didn't stop. She continued calling to Lacey and Bella as the men lifted her to her feet and carried her towards the noose, her boots dragging on the grass. Lacey saw how the Mayor in his wide brimmed black hat nodded to the executioner and the rope was looped around the head. Then, suddenly, the other end was pulled, and her mother was no longer calling her name. Her boots kicked in the air as though she were levitating. Lacey stopped sobbing. The angry crowd grew quiet. Even the wind died down, so that the sound of her skirts could be heard rustling as her legs danced violently, the rope quivering above her.

After a few endless minutes the rope straightened and Alice's body ceased to move. Her toes pointed to the ground. The branch above her creaking slightly, the noise resounding through the crowd. She was cut down and laid in the back of the cart, like a sack of flour. Lacey stared in mute horror as the councilmen, led by the Mayor, began to push her in the direction of The Island. Her mother's skirt hanging off the edge, trailing in the dirt. Before long they disappeared into the wood line. Lacey looked down and saw a little red dot seeping into her new gloves. A few more dropped and landed on her palm. Her nose was bleeding. She stared in silence as the three small spots spread and swelled like blossoming flowers.

CHAPTER ONE

When Lacey first saw the figure she thought it was a Forest Beast. She had lost track of the hour. It was not often that she would still be out at this time, with darkness falling, and the woods still between herself and home. She had stayed too long staring out across the water. Deception Bay was the only point on the mainland where you could see The Island. The mist would break for a moment and then it would reveal itself.

It sat far out, past where the waves rose and fell, past even where they flattened to soft muted glass. It would appear all at once, then dissolve into cloud, only to reappear some time later. Each time shifting a little to the left, or to the right, as though it were moving, floating just above the surface. There might have been birds on it, but from the shore they could neither be seen, nor heard. And in the almost constant fog, that clung and wrapped over the land and sea, it was unclear whether grasses grew, or whether it was all just rock. Only the shape, when the fog parted, was visible. Jagged and uneven, with three sharp peaks. Like a crown, beaten into cracked submission by years of unrelenting waves.

She had sat all afternoon, with her skirts pulled up above her knees, so as not to risk the chance of her hem touching the water. Now more girls were disappearing, she knew that soon she would not be allowed to walk alone in the woods, or along the coast. She moved up towards the sand dunes, chased in by the tide. She felt a wariness of the water here. Fearful of its malevolent, predatory ascent up the shore. Further down the coastline she would not be so afraid. Indeed, were it not such a grey day, where clouds hung above close enough to touch, people might be swimming. Splashing and playing in the tide, but not at Deception Bay. Even on the sunny days, that in truth did not come often, there would still then be no swimmers at this bay.

She had seen, not from the sun for that was too well hidden to accurately tell the hour, but from the progress of the tide, that it was time to go home. She would need a while, before night fell, to wash this morning's pans so that they would be ready before the bakery opened tomorrow. The dusk had caught her by surprise, so it was with a quick, regretful step that she had jumped up from her spot on the beach, the pebbles beneath her revealing the indent left behind from where she sat. She picked up her book, slipping it into her pocket. Then tying her cap tight and pulling her shawl around her, she made her way up the loose shingle to the wood line.

Then she had seen it. It heaved and dragged its round backed shape towards the sea, slouching a little to one side and stopping every few steps to look out at the water, and then back towards the woods. She felt an instinctual jolt of fear, her body reacting before her mind even had time to process it. An uncontrollable shiver of dread ran through her body. She was sure it couldn't see her, you need only take a few steps into the forest, for the dense darkness to swallow you. Here amongst the wet pines, and creeping ferns, she was safe.

She had only happened to look back to take one more glance at The Island, when the movement had caught her eye, making her freeze on the spot. She never saw anyone on this bay, especially not at this time of day, as the sun, hidden by the clouds, had begun to slowly slip below the horizon. When the dimming grey light blurred the edges of things, and shadows began to crawl out from behind them.

She stood, as still and stiff as the trees around her, staring down at the shape in the dim light. It was only a shade darker than the grey rock behind it, walking in the shadow of a wall of slate, that cleaved into the far side of the bay. Lacey squinted, trying to see a little clearer. *There are no such thing as Forest Beasts* she thought to herself, and as though in response, the figure stopped and turned towards where she stood. It's face was hidden in shadow beneath a dark hood. Lacey took a small, silent step backwards. Drawing back behind a low branch, the leaves in front of her face, fluttering slightly as she exhaled.

The Beast then seemed to detach part of its own self and lay it on the ground. It stood stretching its back. It was a man, she could just make out his arms and legs beneath a thick cloak, he had been carrying something atop his back. Something heavy, that had distorted his shape and gait. There came no wave of relief in finding the figure to be of her own kind; she stood still tense, still watchful. It was something in the furtive look of him, the way his hooded head flicked back and forth, something sly and intensely private about his movements, that made her heart beat unevenly in her chest. She lifted a foot and gently took another step back. The noise of the branch snapping beneath her boot sounded deafening in the silence. The dark figure's face snapped in her direction. Not knowing whether she had been seen or not, acting purely on instinct, Lacey turned and ran.

The wood was dark. The trees hung in close, conspiratorial lines, blocking out what little light there was. It was close on dusk, but were it midday, with clouds like this overhead, and fog like this underfoot, no light would have penetrated the forest. Moss climbed almost halfway up the tree trunks. A rich, dark green velvet, soaked in years of rain. Between them weaved Lacey, one hand clasping her shawl to her chest, the other holding her skirt high. The toe of her boot glanced off a root, and she almost stumbled, but just managed to stay upright. She was unable to avoid such dangers in the inescapable mist, that rose in curls above her ankles. She did not look back once, she could not tell if the sound of footsteps were hers alone, or another's accompanying her, only a few steps behind. But though she wanted to, she knew better than to look back, even she who spent many hours in this wood, knew not to lose sight of the path in front of you. It would take only a few steps in the wrong direction for you to find yourself lost in a sea of trees.

With a feeling of an acute, unfastening relief, she came through the other side of the forest. She exhaled in a whistle, tilting her head back, catching her breath. The sky opened above her, wide and calm, with the night just behind the clouds. It took only a few deep breaths beneath it for her panic to fall away. It seemed suddenly silly now, running like that. She exhaled a short laugh and inwardly chastised herself for thinking she had seen a Forest Beast. She was no longer a child; she should stop thinking like one. It had been surely a fisherman, or some other man from the village.

The forest had fallen away in an abrupt, unified line, and below she could see the field, where a few cows grazed lazily. Beyond it, in the dimming light, the sharp edges of the village rooftops were just visible against the sky. The whole scene painted a watercolour blue, with small points of firefly yellow, where her neighbours had already lit their fires, and the light shone through their windows. At the bottom of them, down by the line of the field, sat the bakery where she lived.

Lacey walked unseeing past the bushes studded with berries, were she not late, she would not have been able to resist stopping to pick a few. When she was young every child in the town walked through the streets with purple stained lips and fingertips. The girls, with their skirts pulled wide like fishing nets full of them, and the boys with bulging pockets, where deep red stains appeared, revealing their bounty. But nowadays the children were too afraid to venture out of the village.

Lacey's town of Lower Lynch lay between the edge of the Hooked Forest to the South and the Lakelands to the North. It was established by the First Settlers who came to these shores three hundred years before. All who lived there now were the descendants of those that built it. The closest village, Upper Lynch, was two days' walk, half a day if a boat was chartered across the first, and widest, of the lakes. But almost no villagers had the money to do that. And besides, there not so many boats left on the lake since the fish had all but disappeared. During the winter months the village was totally isolated. It sat frozen in time, waiting, surviving, until the ice thawed and the thin line to the rest of the world was reopened.

From halfway down the field she could see Bella taking down the linen in their back yard. A few blue white sheets still swaying on the line. She nodded to Lacey, her mouth half full of pegs, waiting for her to climb the fence before speaking to her.

'I've finished your washing up,' Bella said, handing Lacey the edge of a sheet so that she could help fold it.

'Oh, thank you Bella,' Lacey sighed in relief. 'I thought I'd have to do it in the dark.'

'I don't need thanks. I need help. I have enough to do as it is, Lacey without adding your chores to my list. It might be nice for you walking around daydreaming, but for the rest of us there is work to be done.'

'I'm sorry.' Lacey glanced nervously towards the house, 'is Father home yet?'

'No, has the bell rung?' Said Bella, stretching her neck to see the steeple at the end of the street, 'I don't think it has, he may still be at Evensong.'

Each holding the end of the sheet they pulled it taut, then came together to fold it, Bella looking into her younger sister's face as she took her ends. 'What's wrong?'

'Nothing.'

'I can tell there is something wrong, you have that little line between your brows. You get it when you are worried.' Bella reached up towards Lacey's face, pointing at her brow. Lacey patted her hand away.

'I have no line.' She said, turning to walk into the house, with her back to her sister, quickly raising her fingers to her forehead to check. Bella walked in behind her, carrying the basket of folded sheets. As they opened the door to go inside the church bell began to ring, the notes rolling in like waves across the mist.

'How have you spent the afternoon?'

'I went for a walk' Said Lacey, removing her cloth cap, careful to avoid her sister's scornful glances at the rebellious curl of her hair. Only with the salty sea air was it inclined to coil in such a way.

'Not on the coast.' Bella said sharply, neither a question nor a statement.

'No,' responded Lacey quickly, making sure not to catch her eye.

'Not on Deception Bay.'

'No,' lied Lacey.

'I should hope not. You know how dangerous it is now. No more walking through the woods alone either. Besides, Father's legs will not last the year, then all the work will fall to us. How will you be able to run the bakery from the woods?'

'I'm here now.' Lacey responded shortly. 'Is that beef?' She nodded in surprise towards a black pot atop the fire. Bella, placing the basket down, crossed the room to stir it, the warm, salty smell of meat filled the little house.

'No. Turnips.'

'Again?'

'Mr Yates was kind enough to give me some bones for the stock. It makes all the difference.'

'It smells nice' said Lacey, masking her disappointment at the prospect of another turnip dinner. She climbed up the wooden stairs to her attic bedroom, stooping below the low ceiling. With both hands she moved the pile of books that had accumulated on her bed to the floor, placing the one in her coat pocket on top and making a mental note to return them to Professor Arnott before the week's end. She sat in their place, leaning down to pick at the laces on her boots, the bed frame creaking beneath her. The two sisters had slept in the same little wooden bed when they were children. It had grown smaller and more cramped as each year passed. In the summer months, the girls pushing and kicking, a mess of arms and legs, desperate for an inch of space. In the winter, curling close, folding around one another like animals, searching for any morsel of warmth beneath the blanket. Before their mother was killed, Lacey could remember her laying extra grain sacks over the two of them in an attempt to keep out the cold. Finally, a few years earlier, Bella had moved to her own room downstairs.

'Do not leave your boots there,' Bella called up to her somehow omniscient in the small house. Lacey swung her legs off the bed, and picking the boots up, carried them back downstairs and through to their rightful place by the front door. The street outside the windows was almost black now, her mind drifted back to the figure on the beach. The way his head moved, as though he were afraid to be seen.

'Lacey,' said Bella, 'get your head out of the clouds. I'm talking to you!"

'Sorry.' Said Lacey.

'I asked do you know what thread Mrs Hall uses?' Said Bella, pulling the plates down from the cupboard and placing them on the little table. 'Does she use a black or brown? I'm in need of some brown thread for the Vicar's hem.'

'How would I know?' Answered Lacey.

'She lives in the house next to Mateo's.' Said Bella, picking a hair pin from the edge of her apron, then slotting it in place at the side of her neat, low, bun. Gently touching it, with the tips of her fingers, making sure of no rogue locks.

'So?' Asked Lacey, turning from the window.

'Do not play coy Lacey, you are there almost daily. You two are inseparable.'

'No we're not,' she responded indignantly, 'and even if we were, why would I have noticed what colour thread his neighbours use? Do you know the thread our neighbours use?'

'Mrs Andrews uses black, and Mr Bradford uses a light blue, a colour far too bright for a man of his age. Oh look, there's that little line again.' Said Bella pointing at Lacey's brow. Lacey exhaled loudly and stalked back up the creaking stairs.

After an hour their father still had not returned. The sky outside was so dark all the windows showed the girls was their own reflection. Lacey sat slumped at the kitchen table, her chin in her hands. She spoke in a low whine. 'Bella, I will starve if we don't eat soon.'

Bella, who had been working on her sewing, stood and looked again at the window. Feeling her own stomach growl painfully, she said 'it is indeed rather late for him to not yet be home. I hope there is no upset in the village. Besides I worry about him walking in this darkness, with his legs as they are.'

'He's probably sitting with Mr Tibbs at the Inn, discussing whatever it is men discuss.'

'Themselves mainly,' said Bella leaning against the sill, peering down the street. 'But no, he isn't there; I bade Mr Tibbs good evening as I was taking the washing down. He was heading home with a rabbit under his arm for supper.'

'Lucky Mr Tibbs.' Muttered Lacey.

Bella didn't respond, only chewed on her lower lip, considering what action might least displease their father. Finally she clapped her hands together and said, 'we will take a quick walk through the village to see if we cannot find father ourselves. Only down Main Street.' Seeing Lacey's eyebrows rise, she added, 'we'll be fine.'

Bella took the time to lace each of her boots and fix her cap in place, even checking in the small mirror that she was happy with her appearance. Lacey, wearing only her indoor slippers and pulling her shawl over her head, did not even bother to wear a cap. She didn't always cover her head when leaving the house. But as she was getting into her later teens, she felt the pressure to do it more often now. Besides she was more likely to draw attention than the other village girls. From birth her hair had a distinct feature, that drew the villager's eyes, and though the years had long since passed where it caused any notable interest, she was still immediately recognised by it. One half of her hair, the left, was a deep black, as dark as a starless night, falling in loose tangles down to the base of her back. The other, though just as long and just as wavy, was white as a pearl. The two colours split down the centre at her parting.

The sisters walked close to the houses along the street, their shoulders high and heads stooped to protect themselves from the cold. They linked arms and trod quickly. Occasionally glancing back when their footsteps on the cobblestones echoed throughout Main Street, bouncing off the dark windows.

The village changed at night. The setting of the sun brought a strange sense of dread to the townsfolk, especially the women. The forest swelled with darkness and pushed at the edges of the town. The shadow of the trees as the sun sunk behind them, spread across every rooftop in the village. Even the air changed. A cold air, creeping down from the coast settled in around the houses. At night you could see how hard the land was. Only this small patch, cut out from the woods, bordered with a fence, could sustain human life. Just beyond, was as dark and unknowable as death.

Each house a uniform, neat square of panelled wood with a low thatched roof and stone chimney. One or two, like Lacey's, had a shop front, with a wooden board above, bearing its name. A few chimneys emitted smoke this evening, and if Lacey looked down the street she could see, between the gaps in their shutters, thin slivers of light coming from the fireplaces inside. As they followed the street round, the noise from inside the Golden Tavern could be heard, and before they turned the corner to it, they could see shadows dancing along the ground outside. Elongated, distorted figures flickering in the candlelight, jugs of mead in hand, heads tipped back in talk or song. The girls were a short way off when the door swung open, the sound of men's voices and the chinking of glass suddenly clear. A huddled figure stumbled out. He didn't appear to notice them and fumbling with the fastenings on his britches, took a few swaying steps round the side of the inn before leaning against the wall and relieving himself.

The two girls walked past, Bella tutting beneath her breath, Lacey stifling a laugh.

'What shameful behaviour,' whispered Bella, 'and so close to the church as well!' Lacey stopped smiling at that, and turned her head slightly to glance up at the church to their left. It sat quiet and neat in its manicured white wood. A loose ribbon of mist wrapping around the base, the steeple jutting into the sky above. The picket fence, newly painted in stark, unforgiving white, bordered the decaying tombstones. Her eyes fell on the piercing points of wood, like a row of shining teeth, and it made the hair on the back of her neck stand on end.

Beside the church sat the town hall. Wide and high, with broad stone steps leading to pillared doors, it stood far taller than any other building in the village. It looked to Lacey as though it was carved out of one single stone. Heavy and immovable, seeming to dwell in the darkness of its own shadow. Apparently it had taken a year to build, with village men working day and night to finish, the Mayor himself laying the last stone.

A tall, thin figure stood at the top of the steps, his face in shadow. One hand held the end of a long pipe, delicately cradling the bowl with the tips of his fingers, the other wiping something from his eyes. He looked out in the opposite direction to the girls and released a long, low sigh, his breath clouding around him in misty puffs, mingling with the smoke. The buckle on his hat shining, so bright in the darkness, Lacey knew immediately who it was; no man in town polished the buckles on his hat and shoes so fastidiously. When they got closer she could see that he was not alone. He was talking to someone, standing in the shadows. They spoke in hushed whispers. Lacey overheard him say, as if repeating to make sure he had understood. 'A stranger?'

Upon hearing their approach, the mayor turned to them quickly, and in that unguarded moment, a strange look flashed across his face. It was something deeper than surprise, something more fearful. But as quickly as it appeared, it was gone, and replaced with a thin, courteous smile. The other figure had vanished back into the shadows. The mayor cleared his throat and tapped the ash from his pipe, the embers fading to black before they hit the ground. He descended the steps towards them, his heeled shoes clicking lightly as he went. He was as tall as he was thin, and his legs had the look of a spider's. His black cloak dragged on the stone behind him.

'Ladies, good evening.' He said, touching the brim of his hat with a gloved finger.

'Good evening Mr Mayor' replied Bella, bending slightly in a bow.

'What are you doing out after dark?'

'We did not want to but...' Bella was interrupted as a peal of laughter came from the Golden Tavern. Each one of them turning their heads to look.

Mayor Abner made a sort of clicking sound as he watched the door of the Inn swing closed. He had a narrow, sharp jaw, beneath which his neck was wrinkled and lined. When Lacey and Mateo were alone he would make her laugh by saying the Mayor's neck looked like the gills of a mushroom. The loose skin tucked neatly into the collar of his coat. 'It is a sadness to me that the laughter we hear is not just that of the men. I understand some of the village women now pass their evenings in the tavern,' he shook his head slowly, and sorrowfully. 'But not you ladies I see.'

'No,' answered Bella, 'we were only out to find-'

'You are missing a father I believe.' He interrupted, looking down and picking an invisible bit of dirt from his cape, with his gloved fingers. Lacey had never once seen him without his hands wrapped tightly within black leather.

'Yes.' Said Bella. 'He is yet to return home from Evensong.'

Mayor Abner nodded, 'he is inside,' tipping his head towards the hall behind him. The blank, grey facade betrayed no sign of there being anyone within. 'He is meeting with the council on...' He paused for a moment, his tongue suspended in his mouth, picking the correct word. Lacey could see, under the shadow of his hat, his wet eyes were lined with thin, red veins, and the skin beneath was coloured a sickly, pale primrose purple. 'On a delicate matter.'

The air seemed to tighten around them. Bella's hand rose to the collar of her coat, beneath which hung her crucifix. 'All is well I hope?'

The Mayor brought the handkerchief once again to his eyes, which suffered from persistent moisture. 'I think it would be best if you were to return home, it is not advisable for young ladies to be out alone after dark. I will be sure to tell your father you called for him.'

Lacey and Bella exchanged a glance, Lacey spoke, for the first time, 'has it happened again?'

Then, as though only just realising Lacey's presence, the Mayor turned to her, his manner changing, his lips pulling back in a yellow toothed smile. Ignoring her question, he said, 'my son Sebastian speaks very highly of you young Lacey.'

Lacey, not knowing how to respond, answered only 'does he?'

Bella being older, and better practiced in conversation, responded quickly 'and her of him Mayor.'

'He mentioned to me only this morning that you are growing to be a fine young lady.'

'Did he?' Said Lacey shortly.

'And he quite the gentleman Mayor.' Smiled Bella.

In order to do anything other than engage further in the conversation Lacey took her handkerchief from her coat and wiped it across her nose. It slipped between her fingers as she returned it to her pocket and fell to the floor. But before it had reached it, the mayor, with the speed of a snake, whipped his hand out and caught it. The white lace even whiter against his black gloves. He held it a moment, his leather clad fingertips tracing over her embroidered initials. *L.E.*

'Lacey Emerson,' he said slowly, in whisper, as though speaking only to himself. Then louder, addressing her he said, 'it would please me greatly if you were to spend a little time together. You and Sebastian.'

The small frown line appeared again on Lacey's brow as she returned the Mayor's gaze. She did not respond, only held her hand out to receive her handkerchief. Bella broke the silence, linking her arm to her sister's. 'A fine idea. I'm sure she would like that very much. Now we will leave you to your important work Mayor. Good evening.' She bowed her head, before turning and walking away. The Mayor nodded slowly, the rim of his hat moving down to eclipse his face.

The girls walked home in silence, their heads to the ground as they passed the dark doorways. After bidding them goodnight and turning to leave, the Mayor had waited a few seconds before calling after them. 'Your father may be a while still, make sure to lock your door upon returning home.' The word *lock* pronounced in such a way that the *k* seemed to echo through the street. Lacey glanced behind her to see his narrow back as he made his way up the steps, the mist curling around his feet, and she thought again of that flicker of fear on his face when he had first seen them.

Once they were home neither girl had an appetite for supper, and they left the stew in the pot, to eat for breakfast the next day. While they waited Bella sat in silence, by the fire, her sewing on her knee, dismissing Lacey's questions of why the council might be meeting. Lacey eventually giving up with a huff and resumed her position at the table.

After a time, Bella laid down her mending and walked towards the backroom, leaning on the door frame, her arm's crossed. 'Did you hear what the Mayor said of his son? And how he talks of you?'

'Yes Bella, I was standing right beside him as it was said.'

'It's clear he has designs on you. I wouldn't be surprised if they waited very little time before a proposal.'

'A proposal?' Exclaimed Lacey raising her head, 'it's too soon.'

'Don't pull that face. You are seventeen Lacey; you are the perfect age. Besides I cannot think of a more eligible bachelor in the village with whom to take the blood vow.'

Lacey exhaled angrily.

'Once a proposal is made there can be no more running around in the woods with Mateo. No more running anywhere with Mateo.'

Lacey sat up abruptly, as scowl across her face. 'If you like the idea of a proposal so much why don't you marry him?'

'If I looked like you I would,' Bella replied coolly. That quieted Lacey. Bella, being too proud to let her see her face, turned and busied herself with folding.

The familiar sound of their father's dragging footsteps could be heard on the street outside, as he reached the front door. His slow, pained gait, more pronounced after a long day, though nowadays even in the morning he walked as though he was ready for bed. Bella, abandoning their conversation, crossed to unbolt the lock. He stepped through, wiping his feet on the mat, handing his hat to her, but shaking his head when she held out her hand for his coat.

'What was your business at the hall Father?' Lacey asked, jumping up, ignoring Bella's disparaging look. 'Is all well? We saw the Mayor, he told us to bolt the door.'

'I saw.' He answered gruffly.

Their father took a seat at the table, unperturbed by Lacey's questions he sat in a still silence staring ahead until Bella placed a bowl of soup in front of him. Now cool, it sat grey and unappetising in the bowl. He took a couple of sips but had little taste for it, pushing it away after a moment.

Frank Emerson had been strong as a young man. Years of kneading dough as a boy had given him muscular hands and arms. He had been a good swimmer too and were a boat in trouble off the coast he could be counted on to help. Twice had he swum out in stormy weather to rescue a local fisherman whose hull had hit the rocks. But time and work and mourning had worn him down. The years sat heavy on his shoulders. His dark hair now all but gone, save for a few patches of grey above his ears and around his temple. His legs and hands were both ravaged by arthritis. When Lacey looked now at his hands, warped like a tree root, it was strange to think that they had ever been strong and healthy. He could hardly knead dough on account of the pain, and now as he held the spoon, it sat awkwardly, half balancing between two fingers.

Frank swallowed, then said in a low voice, 'another girl is missing.'

'No' breathed Bella.

'She was last seen this afternoon at,' Frank swallowed, 'Deception Bay.'

Lacey blinked.

Bella gasped and held her hand at her mouth, then making the sign of the cross on her chest, said 'not again. Dear Lord, so soon. Who?'

'The Morgan's youngest.'

'When?' Asked Lacey, but Bella spoke over her.

'The little girl with the curly hair?'

Frank nodded slowly and closed his eyes as he said the name, 'Mary.'

'When was she seen there?' Asked Lacey again.

'At some point this afternoon. One of the village children saw her there. She probably fell from the slate on the far side, or else paddled too far out in the water.'

Lacey frowned.

'Not another' whispered Bella, her voice shaking.

'It would seem our warnings aren't enough. She is the third girl or young woman this year.'

'*This* afternoon. For sure?' Pressed Lacey.

'Yes.'

Bella, one hand still on her chest, the tip of her index finger touching the cross she wore there, asked 'have you seen Mr Morgan?'

'No, but he spoke to the councilmen. Of course, he is still hopeful that she will be found. But so many haven't been. And those that wash up are...' Their father stopped then, and for one terrifying moment the sisters thought he may cry, which would have been greatly out of character. But he only swallowed and cleared his throat. 'Mr Morgan was by all accounts quite distraught, staying only briefly with the council. He went home to be with his wife, who I hear is overwhelmed with worry. The council then called a meeting of the village men at the hall, so that those of us with daughters may be made aware. The Mayor has reinstated The Watch, for protection.'

Bella exhaled a low whistle.

'Are you certain it was this afternoon?' Asked Lacey.

'Why?' Bella snapped at her, 'why do you keep asking that?'

'No reason' she said, withdrawing with a shrug. 'I was only wondering.' Bella looked at her with narrow eyes, before turning again to their father.

Looking at neither of them he said 'we cannot guess what God's reasons are. We cannot guess why this keeps happening. We cannot know why the village girls do not heed our warnings of the perils of Deception Bay.' In the corner of Lacey's eye Bella shook her head vigorously. 'We can only be grateful that you two know the dangers. And,' he said, lowering his head once more 'we can pray for the safe return of the Morgan girl.'

The family went to sleep in silence. The girls left their father, still in his coat, sitting at the kitchen table, his bible unopen in his hands. Bella dressed for bed, occasionally tutting sorrowfully and shaking her head as though in conversation with herself. Upstairs Lacey lay in bed, with low questioning eyebrows, stared at the ceiling above her. She saw the waves, grey and rolling in the wind. She saw The Island black and dead in the distance. Then, the wide shouldered shape of the cloaked figure, its strange lumbering gait. The misty dark gathering around it like dust. The heavy sack falling from its shoulders, the quick, secretive movement of its head as it looked around.

She dreamt that night of The Island, as indeed she did most nights. The predatory swaying malevolent shape of it, like a shadow in the mist, moving closer. In the wind she heard the voice of her mother, calling to her. As dreams often are, it was a mix of memory and invention. She saw her on her knees in the church, blood smeared all over her. It ran across her dress, staining her forearms and her mouth. White feathers stuck to the blood, some in thick clumps, some stray feathers floating down in the hazy light coming through the stain glass window, finally resting on the floor or in her hair. Her face contorted into a soundless scream, her mouth stuffed with feathers. Then Lacey looked down and she was the one on her knees, wearing a bloodied white dress. She tried desperately to claw it off. But it wrapped to her like a second skin. She cried out as her nails splintered and split as she tried in vain to pull it from her, blood pouring from her fingers. She could hear the men in the yard outside, their horse's hooves, impatient and angry on the street. Their fists rapping in fury on the wooden door.

CHAPTER TWO

In the bakery the dawn arrived in a mist of blue and grey. Lacey watched it lift each shadow in her attic room, leaving it awash with a milky, pale light. She lay with her eyes open, as she had done much of the night. The straw stuffed mattress dug painfully at points into her back. She picked absentmindedly at the patches where the straw poked through, pulling out strands and tossing them to the floor. Downstair she could hear Bella lightly snoring, the sound of it comforted her. Twice in the night Lacey had sat up in her bed to go to wake her. But she had changed her mind. She couldn't quite find the right words, so instead she spent the night sleeplessly watching the walls, blank and ominous reflect her own worry back to her.

No one really knew where the girls were going, they would simply vanish. They were there and then they were not. Some would be seen going on a walk, and never returning. Others it would seem would disappear in the blink of an eye. One, Lacey remembered from when she was a girl, had vanished from her front porch in the time it had taken for her mother to step inside to fetch her coat. When she had returned her daughter was gone. That was when it was one girl every year or two, this past year alone three girls had disappeared from Lower Lynch.

At first it was feared to be witches, then Forest Beasts, but as the years went by rumours began. In the hours after a girl went missing, when every man in the village was out in search, there were whispers that she had been seen walking toward Deception

Bay. Though the origin of the rumour was never clear, after a few bodies were found washed up there, that was enough. The beach was off limits, even for the men.

After each disappearance the town seemed to fold in on itself. The borders were patrolled, outsiders treated with the utmost suspicion, and all liberty surrendered to The Watch. Every mourning mother and father who decried with tear-soaked faces how out of character it would be for their obedient child to venture to the bay, were met with fresh warnings of the wayward mind of girls in the village, fresh restrictions of movement and drawn out church sermons on the risks of not heeding the words of God.

After a while the town would move on, life rolled inexorably forward. Work continued, the fields were ploughed, the sea fished, bread baked. Baby girls were born to mothers who held them tightly and sobbed in dismay. Only a new headstone in the graveyard, like a mark on a tally, to show that anything had happened. But every girl in town, and her parents too, could not help but wonder if they would be next. If their life was to be the one so finally and inexplicably snuffed out.

Pulling her night dress up Lacey bent over the pot and pissed, yawning as she did and hearing Bella below her doing the same. She crept downstairs and seeing her sister still in bed slipped beneath the blankets beside her. Frowning she placed her fingertips on the skin under Lacey's eyes, where the lack of sleep had turned them dark and puffy. 'More bad dreams?' She whispered, so not to wake their father. Her voice was a little muffled as she huddled down beneath the blanket, not yet ready to face the raw cold of the dawn.

Lacey nodded.

'I could hear you up there, tossing and turning all night.'

'I'm sorry.'

'If I can sleep with the miaowing of Mrs Andrews' cat, I can bear sleeping below you.'

'I haven't heard it for a few nights now,' said Lacey glancing at the window, 'perhaps it was eaten by a Forest Beast.'

'Then they will have done us a favour.' Answered Bella wryly.

Lacey usually enjoyed these moments when Bella's matriarchal role slipped, and she was softer, more honest. But not this morning. 'I will thank them when I see them,' she said soberly.

'What's wrong?' Asked Bella.

For a moment she contemplated confiding in her sister. 'I'm... not sure,' Lacey said, semi truthfully, one finger coming to her lips, her teeth gently gnawing at the skin around the nail.

'Well,' said Bella impatiently, drawing back the blanket and sitting up, 'if you won't tell me then I can't help you.' Lacey remained lying as Bella climbed out. 'Come, we'd better start the fire.'

The girls, as always, began their day quietly, in the still sleeping street. Bella stirred their father, who had slept in both his boots and his coat, on his small mattress beneath the shop counter. Though, on the account of his hands, he could no longer bake, he always asked to be woken early. Lacey lay kindling in the grate, which was still warm from last night. It took a little time to nurse the embers into flames again, but before too long she had it properly lit. Feeling somehow more cheerful at the sight of the fire, she tied her apron round her waist and set to work.

The shop had been in the Emerson family for generations and over the years very little had changed. Lacey's father had been born in the back room, onto a sack of flour. His mother had died giving birth to him, she had passed when the doctor couldn't stop her bleeding. In her death she had stained all the flour red. Her husband had mourned not only the passing of his wife, but also his loss of business that month. Now that room was where they kept the proving drawers, two bulky cupboards lined with wool, smelling of yeast. It was also Bella's bedroom.

The front room had the fire, oven, shop counter and a small table and chairs where the family took their meals. The house, due to the almost constantly burning fire, was warm and cosy. The walls sloped slightly at the corners, as though they were bending in old age. The wooden beams warped and whittled away at points, eaten by termites. Sometimes in the evening you could even see mice running along the edges of them.

They opened the shop window by seven, the smell of the first batch of fresh bread floating out on the morning air and spreading throughout the village. Lacey leaned out, with her arms resting on the windowsill and looked down at the street. She saw the black backs of two Watchmen disappearing round the corner at the end of the road, doubtless on their way home to bed after an evening shift. She watched Mr Turner laying out the fish on a table outside his shop, his shirt sleeves rolled above his elbows. He used to sell catch from the lake. Even eels sometimes. But now it all came from the fishermen brave enough to risk the open sea. She observed their little shiny lifeless bodies. Dozens of surprised looking fish heads stared back at her. She was glad to not be a fishmonger's daughter.

Lacey watched as Frank and Bella left to buy sugar from the docks. Bella looping her arm within her father's in support. The street was quiet, no one was visiting the neighbouring shops, no carts passed, nor riders on horseback. Sam Cogsworth, a young boy of eight or nine with short hair matted at the back, rounded the corner, absent-mindedly tossing a ball between his hands.

'Sam,' Lacey called to him, then beckoning him closer. He approached, 'what news is there of the Morgan girl?'

'They've found her.' Said Sam, his eyes still on his ball.

'Alive?' Asked Lacey, holding her breath.

'Nope, she washed up this morning.' He tossed the ball high, his hands cupped to receive it. 'Fisherman Wallace saw her come in on the morning tide. The council and Kinch went down to Deception Bay to collect her an hour ago. She probably drowned, stupid girl.' Lacey closed her eyes as though that might supress the wave of sadness surging within her. She slowly turned and withdrew back into the bakery. 'Got any cakes?' He asked, poking his head through the window. Without looking Lacey took a loaf of bread and placed it on the sill. A small hand snatched it and hurried away.

Lacey sat alone in the empty bakery, staring at the fire. In every flick of the flames she imagined the shape of Mary Morgan's little body, face down in the tide. The Island watching in the distance. The door swung open and Lacey snapped out of her trance. Her mood dropped even further upon seeing who it was. Elisa Littlewood nodded a curt good morning to Lacey, her hair, boot leather black, tucked neatly beneath her cap, her white gloved hands clasped together as if in prayer. If Lacey hadn't already known how old she was, she would have been hard pressed to accurately guess her age. She had the height and frame of a child, but the drawn, tight face of an older woman. She took her time to orbit the shop, picking up loaves and buns and prodding at them with a gloved finger before dropping them in distaste.

'Have you nothing sweet?' She asked eventually, her voice high and tight.

Lacey, in an attempt to avoid conversation, was needlessly rearranging the jars on the shelf above the counter. Without turning, she answered solemnly, 'No, we are low in sugar.'

Hearing her desolate tone, Elisa's eyes flitted eagerly in Lacey's direction. 'So, you've heard the news of the Morgan girl.'

'Her poor parents,' said Lacey quietly in response.

'Her parents should count themselves lucky. Most don't get a body to mourn.'

'They aren't lucky Elisa.'

'These girls know the dangers well enough. But even the ones our age don't seem to heed the warnings. How old was Eleanor? Sixteen? Only a year our junior, her body never even washed up. Time after time they are told that the villagers are forbidden from Deception Bay. If they don't listen it is their own sorry fault. They are getting more unruly, it wasn't like that in our day.'

'Girls disappeared when we were young.'

'Not as many. Besides that was different, that was witchcraft...' she hesitated, slyly pleased she had happened upon a point of pain. 'Well I don't need to tell you.' Lacey stiffened, clenching her jaw. 'Apparently Commander Kinch is to announce a curfew.' She poked her finger into a rye loaf, feeling at the crumbs. 'At least the boys have more sense. They never disappear. Once you have your sugar will you be making spiced buns?' Lacey, sensing anger rising in her chest, not trusting herself to speak, only shook her head. 'What about apple cake?' She asked, bending to squint at a roll, 'Mother and I have a gentleman coming for tea, apparently he has a taste for sweet treats.'

Since rumours had begun that Sebastian Abner had taken a liking to her, Lacey had come to accept comments such as these from Elisa on a regular occurrence. Over recent months Sebastian would loiter outside the bakery almost daily, leaning against the wall opposite, plumes of pipe smoke engulfing his face. He was in no need of bread, loaves were shipped to the Manor from the Upper Lakes at the beginning of each week. It was her he came to see. Having the idea that the Manor might start buying their bread from them instead Lacey's father was most pleased with his presence. Lacey was not. Something about the way Sebastian watched her through the window made her feel like a fish in a barrel, having had its lid prized open with a fisherman's head over the rim, inspecting his catch. Eventually she had come to tolerate his being there as one of her daily chores, making a point of never looking in his direction.

'Even if we had the sugar we don't bake sweets on a mourning day,' Lacey said, turning to Elisa, 'perhaps you can make your own. I will happily sell you a bag of flour,' her eyes travelled purposefully down the girl's bird like frame, 'though you might need help carrying it.'

Elisa's eyes narrowed, one brow arching cruelly, the mock sweetness gone from her voice 'I wouldn't be seen walking down Main Street with you Lacey Emerson, even if you were carrying my flour.'

'Then perhaps you should ask your gentleman to carry it.'

Elisa glared at her. 'Sebastian might be momentarily willing to overlook your family history. But we aren't, the people of this town have long memories, no one has forgotten what your mother did.'

Lacey blushed from her neck to her cheeks, she looked down at her flour covered hands. A pulse beginning to throb in her neck.

'Never mind,' said Elisa after a moment, her tone returning. 'I'm sure I will be sweet enough for him.' With that, she turned and walked primly through the door and out onto the street.

Only once she heard the door close did Lacey look up. 'I'm hope you are,' she said to the empty shop.

Soon Frank and Bella returned, but by the time noon arrived they had served only a handful of customers. Lacey had drawn up a chair to the counter and was reading her book. Frank sighed as he sat down, and, reaching behind his back, untied his apron. He stretched his swollen fingers, thin strips of flour embedded in the crease of his red knuckles. 'Another quiet day,' he muttered beneath his breath.

In an attempt to appease his mood Bella said 'almost no one is out on the street Father, and those that are are not wanting bread. Death takes a toll on people. I saw Mr Lewis that day last year when he found the Grey's daughter washed up.' Frank gave no response. Talking nervously, fearful of her Father's silence Bella continued, 'he had the look of a haunted man. He didn't eat for a week.' Tentatively she pulled up a stool to sit beside him. 'It is only to be expected Father, the whole town is in mourning.'

'I know that!' He snapped suddenly, slamming his fists against the table. Across the room Lacey shut her book quietly. The sudden flare in his temper causing Bella's pale cheeks to flush a deep, mottled rose. His voice, like gravel in a barrel, his low, lined brow, compressed into a frown. Bella hovered, for a moment, like a scolded child, unsure of whether or not to take a seat. From across the room Lacey heard her swallow.

'I know that Annabella,' Frank said again, this time his voice a little softer, a little less stern. But his hands still locked in fists. Bella eventually lowered herself, shifting the stool a little further from him. His face now rearranging itself back into its usual shape, the heat of his anger draining away, replaced with his usual look of stern weariness. 'We haven't taken even half what we might have last year. Before next winter I will be...' He trailed off, looking down at his legs. It was at this table Doctor Prior had told Frank he would be likely bed bound before they year was out. 'What will become of us then?'

'We will make do' said Bella her voice shaking slightly, 'Lacey and I have taken on more laundry and sewing. That will bring in extra money. You are doing all you can, remember it is under doctor's orders that you must not exert yourself.'

'I will not succumb to idleness.' Said Frank bitterly, shaking his head.

'It isn't idleness Father, your hands-' She glanced down at his hand, lying like a knot of rope upon the table.

'Enough.' He interrupted her, closing the topic in a word and pulling his hands down to rest upon his lap.

'I will pick us some blackberries' suggested Lacey, changing the subject, 'we might make some pies this week. Pies always sell well.'

Frank sighed and beneath the table stretched his fingers. He nodded once in consent. 'But only those from the field here. The woods are too dangerous. There are dangers there you will not learn from your reading.' He gestured with contempt to her book.

'I will be alright Father.' Said Lacey.

He turned then and looked up at her. 'Do as I say,' he said quietly. 'Are you listening to me? Not in the woods.'

Lacey nodded.

Frank took a loaf wrapped neatly in a handkerchief and tied with a black ribbon to the Morgan's house. He walked off down the street holding it carefully in front of him as though it were made of glass. Once he had left, Bella turned the shop sign to closed and began work on the mending. Her fingers deftly moved in the light from the open back door. Lacey, unable to concentrate on her book, took her coat from the hook on the wall and left too. She walked aimlessly for a time. Strolling along the edge of the field, looking at the cows chewing grass, staring ahead with their hollow, blank eyes. She held her hand out and stroked the soft domed heads of the calves who were less weary of human touch than their parents.

Most of the trees had turned now, their leaves curling, as though on fire, changing from their vibrant, summer green, to a bright, glowing orange. Beyond the village a thin carpet spread across the forest floor, making a sweet, crisp, crunching sound underfoot. The woods were ablaze with autumn, you could taste it in the air, that sweet, nutty scent of decay. The sun was slowly retiring. The year was winding down, every night arrived earlier and stayed later than the one before. The endless, optimistic heat of summer had been exchanged for the gentle cool of autumn, the buffer before the knife edge cold of winter.

Lacey turned and walked into town, though not along Main Street, for though she didn't admit it to herself, she was afraid to pass the Morgan house. At the beginning of the year she had attended the service of Lucy Cobb, the last girl lost at Deception Bay and she hadn't forgotten the looks on her parent's faces. The raw mask of anguish and pain had filled her with a dread she could feel even now.

Beside the village green a small group of children held hands, dancing and singing in a circle. The Old Oak Tree swayed in the breeze above them, the wind rustling its leaves, its acorns scattered around their feet. Lacey glanced up once at its branches before swiftly looking away. The girls already wore little black mourning bows in their hair, their voices carrying through the quiet street. Lacey knew the tune, they had sung it when she was a child, it turned her blood to ice.

Don't step foot on Deception Bay
Or your sisters will wash away
Don't step foot on Deception Bay
Or the water will take your daughter

The children always came out on the street to sing the nursery rhyme on the days after a drowning. She watched them, their hair ribbons trailing behind them as they danced. One girl of about eight had her long auburn hair tied in a black bow, it came loose, falling to the ground at Lacey's feet.

Lacey scooped to pick it up. The girl broke from the dance and approached her. She looked up hesitantly at Lacey. She had a smattering of freckles dotted across her nose and cheeks and eyebrows that pointed pleasantly upwards. Lacey knew her name to be Jessica, an orphan who, along with her brother, had been fostered by multiple families in the town.

'Thank you' she muttered, taking the ribbon from Lacey's hand.

'I sang that song when I was a girl.' Said Lacey.

'It's a silly song really,' said Jessica, running the black material through her fingers. She spoke still with a childish lisp and her face had yet to grow out of its infantile roundness.

'Why do you say that?'

'None of us ever play on Deception Bay, we're too scared. We don't need a song to tell us.' She hesitated, her tone eager, conspiratorial. 'I have been though, once, when I was younger.' She said, as though she were a woman of many years. 'I saw The Island from there.' Her eyes widened at the word. 'My brother says that if I touch his toys they'll hang me and send my body to The Island.' Jessica threw a scornful look at a pug-nosed red-haired boy playing behind her.

'Jessica do you know which child told the council they saw Mary at Deception Bay yesterday?'

Pulling the ribbon tight she answered in a matter of fact voice, 'no-one did.'

'Someone must have.'

'Then someone is lying. Mary would never have gone there; she was the most afraid of all of us.'

With her bow tied Jessica ran off to re-join her friends. Lacey waited a moment then called after her, the girl turning in response. 'They don't hang people for touching their brothers' toys. And if they did,' she added, 'they would bury them in the church, not The Island.' The little girl nodded then skipped away. Lacey knew that some parents still used The Island as a threat of punishment for their children. Even though it was more than ten years since the execution of her mother, who was the last person in the village whose crime was deemed so heinous her soul was not granted the luxury of resting in peace. Lacey turned and walked slowly down the street, heading towards the lake, the voices of the children growing quieter until they were lost completely.

She walked past the dock lined with crayfish traps and piles of rope, where a few empty boats sat bobbing on the water. The few fishermen that still fished the lake never sailed on a mourning day. Her father often said that the view of the lake from here was the same as the First Settlers would have seen. The men even fished with the same style nets as their ancestors, most of whom had died in the first few winters, the harsh climate had squeezed the population down so that only the strongest survived. The villagers were proud to have be the ancestors of such resilient men.

Finally, at no point having admitted to herself that this had been the purpose of her walk, she arrived at Mateo's house. His home was one of a few built on wooden pillars above the water. Though once seen as a solution to the issue of town expansion (the forest was thought too dangerous to build in) the houses soon proved a failure. The damp had been the uppermost problem, now most were used by the fishermen during winter to store their sails and skiffs in need of restoration. On top of that it was a convenient place, as Lacey and her sister had been witness to last night, for the punters at the Tavern to relieve themselves. No amount of rain could ever quite wash the smell away.

Lacey paused, casting a furtive glance up and down the dock, making certain no neighbours were watching, then knocked gently, and not waiting for a reply, pushed the door open. The house had the unmistakable markings of a young man. Shirts and trousers lay hanging off chairs or crumpled on the floor. Half eaten apples sat in varying stages of decay atop scraps of paper. Mateo's diet consisted mainly of apples and loaves of bread gifted by Lacey. Thick curls of sawdust covered the chairs and the work bench, in the corners of the room it gathered like snowdrifts. The light shone through the gaps in the boards below, casting watery ripples across the walls.

A ladder stood at the corner of the room leading to a small landing beneath the eves, not much wider than a mattress, where the sleeping Mateo now lay. His arm hanging in the air, visible from below. As she climbed the last few rungs of the ladder Lacey considered taking it by the wrist, and placing it on his chest, but stopped herself. He didn't quite wake, only stirred a little and shifted over to make room for her. She felt the warmth of his legs against hers through the bedsheets. Picking up one of his books she thumbed the dry, dusty leaves full of carpentry diagrams.

After a time, and without moving, Mateo spoke. 'Did they find her body?' He said, half into his pillow.

'Yes.'

He sighed. 'You shut the bakery?'

'Yes, no one was wanting bread.'

He turned slowly, and lifted himself onto his elbows, 'the wife Morgan can be heard crying three houses down.' Lacey didn't answer, only looked unseeing at the book in her hands. Mateo rubbed his palm across his face, pushing the sleep from his eyes, the imprint of the pillow still embossed on his tanned cheek. His eyes set deep below shadowy brows, locked in an almost constant frown, not of worry or anger, but concentration. As though at any moment he might be working on a puzzle.

'You'd read anything Lacey.' He said shaking his head. 'Interesting book is it?'

'Very' she answered, her eyebrow flickering minutely.

He stretched, lengthening one arm into the air, until it reached the sloping, wooden roof. His face twisting in discomfort. Seeing in her peripheries that he was shirtless, Lacey kept her eyes trained on the book. He groaned, 'I spent all day bent over, working on that new plot off Main Street.'

'How is the progress?'

'Just finished the staircase yesterday, polished oak.' His eyes widening at the words, and his lips pursing in a whistle. 'Must have cost a fortune, but I suppose the Abners aren't short of money. The foreman's already got me laying the floor and now my back is killing me. I will be walking like an old man for the week.'

'How is your new apprentice?'

'Shit.' Said Mateo with an honesty that caused Lacey to giggle. 'Eli doesn't know one end of a hammer from the other. I tell you, if I'm found dead from a blow to the head have him shot and sent to The Island.' He stopped suddenly, glancing up at her. 'Sorry,' he said.

She gave a small, dismissive shake of the head as he quickly changed the subject. 'Anyway I would rather spend my days with him than having to endure the Barrick brothers' conversation.'

Lacey rolled her eyes. 'They stumble out from the Tavern passed noon, stinking of ale and chewing tobacco, to sit on their arses at the site doing less than nothing. They smoke and fart and occasionally annoy one another to the point of wrestling, I don't understand why the Mayor would keep them on.'

'They are Sebastian's friends, at least Lek is.'

'What a charming pair those two must make.'

'Thank God I didn't have to endure school with them, one of the benefits of being a gypsy.' Winked Mateo.

'Lek is cruel.' Said Lacey, her mind in the past. 'In comparison I suppose Eli doesn't seem so bad.'

Mateo smiled and yawned, 'how are you? Has Bella been bossing you around?'

'No more than usual,' Lacey shrugged. Bella's nagging had increased of late. Since their father's condition had worsened and the girls had been forced to taken on the extra work, there seemed to be no amount of chores Lacey could accomplish that would satisfy Bella. But knowing Mateo still mourned his sister, she always felt uncomfortable complaining about her own.

'Not visiting the Professor today?'

'No,' answered Lacey, picking the book back up and opening it to a random page.

Mateo frowned, 'normally when you have a day free, and you aren't reading at the Professor's, there is one place you are sure to be found.' Lacey didn't look at him. Mateo persisted, his eyes narrowing, 'I thought of you yesterday when I heard the news of the Morgan child. I would have thought with your day off work that you would have been at Deception Bay.' He left the words hanging in the air between them, staring at her, but Lacey didn't look up.

'Don't you know us girls are banned from the bay?' She said wryly.

'Ha,' he snorted, 'as if that's ever stopped you.'

Seeing she didn't return his smile he paused, and asked 'what's wrong Lacey?'

'Nothing,' she mumbled staring at the pages.

'I know your face well enough to know when you are lying.' Beneath the sheets he nudged his knee against hers. Lacey shut the book with a snap and sat up, 'will you come with me for a walk?'

Mateo fell back onto the bed with a groan before answering, 'if you wish.'

'Good' she said, swinging her legs down onto the ladder, 'you will have to find a comb, your hair has the style of a farmer's dog.'

Though the wind had cooled, Lacey kept her hood down as they left Mateo's house but she made sure her cap was tied as the pair made their way through the village, walking on opposite sides of the street. They walked as though strangers. Neither said a word or even acknowledged the other's presence until they reached the privacy of the woods. Though they may have done so this time last year they would certainly not have walked down Main Street together today. Since they had begun nearing adulthood the villager's reaction to their friendship had changed. They couldn't meet in public without scornful glances or indignant frowns. More than once she had returned home to be chastised by her father who had heard reports that she was cavorting with a man in public. Their childhood closeness no longer felt suitable. So without discussion or acknowledgement of the changes, they only met now where they were sure not to be witnessed.

But as they entered the forest, leaving behind the watchful eyes of the town, they were drawn to each other's sides once more. The two strolled in an easy silence through the wood, the light coming gently through the orange leaves. Suddenly there was a noise, like a cracking branch, coming from a little distance away. Lacey jumped, they both stopped immediately and stood very still. Never too long would the woods allow you to relax. Their eyes hastily scanning the spaces between the trees, the forest unmoving around them. Both stood, poised, ready to run. A small red fox stepped out a few yards ahead of them. Seeing them it sniffed the air a moment, unafraid before wandering off, it's nose to the ground. Mateo laughed and started walking again.

'I thought you didn't believe in the Forest Beasts,' he said.

'I don't' snapped Lacey.

'Your hair is quite white with shock' he joked, reaching out to stroke the light side of her head. She deftly ducked away from him.

'You are the one who believes in Forest Beasts, Mateo.'

'That is true,' his tone earnest, 'only a fool doesn't believe in them.'

'Then why don't you carry a sword?'

'It would do no good' he said quietly, reaching out and snapping a twig off a branch.

A tree had fallen across the path ahead of them, its roots lying exposed, Lacey didn't move to go around it, only lifted her skirt a little and climbed on top of it. Mateo didn't follow, he looked up at her standing high on the decaying trunk, the afternoon light falling behind her in such a way that one side of her head seemed to shine. Small pieces of dust and pollen danced around her in the sun. She frowned down at him questioningly. She had been quieter than usual and he could tell there was something wrong. Finally he said, 'you were upon Deception Bay yesterday, weren't you?'

She paused a moment before answering 'I was.' She spoke quietly, cautiously. Mateo crossed the distance between them in two wide steps, jumping nimbly up onto the tree so that he was level with her. He looked into her eyes.

'Lacey did you see the poor girl drown?' His stare so deep and intense she thought she may be crushed under the weight of it.

'No' she whispered, he didn't hear her.

'Tell me what happened.'

'It didn't happen,' she said, looking straight at him, 'not like that. It couldn't have, well not exactly, not in the way they say.'

'In what way? What did you see?'

'I don't know what I saw, not the child Mary though. I saw no child, I saw...' She chewed anxiously on the soft inside of her mouth, her brows two arrows pointing downwards. 'I saw a man. I think. I don't know.'

'A man? Who?' Said Mateo, blinking his dark lashes.

Lacey huffed in frustration. 'That is the point Mateo, I don't know who, it was too far and too dark. If he were closer or it were lighter I could tell you, but it wasn't. So that's all I say. I think I saw a man on Deception Bay yesterday, holding... something. But either way I was there all afternoon and I saw no child.' Lacey looked down at the mix of leaves embedded like pressed flowers on the forest floor. She drew her lips inside her mouth and pressed down on them between her teeth, then she said, 'and he wore a hood.'

'A hood?'

'Yes, a long black hooded cloak.'

Mateo turned a paler shade than she had ever seen. His eyes narrowing to fine slits he said, 'I... I don't understand.'

'Neither do I.' She said, looking up, 'that is why we are here. I want to see Ma.' With that Lacey turned and jumped down the other side of the log, continuing on the path. She didn't look back to see if he was following, but after a few moments heard his footfall on the ground behind.

CHAPTER THREE

The axe flew past Lacey's head with such speed she felt the rushing of the air around it. It embedded itself into a tree between her and Mateo with a deep, resounding crack, which echoed around the forest. A few shards of bark splintered off and fell to the ground. The pair spun around in shock. Commander Kinch strode towards them, shaking his wide head, his jaw jutting forward in anger.

'What are you doing?' Yelled Mateo, 'you could have killed us!'

Walking between them, forcing them to break apart, Kinch took the axe by the handle and yanked it from the tree. The shining head must have been buried at least two thirds of the way in, but he pulled it out with ease. He turned to Mateo, whose expression of anger subsided somewhat beneath the tall man's stare. 'Take it as a lesson. A beast would move twice as fast, it would have had your gypsy head clean off.'

'We are just going for a walk Commander,' said Lacey, taking a small, defensive step towards Mateo, at whom the man stared at with such distaste that it drew his mouth into a snarl.

'Well a walk can get you killed, you have to keep your eyes open in these woods. There is danger here.' He turned his massive bulk to Lacey, his axe still in his hands. The handle tucked as naturally into his forearm as though it were an extension of his own body.

He dragged a wide palm across his shaven head, then down to cup his jaw, moving it left and right as though it were not connected to the rest of his skull. 'Now The Watch are back, soon there won't be any more wandering around in the woods. The rules are changing, especially for your type.' He said nodding at the two of them.

'And what type might we be?' Mateo asked through clenched teeth.

'A dirty gypsy and a witch's daughter.'

Mateo's cheeks flushed with anger and he took a step forward, but Lacey held her hand out calmly. 'We are visiting his grandmother,' said Lacey, 'that is still allowed.'

The Commander sucked at a piece of tobacco, softening at the back of his mouth. Then slotting the axe into a loop on his belt he said, 'we'll see.' The leather of the belt strained slightly at the mass of him. He was neither pure fat nor pure muscle but a combination of the two. Which gave the effect of him being carved from stone. An immovable boulder.

Making sure Mateo was beside her, Lacey turned and walked cautiously away. Feeling Kinch's eyes on them every step. Once they were out of earshot, and sure that enough woodland was between them and him so not to be seen, Lacey looked up to Mateo, 'are you all right?'

'Let's just forget it.' He frowned, walking swiftly on.

Ma's house, if you could call it a house, was as wide as Lacey was tall. Buried deep in the forest, you would only find it if you knew exactly where to look. It was a tradition originating from the First Settlers, though rarely observed any longer, to leave the village in your very last years, and live alone in the woods. Family and friends, if you had any, would visit bringing wood and dried meats. But otherwise you would live alone, with God. The Southerners, and especially the people of the Lakelands believed that your last years on earth should be spent repenting for whatever sins you may have accumulated during your lifetime. Ma didn't believe so strongly in God, Lacey couldn't remember seeing her in church ever. But she had no appetite for society, preferring her own company and occasionally that of Mateo, who brought her meat, smoked fish and parcels of the Emersons' bread. Ma was very old, older than she herself knew, but old enough to remember the Thousand Day Winter that killed her parents, and the Great Fire that killed her daughter and granddaughter.

The tiny, windowless cabin had long been fighting a battle against nature and was now officially losing. The forest had crept upon it and was reclaiming the wood as its own. The roots of the tree behind it had, as it grew, begun to push up beneath the floor, eventually picking the entire house up and tilting it to the left. Upon stepping inside the visitor immediately had have the discombobulating feeling of standing at odds with the outside world. Moss grew on the roof, and ivy wrapped itself, like a fist, around the exterior walls. Green glass jars and lanterns hung all about it, shining and chinking in the breeze. Some, the higher ones, had collected rainwater for drinking and cooking, others had lids and half melted candle wax inside. One or two held insects Lacey didn't recognise, buzzing and rattling against the glass.

Lacey raised her hand to knock but before she could a thin, silvery voice came from within. 'Hello children. Mateo, I wouldn't have recognised you as my kin. Have you no brush for your hair?' There was no way of Ma seeing them from the outside, but both knew her well enough to question how she seemed to know the unknowable. Lacey raised an eyebrow to Mateo as he tried, with the palm of his hand, to flatten his unruly locks. She pushed the door open and they stepped inside.

The smell never failed to take Lacey by surprise, forcing her quickly to adapt by breathing through her mouth, abandoning the use of her nose entirely. The odour was a cross between animal blood, wood smoke and something thickly floral Lacey was unable to place. A small fire burnt low in the grate, crackling and hissing below a smoking pot. Although the bed was less than a few inches off the ground, Ma's legs hung in the air, failing to reach the floor. She had the frame of a bird. A loose woollen shawl hung limp off her arched back. Her hair, split and tangled and the same colour as the wool around her shoulders, seemed to knot itself into the weave. But her eyes, young and playful, darted and danced around the room in a way her body was unable to. She patted at the straw mattress, that was even more threadbare than Lacey's, and gestured for her to sit.

Mateo pulled up a stool glancing quickly at the tiny fire. 'You need more kindling Ma,' he said, 'I will chop you some next week.'

'I can chop my own.' She answered. Mateo supressed a smile. 'You think I cannot lift an axe? I still have the strength of ten men.' She raised a twig-like arm and made a fist, her eyes twinkling.

'I don't doubt it' smiled Mateo.

With a gnarled length of wood that she used as a walking stick, Ma skilfully hooked the pot from the fire. Then, with a practiced twist of the wrist, poured out the liquid into three small, glass cups. The steam hung in the air making Lacey's eyes water, but not wanting to be impolite, she held the warm cup to her lips.

'It has been a long while since your last visit young Lacey.'

'I'm sorry Ma, I–'

Ma's thin hand rose slowly into the air stopping her. 'No apologies please. I'm old and may die at any moment. I don't want the last thing I hear to be the word sorry. I would prefer something a little more... exciting.' She took a gulp of tea, smacking her thin lips, then wincing slightly at the acidic aftertaste, 'ahhh, delicious. Now, tell me how you are.'

'I'm well, I think.' Said Lacey, staring down at the leaves floating at the bottom of her tea.

'Miss Lacey,' said Ma, poking at the fire with her stick, 'now that you are a woman, you must learn take ownership of your feelings. You must say *I am well, I am happy* or else *I am miserable and had I the means I would pack my bags and sail out onto the sea and never return!*'

Lacey laughed nervously, 'I feel all those things Ma.'

'Very good,' said Ma with a smile, 'a balance. How is your sister?'

'She is well. Not much changed. She has joined the choir in Mrs Ward's place'

'Good, I cannot imagine a God who would enjoy the sound of Mrs Ward singing. Still I can think of better things Bella might be doing with her time. Singing hymns is just praying but to a tune. They would have us pray in our sleep if they could find a way. And your Father?'

'He is tired.' Lacey said, thinking back to that morning, the rash of anger on his face.

'Yes. That happens, the tiredness creeps in like ivy through a window. But he is strong. I remember seeing him swimming as a young man off the rock at Twilight Bay. He has strength in him. You tell him I can still recall the shape of his arms after a swim!' Ma cackled at that. A hoarse, smoke filled cackle, strangely unlike her speaking voice. Her bony legs swung like a child as she laughed. Lacey watched her and wondered how old she was.

'Ancient,' Ma read her mind as she took another sip of her steaming tea. Lacey stared at her in amazement, but before she could speak, Ma took up her hand. She thumbed at Lacey's naked ring finger.

'No engagement yet I see.'

Lacey withdrew her hand quickly; she didn't look up to see it, but she felt a scowl spread across Mateo's brow. He grabbed another log and tossed it angrily into the fire.

A few sparks spat angrily in response, skittering out onto the floor, he stamped them out purposefully with the toe of his boot. Ma's hand reached out to stroke his hand. Hers seeming skeletal in comparison. 'Be careful.' She whispered. Mateo looked at Ma then and it seemed to Lacey that he was a child again. Lacey thought immediately of his parents. Of him, as a newly orphaned boy. His face stained with blood and soot, his burnt pyjamas, crying beside his still burning home.

'No, no engagement yet' said Lacey, unable to bear the moment any longer. 'Or ever I hope.'

'The Mayor is a very determined man.' Answered Ma simply, turning to talk to her once again.

Lacey pressed the flesh of her ring finger. 'It would seem so.'

'A man with such a marked history as his needed conviction in order to obtain the power he desired.' Ma ran her small eyes over Lacey, 'I must admit I spat out half my tea when I heard he had his eye on you Lacey.'

'Good to know you are up on your local gossip,' said Lacey flatly, shooting Mateo a suspicious look.

'Well you aren't exactly the bride I would have expected for an Abner.' Continued Ma. 'Not only because you are far more likely to be found with your head in a book than at a village dance. But because the Mayor's son marrying a girl who not only has a poor baker as a father but also a mother who was a witch is a surprise.'

'Ma!' Exclaimed Mateo, open mouthed at her frankness.

Lacey's insides twisted in shame. It wasn't only the word *Witch* that knotted her stomach, but *Mother* too. Her name was all but forbidden in the bakery. Other than her chats with Ma, Lacey could convince herself the word existed purely inside her own mind. 'It's alright,' she said quietly, 'there isn't a soul in town who doesn't share that opinion Ma. Never have two families so unalike taken the blood vow together.'

Lacey most of all was surprised when she learnt of the possible union. From pressing her head so close to the back door that it hurt, she had heard, with a feeling of dread, the Mayor suggesting the idea to her father. It couldn't be said that her suitor was an ugly man. Sebastian had the height of his father, plus an inch or two, he was so tall he had to stoop to enter every home in town. But where his father was slim, he was broad, with wide shoulders that stuck out from his neck at a right angle. His hair, left to grow long, was often tied in a knot that sat atop his head beneath his hat. Or else, often on a Sunday, he would leave it out to flow in golden locks around his shoulders. He was proud of its length and softness. It was said in the village that the woman who had been his nanny as a child, and still resided at the Mayor's manor, would still brush it nightly, with a comb dipped in lavender and witch hazel. So that you might smell him before you had seen him, sitting high atop his horse, riding through town, his sword glistening at his side.

Lacey cleared her throat and said bitterly 'you would think the shame of having a witch as a mother might spare me such a union. It seems she wasn't content only to ruin my childhood, but she must now deprive me of a happy future too.'

Ma pursed her lips. 'You say witch as though it were a bad thing. It is the way of all living beings to commune in some way with the nature around them. To be a witch, is only to feel that relationship a little stronger. To feel the elements at one with your own body. The water in the lake, the earth beneath your feet, the wind between the trees, and fire too,' she gestured to the hearth. 'It is all merely an extension of yourself. Only witches know how to control it.'

Mateo rolled his eyes at Lacey and she suppressed a smile. The two had often sat at Ma's feet as children and listened to her talk of these things. Even as youngsters they had known it to be fantasy, but blasphemous fantasy all the same.

'But the men fear such a power. They hung your mother for being a witch. Accused her of murdering children as sacrifice. With only the slightest of evidence. And still the girls continued to vanish, even after she was executed. They do not apologise for making a mistake, they do not even acknowledge a mistake was made. Only say it is something different now. First, they say it is Forest Beasts. Then they say girls don't listen, say they play on the Bay when they shouldn't.' She waved her withered hand, as though the concept were idiotic. She took a long sip of tea, pulling a dark green sinuous leaf from her mouth and placing it back in the cup.

'Lacey,' continued Ma, 'when you are alone as much as I am all you have are your memories. I think often of the happy times I had with your mother here. Do your memories of her bring you no comfort?'

'I don't want to remember her Ma.'

'She loved you Lacey.'

'You would be called before the council were anyone to hear you speaking like that in town Ma.' Said Mateo.

'But we aren't in town now, grandson. Out in the woods only the trees can hear us, and they are on our side.' She turned back to Lacey, 'let the memories in child. You will see you are more like your mother than you think.'

The room fell silent. Mateo shifted a little on his stool, Lacey stared at the tea leaves circling in her cup. Ma leaned back and closed her eyes. Eventually she said 'Lacey you would be best to come right out with it dear, I'm somehow even older than when you first arrived.'

'You don't have a monopoly on ageing Ma,' said Lacey lightly.

'I do in this house,' Ma replied. 'Now, out with it girl. I think you want to ask me about Deception Bay, am I right?'

Mateo, who had been staring at the fire, looked up.

'Yes,' answered Lacey, dumbfounded, but knowing there was no point in questioning how Ma knew.

'There has been another girl lost?'

'Yes Ma.'

Ma shook her tiny head dislodging dust and a few small twigs from her hair, she made a clicking sound with her tongue, just as Bella had done. Then in her small, thin voice she whispered a short gypsy prayer. Unable to understand the words, Lacey watched the woman's small, puckered, petal-like lips moving, her words as quiet and soft as smoke.

Lacey thought of the figure in the hood. 'Something is wrong.' She said.

Ma's eyes rolled and closed, her voice was suddenly ethereal and distant, she whispered 'see how the waves fall on The Island Lacey? See how in the mist it seems to move and avoid the eye? It isn't at all a natural place.' The insects in the jars seemed to beat their wings more violently against the glass. An insistent, hypnotic thrumming. 'It is a place of death. The leaves on the trees grow red with blood. It has soaked into the earth. The dead there cannot rest.' She blinked, pulling herself back to the moment, the strange look gone from her eye, the insects resting once more behind the glass. 'Yes child, there is something wrong. In the past when the girls have occasionally washed up, they have had marks upon them. Unnatural marks, unlike those you get from drowning. The evil in these lands isn't young, to find the root you need to go back to the beginning. To the very start when the First Settlers came to these shores. It is with them you will find its foundations. You were right to come to me Lacey, your mother said one day you would.' Both Lacey and Mateo stared round eyed at her.

Lacey's started once more to speak, but before she could respond, Ma closed her eyes and said, 'I'm tired now.' It was enough to stop Lacey's questions before they reached her lips. The pair remained sitting, eager to hear more. But the little old woman stayed perfectly still, with her eyes and mouth firmly closed.

Eventually Mateo, half in frustration, half in acceptance sighed and stood. 'It's getting dark, I want to be out of the woods before sundown.' He leant and kissed the old woman on the cheek, then in turn bowed his head so that she may kiss it. Ma, raising herself as best she could, stamped a tiny kiss on his forehead like a pecking hen.

Lacey, still speechless, mumbled a thank you to Ma as she was guided out by Mateo. She wanted to stay, wanted to ask her what she meant, but she was also longing for the fresh forest air. She couldn't see her thoughts clearly in the smoke from Ma's fire, so she allowed Mateo to lead her away. As they were leaving Ma whispered into her tea, 'watch your backs young ones, there are beasts between the trees.' The door shut with a creak behind them.

CHAPTER FOUR

Once home Lacey shut the door behind her, leaning her back against it for a moment, before taking off her coat. The house was still and silent; she was glad Bella and her father were both out, glad to have the time alone to collect her thoughts. She dealt with a few light chores, picking up the broom she circled round the small house, sweeping up the dust and flour. Then she set about folding the clean linen that lay in a basket on the chair by the fire. The house sat silently while she worked, her hands busy, while her mind was elsewhere.

Although a number of times, Mateo had tried to strike up a conversation, Lacey hadn't spoken on the walk home, after a while he had fallen into silence beside her. Eventually they had arrived at her back gate, Lacey turned to bid him good night. She found his face marked with concern, his eyes wide with worry and his bottom lip slightly swollen from where he had been chewing upon it. For a moment she had the urge to stroke his face, wipe the worry from it with her hand, feel the softness of his cheek beneath her palm. But the feeling rose like a wave, then ebbed away. The moment passed and giving him little more than a half smile she turned towards the door. He caught her wrist in his hand stopping her. His fingers, brown with dirt, pressed into her skin.

'Lacey.'

'Yes?' She responded. He leaned close to her then, closer than he normally would in the village. She felt his breath against her cheek. The sky and woods behind him blurred out of focus, but she could pick out every detail on his face, each freckle, each dark hair in his furrowed brow. A few small scars traced in lighter skin around his jaw and forehead. Some from the fire that killed his family, some from playing as a boy. In the fading light they shone against the darkness of his skin. She felt something inside her chest twitch as though it were coming to life.

He whispered with sincerity, 'don't tell anyone about what you saw.' He paused, searching for the words 'or what you didn't see yesterday. Just don't tell anyone.'

'I won't.'

'Promise me Lacey. Not a word. Don't say anything about the hooded figure.' His voice was tightly wrapped in fear. But in a vain attempt to disguise it, he smiled. However it was forced and strange and the sight of it made Lacey even more afraid.

She paused, looking at him before answering 'I won't. I promise,'

Mateo relaxed his grip and her hand fell through his, but not before he caught her fingertips and gave them a quick squeeze.

His words hung above her head as she worked. The strange note of warning in his voice, the reluctant promise she had made because of it. She frowned at the white linen squares as she folded them. She heard Ma's words too, of how The Island was a place of death. It was where the damned were dispatched to an afterlife of eternal loneliness. Not for them, the peace of the churchyard, instead a neverending limbo, tormented by your own crimes. Even as a child, before her mother's execution, she had been afraid of The Island. Afraid of those three sharp peaks, unforgiving and cruel as a grave. It haunted her, even now as she worked, the image burnt into her eyelids, visible on every blink. She stoked the fire, then pulling herself up, sat in her apron on the countertop and closed her eyes. Her long legs hanging over the side, her heels knocking at the cupboard door.

Cool, grey waves rolled in from a fog lined horizon. She could smell the seaweed and feel the salt tightening the pores of her skin. White foam lined the edge of each crest as they rose and broke before her, pulling desperately at the pebbles as they went out. Behind them new waves swelled in expectance, waiting for their turn. Then, in the distance, the fog seemed to dissolve, and The Island appeared. Even in her imagining it swayed from left to right. 'Stay still' she whispered under her breath. She envisioned each misty mile of water, rising and falling, swelling and ebbing, and the parts that never moved at all. She wondered how far it was, six miles, seven maybe. She wondered if the skiffs the fishermen used could make that distance. What had the Mayor and his men taken her mother out on? A boat larger than that she knew. They had tied her body to the outside.

The last time Lacey had seen her mother was not beneath The Old Oak Tree, nor in the back of the councilmen's cart. She had stood at her father's side whilst the crowd dispersed, most of them going to mix their grief with ale within the walls of the tavern. Frank's hand lay firmly on Lacey's shoulder. A man had come to greet him, reaching out an open palm to shake. The second her father's hand was off her, Lacey had run.

She had the speed and agility of a hare. Her plaits flying in the wind behind her like the tail of a kite. Frank called out to her, so did Bella. Their voices angry, afraid. But in a few quick moments her little legs had crossed to the wood line and like the extinguishing of a flame, her small shape vanished between the trees. In the woods she ducked and weaved through the undergrowth, she did not think then of the Forest Beasts, the fear of which had kept her awake many nights. She thought only one instinctual, animalistic, rhythmic thought. *Mother, Mother, Mother.* She moved fast, trying to close the gap between them that seemed with every passing moment to be splitting her in two.

Lacey burst out onto Deception Bay, the shingle skittering beneath her feet. But the boat had already left. It looked to her like a toy boat, floating atop the cresting waves. She could see the black figures of the riders, rowing diligently. And bound with thick fishing rope, tied to the side it, was her mother's body. They had taken her hood off, or perhaps the tide had torn it from her. Her hair soaked and stuck to her face. Each time the boat crested a wave, her head submerged beneath the surface. One arm, white against the grey of the sea, hanging down from its bindings, dragged lifelessly in the water.

Lacey couldn't remember how she got back home. She was found sometime later sitting at the top of the field. Her hair full of brambles and leaves. Deep scratches across her face. A few thorns still sticking to her tear stained cheeks.

Bella burst through the front door in a fluster. Her fingers desperately picking at the ribbon under her cap, her cheeks flushed pink from haste. Lacey's eyes shot open, her daydream instantly evaporated.

'Lacey! We have a visitor! Father and Sebastian are coming from the church, they aren't twenty steps behind me. Off, off with that!' Lacey looked at her blankly but raised her arms to allow Bella to untie her apron. 'Oh, your hair Lacey! I don't know how you manage within the small hours God gives us in a day, to ruin it so.' Bella, pulling her sister down from the counter, began plaiting Lacey's hair, her nimble fingers weaving the contrasting strands, ignoring Lacey's cries of 'Ow!' when it pulled on her scalp.

'Why does it matter how my hair looks?'

'When you are my age you will understand.'

'You are only five years older than me.'

'Five years is a lifetime to a woman.' Said Bella, two hairpins sticking from her mouth. Then, with a rag from the basin, she tried, mostly in vain, to rid Lacey of flour.

Footsteps could be heard outside. In the last moment Bella, taking Lacey's face in her hand said in earnest desperation 'Lacey, please be good.' At the sound of the bolt drawing back, she threw the cloth behind her where it hit the wall with a slap and slid to the ground behind the counter, just as the shop door swung open and the two men stepped over the threshold.

Sebastian Abner stooped below the low, wooden frame, his hat in hand. His buckles and knife winking at her in the light from the fire. He looked to Lacey like a child playing dress up. Bella promptly stepped forward.

'Welcome Master Sebastian.' She beamed.

'You have a quick step Miss Bella.' He said, in his soft, pleasant tone.

Bella, her breath still slightly uneven, answered, 'I thought it prudent to walk ahead in order to ensure the fire was properly lit.'

Sebastian held his hand to Lacey who in return placed hers upon it. He raised it to kiss, his eyes cut like narrow slits in his head, stared down at her. They were a cool, icy blue, the only thing of colour on his pale face, below white, almost translucent, eyebrows. Even his lips, which, unlike his father's, were plump, had the same exact colour as the rest of his face. As though he were wrapped in an extra layer of skin, which somehow, in comparison, made his eyes seem an even deeper blue.

'You did not attend Evensong, Miss Lacey.'

'I had work to do,' she replied, retrieving her hand.

Sebastian's lips spread into a smile revealing a row of teeth, too small for his mouth. They sat, as small as a child's milk teeth, studded awkwardly in his gums.

'Indeed. Quite the homemaker.'

'Not really.'

'Oh, come now Lacey, you are very adept at housework,' said Bella while placing a pot above the fire.

'You said last week I was half as useful as a one-legged dog, but cost twice as much to feed.'

Bella, her usual colour only just having returned, blushed deeply. She glowered at Lacey.

'And quite the humour too.' Said Sebastian.

'She is quick of wit.' Said Frank unsmiling, hanging his cloak on a peg by the door. 'I don't know where she gets it.'

Then, without thinking and taking even herself by surprise, the words seeming to rise of their own volition, Lacey said 'from Mother perhaps.'

The room froze. There was silence but for the crackle of the fire. Bella stared at her in pure astonishment and Sebastian had the courtesy to look down at the sharp toes of his boots. Lacey didn't dare look at her father so didn't see the expression on his face, but had she done so she would have seen sorrow. Having trespassed over such a crucial, but unspoken rule, Lacey felt her chest seize.

After what seemed an eternity Sebastian said, 'people say I have my mother's hair.' Offering the words as a small scrap so to feed the starving silence. Lacey glanced up at his face, it was, she thought, a small and unexpected act of kindness from him.

'Really?' Responded Bella quickly, grateful for the interruption.

'Well it certainly is not from my father.'

With a note of relief Bella answered 'nonsense, I'm sure the Mayor has a fine head of hair. Although in truth I cannot ever remember seeing him without his hat, nor his gloves.' Sebastian smiled thinly. 'Were it not impolite I'm sure he would wear them from dawn to dusk. Maybe even in bed.'

Bella laughed, more in relief than humour, and moved the laundry, folded in the basket, off the chair. Frank kept his back to the room a few moments longer, using the pretence of smoothing the creases from his coat. Then, with his eyes cast to the ground, he turned and fetched a stool for himself, while Bella busied with the tea.

'How was church?' Lacey asked Frank.

'Annabella did well in choir, she is a competent replacement.' He sat uncomfortably on the stool and directed his answer to the corner of the room, unwilling to catch her eye.

'How nice,' said Lacey in a clipped voice, his reluctance to look at her putting her on edge. She could tell by the stiffness with which he held himself, that he was still recovering from her mistake. But there was something else too. She felt an uneasy sense of something slipping away from her, but she wasn't sure what. Frank, then turning to Sebastian, asked a question about his stallion, and for a while the men spoke of horses. Lacey sat straight backed, looking nowhere in particular. Beneath the table her fingers drummed a tight rhythm on her knee.

Finally the kettle whistled, drawing the men's discussion to a close, and it was with a palpable feeling of relief from Lacey that Bella returned to the table with a tray of tea. She set it down, then reappeared a moment later with a plate of spiced biscuits, stacked neatly atop one another. They sipped at the good china cups, and Lacey wondered where Bella had magicked them from.

Perhaps she kept them secreted in her skirts, ready and polished for just such an occasion.

'A fine cup of tea,' said Sebastian holding the cup to his lips. 'You are quite the housewife.' Lacey glanced at Bella, seeing her eye's flicker at the misplaced compliment. Afterall Bella was no man's wife. The conversation moved from horses to fishing, Bella chiming in at times, but for the most part letting the men talk. She had perfected the art of supporting, but not intruding upon, the talk of gentlemen. Lacey on the other hand just nursed her tea, never allowing it too far from her lips, as though it were a shield. After a time Frank cleared his throat and said, 'the flowers were most beautiful this year, the church had many charming displays this summer.' Lacey frowned over the rim of her cup, she hadn't once heard her father talk of flowers.

'Indeed,' replied Sebastian, taking a handkerchief from his breast pocket and dabbing at his top lip. 'Miss Lacey,' he turned his cold gaze in her direction, 'your father mentioned you have quite the rose garden in your back yard.'

'Did he?'

'He did, and he said one or two buds were still in bloom. I have an interest in gardening myself. I wonder if I may be permitted a quick tour?'

'It is really just one plant,' protested Lacey.

'But quite the beauty.' Chimed in Bella. 'Plants like Lacey, under my watch they seem to shrivel, but Lacey is green fingered' she said, gently leaning her leg against her sisters.

'Nothing sweeter than a rose in bud,' said Sebastian, taking a sip of tea, his eyes looking up at her through blonde lashes.

The pair walked out into the twilight together. Lacey took a slow, deep breath. The air was slightly milder this evening, the sky a low, bruised purple, thick with clouds. She sniffed, Mrs

Andrew next door must have planted a new bush of lavender. The rose in question was indeed a beautiful plant, its tangled, snakey stems, wrapping around the back door and up the side of the house. Even in the dim a few flowers could be seen, peaking from between the leaves. Lacey couldn't remember when it had become *her rose*, only that once she had taken over from Bella in the watering off it, it seemed to blossom more fully. Now, in the summer months, when she slept with the window wide open, she could smell the perfume from her bed.

Sebastian walked past the rose and straight to the fence, not bothering to look back. Lacey, having paused, expecting they might discuss it, followed a moment after him. He leant one arm against the wood, then, with his pipe between his teeth, pulled a match from his waistcoat and struck it against the post. He dropped it, still burning, to the ground, where it hissed on the dewy grass. The wood pigeons cooed melancholically in the trees. Lacey looked out at the soft blue of the field in the fading light.

'I have no interest in gardening.' He said, shaping his mouth into a wide *O* and exhaling a ring of smoke.

'No?' She said sceptically.

'I cannot understand the compulsion to do something when you can pay someone else very little money to do it for you. I don't sew my own shirts, do I?' He waved his hand behind him towards the house, 'or bake my own bread. I cannot imagine a less productive use of my time than scrabbling around in the dirt for one measly flower, only for it to die in the vase a few days later.' There was a shift in his manner in coming outside, as though he had shrugged off his courtesy like a coat.

'Why does my father think you are have an interest in gardening?'

'He doesn't. He was just using it as an excuse, so we may have time alone.' His pipe crackled as he sucked on it. 'My interest is in you.'

Lacey felt herself blush and was grateful for the dim light. She felt the same uneasy feeling of something slipping away. Sebastian's eyes tracked the change on her face, pleased that his words elicited such a response.

He smiled and whispered 'I must say, there is such a curious pleasure watching your reaction to my words. Does it take a great effort in ignoring my stares through your shop window?'

'Sebastian I don't –'

He interrupted her before she finished the sentence. His voice returning to the same, even, cool tone, his lips still curling lightly at the end of each breath. 'I know you are an avid reader Lacey, almost every time I see you you have a book in your hand. But I wonder do you read the newspaper?'

Taken aback by the shift in conversation Lacey shrugged, answering 'Father does. I prefer fiction.'

'Why?'

'I like the escapism.'

Sebastian made a noise, somewhere between a sigh and a laugh. As though the concept of escape was absurd. Though the night was still the roses around the door stirred a little, rustling against their leaves. 'Perhaps you would enjoy the newspaper, it is mainly fiction anyway. They don't print the real news, what is of real interest to the Southern towns.'

With the feeling that their conversation was being pulled purposefully in one direction, Lacey responded only with, 'No?'

'Not at all,' Sebastian shook his head, a silver lock of blonde hair falling about his brow, his hand instinctually tucking it behind his ear. 'They don't write, for example, of the heightened cost of flour across all the Lake Lands.'

Lacey, unmoving, shifted her eyes suspiciously to his face. He continued, 'they don't report that it has crippled farmers from East to West. It is quite a shame.' She could hear his soft voice trying to bend to the sound of sympathy, but not quite managing, his mimicry sounding forced and unnatural, his tone slipping so easily into teasing.

'I haven't heard of this price change,' she said.

'No, of course not. It is a matter for the men to manage. Unfortunately for them they haven't a Mayor with the political cunning of my father.'

'No,' she said, neither a statement nor a question.

'No,' he answered, drawing smoothly on his pipe, his breath not changing rhythm. 'Thankfully my father has made it a priority to keep the price the same in Lower Lynch, although this has been no small feat. He has in fact invested a lot of his personal time in, as, you might say, a favour to your family.'

Lacey twisted the fabric of her skirt between her fingers, her eyes set upon the forest. She wondered if there were Forest Beasts and one appeared now, how quickly it would be able to cross the field to reach her. The trees swayed gently in the wind, thin slices of darkness lying between them. On dark nights when there was no moon and no stars, Lacey would lie in bed and imagine she was in the woods. When the darkness was so thick and impenetrable that she could not see the edges of her room she imagined that they didn't exist at all. In her mind the walls disappeared and the blackness that she stared into stretched out past the house, past the meadow and into the woods. Until her mother died the worst thought she had ever had was to be alone in the forest at night. Or perhaps she was afraid that she would not be alone.

She had found the knot at the centre of their conversation. He seemed to sense her discomfort, the corner of his mouth twitching into a half smile, as though he found it charming. 'I must say you aren't the conversationalist that your sister is.'

'She has a way with words.' Lacey responded through clenched teeth.

'But you are honest' he said looking down at her. He said it in a way that it sounded like the greatest compliment. He blinked his long pale lashes. His face unguarded.

In a moment it changed. His back stiffened. Sebastian tapped out his ash on the edge of the fence. From the inside of his coat he pulled a fresh linen handkerchief, and set about precisely cleaning the pipe with it, before placing both back inside his pocket. Lacey wondered if it had been her hand or Bella's that had ironed it so thoroughly. 'The true reason for my little intrusion tonight Miss Lacey was I was hoping that you might accompany me to the lake this Saturday. The weather being fine, I had thought I may take the boat out and would be very grateful of your company.' He paused, 'It would be a *favour* to me.'

The words sounded rehearsed and unnatural as he spoke them and only upon completion, did he finally look at her. But the word favour seemed to fall a little heavier than the others, as though it were written in bold.

'I will think on it and let you know' she said primly, crossing back towards the door. His long arm came up quickly and caught her around the wrist, stopping her mid step. She twisted round to him, her pulse drumming against his thumb. A thorn from the rose bush reached across the garden and caught in a strand of her hair. It was growing larger every day. Sebastian stared down at her.

'You wouldn't want to be ill-mannered in not returning the favour my father has paid your family.' He glanced behind her. 'I'm not sure the bakery would survive another quiet year, especially if the cost of flour were to rise.' He looked down at his hand holding her arm. Her blue veins visible through her flesh. His hold softened, his thumb stroked the inside of her wrist. Looking back at her, his head cocking to the side, he added in a whisper 'it's just one afternoon Lacey.'

It wasn't the neighbour's flowers she could smell after all. The thick, sickly, floral aroma was coming from him. He had pulled her inside the cloud of perfume that surrounded him, and she felt she could hardly breath. She thought of his nanny brushing his hair for him before bed. Her eyes went to the white blonde mane, pulled straight back from his forehead. She remembered how Mateo had squeezed the tips of her fingers as they had stood on this spot less than an hour before. Then she thought of her father's hands, holding the teacup so awkwardly and she said quietly 'if you wish, I will join you.' Sebastian smiled then, a broad, flawless grin. Like a child who had won a prize.

Once Sebastian had been bid goodnight, the tea cleared away, and their father departed for the Inn Bella ran up the stairs to Lacey's room. 'What did he want?'

'To go to the lake,' Lacey sighed as she fiddled with the ties on her corset.

'When?'

'The day after tomorrow. Here help me with this.' Lacey raised her arms so that Bella could untie the knot.

'How romantic,' whispered Bella into her back, Lacey could feel the excitement in her breath against her skin. 'Will you take the boat?'

'Hmmm.'

'How romantic,' she repeated.

Lacey, with her arms still raised in the air, looked down at her older sister. 'Did you know the price of flour has risen in all the Southern towns but ours?'

'No. Why do you say that? Ah, there it's done.' The corset came loose and Lacey, one arm across her breasts, reached for her nightdress.

'Sebastian told me. He said many bakeries across the Lakelands are closing down because of it.'

'I don't see how you had the time to discuss the economy in the few minutes you were outside. Anyway, if he says it I'm sure it is right, men understand these things. We are in hard times at the moment.'

'He said the Mayor was the only reason our prices were unchanged. It felt as though...' She paused, thinking of the right word. 'It felt like a kind of threat Bella.'

'Lacey you think everything is a threat.' She sat down on the bed, 'he was just talking, I'm sure. Showing off perhaps, he wants to impress you with his family's power. Father is very pleased.'

'Really? He never seems pleased with me. Sometimes,' Lacey rubbed her tied eyes, 'sometimes I don't think he even likes me.'

Sighing, Bella patted the space beside her. Lacey sat, Bella touched the ends of her black and white hair, rolling the tips between her fingers. 'You know the most distressed I have ever seen Father, in all the years, was when you went missing once as a baby. You crawled off, only for a few hours, you never did stay still, someone would put you down and within a blink you were gone. Anyway they found you before long. But I will never forget the fear on Father's face. He loves you Lacey, very much.' She playfully tugged on her hair.

'Was mother worried?'

Bella's hand dropped immediately, though they were alone in the house her eyes moved instinctually to the door, then with scorn back to Lacey. 'I don't know what has gotten into you with that talk Lacey.' She hissed. 'Don't allow your compulsion for disobedience to sabotage this opportunity. You should be pleased, it is a blessing that a man of Sebastian's standing would show such interest in a girl from a family such as ours. With our *history*.' She said, her eyes widening on the last word. 'He has you in his sights. You should be grateful. We might finally be able to give the villagers something better to speak of when our name is mentioned. If the Abners have shown us anything it is that it is always possible to turn misfortune around. To have our family joined by blood to theirs would be the saving of us.'

Lacey sighed, 'but he would be far better suited to any of the other village girls. Why would he want me?'

'You are the beautiful one,' said Bella not as a compliment but a fact. 'Sebastian likes beautiful things. His heart is set on you.'

'I wish it wasn't. I wish things were different.'

Bella stood and before closing the door behind her said under her breath 'me too.' Lacey picked up a reading book but too exhausted to read lay down instead, pulling the blanket around her and closing her eyes. She thought about Bella saying 'our history.' An image of her mother rose into her thoughts. It was a happy memory. Alice Emerson, her hands stained red with beetroot juice chasing Lacey through the bakery. The young Lacey shrieking with laughter and delight. The joy of the memory stung like a nettle and snapping her eyes open Lacey tore it from mind.

The ceiling above her was a wide black mass. Shadows leaked out from the edges of it and slid down the walls. The splintered roof beams vanished into it like oars in the sea. The house had begun to betray her at night. Rooms that in the daylight had been so plain, so ordinary, now filled her with a kind of dread. Draped in untrustworthy shadows that seemed to move and shift in the corner of her eye. As she got older she was becoming more afraid, not less. She had naively thought the fear would diminish as she got used to being alone in the room, but that was a few years ago now. When Bella had slept beside her she had felt safe. Comforted by the sound of her snoring, the warmth of her body. Lacey would rest her head against her back, feeling the rise and fall of her breath. Now when she was alone it felt like there was no life in the room at all. Now she moved around the space quickly, silently, making sure not to tread on the floorboards that creaked, so not to disturb the darkness.

There was a noise in the room. A dry, scratching sound. Lacey froze, her body brittle with fear. In the top corner of the room, at the edge of the candle light, with an agonising slowness, two booted feet lowered from the darkness. The heel of one scraping against the wall, the rest of the body obscured by shadow. Lacey's heart halted inside her chest, her face aghast and white as bone. Suddenly the feet spasmed, the toes kicking wildly in the air, rustling the mud-stained skirt, the laces of the boots whipping loose from the eyelets. The flame of the candle flickered in panic as though trying to escape the wick. The room filled with a sharp creaking sound. The same she had heard from the branch as her mother had hung from it. She had looked as though she were dancing when she died. The sound grew so deafening Lacey clamped her hands to her ears and squeezed her eyes tightly shut.

When she opened them again she was in darkness. The room was silent, the candle was out, its wax cold and hard, her reading book still open on her chest.

CHAPTER FIVE

Lacey lay in the pre dawn light of her bedroom. She opened her eyes just enough to see that there was light coming in through the window. Though it was not day yet, the dawn would not be breaking for another half hour at least, it was mercifully no longer night. Thin cool fingers of blue stretched across the sea and the forest to come through her attic window, and for them she was grateful. The nightmare of the night before fading with the new day. She exhaled which turned into a yawn and for the first time all night was able to fully relax. Her legs stretched out to the bottom of the bed. Her feet poking out beneath the sheets and hanging over the edge, something she would never do at night.

Lying in such a way, a memory from the previous summer that she had pushed aside drifted into her mind. She was sitting on the edge of the dock, her bare feet swinging in the water below, the tip of her toes skimming the cool surface. The setting sun breaking through in patches and igniting points of the lake, casting long silver slithers across the horizon. Mateo sat by her side. In a moment he jumped to his feet, pulling his shirt over his head in one swift movement. Lacey's eyes, unbidden by her, were drawn to the shape of his arms and the smooth dark arc of his back. His scars spreading across his spine, like a vast spiders web. The last time she had seen him shirtless he had been a boy. Tall and scrawny, with legs and arms too long for his body, but now he had changed. The indecent furrow of black hair just above his trouser line shocked her into turning her head. It had only been a moment, a second later he had dived in, but the image of him burnt into her memory, skirting around the outside of her mind, like a dog whining at a door, waiting to be allowed in.

She shifted in the bed, but her thoughts filled with the sight of him on the dock, she could smell him too, sweet with sweat and sawdust. Then her mind created a whole new illusion. She imagined him beside her now, his chest pressed up against her, feeling the weight and heat of him. His body warm like a stone in the sun. She imagined him staring down at her through locks of dark brown hair, her bedsheets draped across his back. Something at the base of her stomach flickered and she turned over suddenly, kicking the sheets away, exhaling forcefully as though expelling the image. She lay frustrated, angry that not only did she seem to not have any control over her own thoughts, but now of her body too.

Lacey pulled herself downstairs and got to work. Though she was tired she worked hard. Her feet were sore in her boots, the soles of which had worn down so much when she held them up she could see the light through them. Nowadays her back so stiff it felt as though her muscles at the base were locked around her spine. She wondered how long it would be until she stooped like her father and her joints began to lock in place like cooling iron. Her hands worked automatically, sifting the flour, whisking the eggs, kneading the dough.

Her mind of late, during these repetitive motions that she had done every day since she was a little girl, had the habit of untethering itself from the rest of her body. It was worse since the nightmares had started. She would lose herself in her revelries finding that whole tasks had been completed without her having noticed. It was not that which bothered her so, she had always possessed a wandering mind. It was what filled her mind that scared her. The Island. She could lose whole hours now thinking only of it. It filled her vision, spread to the very edges of her eyes. The unnatural bending of the light around it, it's predatory descent from the horizon towards her. She would be staring at her hands in the dough then feel it pulling her in like a rip tide. Then in a blink she was sitting in the kitchen. The doughs finished, proved and baked, the dishes clean, the work tops wiped, the bread sitting in the window ready for purchase. And not once had she considered a single action along the way.

That afternoon alongside Bella, Lacey walked across the field to the well. Their skirts blowing gently in a breeze that held the faint scent of autumn. Close by a few cows looked on in mild disinterest, one or two approaching the sisters in anticipation of milking. Lacey reaching out and stroking them as she passed.

'I saw him blush at just the sight of you,' said Bella, reaching for the rope to tie the bucket to the top of the well, 'though I hear Nanny does rouge his cheeks each morning.'

Lacey leaned over the well wall watching the pail sink into the darkness, her voice echoing lightly. 'If he proposes then what, what will happen to me?'

'You will be wed.'

'But then what?'

'Then children.'

'How do they come?' Lacey asked cautiously, glancing sideways at her older sister. Lowering the rope Bella shot her a sardonic look. 'I know they come out of me' said Lacey quickly, 'but how do they get in there? They aren't in there now.' Lacey thought then of a row of tiny babies inside her tummy, curled and pale like a shelf of proving doughs.

'No' snorted Bella.

'Don't laugh at me' flared Lacey, her cheeks blushing in annoyance. 'Oh forget I asked.' She spun round to sit on the well, digging the toe of her boot into the ground.

'No,' said Bella supressing her smile, 'I forget your age when...' The word mother floated noiselessly above them. 'When she died. I can tell you.'

'Don't bother if you will laugh,' glowered Lacey, behind a lock of black hair.

'I won't.'

'Very well' said Lacey lifting up her chin and watching her sister with thin, distrustful eyes.

'Men and women are different between the legs.'

'I know that.' She interjected.

'Don't interrupt, you were the one who asked me' snapped Bella.

Lacey acquiesced.

'So, they have different parts and when those points touch a baby is made.'

The sound of the bucket hitting the water echoed up through the walls of the well. Bella allowed the rope to slacken in her hands before pulling it back.

Lacey wondered for a moment in silence before saying 'it hurts when the baby comes out. Sometimes sows die of that don't they. Father's mother died of that, people *can* die of that.'

'Yes, sometimes' sighed Bella, passing the rope to Lacey and flexing her fingers.

Lacey stood and began pulling, stating frankly 'I don't want to.'

'Nobody wants to die.'

'No I mean I don't want to have a baby.'

'Don't be ridiculous' retorted Bella flatly, reaching for a hair pin in her apron pocket and slotting it into the edge of her cap.

'Does it hurt when the baby goes in?'
'I don't know. Maybe.'
'Why do people do it?'
'Because babies are a blessing.'
'Does it hurt the man?'
Bella looked up to the clouds above, squinting in thought. 'I don't think so.'

'When I bleed it hurts, it aches I mean. Is it worse than that?'
'Does it matter if it hurts?'

A thin rippling disk of reflected light had appeared out of the gloom, Lacey fastened the rope and grabbing the pail untied it, then rested it on the wall. 'I'm not doing it Bella.' She stated looking at her, 'I don't like babies really. They cry so much.'

'You have no choice, it is the husbands choice and men always want babies. Especially boys.'

'I have felt and there is no space on me big enough for a baby to come out.'

'How do you know?' Bella's eyes narrowed. 'You must only feel to wash otherwise it is not allowed.' She said sternly 'it is ungodly Lacey.'

'It is ungodly to think that the head of a baby might fit through there!'

'That part belongs to God and your husband.'
'What part?'
'Between your legs' hissed Bella gesturing to Lacey's skirts.

Lacey considered this a moment, her face drawn in thought. She could tell Bella wanted to return to the bakery, but Lacey stood unmoving, her hand on the heavy pail.

'Who does my mind belong to?'
'Your mind and the thoughts inside it are Gods.'
'And what of my breasts?'

Bella's patience had reached its end, 'pass me the pail.' She stretched her hand out, 'you are talking nonsense.'

Lacey jerked the bucket back, a little water sploshed over the side, she raised her eyebrows.

Exhaling loudly Bella answered, 'they will be your childs and maybe your husbands.' Honest of the limits of her own knowledge she added, 'I think.'

'So some of me is Gods, some my husbands, and some my baby's. What of my hands?'

'Nobody wants your hands.'

'Those are mine?'

'Yes.'

'And might my husband want my elbows, or God want my neck, or the space here between my lip and my nose,' she pinched the spot, 'who might that belong to?'

'You are talking nonsense' repeated Bella.

'Perhaps the baby wants that' muttered Lacey, gripping the handle of the wooden bucket and dragging it off the edge. She stood there holding it with both hands the weight of it arching her forward.

'Have I answered your questions to your satisfaction?' Asked Bella, her hands on her hips.

'Oh yes, Thank you for blessing me with your knowledge, now I know all' Lacey said sarcastically, blowing a lock of white hair away from her face in frustration.

'Good then you can carry that water back with your very own hands.' Bella turned on the spot and walked primly across the field in the direction of home.

*

The sound of the laundry cart echoed down Main Street. Lacey took care to avoid any potholes. Last month she had run over one and cracked a wheel which resulted in her and Bella having to carry the laundry on their back for a week whilst it was being mended. She made two home deliveries, returning fresh sheets, before climbing the hill to her last stop.

Before long she was on the other side of the village, approaching the Manor's boundary wall. Two stone wolves stood guard either side of a heavy oak gate. They stared into the distance, their lips raised, their sharp, grey teeth bared in an infinite snarl. With her cart still in hand, Lacey turned awkwardly. Walking backwards she struggled through the gate and out onto a wide flagstone courtyard. There were no potholes here.

The yard stretched before her, almost as deep as the field outside the back of her house. A few people moved busily around the space. From within a set of stables to her right she could hear the sounds of spades striking stone. Outside, a young boy with his sleeves rolled up, stood stroking down a tall stallion. He brushed it with appreciation, standing on tiptoe to reach the top.

Ahead of her the Manor loomed. It was built of chalky, white stone, shipped in from across the lakes. Three storeys tall and twice as wide, with chimneys running the length of the roof, it sat proudly in its place. Each wide, perfect window with nine perfect panes, was decorated with ornate cornicing. Lacey walked round to the side entrance. Leaving her cart at the door and carrying the sheets inside.

She made her way through a thin alley and into the manor kitchen. It was a high-ceilinged room, with copper pots and pans hanging from great racks. A fire crackled with a small tree's worth of logs, a chicken hissed on a spit in protest above it. Its siblings hung half plucked to the side. Their soft pink shocks of flesh showing between plucked feathers. At the table a meek girl with black hair peeking from the edges of her cap nodded at her.

'Morning Ann,' said Lacey.

'Good morning Lacey,' she replied, her hands red with blood. The chicken heads and feet lay in a pile beside her knife. 'Nanny's in with the young master.' The household staff still had the habit of calling Sebastian, though well into his twenties, the young master. 'She said to take the laundry straight up to The Master's room.'

'The Mayor's room?' Lacey asked, pausing. 'I normally just leave them here.'

'At the top of the stairs,' Ann said, nodding towards the staircase. Pulling another bird onto the chopping board and bringing down the blade with a whack, she added 'you can't miss it.'

Lacey climbed the servants' stairs. They snaked and darted around the edges of the building. At the top she opened a door and came out onto a landing. Her steps suddenly silent on the thick carpet. She was no longer in the servants' area, and nervous that she might have mud on her boots, trod lightly. The landing wrapped around the top of a wide staircase, leading to the floor below and all the way down to a polished entrance hall at the bottom. The walls were adorned with great oil paintings. Unknown landscapes, decaying fruit, angry looking men. A glass chandelier hung above, its sharp crystal glittering like icicles.

Lacey crossed quickly to a double door, the only other door on this floor. Balancing the sheets on one arm, she knocked gently but loud enough to be heard. A single word answer came from within.

'Come.'

She tentatively pushed the door open and stepped inside. This room was not carpeted. It was, if anything, jarringly bare in comparison to the landing. In here there was no wallpaper, no ornate paintings, no chandeliers. Only a single bed, and a dresser. It had the punishing bareness of a prison cell. Standing there she had the feeling she was trespassing. The Mayor, thankfully, was not inside, but he had left the anteroom door ajar and she could hear the sound of water in a wash bowl coming from within.

'Just dropping off your laundry sir.'

'Take the dirty with you.' He answered. Lacey looked and saw a small pile of clothes on the bed. She lay down the fresh folded laundry and hastily scooped the rest up.

'Thank you,' she said quietly before leaving and closing the door behind her, eager to leave the cold room.

Lacey was halfway back down the servants' staircase when she realised her mistake. She had glanced absentmindedly at the pile in her arms when she had seen the shine of black leather. Her footsteps stopped abruptly, their echo ceasing a second later. At the top of the pile of dirty laundry was a pair of black gloves. The Mayor's gloves.

She was immediately certain of her error. There was no chance he had meant for her to take them. He was never without them, besides it wasn't the job of washerwomen to clean leather. He must have lain them on his bed when he had gone to wash his hands and she had picked them up with the rest of the laundry. She turned on her heels and raced back up the stairs cursing under her breath. Again she crossed the padded landing. Knocking lightly on the bedroom door, though not waiting for a response she pushed it open.

Lacey froze on the threshold, one foot in the hall the other inside the bedroom. The bedspread, which, less than a minute ago had lain neatly tucked atop the bed was strewn across the floor. A water jug that had sat beside the bed lay smashed. The broken glass protruding out of the pooling water like shards of ice. The room, which a moment ago had been as still as a crypt was in sudden disarray.

The mayor stood with his back to her, his arms frantically ripping the bottom sheet from the mattress. He spun round in shock, at the sound of her entering. It was the appalling whiteness of them that drew her eyes to his hands. A startling paleness, beneath the black cuffs. Not white like a new thing is white. It was an old, dead white, like the fat of a cut of pork. But soft like fungi on decaying wood. It looked as though if you pinched it the skin might pull right away from the hand in one piece. Each fingertip wrinkled and puckered as though left in water too long.

But it was not only that which widened Lacey's eyes and caused her heart to skip a beat. On the back of both his hands was a tattoo. Black, but greying and even greenish at the edges. A single, continuous line, the unmistakable shape of the of The Island. Three, crown-like peaks.

Lacey's eyes took all this in before he could whip his hands behind his back, the sheet falling limply onto the mattress. When she looked up and her eyes met his, his face wore a look of vicious anger. His blood shot eyes burnt red at the edges, his nostrils flaring in rage. Though he said nothing his fury was palpable. Like a wolf behind a window, its breath misting the glass. Lacey's cheeks flushed pink, her throat seizing in that familiar child-like way before crying. The two stood facing one another, the moment so painful it seemed to stretch into hours.

Finally, he broke the spell. 'Put them on the dresser.' He whispered, the words shaking at the edges.

Lacey did so quickly, then returned to the door. 'I'm sorry,' she muttered as she made her retreat, the tears pricking painfully at her eyes. She left the mayor standing there with his hands still hidden behind his back.

But before she had crossed the landing she heard his bedroom door reopen. Her stomach dropped, with her head down she continued on without stopping.

'Miss Lacey' he said, his voice strong enough to reach her, but no further. 'Miss Lacey.'

She stopped, taking a deep breath before turning to him. 'Sir?'

He took a few steps closer to her. His face having reshaped itself into its usual look of placidity unnervingly fast. His eyes like cool stone. She glanced down to see his hands once more encased within their gloves. 'I apologize for my tone.'

'It's nothing sir,' she said moving to leave.

'It was impolite.' He said, stopping her, his eyes locking upon hers. 'I apologise. I did not mean to snap at you, most of all.'

'Most of all?' She responded.

'Well,' he said, clearing his throat, 'I hear you will be returning to the manor as a guest in a few days. Sebastian has invited you for a trip to the lake.' When she was late to react, the Mayor looked suddenly uncertain. 'Did he not?'

'No, he did.'

'Oh,' he said, reassured, 'that is good then.' Lacey wanted to leave, but found she could not. His stare upon her had the same effect as if he had his foot on the hem of her dress. Finally, he granted her mercy. Blinking once, he said 'good day miss Lacey'

Lacey nodded and turned. Though she wanted to run, she forced herself to walk slowly down the servants' staircase. She didn't want him to hear her run. But once she was outside and on the other side of the gates, she grabbed her barrow with both hands and walked in the direction of Mateo's house as quickly as she could.

CHAPTER SIX

For the second time that day Lacey opened a door before being invited inside. The watery reflections shimmered and danced across Mateo's walls. The air thick with the scent of beeswax. Mateo was bent over his trestle table, a pencil behind his ear, sanding a piece of wood back and forth. Clouds of curled wood shavings settling in piles across the table and at his feet. An unfinished rocking chair sat behind him.

'Good morning Lacey,' said Mateo, not looking up. 'Don't you know it's bad manners to enter a room without an invitation?'

'I'm learning that,' Lacey sighed, kicking the door closed with the heel of her boot, before sitting on the bench and plucking her gloves from her fingers.

Glancing at her Mateo said quietly but firmly, 'hood off.'

'Sorry,' said Lacey, quickly removing her hood. Her mind so far away she had forgotten his house rule. She remembered once when they were young, he had come for dinner at the bakery, as he often did after his parents died. It had been a stormy night and the two of them were playing ring toss on the floor as her mother worked. Lacey's father had arrived home, stomping his muddy boots on the doorstep, walking through the door, his hood still atop his head. Mateo had screamed, a wild, frightened wail, his face a sudden tortured mask. He had skittered across the floor, away from Frank, like a frightened cat. Only when her father had removed his hood, and her mother had held him and rocked him a while, had he stopped crying. Ma had come to collect him not long after and, not wanting to upset him, Lacey had never asked him about it again.

'Do you often walk into houses unannounced?' He asked her, taking the pencil from behind his ear and marking a point on the wood. 'What if I'd been naked?'

'Then Mateo I would have screamed and run. For the mere sight of a naked man would send me half mad.' She said, dramatically feigning fainting, holding the back of her hand to her brow and lying back on the bench. Smiling wryly Mateo continued his work.

Lacey dropped her hand but remained lying, staring up at his ceiling, her face settling into a frown. They stayed that way a while, the only sounds Mateo's sanding and the gentle wash of the lake water beneath them.

'Come' said Mateo, not looking up. Lacey stood and walked to him. She saw that he had been sanding the back of the chair. It was a lovely pale oak, sanded as smooth as porcelain. She followed him as he carried it over to the unfinished piece. 'This is the best part' he said, then handing it to her, directed her to slot it in. Each spindle of the rocking chair aligned with a small hole on the back piece. Standing behind her he helped her move the section in place so that it fit perfectly. She could hear his breath just behind her ear, and for a second her eyes flickered shut. She felt suddenly aware of the skin on the back of her neck where her plaits parted. Putting his hands over hers he gently pushed the piece down and the wood made a satisfying sound, slotting in place. Neither moved, Lacey felt his eyes shift from the wood to her.

'You smell like washed linen,' he said. She smiled. Gently, quietly, Mateo began to sing

'Oh washerwoman Oh,

There's pain in my heart you know.'
Taking her by her shoulders he spun her round, half smiling
she allowed herself to be turned. With one hand holding hers and
another around her waist, Mateo pulled her into a slow dance.
Smiling he sung to her the old gypsy song. Their feet marking
their progress in the sawdust.
'I loved you but now,
You've married my brother.
So stay and wash my tears away
Oh washerwoman Oh.'
She felt the pressure of his touch against the narrowest point
of her waist as she had felt his breath on the back of her neck.
Her nerves around it began to flicker, the feeling spreading, until
her body seemed to be ignited. He finished the song, grinning.
Their footsteps slowing to a halt, but still his arm stayed around
her waist. Lacey watched his smile flicker and fade, his gaze
dropped from her eyes to her mouth. Instinctually, protectively,
she drew the corner of her bottom lip into a bite, pressing the
flesh between her teeth. His face began to shape itself back into
its natural frown, but, before she knew what she was doing,
Lacey's hand rose up. She ran her thumb along his brows as
though smoothing them out. Then, with her fingertip, she pushed
a lock of dark hair behind his ear. For a pair who had touched
each other only as children do, with the roughness of siblings,
the act was shockingly unfamiliar in its intimacy.

Every breath he exhaled, she inhaled. Lacey had the feeling
of standing on the edge of a cliff. She swallowed. There came
a noise outside; simultaneously Mateo released her and Lacey
swiftly took a step away. Two men, fishermen most likely, talked in
deep tones, the sound of their footsteps nearing, then diminishing
as they passed. Lacey's mind suddenly went to her barrow, she

wished she had brought it in, rather than leaving it outside. What if Father were to see it and know she was here?

The frown she had wiped from Mateo's face sprung back, and she exhaled, as though she might blow the atmosphere from the room. She had. The moment passed. Not catching each other's eyes, they both turned away. Mateo retreating to his chair, Lacey back to the bench.

Lacey watched him a while before speaking 'Mateo?'

'Hmm?'

'Do you think God can see my thoughts?'

Half smiling he said 'I know little of your angry God' and reached for a jar of wax and a cloth.

Lacey squinted up at the watery reflections above her, 'I wonder if he can see them now, or only when you die. Perhaps only after death are you revealed as a sinner.' She bit at a nail with the corner of her mouth.

'Do you think you have sinned?'

Lacey did not answer. She thought then of that morning, how she had lain in bed awake and thought of him. Why did her mind bring him to her? This unanswerable question. What did she want?

Biting hard Lacey ripped the hang nail free from the bed, feeling the acidic sting of torn flesh. 'My thoughts and my body seem to be conspiring against me in sin' she sighed sucking at her finger.

Mateo, engrossed in polishing, smirked. 'Your God is more concerned with sin than mine, so I may not be the best to advise you.'

'So you can think what you like without fear it is wrong?'

'I can.' He nodded, then glancing up at her added, 'I do.'

Unaware of his glances Lacey fiddled with her finger, building the courage to address what had brought her half running here in the first place.

'Do you have any tattoos?'

He cast her a quizzical, smiling look, 'do you not know me well enough to know that I do not?'

'Well I don't know your whole...' she gestured towards his body. But sparing her her blushed cheeks, Mateo interjected.

'It is bad luck for gypsies to mark their skin before marriage. A tattoo is the last thing I need. I stand out in this town enough as it is. Besides no-one in the Lakelands has tattoos.'

'The mayor has two tattoos on his hands.' She said softly.

'Ha!' Chuckled Mateo, but then looking at her face and seeing it was not a joke he stopped smiling. 'No he doesn't.'

'Have you ever seen him without his gloves on?'

'Well,' he said contemplating, 'no. Have you?'

'I saw him without his gloves this morning.' Responded Lacey inwardly repressing a shudder.

'Why?'

'I took them,'

'You took his gloves?'

'I didn't *take* his gloves. It was an accident. I was collecting laundry at the manor and I took a pile of clothes off his bed. In error I picked the gloves up too. Anyway, when I went to return them, I saw his hands. He tried to hide them, but I saw. They were,' she winced, recalling their sickly condition, 'so pale. Unlike anything living.' She kept his later apology and mention of the lake trip to herself.

'What were the tattoos of?' Asked Mateo, wrapping and unwrapping the cloth around his knuckles.

'That was the thing,' Lacey tucked a strand of white hair nervously behind her ear. 'They were of The Island. The three peaks.'

Mateo blinked, processing the information. As though translating it from some foreign language. His hands stopped moving. 'That can't be right. Are you sure?'

'I am certain. I know the shape of that land better than any other thing. I see it every night in my dreams.'

Mateo dropped the cloth, turning to look full at her. 'That makes no sense. What reason could he possibly have to mark that nightmarish place upon his skin? That place is unholy... evil.'

'Evil? What is evil about the dead?'

'You know what I mean,' said Mateo, his eyes shifting uncomfortably around the room. 'It is where one's soul is tortured.'

Lacey saw in her mind the image of a hooded face, the material sucking around the mouth, blindly gasping for air, the rope around its neck. Could her mother see any light from inside the hood, or was it all just blackness? Lacey forced the thought out of her head, standing to leave, as though she could no longer be in the same room as the idea.

Speaking to himself as much as to her, Mateo said, 'no wonder he always wears gloves.'

CHAPTER SEVEN

The afternoon the villagers laid Mary Morgan to rest was cold and overcast. Dark, slate coloured clouds, sat in low, ominous lines on the horizon. The cows in the field, sensing the approach of rain, surrendered and lay down on the grass. The air had the taste of salt, a strong wind was blowing in off the sea, bringing the bay a little closer with every breath. The day held that strange, thick, electric energy that always came before a storm.

The procession walked slowly down Main Street, their heads to the ground, the heels of their boots dragging with every step, as though it were they who were destined for the grave. The women wore their black cloth caps and gloves, the men, held their hats in their hands. Only Mayor Abner, who stood at the front with the Morgans, kept his hat on. From where she stood at the back of the procession, Lacey could see its peak above the bowed heads of the other mourners.

The procession had walked to the top of the village and round to enter the churchyard from the back. The tombstones looked out onto the hills beyond, it was a pleasant view, the type that hadn't changed since the creation of the world. Lacey wondered if the dead ever tired of it. The line of mourners transformed into a circle around the empty grave. Mary Morgan's body lay in an open casket beside it. She wore a white dress, like a little bride. A few strands of her hair flickered around her porcelain doll face. Her expression was so peaceful she might have been asleep.

The wind swept down off the hills, and the crowd huddled a little closer. Mrs Morgan blew her nose loudly into her handkerchief, Mayor Abner, leant, ever so slightly away from her. He had an aversion to germs, his eyes watching the tissue as though it were a loaded pistol.

The Vicar, standing to the other side of the grieving widow, had the look of a man who would much rather still be tucked up in bed at the Vicarage. His mouth turned down at the edges, his chin stuck firmly to his chest. He cleared his throat and began to speak, 'It is with great sadness that we find ourselves gathered here this morning. Another one of God's daughters has been called to sit by his side. We will mourn the loss of her and ask why she heeded not the words of her parents. We will pray that the other girls may listen, and that the protective actions our good Mayor is implementing may keep them safe. We may too take comfort in God's plan. That all our girls, along with Mary, are together now in the eternal Kingdom of Heaven.'

Lacey looked around her at the sniffing women, who held handkerchiefs tight to their mouths, and the men who didn't cry, only stared in blank remorse. She wished Mateo were here, but he rarely attended any of the village gatherings. She spotted Lek Barrick standing beside Sebastian, a chewed matchstick sticking from his mouth. Lek had, of late, concerted most of his energy into growing a beard. But the thin strands of wispy hair that blew forlornly in the breeze couldn't in all good faith be called a beard. He shifted uncomfortably on his feet, his hands deep in his trouser pockets, he wore no coat, only a thin jacket, his shoulders arched against the wind. Most who knew Lek, would say he had the face he deserved, and it wasn't improving with age. Both his nose and chin had an unfortunate curve to them and as the years passed they showed every indication that they may one day meet.

But Lacey could remember him as a young boy, before he had fallen in with Sebastian, he had had kind, smiling, moon shaped eyes. He had been sweet on her then, picking wildflowers to leave in bunches at the bakery, bringing her butterflies and ladybirds in glass jars as gifts. He even asked her to dance once at the feast of midsummer, but she had declined, instead spending the evening with Mateo. That was when he had changed towards her. His eyes no longer kind, but surly and cruel, his voice became one of the loudest in the chorus of local children who called her *Witch*.

Behind him stood his brother Bran, who was shorter and stockier, with none of the sharp malice of Lek, but instead a dull brutishness like a dog who had too often taken a boot to the head.

Lacey's gaze moved lazily through the crowd of familiar faces, suddenly she came upon a pair of eyes staring straight back at her. She started, as though she had been burnt, their focus so intense and piercing, she felt as though he might be looking right through her. However she didn't immediately look away, she held Sebastian's stare for a moment, before dropping it and turning, ever so slightly, towards Bella. He was wearing a long cloak, held together with a small, silver clasp in the shape of a sword. It sat horizontally across his chest, in line with his collar bone, making his shoulders look even broader than usual.

She felt Sebastian's gaze upon her long after she had looked away, it had the pressure of someone pushing on her forehead with the tip of their thumb. But she was practiced in ignoring men's stares, or at least in giving the impression of ignoring them. In the last few years Lacey had felt a change in the village men. Gone were the days of paternal smiles or innocent nods. It was with the eyes of wolves that they seemed to watch her now.

Their stares heavy with waiting. Whether it was small, secretive glances as she passed them in the village, or the brazen boldness of glaring at her across an open grave.

She had begun to feel, in turn, more conscious of her appearance. More aware of the shape of her hips within her skirts, of her breasts beneath her apron. She had the strange feeling that she was doing something without fully meaning to do it. She would catch the eyes of the men who came to buy bread, they would scan her as though she herself were a loaf. Appraising her shape, her weight, the lines of her. And their wives would frown at her or else give her a small half-smile, in comprehension, as though Lacey shared with them a secret she couldn't quite understand.

The Vicar continued his address, his slow measured voice struggling at times to be heard above the increasing wind. The pallbearers moved to place the casket lid over Mary.

Mrs Morgan wore a black shroud over her face, it shook with grief. With a cry she dropped suddenly to her knees, her hands reaching inside the box for her daughter. The crowd gasped in unison. The veiled mother pressed her wailing head against the dead girl, her hands grasping at her, feeling in desperation, the shape of her one last time. Her knuckles a shocking, raw pink. Lacey knew that she too brought in a little extra money washing clothes, you could always tell a washerwoman by the condition of their hands. Lacey's own hands were growing redder by the day. As Mrs Morgan grappled with her child's stiff body, Mary's little white dress was pulled up. Just above her pale knee Lacey saw something. It caught her eye. A birthmark perhaps.

Mr Morgan, stony faced, dead eyed, reached forward trying to pull his wife away. It was too fine to be a birthmark. Lacey's eyes narrowed, trying to focus on it. Finally Mrs Morgan was restrained by her husband and pulled back to a standing position. The Vicar hastily rearranged Mary, pulling her dress down, pushing the hair back from her face. But not before Lacey had made out the strange scarred mark on the girl's sallow thigh. Three sharp peaks. Lacey's mouth dropped open, The Island drifted into her mind. Then her eyes shot across to the Mayor's gloved hands. He held them clasped together, as he whispered a word in the Vicar's ear.

Composing himself, the Vicar straightened his green stole, and nodded to the pallbearers who placed the lid over Mary. With the methodical movements of a choreographed dance, they hammered each nail into the coffin. Then, holding the ropes taut, they lowered the girl down into her narrow grave. Mrs Morgan gave a small strangled sob and raised her handkerchief beneath her veil.

'The greatest gift we can give those who leave us, is a place for their soul to rest in peace,' the Vicar intoned. Lacey thought of her mother's soul on the Island. *The dead have no peace there*, was that what Ma had said? The Vicar went on 'in the midst of life, we are in death.' He dropped a small handful of earth into the grave, even above the whistle of the wind, the crowd could hear the hollow sound it made as it hit the casket. 'Earth to earth, ashes to ashes, dust to dust.'

The pallbearers set to work filling the hole. A muscle deep inside Lacey clenched. I might scream, she thought, I might yell out. The wind pushed harder at her back. For a moment, her body seemed to lift, just a little, raising her on to her toes. Her shawl whipped at her side, she grabbed it and held it close to her. She felt a sudden pulse of anger at the crowd around her. They seemed to resign themselves so effortlessly to staring at the ground, with such ease had they donned their black caps and gloves. They had their eyes so tightly shut they may as well all be wearing a veil as thick as Mrs Morgan's. Even the Vicar looked relieved to be burying her. Handing her over to the next life in a neat little box. Better the dead deal with the complexities of death, so not to allow it to seep into the world of the living.

Lacey looked down at the little mound of wet earth, a fresh brown scar on the grass. Her anger rose like a tide inside her as she stared at the soft new soil. It filled her vision, the sound of the wind and the voices falling away. Her heartbeat quickened, her pulse throbbing beneath the skin of her neck. Suddenly the earth seemed to start moving. The wet dirt vibrated and shook, small clumps on the surface quivering, falling down the sides. Little rivers of rainwater snaking their way down the shaking grave. Her eyes widened.

'Lacey?' Lacey looked up at Bella in shock as though returning from a dream. Without her noticing most of the procession had dispersed, only a few mourners remained. Lacey looked back down at the new grave, still and silent and final.

'Come,' she ordered, looping her arm into hers.

'Where is Father?' Asked Lacey, slightly disorientated, her mind still returning from a distance away.

'He left with the others, for the wake. Come now, we must join him.'

'Did you see a mark on Mary's leg?'

'No. What kind of mark?'

Lacey shook her head. 'Maybe I imagined it.'

'You are always in a daydream,' Bella said with annoyance, pulling her away. Allowing herself to be led, Lacey turned from the fresh grave and moving amongst the tombstones headed back into town.

CHAPTER EIGHT

The air inside the Golden Tavern was warm from the throng of bodies and thick with the smell of rum and breath. Candles shone brightly behind the bar, their wax dripping silently down onto the bottles below, creating strange stalagmite sculptures. A swathe of black mourning cloth hung in a wide crescent across the beam above Mr Carter, the Innkeeper's head, tied at each end in a bow. The material had sagged slightly and at points he had to bend down, in order to serve a punter, of whom there were many. Lacey guessed at least two thirds of the village had crammed themselves between the thick walls of the Inn. They lined the bar, crowded round tables, sunk into the shadows at the very back. A few looked up at the sisters as they walked in, whispering to their companions of their arrival.

Lacey always felt more anxious being amongst the villagers the days after a disappearance. She knew they were talking of her mother. Her cheeks pricked with shame and she made sure to catch no one's eye. She missed Mateo, for not one friendly face looked back at her. A nudge of his shoulder or a conspiratorial wink would have been enough to comfort her.

A few years back, when one of the fishermen had married, the Inn had been almost as crowded as this. The village had rejoiced in the celebrations. It had been a hot, summer night, even the bride had taken off her shoes and danced barefoot. Lacey had sat all night with Mateo, who after her pleading had joined the festivities. Though it was only a few years ago they were children then, before strangers stamped their stares upon them. Before Frank minded them being together. The groom had quieted the fiddlers and raised a toast to his new bride. Lacey could see the red gash upon the palm of his hand from where he had made the blood vow with her family only a few hours earlier. After speaking for a while, the man then paid his respects to his mother. The Inn stayed silent for his words of love and gratitude, the old lady sat listening with her eyes full of tears and pride. Her blood vow scar behind a pair of gloves, though Lacey could see a red stain drying at the corner of her wrist. The two motherless teens had listened to the speech with a sudden sadness. Mateo glanced at Lacey, then stealthily taking her hand in his had pulled her out into the darkness. The rest of the night they had sat together on the edge of the dock beneath a yellow moon, whilst the villagers inside drank late into the night.

'We should find Father,' Bella spoke loudly into Lacey's ear. The two began to awkwardly push their way through the crowd. The wall of backs seemed impenetrable. The mass of bodies impervious to courteous nudges.

'Move aside,' a familiar voice rang out, Lacey looked up. Sebastian had appeared as if from nowhere. He held out his hand for Lacey. The villagers jostled aside, drawing back to make way for them. She was suddenly grateful that Mateo was not here and with a mix of reluctance and gratitude looped her arm within his. The crowd watched as Sebastian escorted the two sisters to a table at the back, where Frank was sitting. A thin veil of politeness masking their looks of surprise.

Frank rose to greet them from his place by the fire, pulling up a little bench for them to sit.

'Thank you' said Bella graciously. 'We would not have made it through the crowd without you.'

'You are most welcome' he responded, then turned to Lacey. Bowing, he said 'Miss Lacey.' Not breaking eye contact as he bowed, staring at her through translucent lashes. Then, quickly, so that only she could see it, he gave her a small wink. Against her will, Lacey felt her cheeks blush. Though she looked away as quickly as she could, giving him only a perfunctory bow of the head, she knew he noticed. Sebastian's mouth twitched in satisfaction, then he turned back into the crowd. Feeling him move away, Lacey allowed herself to watch. She saw him return to sit beside his father, whispered something into his ear. The Mayor not bothering to look at his son, gave a short, curt nod.

'Thank you, Father,' Bella said, then turning to the rest of the table, 'Good evening Mr Turner, Good evening Mrs Turner, what a sad occasion.'

'Indeed it is Miss Bella,' answered Mrs Turner, as Lacey sat, 'terribly sad.' She didn't greet Lacey, only cut a disapproving glance in her direction. Though she was one of only a handful of people who would even sit at the same table as the Emersons, Mrs Turner avoided speaking directly to Lacey.

Bella had been welcomed into the circle of housewives, who often bemoaned their hard work and the inconsiderate behaviour of their husbands. When they spoke of tiredness and irritation with their spouses, Bella found she could attribute much of that to her father and strike a bond of understanding between herself and them. As the eldest, many of the motherly and wifely jobs fell to her. The women of the village had found a familiar role to attribute to Bella, that of a widow. Not one who had lost an actual husband but had instead lost the chance of a husband. Furthermore, where Bella had a more appeasing, social nature, Lacey seemed peculiar and distant. Her strangeness, on top of her mother's history, made her an unappealing character in many villager's eyes. Unlike her sister, they had not found an archetype to comfortably fit to Lacey.

Mrs Turner tutted loudly. Her hair, curled around a hot iron all morning, now hung in forlorn ringlets that bounced as she shook her head. She wore a touch of powder at each cheek. The ladies of Lower Lynch had seen the occasion, although a wake, as an occasion none the less. Many of them spent much of the days with their aprons around their waist, their hair pulled back, sleeves rolled, arm deep in soapy water, sacks of flour, or, like Mrs Turner, fish guts. Or else they sat nursing a fat baby, whilst another two cried in their cots for more. So, upon the occurrence of a wedding, Midsummer's eve, Christmas, or even a wake, they seized the opportunity and cast their aprons aside for their finest dresses, their cousin's lip stain, and the blush of their neighbour. But the persistent scent of fish, fully distinguishable, still rose from beneath Miss Turner's layers of rose water.

'Terribly sad,' she repeated. Her husband only stared, grim faced at the fire. However when Frank excused himself to fetch the girls a glass of mead Mr Turner's eyes flitted to rest upon Lacey's chest. Only moving occasionally when he felt his wife's attention turn to him. Aware of this, Lacey angled her body away from him as best she could, resting herself beside the hearth and allowing her concentration to relax a moment, until she heard Mrs Turner's question.

'Have you met the stranger?'

'What stranger?' Asked Lacey, sitting up a little.

Ignoring her, she addressed her answer to Bella. '*The unknown man*' whispered Mrs Turner, leaning forward, relishing the words in her mouth, 'he is a stranger in these parts. A fisherman from the Upper Lakes, staying upstairs for a while after his boat broke its rudder coming down the coast. Quite a handsome man,' she added, her cheeks flushing beneath the powder. 'All the women in town think so.' Mr Turner sipped his ale and stared at Lacey.

'When did he arrive?' Asked Lacey.

'Three nights ago.' Mr Turner answered, speaking for the first time.

'It isn't becoming of a young lady to take such an interest in a gentleman,' snapped Mrs Turner to Lacey without irony.

Lacey moved her eyes around the low-ceilinged pub, there was a little more space now. The men, with a few drinks inside them, had found the cool night air outside, more agreeable, and stood in groups, emitting blue clouds of pipe smoke. Between the remaining mourners Lacey could see the Mayor at a table in the corner, with a group of men, Lek and Bran sat at the bar, their glasses never long from their lips, her father too, paying for drinks. Then she saw a man, with a beard, more grey than it was black, sitting alone at a small table, nursing an ale. His brow low and furrowed in thought, his hair swept back, as though years of staring into the wind had frozen it in that style.

'Is that him?' Lacey asked, staring at the man. She couldn't see, whilst he was seated, what height he might be. The image of the figure on Deception Bay, grey and blurry, appeared in her mind like an apparition.

Obviously irritated at having to talk to Lacey, Mrs Turner looked up and answered simply, 'yes,' before returning to her conversation. Lacey felt Bella lean her weight back a little so that she might get a better view of the stranger. It wasn't often there was a visitor to Lower Lynch, less often still that the ladies would catch a glimpse of him. Frank appeared with two small glasses in each hand. The conversation moved gently between the usual topics, the weather, the fishing, the farmlands. Lacey sipped the sweet drink, occasionally glancing up to observe Mr Warren.

It was a cousin of Mary Morgan, Daniel, who started the initial upset. He sat with a few of his friends, field workers mainly, whose earth-stained shirt cuffs peeked from beneath their black coats. They had drunk rum all night, calling for Mr Carter to bring a bottle to their table and leave it there. Their voices, soaked in alcohol, gradually growing in volume and intensity.

Daniel had begun by talking of the old days. 'The girls in our day could swim anywhere,' he slurred, 'they weren't afraid! He pointed over to the fisherman Douglas who sat with his wife on the other side of the room. 'You and your sisters swam those waters Douglas, did you not?' Daniel's eyes shone and his breath, beneath his words, came quick and uneven. He threw the question across the room, as though casting a net, everyone turned to watch.

Douglas shifted a little awkwardly in his seat, uncomfortable with the sudden attention of the room. He tugged gently at his white beard. 'Yes,' he said quietly, 'we swam there.'

'Yes!' Cried Daniel, in satisfaction, still pointing a finger at Douglas, rum glass in hand, the liquid spilling and running down his arm. 'We swam all over. We were never afraid of that Bay. Now,' he leant back on the stool, moving his finger around the room, pointing to each corner in turn, 'can any here still say the same?' The room was silent. To Lacey, though no one had lain a new log since her arrival, the noise of the wood crackling beside her in the fire seemed suddenly deafening. The heat pricking at her back beneath her corset. 'Can you say the same today? Can your daughters say the same today?'

He sighed and lowered his arm, exhaling deeply. 'What happened to our Mary ain't right. Nor to the others, little Lucy a few months back, and Lizzie before her. More and more each year. It ain't right. Our Mary wouldn't never have gone off alone like that, she wouldn't never have gone through the woods alone, nor into the water alone. She was afraid of The Hooked Forest, little thing cried at night for fear of Forest Beasts. And never would she have gone on Deception Bay, she was told each morning, warned by her parents of the perils. It wasn't in her nature.' His voice, grew strained, and he stopped abruptly, clearing his throat and holding his neck as though the words had gotten stuck. In his silence one of the field workers, a man called Tobias, with a lip that curled into a scar on one side, sat up.

'No, no it ain't right!' He slammed a fist onto the table. The door opened, and those returning from their pipes quickly realised the changed atmosphere of the pub and filed in silently, standing against the wall. 'It's wrong, something's wrong here.' Suddenly, beside Lacey a log fell away and crumbled into the embers causing a burst of flames to rise up into the chimney. In the light, she saw the Mayor at the end of the Tavern, shift a little in his seat. A few more voices joined Daniel and Tobias, thumping their fists against the tables. 'And what's the council doing about it, I'd like to know? Our appointed councilmen!' Commander Kinch, who stood arm's folded by the door surveying the scene, made a move to silence them.

It was then that the Mayor moved noiselessly from sitting to standing, no one but Lacey noticed, as they continued their yelling from one end of the tavern to the other. He took from his coat pocket a cream lace handkerchief and held it against both eyes for just a moment. She stared at his gloved hands as though she might be able to see the tattoos beneath. 'Gentlemen' he said, his voice, no louder than if he were speaking to one man alone, still it silenced every cry. A few, who had stood in passion, sat, those who had thumped the tables unfurled their fingers and turned to hear him. Even the fire grew low and quiet in the grate. He looked around the room then, his pointed nose, like that of a bird, scanning the crowd, making sure of everyone's full attention. His voice, lower and quieter still. 'Stand up.' He said quietly. Nobody moved. Then he said again, 'stand up councillors, Mr Morgan and I call upon you to stand.'

There was silence, and then the tentative scraping of chairs on the stone floor. Around the room the four men stood. Professor Arnott and Dr Prior stood beside their table, the scholar's glass empty, the doctor's not yet touched. The Vicar stood at the bar his hands frozen, halfway through cleaning his spectacles. Mr Lewis, the cobbler, stood alone beside a stool, in the shadow at the corner of the room, his bald head glistening in the candlelight. All had the slightly surprised look of having the whole tavern turn their attention unexpectedly upon them.

'Gentlemen you have been accused of not doing enough to stop the drownings of these young girls.' Said the Mayor quietly. Daniel Morgan interjected, attempting to speak, but the flick of the Mayor's hand in his direction froze the words in his mouth. 'After all, why not lay the blame upon your doorsteps, when the truth is so much harder to face.' Lacey shifted uncomfortable in her seat. 'The blame isn't upon the shoulder of any of these gentlemen, who not only dedicate their lives to their work, but also to that of the betterment of the village.' He looked down then at Daniel Morgan, his glare cutting across the room, 'and nor does it rest upon the families. It is a hard pill to swallow, but the blame rests upon the girls themselves.'

The Mayor sighed, 'I too know the acute agony of grief. I too know, the anger, the heartache of losing someone I...' He paused, seeming to inspect the lace of his handkerchief before the word surfaced, 'loved.' The councilmen shifted on their feet. 'When my son lost his mother, I didn't leave my room for a month. I hung mourning cloths from every window in the manor.' He shook his head, rolling the lace back between thumb and forefinger, 'I gave up, laying myself as a sacrifice to my sadness. Laying the blame at every door, except where it belonged.'

Mayor Abner's head jerked in reflex up at the black cloth behind the bar. 'Deception Bay is a dangerous place, the Hooked Forest is a dangerous place, there is peril in this town. There is peril on the coast, we have already had enough girls wash up to know this, those whose bodies the current did not take. That is why I have advised Commander Kinch to reinstate The Watch, and from tomorrow they will be putting some changes in place. Most notably there is now a curfew, it is forbidden for all girls and young women to leave their homes after dark. There will be a daily bell at dusk to alert you.' A few women in the tavern began to mutter in protest, the Mayor paying no attention, continued. 'And there is a ban on anyone, man or woman, from entering the Hooked Forest. These may seem like harsh rules, but these are harsh times.' He took the lace tissue, holding it at each corner with the tips of his gloved fingers, and gently folded it into a small square.

'Mary Morgan wandered from the village and walked through the woods to Deception Bay. She decided to swim or else paddled a little and was caught by the current. Either way, it isn't for us to tear one another apart in grief. We cannot help the girls if they don't follow the rules. If they don't do as they are told.' He slotted the little white patch of cloth into his inside pocket. 'Sit down gentlemen' he said, nodding to the councilmen, 'you are good men, the blame does not rest upon you.' Each man sat in relief and the Mayor moved to join them. Daniel Morgan hung his head low and stared bleary eyed at a point in front of him. A low, sombre silence had befallen the room, then one, unfamiliar voice, spoke.

'The current wouldn't have taken them.' It said. The villagers turned their heads in unison, to look in the direction of the unknown man, Mr Warren. He sat, staring at his ale glass, turning it slowly atop the table, on each rotation the handle catching the light from the candles. Eventually he raised his eyes and cast his stare around the tavern. Then, slightly shaking his head he said, 'not on that bay.' The mourners, unsure of what to do, looked back at Mayor Abner, who, half crouching towards his stool, stood up fully again, but said nothing.

Mr Warren continued, 'I take it you folk see the bay as dangerous, or cursed and so none of your fisherman fish from that shore. But I, being a stranger of these parts knew of no such danger. I brought my boat in onto the bay where the girl...' he broke off, evidently uncomfortable at forming the words. 'Well, anyway, I sailed in there when my rudder failed, and, begging your pardon,' he said, nodding towards the Mayor, 'it doesn't make sense.' The crowd, as though they were painted figures at the back of a stage, moved not an inch. Mr Warren continued, 'it's the shape of the cove, the way it crescents out at one end.' He moved his finger in a semi-circle to illustrate. 'There aren't any currents there, not strong enough to take a body out. If anyone fell in there, they'd just wash back up onto the beach. You say only a few of your girls have washed up there.' He shook his head. 'If someone fell into that bay, the sea would spit them back out. Every time.'

Mayor Abner blinked once or twice, and finally spoke, his voice as flat and smooth as glass. 'What is your name stranger?'

Mr Warren turned to face him fully. 'Warren, John Warren. As I said I'm a fisherman sir-'

The Mayor interjected, 'and from which village do you reside?'

'Redford sir, born and raised.'

'Redford?'

'Yes sir.'

'I am familiar. Your port is something to be boasted of, is it not?' From where she sat Lacey could see Mr Warren shift a little on his stool, unsure of this line of questioning.

'That is true–'

Mayor Abner looked up to address the room. 'Those who may not be familiar with Mr Warren's hometown, may, perhaps, know it by another name. Rumford.' A laugh rippled across the room. Lacey, not understanding the joke, looked between Bella and Frank, who both smiled broadly. 'I'm not sure we will be taking advice from a man who professes to be from the most prolific rum port within five hundred miles.'

'Sir the shipping industry of my town has nothing to do with my professional opinion.'

'Can a resident of Rumford have a profession, other than propping up a bar?' Again, the crowd erupted in laughter, the tone cruel and cackling. The stranger drew a broad palm across his bearded jaw, shaking his head slowly. He stood abruptly, the sound of the stool scrapping against the stone floor, silencing the laughter. He leant forward, resting his knuckles on the tabletop.

'I'm a stranger here. I have no quarrel with any man from the Lower Lakes, in a few days time my own boat will be fixed and I will most likely see none of you again. But I heard what is happening to your girls, and I can say on my reputation, which in my land is held in the highest regard, that if she drowned, it wasn't there. Not on that bay. You would need a boat to take you far enough to catch a current that would carry a body away. You sir,' he said, addressing Daniel Morgan, whose hair had fallen in thick locks over his eyes. 'You weren't wrong sir, something is ill in this town.' Then taking a large gulp of his ale, Mr Warren placed the glass down and, passing the Mayor, walked out into the night.

The room stayed silent for a moment, then, in a quiet, relaxed tone, Mayor Abner said, 'Mr Collins are you very busy this week?'

Mr Collins, a sandy haired boatbuilder, stood a little straighter. Clearing his throat, he answered, 'no, not particularly sir.'

'Very good, then perhaps you might see to Mr Warren's vessel as quickly as possible. I agree, something is wrong in this town, and the sooner his boat is fixed and he is upon it headed straight back to Rumford it will be righted.' Then taking his glass from the table, he drew his hand up. The crowd in turn held their glasses aloft and shouted in agreement. A few even clapping in applause. Only Lacey, watching from across the room, saw the Mayor lower the still full glass, not letting a drop of the liquid touch his lips. She had seen too, that Mr Warren, a man of well under six foot, couldn't possibly have been the figure on the beach.

Another half hour passed and the mood in the Golden Tavern relaxed once more. A fiddle was brought out from behind the bar and a few sorrowful songs were sung. Eventually Frank had had enough and the girls wrapped their shawls around them and bid the Turners goodnight. Outside the cold gripped tightly and the three, huddling close, set off briskly towards home. When something caught Lacey's eye, she glanced down the alleyway to see a plume of smoke glowing silver above the back of a man.

'I have forgotten a glove' she said suddenly, drawing back, 'go now I will just run and fetch it. I won't be long, I know where it is. You go on,' she said, seeing uncertainty on her father's face. 'I will be less than a few steps behind you.'

Feeling the cold he answered 'very well, be quick,' and with Bella on his arm, he hobbled down the street. Lacey stood for a moment, watching them, then she walked back a little way and turned down the alley.

CHAPTER NINE

Lacey approached the tall back of the stranger Mr Warren as he stood alone in the darkness of the alleyway smoking his pipe. She felt her courage wavering as she went to address him and as she had opened her mouth, her voice betrayed her, shaking like a struck bell. 'E-excuse me sir?' He turned a little, the shark like profile of his face highlighted in silver against the backdrop of the lake. Black and infinite, sucking and consuming the light of the town.

'What is it Miss?'

'Excuse me sir, we haven't met.' She said, her voice still thin, one hand squeezing the fingers of the other.

'No we haven't, and after the interaction with your Mayor I can say I'm glad of it. No man in this town has treated me with any kindness.' He shook his head, exhaling in a humourless laugh. 'Not a single one.'

'But I'm not a man.'

He turned full to look at her then, her face open and young and expectant. 'No,' he said, 'you aren't. What do you want?'

'My name is Lacey Emerson. I want to ask you about Deception Bay.'

'I have said all I wanted to say, Miss Emerson.'

'Please tell me,' Lacey's face knotted into an anxious frown, inwardly cursing herself for not being able to find the words, 'how certain are you that what they say happened on Deception Bay cannot be so?'

Mr Warren took one broad step towards her, crossing the distance easily. She could see each coarse grey hair on his face. 'What do you want girl?' He growled at her, his teeth, sharp points within his mouth. Perhaps this was what Mrs Turner, and the women in town had found so handsome. It made Lacey's heart tighten with fear in her chest.

'I want to know the truth.' She whispered the words, her breath materializing as mist, then disappearing around his face. Suddenly the tavern door swung open and three men stumbled out, their pipes already resting between their teeth. Mr Warren's eyes narrowing at their arrival, before dropping back down to Lacey's.

'The truth?' Mr Warren, exhaling through his nostrils, shook his head. 'This may not be my town. But really you see the same folks everywhere, no matter the town. Up and down the Lakelands and further even. People are mostly good. But there is bad too, you learn to recognise it.' He paused.

'You see bad here?' Prompted Lacey.

The men outside the tavern guffawed at an unheard joke, but the stranger's eyes did not leave Lacey's as he said with finality 'there is evil here.' And with that he marched abruptly off and in through the side entrance of the tavern, under the scornful eyes of the village men, smoking as he passed.

Lacey stood a moment, looking out into the darkness. She could hear the water lapping gently at the sides of the boats, though she couldn't make out a single one in the gloom. She exhaled in frustration then turned to leave when suddenly, from the corner of her eye, she saw a movement. Something was hiding in the darkness, watching her. From the shadow of a doorway at the other end of the alley a hooded head leant forward. It was no longer hiding. Lacey gasped. It emerged slowly, its actions calculated, deliberate. It moved as though it wanted to be seen. Wanted her to see it. It stood front on and stared at her, though no features were visible beneath the hood, only a hollow empty void. The weak lantern light above the Inn, no match for the shadow. Its cape hung down in thick black swathes to the floor. For a sickening moment the faceless figure stayed still, just looking at her. Then slowly it turned and slipped away into the night.

Lacey's mouth opened as though she might call after it. But her body could make no sound. She stood still, a statue fused with the cobble stones. Frozen by the sinister, considered movements of the figure. He had not run. He had wanted her to see him, and once she had he had calmly returned to the night. Her thoughts were unformed and fluid with fear. But at the fore of each one was what she had seen as he had turned his back to her. By the yellow gold lantern light she spotted a symbol embroidered on the back of the hood. Three thin, jagged peaks.

*

The next day Lacey stood at the kitchen counter with her sleeves rolled up, making the filling for a blackberry pie. She pressed her hands into the rich, purple mixture, the berries bursting and squelching under her pressure. She squeezed her fingers together, feeling the juice rush between them. After a few minutes ever berry was decimated, crushed to a thick jam, the ant like seeds floating on the surface. Her mother used to do it like this. Tearing off little shreds of wildflowers and spices she kept wrapped in brown cloth, whispering to herself beneath her breath as she did so. Lacey would sit on her lap and watch as the pie baked in the oven, seeing the pastry on top start to brown.

'We have a pestle and mortar for that,' said Bella, neatly cutting an apple into thin, crescent shaped slices.

'I prefer it this way,' replied Lacey, leaning into the bowl, a satisfying wet, sucking sound coming from inside.

'Lacey! You are getting juice on the sleeve of your dress. It will stain.'

'What is the point of wearing a blue dress if you cannot get a little blackberry juice on it?'

'Blackberry juice is purple, not blue.'

'Close enough,' said Lacey, emptying the bowl into to the pot above the fire, and stirring in cut lavender. 'Do you think Mr Warren will leave today?'

'You seem half obsessed with Mr Warren, Lacey.'

'Not at all, I'm,' she paused, plunging her hands into the washing bucket, 'I'm only interested that's all. Did you not find his words interesting last night?'

'I found the Mayor's spectacular dressing down of him interesting. He has a mind sharp as a tack that man, not many get past him.'

'So, you think Mr Warren a liar?'

Bella frowned as though frustrated at having to explain this to her. She sighed like a woman of many years. 'No, not a liar, sister, a drunk.'

'Because he is from a town where they ship rum? Aren't they quite a wealthy and well educated town too?'

'Lacey, a man from Rumford who knows nothing of our lands can expect to be reprimanded when trying to school the gentlemen of Lower Lynch on the area of their birth.'

'But the men of Lower Lynch are very superstitious about Deception Bay.'

'As they are right to be.'

'Yes, but it means that they never sail their boats there. Whereas Mr Warren, being unaware of such fears and so unafraid to venture into the waters may know a little more about their currents. Don't you believe that to be so?'

Bella exhaled in vexation, placing the knife down flat against the board. 'I believe that Mayor Abner and the rest of the gentlemen know what is right. That is what I believe.'

Lacey rested her spoon within the pot and took a deep breath. 'Do you ever think if it was Deception Bay killing girls all along, then perhaps Mother was innocent?'

Bella stood staring down at the wooden chopping board. Her expression blank, her eyes black and unfocused. There was a long pause before she whispered 'Mother was a witch. No amount of neighbourhood girls going missing can change that.'

'But-,'

'Enough.' She snapped. 'I don't know what has gotten into you saying her name under this roof. I am grateful for your sake that Father was not here to hear it. Enough now. Keep your mind out of the past and put it to what is in front of you.' She picked the knife back up and resumed her cutting. The sound of the blade cracking against the board.

Lacey washed up in silence, leaving Bella to finish off the pie. After laying each dish to dry against the rack she untied her apron and pulled on her coat and cap. It being her afternoon off from the bakery, she had planned to spend it at the The Proffesor's, as she often did. Although this afternoon, as she made her way through the village, she detoured, veering off toward the Golden Tavern.

She glanced down the alley, remembering with a shiver the figure she had seen the night before. But in the daylight all menace had faded. She had then the fleeting and frightening thought that she had imagined it. Surely that was a sign of madness, seeing things that aren't there. The Golden Tavern sign swung lazily in the breeze, behind it a few anchored boats bobbed on the lake.

Leaving her cap on, Lacey pushed through the doors of the pub just as she had done the previous evening. The room smelled sticky, of old alcohol and wet wood. With relief, she found no Mr Carter behind the bar, only the noise of bottles clinking in the cellar. She turned swiftly and noiselessly through the door and up the little staircase behind the bar. The bare stone walls crumbling and smelling of chalky decay. At the door of the little guest room she inhaled deeply and raising her gloved fist, knocked upon it.

It swung open immediately and to her surprise Dr Prior stood before her. He took a small, but calculated step towards her, and, as though they were tied by string, Lacey stepped backwards too. The door, in response closed behind him, shutting with a firm and final click.

'Oh! Good morning Doctor.'

'Miss Lacey.' He answered shortly, pushing a few bottles into his bag and drawing it closed. He was in fact younger than his face or conduct suggested, but this was by design. He had begun on his moustaches during his days at medical school, across the lakes, and now treasured them as a mark of his intelligence and professionality as much as the certificate of medicine he returned with. 'How can I help you?'

'Is Mr Warren ill?'

The doctor looked at her, allowing his eyebrows to raise. 'What business have you with the stranger?'

'He wasn't ill yesterday,' Lacey said, ignoring his question.

'He has a flu.' He said, as he drew a long thin key from his pocket and turning his back on her, locked the door behind him.

'I am securing the contagion until it has passed.' His tone was clipped, his face stony and indignant.

'May I have just a quick word with him?'

'Certainly not!' He said, dropping the key back inside his pocket, Lacey followed its path with her eye, seeing its thick outline inside the material of his coat. Looking up she found he was staring directly at her.

'I understand that things must be difficult for you and your sister. Whenever another girl goes, the past is brought up. And perhaps it is exactly because you have no mother that you don't know how highly improper it is for you to be meeting alone with a strange man.' He leaned forward then, his voice lowering to a clandestine whisper. 'You are no longer a child Lacey, you are,' he paused, pulling the word from his mind, 'you are *changing.*'

The word made Lacey's insides twist. With a thin fingered hand, he turned her body and guided it back down the staircase. 'Your behaviour must change too. You may consider it a favour that I'm not informing your father of this. I won't inquire into the nature of these words you were planning to have but they won't take place now. The stranger isn't to be seen, and once he is well he will return to his own village, and that will be the end of it.'

'There was no impropriety Doctor. I was only wanting –'

'Get yourself back to the bakery now. You should know, especially after yesterday, what dangers girls are at risk of when they don't do as they are told.' With a gentle, but firm push to her waist, he dispatched Lacey back down the stairs. Frustrated, but knowing better than to say anymore, Lacey allowed him to guide her out onto the street.

She felt his stare heavy on her shoulders as she walked away from him. The dense rainclouds, that had lingered at the periphery all morning, had now gathered and hung overhead. The storm had held on through the night, but was now on the verge of breaking, Main Street was dark with shadows and fog. Lacey headed in the direction of Professor Arnott's house, promising herself she would knock again for Mr Warren in the morning, no matter what the doctor said. She wanted to know more from the stranger.

Ahead she saw the Morgans' home, steeling herself as she approached. The image of Mrs Morgan's shaking veil from the day before, echoed in her mind. She saw on their house the sign of mourning, a thick, black diagonal line across their front door. The paint had run in droplets down the wood before drying. Small bunches of flowers lay on the doorstep. Their stems still wet, as though only just this morning torn from the ground. The curtains were drawn at every window.

Amongst the wildflowers, sitting up as though placed with care, someone had left a doll. It had two black plaits and a green dress, with yellow stitching at the rim. Her head lolled forward, onto her body. Before Lacey knew what she was doing, she had stopped walking and bent to pick it up. Her mother had made one, just like this for Lacey when she was a little girl. She had adored it, carrying it everywhere. At night it would lie beside her on the pillow, as Lacey would rub its hair between her fingers.

The doll lay limp in her palm, its lifeless eyes staring into nothingness. Its hair and skirts blowing gently in the wind. She felt at the fabric with her thumb, it was soft, soft enough to lie in the cot with a newborn. Two small drops fell on the dress and soaked into the cloth. Lacey wiped her tears away on her shirt sleeve, and, careful not to upset the flowers, lay the doll where she found it. Suddenly, noiselessly, the front door swung wide open. Lacey jumped back in fright.

From within the gloom of the dark house came the figure of Mrs Morgan. Her plump face drawn and pale. The skin below her eyes raw and blistered from tears. Her veil had been discarded, however she still wore her mourning dress of black lace, but at some edges, where the dye hadn't quite down its work, it was a lighter brown, even white. Lacey could see that the woman, not being wealthy, had dyed one of her own dresses black, rather than buying new. Perhaps it was her wedding dress.

'What are you doing with that doll?' Mrs Morgan snapped, her voice harsh and brittle from crying.

'I'm, I'm sorry' Lacey stuttered, 'I was only taking a look. I'm very sorry for your loss.' She lowered her head and began to step backwards.

'What business have you with our Mary's doll?'

'None, I...' But the older woman cut her off.

'Looking to pinch it, were you?'

'No!' said Lacey, aghast.

'You've come to steal from my home have you? What type of a girl comes to a house in mourning with treachery in her heart?'

'I wasn't stealing the doll. I had one like it as a child. That was all'.

'Oh?' The woman paused, and her face changed. She wore the look of the cat that had finally spotted the mouse. Something in the sound of her voice made Lacey's stomach tighten in anticipation beneath her corset. 'A gift from your mother?'

Lacey didn't answer, only stared back at her. Mrs Morgan's sore eyes narrowed, as though in eager relief to feel anything but grief. Lacey could see her tongue working inside her mouth, feeling at the word before she spat it out. When she did it sounded like a smashed plate in the quiet street.

'Witch!'

Lacey's eyes widened in horror. 'No,' she breathed.

'Witchwork!' cried Mrs Morgan louder still. A young boy from Mr Tibbs's farm, passed with a cart full of straw, he stopped and looked at them. The neighbours either side of the Morgan house swung their shutters open and poked their heads out, intrigued by the commotion.

'You are like your mother. You have a witch's heart, Lacey Emerson, I always knew it. We all knew it.' A chubby hand, still grasping a balled handkerchief, poked at the air in front of Lacey. Lacey shook her head in shock and dismay.

'No! I, I'm so sorry,' she stammered.

'Take your sorrow elsewhere witch!' The boy with the cart leant against it and guffawed. 'What evil plans had you with our Mary's doll? Spells learnt from your mother I say. Tell me?!' Her voice grew louder and filled with tears. The sound of her grief echoed off the houses and down the street. Lacey, feeling the stares of the neighbours, more of whom had come out of their front doors, wished that she might disappear.

Then, behind Mrs Morgan, came the sound of hurried footsteps and Mr Morgan appeared in the doorway. His hair, usually combed neatly behind his ears, stuck out in wiry, grey clumps, patches of dark stubble grew around his chin. He looked as though he might have been asleep and startled awake. He placed a thin arm around his wife.

'Miss Lacey my wife is very upset. Please leave.'

'Oh Harold!' wailed Mrs Morgan, burying her face in her husband's chest, her voice suddenly soft and weak. The sound of her crying was somehow more unnerving than her yelling had been.

'I'm sorry. I really was just looking at it,' Lacey mumbled, feeling her throat tense, as a sob wrapped like fingers around her neck. Harold Morgan closed his eyes and nodded his head slightly, then gently guided his wife back inside the dark house, the door closing behind them with a muted click.

Under the watchful eyes of the neighbours, Lacey turned and walked away. She walked quickly, with purpose, and staring resolutely at the stones below her she concentrated on not crying. Not in front of these people. She wouldn't give them the satisfaction to finish this story, when they retold it this evening over an ale in the Tavern, by saying that she ran away with tears on her face. So she held them inside, though they stung her eyes and grew as a lump of ice in her chest. Still the word *Witch* resonated in her mind like a slap to the face. She heard it repeated in rhythm with her footsteps *Witch. Witch. Witch.*

The first few heavy drops of rain began to fall as Lacey turned the corner to see Professor Arnott's house at the end of the street. The building was slightly taller than its neighbours, built of black wood beams and white panels, the timber in the centre bowed slightly, beneath the weight of itself. The diamond shaped windows sat a little crooked in their panes, each reflecting a slightly different view of the street. Some where the glass was cracked, were papered over, unlikely to ever be repaired. A heavy shoulder jostled hers and rebalancing herself she looked up to see two Watchmen walk past. The muzzles of their rifles poking from the top of their cloaks. The man who knocked her, not stopping to apologize but watching her as she passed, spat a thick glob of tobacco onto the street. Lacey lowered her head and averted her eye.

Lacey gave the door two perfunctory knocks before reaching for the handle and allowing herself inside. She placed a package of two waistcoats, freshly tailored with extra room at the sides, on the stool in the hallway. She had sewn them in bed late last night and would not be expecting payment. Since she was a little girl she had engaged in a private transaction with Professor Arnott. Free mending and tailoring in exchange for access to his collection of books. She quickly lit a candle and was grateful for the light as the sky outside had darkened and above her she could hear the increasing tip-tap of rain against the gabled roof.

The house was empty, as she had expected it to be, recently she had come to plan her visits at the time of day when the professor was most likely to be out. Taking the candle she passed the grubby fire-side bed adorned with a moth eaten blanket around which empty wine bottles lay like flowers beside a grave. She climbed the creaking spiral staircase to the first floor. When the professor's family made the voyage to this land with the rest of the First Settlers all they had brought with them was their collection of books. They were one of the wealthier families in town and though the professor had squandered what last pennies his ancestors had bestowed upon him at the Inn he was still in possession of their books. But to the religious villagers of Lower Lynch such a collection of enlightened thought had worth only in as much as they might be used as kindling.

Literacy was uncommon for the woman of The Lakelands. Lacey's mother had taught her how to read, just as her own mother had done to her, under the pretext that she may better understand the teachings of the Bible. When Frank had protested, Alice Emerson had the shrewdness to placate her husband with the idea that it might be beneficial to the bakery were Lacey able to read more advanced recipes. So he had begrudgingly accepted the endeavour, though Alice had never once given her daughter the Bible nor a single cook book to read.

Though familiar to her Lacey still marvelled at the admittedly neglected but nonetheless vast collection of books. Row upon row of them, from medicine to the arts, stacked from floor to ceiling, from narrow three-page pamphlets to encyclopaedia's wider than a man's arm. Some were indecipherable on the account of the mould, and upon opening Lacey would find whole pages falling apart in her hands. Others so beautiful they could have been works of art, with intricate designs on the spine, lined in gold leaf.

Here was where she had spent hours poring over book after book, her favourites being the travels of voyagers many seas from here. The men who roamed the earth in search of discovery and new worlds. Those who existed on the very edge of life, living by no law but their own. Those who had taken their courage, leaving behind all they knew, in search of the undiscovered. As she walked past, her hand reached out, stroking the dusty spines.

She walked along, to the section where she knew there to be history books. Ma had mentioned the First Settlers when Lacey had told her of Mary's death. If she wanted to find more information about them, she would find it here. She traced her fingers over the books, stopping occasionally to pick one out, the spines peeling as they arched their backs towards her. The earthy, stale smell of the pages, so familiar and at the same time a little thrilling. She stopped, going back a step or two, seeing something that caught her eye. A thin, green spine embossed with a series of curved dashes. She felt at the indentation of the markings with her fingertips, before sliding the book from the shelf. It brought with it a large plume of dust. Coughing a little she carried it to a table and placing the candle holder beside her, Lacey opened the first page.

She knew there to be many texts written in the Lost Language, going back through the years. Though now only gypsies still used it. She remembered when they were young she and Mateo would play at Ma's hose and she was amazed how different his books looked to hers. They would spread them out on the floor and lie side by side, flicking through the delicate pages. She would marvel at his ability to read from both. There were many dialects of The Lost Language, Mateo knew the type Ma had taught him, but most were now almost entirely extinct. Countless books remained untranslated and looking down at the pages filled with strange curved lines, punctuated throughout with small crescent shaped markings, Lacey wondered if this was the dialect Mateo could read. Her eyes scanned the unfamiliar, disjointed scrawls spread across the paper. She didn't know exactly what she was looking for and was about to put the book aside, when she turned the page and her eyes widened in surprise.

Amongst the curved, illegible symbols, one word, written in her own language, stared up at her. 'Witch' Lacey mouthed, her gaze moving across each letter. She blinked down at it. Finally, as though they were magnetised to the text, she managed to pull her eyes away. Looking across to the left hand page where an illustration, scratched out in thin black ink, peered out at her. She tilted her head, trying to make sense of the lines. It was a tree she thought, but the wood was warped into a screaming face. Two hollow horrified eyes, and a mouth frozen in a gasp of agony. The image filled her with an icy fear. Then something moved behind Lacey's back, its large shadow falling across the page.

CHAPTER TEN

Sensing a presence, Lacey turned quickly, just as a hand was laid on her shoulder. She jumped, her chair screeching on the floor.

'Oh!' She cried, then exhaled in relief, her hand coming to her chest.

'Young lady, you must have been a world away,' came the soft voice of Professor Arnott.

'Yes,' she said still a little breathless from the shock. The professor pulled over a stool, its legs creaking under his weight. He was a regular at the bakery, favouring their sweet buns and spiced biscuits. The buttons straining against the fabric of his waistcoat were testament to that.

'So how is Miss Lacey keeping on this rather wet and tempestuous day?' He looked at her over a small pair of spectacles, and as he spoke, his neck, which was covered in a goatee, the growth of which didn't stop at his chin, shook like whale blubber.

'Well thank you,' she smiled weakly. 'Glad not to be out in this rain.'

'Ah well I'm glad my little library might serve as some sweet sanctuary,' he gestured to the walls around him, stretching out his chubby fingers with their long nails. 'Often I think books owe their popularity to rainy days. When the young men cannot chase the girls in the fields, nor swim in the lake, perhaps they will go indoors and leaf through a book. Many times I have found succour in my collection,' looking out through the smudgy window panes he added, 'alas today I believe we need more comfort than ever. It is a sad week for the village.'

'Indeed,' she said, recalling how nervously he had stood the night before in the Tavern, shifting his weight from one foot to the other beneath the stares of the mourners. None of those insecurities apparent now as he sat in his own domain. 'I saw the Mayor call on you to stand last night.'

'Well, I admit my natural habitat is not in front of an audience, but when the Mayor calls on you...' He left the sentence unfinished, unhooking his spectacles from his ears and wiping them on his handkerchief. His eyes, naked and mole-like without glasses, remained shut, only reopening once they were back in place. He shook his large head slowly. 'They are dangerous times we live in now Miss Lacey, sad and dangerous times indeed. I admit as a child I wasn't a great one for swimming, preferring to spend my time with my nose firmly nuzzled between the pages of a book, but still I have one or two fond memories of dipping a toe on a sizzling summer day. It is a loss that now all our youngsters may not enjoy that, Deception Bay is by far the most beautiful. Sad that the girls seem incapable of heeding our warnings.'

'Only it wasn't a summer day when the Morgan girl drowned. It was an overcast autumn day.' She said.

'Well,' he paused a moment, 'a girl's mind is indeed a rare and beautiful mystery. Who is to say what their motivations are? If they aren't off swimming where they are not allowed they are stealing ale from behind the bar at The Golden Tavern. Actually, I fancy Mr Carter will be lining his pockets quite nicely this week, there is no sorrow that cannot be drowned at the bottom of a good bottle of rum.'

'Mr Carter?' Lacey was only half listening to the professor, her mind still distracted by the book.

'The proprietor of The Golden Tavern Miss Lacey.'

'Yes of course.'

'Do you mean to sit before me a young woman of the fairer sex, and tell me the ladies of the village of Lower Lynch aren't acquainted with the owner of the Inn? Come, come, you won't make pretend that you are all as innocent as that are you? You forget I too was a young man once, younger and,' he patted his tight belly, 'somewhat more svelte. You would hardly have recognised me Miss Lacey, but when I stepped out onto Main Street of a balmy summer evening, I would have the eyes of many a fair maiden upon me. But time is cruel and summer is fleeting. Now I settle as an old man in the autumn of life with little but my books as company.' The rain drummed on the roof above them and somewhere Lacey heard the tell-tale tip tap of a leak coming in through the thatch. 'Still, one mustn't complain.'

He reached forward and half closed her book so he might read the title, she moved it quickly aside. When she thought back, later that day on why she did so, she couldn't quite summon an answer. She knew only that she had acted upon instinct.

'Professor,' she said smiling, and shifting slightly so that she was in his eye line, 'do you have many books on the subject of the First Settlers to the Lakelands?'

He looked at her then, appraising her, his eyes twitched slightly at the corners. 'That is indeed a specific request.'

'It was only that I was wondering if there would be any recipes in them, for the bakery. Bella and I had wondered how the techniques might have changed over the years.'

The floorboard beneath his stool bowed slightly as he sat back, his manner relaxed again. 'A very interesting period for baking, not too much changed I'm sure, but still some stimulating points. It was indeed a fascinating time, although not many books written about those early years, they were more preoccupied with the effort of staying alive. Still, if that tickles your fancy I might be persuaded to hunt down a few.'

'I would be very grateful.'

There was a sudden white flash of lightening, illuminating every inch of the room, followed moments later by a heavy, ominous groan of thunder. A cold draft blew through the house, the candle flickered but stayed alight. Professor Arnott reached inside his waistcoat for a small, silver flask. Unscrewing the cap, he took two large sips. The smell of rum, sharp and sweet, and so strangely incongruous amid the dusty books, filled the air around them. He held the flask aloft for a moment, like an unanswered question, before shaking it at her, the sound of the liquid sloshing inside.

'Oh, no thank you Professor.' Lacey shook her head. They had sat and talked many times, but she had never seen him drink alcohol. Indeed, beside her father, she had never been alone with any man drinking alcohol.

'Come, come, Miss Lacey you are a grown woman now.'

Lacey set her jaw, lowered her eyebrows and looked at him, the candle reflecting in his glasses made it seem as though his eyes were on fire. 'No thank you,' she said, her voice void of its earlier courtesy, 'I haven't the taste for it.'

He chuckled, resting the flask on his round knee, 'A good thing I'm sure. A true lady.' Then he raised the flask again, this time in salute and tipped all the contents down his throat. His stubbly Adam's apple bobbing up and down like a buoy as he swallowed. 'I'm sure you are glad to hang up your apron and become a married woman.'

She stared at him, 'I'm not engaged to be married Professor.'

A flare of mottled rose came to his cheeks, 'Oh. Forgive me,' he said clearing his throat, 'forgive an old man his error. I must have been thinking of someone else.'

Lacey said nothing, only watched his face. She could not say why but felt with an immediate instinct that he was lying. Lightning struck again; the wind whistled through a gap in the door below. With the gentleness of movement of a man half his size, Professor Arnott dropped to his knees. Lacey stiffened in her seat, her back as straight as though her corset were pinned to the chair.

'Now if I'm not mistaken, I do believe we have a book on early cooking techniques down here somewhere.' with a wheeze he bent forward and started rummaging beneath the desk. Holding her legs so closely together her knees began to hurt, Lacey angled her body away from him.

But she didn't want to waste this opportunity. Something deep inside Lacey wanted desperately to know what was written on the page around the word *Witch*. The idea of asking the professor if she may borrow it seemed unthinkable, she knew that she didn't want him to know she was reading it. However she knew too that she wasn't leaving without it. Then a thought came to her. Lightning lit the sky, in her head Lacey began to count. Four, five, six, the thunder rolled in, shaking the windows in their panes. It was getting closer, she ran her thumb down the page. Heavy breathing came from beneath the desk, Lacey could feel a draught beneath her skirt.

'Yes, this is just the one' he said. Lacey glanced nervously down at his curved back.

Then once more the lightening came. She turned in her chair ever so slightly, tensing her finger and thumb either side of the page. The Professor had hold of the book and was starting to pull himself back to a sitting position. She counted to four, then praying to God her estimation be correct, she reached the fifth second and pulled. She ripped the page from the spine in one sheet, but all that could be heard in the room was the roar of thunder. She had been accurate in her timing, and not wasting the good fortune, swiftly folded the paper and hid it inside her boot.

She closed the book just as the Professor popped up and handed her the one he had just found. 'Please excuse a gentleman from breaking a sweat around such beauty,' he said, gesturing to the books, but his eyes coming to rest on her. Then wiping his brow with the back of his hand said, 'this is most interesting. It records the farming patterns of the First Settlers and how they dealt with the harsh winters.'

Lacey listened and nodded, unhearing, as Professor Arnott read from the first page of the book. She could feel the folded paper scrape against her ankle. He turned to the second page and taking a breath continued reading. Lacey interrupted 'I should make my way home, the hour is later than I thought. Thank you for reading that to me, it is most interesting. I have left your mending downstairs.'

She picked up the books she had been reading, placing them back on the bookshelf. She struggled with the last one, a large red leather-bound novel. The neighbouring books having slipped to the side, she was unable to fit it back into its space. Professor Arnott crossed the floor between them in silence, for such a large man he had a light, nimble tread, as though he had lamb's wool on the soles of his shoes. Within a moment he was behind her, she felt the soft pressure of his rotund stomach pressing lightly against her back.

'Allow me to assist you.' With a push the book was returned to its place. One of his plump, little fingers rested on top of her own, the tip of its long nail touching hers. Her hands were still stained a light purple from making the blackberry pie. His voice a low, slow whisper, close enough for her to feel it on the back of her neck, 'have you been picking berries?'

Lacey immediately shrunk away and, turning, ducked under his arm. She grabbed her coat and gloves which hung off the back of the chair. 'Thank you Professor,' she said briskly, 'good day.' But he side-stepped and placed himself at the top of the staircase, blocking her path. He was, she thought, perhaps a little uneasy on his small, polished feet. The heels of his shoes edging over the narrow top step.

'Now, now Miss Lacey, look at the weather. This rainstorm is full upon us. Surely us mortals are paying penance for some trespass against the wish of the Gods. It falls in sheets! You may catch your death should you walk home at this time.'

'I'm sure I will be quite fine.' She buttoned her gloves and pulled her arms through the sleeves of her coat.

'What should your father say, were I to let his most precious possession come to harm under my supervision? I'm sure he would roam this earth, vengeful for my blood!' His eyes glistened behind the thin spectacles. The smallest glimpse of a tongue protruded from his mouth at the edges, wetting the cracked skin there. He swayed slightly, his toes balancing on the brink of the top step.

Lacey, holding her breath inside her lungs, released it slowly and relaxed her arms. 'Perhaps you are right,' she said, looking out at the dark clouds 'perhaps I should stay until it passes.'

The Professor exhaled deeply, the smell of rum and something else, onions perhaps, stinging the inside of her nose. A small, eager smile pushed at the corner of his fat cheeks. 'Quite right, now come back and I will finish the chapter. And perhaps we can find something more to your taste to drink.'

He stepped away from the top of the stairs and walked back to the table, gesturing for her to accompany him. Lacey followed. Then, as quick as she dared, she spun on her toes and darted back to the stairs, saying quickly, 'I have just remembered it is my turn to close the shop.' He called after her, but she didn't stop, the stairs creaking as she bolted downstairs. 'I mustn't be late, as you said Professor we wouldn't want Father to be worried.' She reached the ground floor, and walking as fast as she could without running, made her way quickly towards the door and out to the street beyond. She did not wait to hear the man's reply.

Lacey opened the door, the rain hitting her face with force. Pulling up her collar she ran full tilt in the direction of home, feeling the folded paper press against her ankle with every step.

CHAPTER ELEVEN

It rained in Lower Lynch the whole of the next day and two days more after that. On the third night Lacey sat in bed reading. *Knock, Knock.* She sat up suddenly, her head moving with the alert nervousness of a deer. She squinted up at the black blanket of darkness above her. The noise sounded again, it was coming from the window. Cautiously she crossed to it and with her teeth clenched she pulled back the curtain. Mateo's face looked back at her through the glass. Lacey's muscles relaxed, she lowered the candlestick and exhaling opened the window.

'You scared me' she whispered.

The cool night air slid past him and into her bedroom. He rubbed his hands together, then holding them to his mouth warmed them with his breath. Smiling, he said 'I don't think Forest Beasts knock Lacey. Were you asleep?' He asked looking down at her nightdress. Lacey, suddenly remembering she was standing in her nightdress, crossed her arms protectively in front of her chest, 'not yet.' Mateo looked up at the roof as though there might be something there of great interest. Lacey gave a half smile and shifted her weight from one foot to another.

'It's stopped raining,' he said, and looking past him Lacey could see that he had lain a blanket out on the flat part of the roof outside her window. Unbeknownst to Bella and Frank, Mateo would sometimes scale the side of the house and visit her at night.

With Mateo's blanket beneath them and her own on top, the pair lay down together in silence for a long time. After a while, feeling the cold, Lacey turned on her side, curling her body round and pulling her knees in towards herself. She looked at Mateo looking at the stars. His arms folded behind the back of his head, the short tufts of hair on his chin silhouetted like a tree line on a distant hill.

It had not been just for the rain that Lacey had spent the last few days within the safe walls of the bakery. The Professor's behaviour had unbalanced her, frightened her. For a moment she wanted not to be seen by any man. When, in past years, she had complained about men's stares to Bella, her sister had responded that they wanted to kiss her. But she didn't think the village men were thinking about kissing when they stared at her breasts. Breasts are for feeding, they were perhaps contemplating whether she could suckle well. She wished hers were smaller, or that they had not grown at all. Bella still wore the same corset she had as a twelve year old, mens stares did not seem magnetised to her chest. Looking at Mateo she wondered did he ever think of her in that way? She didn't think so. His eyes did not linger on her breasts or hips. Although sometimes they seemed to float down to her lips when she talked.

'I can see the moon in your eyes.' She whispered. Every word between them contained in a cloud of silvery frozen breath.

His brow flickered, 'Ma says I have my mother's eyes.' He blinked, the tiny shiny crescent vanishing then reappearing. 'She says I am like her in character too.'

'I'm sure you are.'

'She was kind.'

'Then I'm certain you are.'

Mateo sighed contentedly, his eyes creasing into a smile, before asking 'are you like yours?'

The question floated perilously in the air above them a while, as though it were made of glass. Mateo, unsure of whether to have asked, Lacey unsure of how to answer.

'I fear so.' She said.

'What are you afraid of?'

With the uneasy feeling of stepping out onto crumbling ledge, she breathed 'madness.' She spoke so quietly, as though in saying it aloud she might summon it into reality. 'If my mother was not a witch then she was mad. I am afraid I am mad. I fear at the core of me there is a rotten seed, that only now as I grow is making itself apparent.'

'You are not mad.'

'You don't know' She whispered into the sleeve of her nightdress.

Mateo exhaled, blowing his misted breath out as though it were pipe smoke. 'There is a lot that I don't know. I have not read as many books as some, I never went to school. But I know somethings,' he said gently, turning his face to hers 'and the one thing I know better than any other is you.'

'You believe so?' She asked, glancing up at him through her lashes.

'Yes. I know you Lacey Emerson,' he nudged her playfully with his shoulder before adding, 'fearing ones own nature is the true madness. It is of that which we should be afraid.'

The clouds above had gathered once more and as the pair sat up and folded the blankets the rain began to fall again. Making sure to tread on the boards that did not creak Lacey climbed back inside her bedroom.

'I have something for you,' she whispered going to get the scrap of paper she had torn from the book.

'Actually Lacey,' he said stopping her, 'I have something for *you.*' He reached into his pocket and pulled out a small parcel wrapped in linen. He passed it through the open window without looking at her.

'Is it my birthday and nobody has told me?' She smiled.

'It's nothing' he murmured.

The fabric fell open in Lacey's hands to reveal a small rectangle of wood, shaved down so fine you could almost bend it. Upon it was carved the most intricate and detailed etchings of wildflowers. Small snaking vines entwined with buds ran up the length of it. The finest whispers of indentations marking out the leaves and petals. Turning it over, in thin looping letters, so smooth they looked as though they had grown from withing the wood, she read the word *Lacey.*

'A bookmark' muttered Mateo, his eyes still turned away, 'you said you kept losing your page.'

'I did' responded Lacey staring down at the little cut of wood, feeling her cheeks blush. 'I love it,' she said to him, though in his shyness he had all but turned his back on her. 'Mateo,' she urged, reaching out for his hand. Finally, he looked at her, his eyes glowing at her touch. 'I love it,' she said again.

Then suddenly, unexpectedly as much to him as to her, he pulled her hand to his mouth and kissed her open palm. Lacey's heart skipped a beat.

As though remembering himself Mateo nodded briskly and mumbling a goodnight turned and was gone. Lacey stood, with her arm still extended, her hand hovering in mid-air, still holding onto the kiss. She heard the sound of him climbing down the trellis then, his footsteps fading as she stared out into the darkness. She stood a long time like that, looking out at the black sky, listening to the rain. It occurred to her that the night didn't seem so frightening knowing he was inside it.

As she climbed back in bed she realised she hadn't given him the paper. Never mind, she would do it tomorrow. She stroked the palm of her hand as if she may still feel the kiss upon it. She remembered again him on the deck without his shirt. She thought about what Bella had told her at the well, of the different parts of men and women.

As she closed her eyes she had the strange feeling of slipping into a river. A current taking hold of her. It was not up to her the direction, she only moved with the flow of the water. She felt her body warm below the blankets. There was the sensation of sparks beneath her skin, running up and down her stomach. She moved silently and smoothly like a hand over soft dough. But then it was not calm, the river moved with urgency. There was a curious, instinctual need that guided her. She thought about Mateo, her brow knitting in frustration at the unfocused blur of his body. But she could see his hands clearly. Lined dark fingers, nails cut and smooth with sawdust between the beds. She imagined her hands to be his. And it was that which led the river to the edge of a waterfall, upon which her body tipped finally, gratefully, over. To be consumed in the rolling cascading, tormented torrents of water beneath.

In the darkness Lacey reached for the bookmark and placed it beside her on the pillow, feeling at the indentations of the carved flowers as she fell asleep.

CHAPTER TWELVE

Lacey couldn't breathe. Water flooded her mouth, her lungs. Salt stung her eyes as she looked up at the surface of the water moving further and further away. She could make out the malevolent shadowy shape of The Island above her. Its three black peaks staring down at her, watching her struggle. Her skirts, waterlogged and heavy as stone, dragged her down, her legs kicking limply, feebly, tangling in the fabric. The light above her shrunk to a small, rippling circle. It felt colder down here and as silent as a grave. Though she screamed and cried in desperation all that came from her mouth were streams of bubbles that rose noiselessly to the surface. Then, from somewhere unseen, she heard her mother's voice crying out, 'wake up Lacey!'

Lacey's eyes opened and she lunged forward, gasping for breath, her hand at her throat. She inhaled desperately, swallowing great mouthfuls of air. She was soaking. Her hair hung about her face in thick monochrome strands, droplets of water running off them and falling onto her bedsheet. Her nightdress clung to her skin, drenched and deathly cold. Even the mattress beneath her was sodden, the smell of wet hay rising from it. She looked up at the roof of her bedroom, no hole, no sign of a leak. The window too was just as usual, the handle locked. Lacey, her heart still thundering, her breath still uneven, stared around her in astonishment. For a long while she sat there, unable to make sense of it. Biting her lip she tasted brine and then came to realise the room was thick with the smell of the sea.

Shaking, she extricated herself from the bed and stood, water dripping from her, running in streams down her legs and pooling on the floor around her feet. Her thoughts suddenly pivoted from trying to figure out what had happened to making sure no one discovered it. She moved in haste, tearing her nightdress off, bundling it into a ball with her sheets she put them at the end of her bed. Naked and afraid she resigned to dealing with them later, when Bella was out. Then wringing her hair out she dressed herself. She did not know what to think, she moved as if in a dream and tried not think at all. As though even contemplating the thought was an invitation for madness.

As she plaited her hair she realised what day it was, she was due for tea at the manor with Sebastian that morning and for the first time since waking felt that she might succumb to panic. Then a thought occurred to her, after the rain perhaps the lake had flooded and she wouldn't have to go after all. Lacey crossed hopefully to the window. She drew back the curtain and saw with a sense of dread the green field outside below a calm sky. Not a raindrop in sight. Crestfallen, she leant her still damp forehead against the pane and sighed, her breath clouding the glass.

A few hours later, Lacey arrived to knock on the door of the Mayor's mansion. Though she wore her usual blue dress, she had taken off her apron and allowed Bella to tie a teal coloured ribbon in her hair. It was fastened at the bottom of a plait, her white cap sitting neatly on top. Bella had also confiscated a reading book from Lacey's pocket, as it ruined the line of her dress. Lacey had shut the door firmly behind her, just as her sister who, buoyed by the victory of the ribbon, had approached her with a powdery concoction comprising of beet juice and cornflour, in an attempt to rouge her cheeks.

Though the lake hadn't burst its banks, it had swelled in threat and then, just before dawn, the rain had stopped. The villagers had come out, as they often did in the days after a storm, to discuss the event. Some of the older men, leaning upon their sticks, peered into the water suspiciously, and stood for hours talking it over. How might it affect the fish? Perhaps it would rain again? They chewed and spat tobacco whilst reminiscing about the rainstorms of their childhood.

The ladies of the village kept to their post-storm rituals too, standing in small groups outside the shops, wearing their starched white caps and gloves. Their eyes flitted protectively in the direction of their daughters every few moments. As Lacey walked past they moved to stand a little closer to their children. The shiny bow in her hair had caused one or two to turn their heads in curiosity before returning to their conversations. She imagined them thinking *where might the witch's daughter be off to dressed so prettily?* Or, *so even witches wear bows in their hair.*

She had taken a small detour to give the torn page, along with a hastily scribbled note, to Mateo, with a hope that he might be able to translate it. She had raised her fist to knock for him, but an unfamiliar anxiety had stopped her hand mid-air. She had stood outside his door a moment, conflicted. She wanted to see him, wanted to go inside and sit on his unmade bed, wanted to hear his voice, even just for a moment. Then she imagined him greeting her and seeing the bow in her hair, realising that she was meeting Sebastian, and she had hastily pushed the note beneath the door and half run away.

Lacey walked across the Manor courtyard, heading automatically for the servants' entrance, then correcting herself, doubled back, to climb the stone steps leading to a white varnished front door. Adjusting her cap, the tie sitting awkwardly under her chin, she pulled the bell. A minute passed before Nanny opened the door. As a child, Sebastian had been taught at home, but occasionally he would be seen walking the village with a teacher in tow. And a few steps behind, as present as his shadow, there would be Nanny. She was older now, her once plump skin sagged at the edges of her eyes and mouth. Two deep lines had grown either side of her nostrils, creasing beneath the weight of her cheeks. Her teeth, having continued to grow, poked out between her lips, even when her mouth was closed. She looked a little like a wood pigeon, Lacey thought. Perhaps it was her way of walking, her little head jutting forward with every step, or maybe it was her wide, sloping breast, perpetually covered in a grey apron. She held a small towel and the edges of her sleeves, which had been rolled high up her ham-like forearms, were slightly wet.

Nanny made no move to welcome Lacey inside, she stood in the hallway, a grey boulder, blocking her path. If I were to topple you over Nanny, you might just roll away and never stop, thought Lacey. But she didn't say that, instead she said, 'good morning.'

'Miss Lacey,' came Nanny's short, clipped, schoolmistress voice, 'your cap isn't straight.' Again, Lacey pulled the string from her neck, the bow refusing to align itself properly. 'Come child, that isn't how you do it,' chastised Nanny. With a push of her finger Nanny raised Lacey's chin, her eyes looking up at a large, glass lantern swaying slightly above her head. Nanny fiddled with the strap for a moment, then stepping back, said 'if you had only taken a minute Miss Lacey, you would have had it straight. Does your father not provide you with a mirror? It matters less when you are here to collect the linen, but when you are a Manor guest you must dress appropriately.' Lacey moved to answer, but before she could Nanny had already turned and walked off into the hallway, waving for Lacey to follow. 'Never mind,' she called, 'you are indoors now, it is polite to take off your cap and gloves'. Lacey hastened to chase after her, Nanny's feet on the polished floor, so delicate they sounded like the ticking of a clock. Unlike the courtyard that seemed to be alive with action, in here it was still and quiet. Lacey felt that she could hear every one of her breaths as she exhaled. At the centre of the hall sat a wide, wooden staircase which curved around the room all the way up to the third floor. It had thin white banisters and deep cherry wood steps varnished to a glassy shine. Glancing up Lacey saw the closed door of the Mayors bedroom above.

She followed Nanny's bobbing shape through a wide domed doorway that led to the main room. Lacey held her breath at the lavishness of it. Never before had she laid eyes on such luxury. The space could have held four bakeries, and still had room leftover. A dark pink wallpaper wrapped around every inch, painted on which, in meticulous detail, red and green birds perched atop golden branches. A wide, deep fireplace with heavy marble mantels sat at each end. On top of the one closest to her, a clock ticked loudly and impatiently. The furniture, stuffed with duck feathers to the point of bursting, was upholstered in dark red velvet. The feet, golden claws with sharp, pointed nails, digging into the panelled floors. And across the length of the room, windows stretched almost from floor to ceiling, behind which lay the lake.

With distaste, Nanny watched Lacey survey her surroundings. 'Sit here Miss Lacey, you are early. Master Sebastian has only just begun on his bath.'

Lacey nodded and sat on the edge of one of the chairs. But then, rather than leaving, Nanny leaned in close to her, her corn coloured teeth inches from Lacey's face. She spoke in a soft whisper, 'you should count yourself greatly lucky,' her breath smelt like decaying flowers, 'not every girl in the village has had the privilege of being the Young Master's guest.' And with that, Nanny snapped upright and walked away. Lacey, wide eyed, watched her bobbing head as she departed.

Just as her rotund figure turned the corner, Lacey called out, 'The Mayor isn't home is he Nanny?'

The woman stopped, half her face obscured by the doorway. 'Mayor Abner isn't expected home until sundown.'

'That is a pity,' said Lacey, in her sweetest voice, 'I was hoping to see him. Thank you, Nanny,'

Nanny retreated towards the kitchens, her tapping feet echoing as she went. Lacey stood and walked slowly around the room, her hands held behind her back. She smiled at the birds on the walls, they were so lifelike in their detail. Each feather so delicately observed with a fine, sensitive brush stroke. The shining branches beneath their feet a bright, rich gold. Three stuffed wolves' heads hung above the mantel piece, made somehow more alarming framed by the pink wallpaper, snarled with distaste at the birds.

Lacey walked to the far end of the room where, beside the mantelpiece a door was cut out of the wallpaper. It sat flush with the wall, the only sign of it actually being a door, was a simple gold handle. Lacey had seen the Mayor's bedroom. There was not even a writing table inside. Which had left her with a question rattling around in her mind. Where is the Mayor's study? It was that question which had impelled her to arrive early for her appointment today.

Waiting a moment, and hearing nothing, Lacey took hold of the door handle and pushed. It opened onto a long corridor of grey exposed stone, the temperature far colder than the rest of the house. It was windowless, with the only light coming from the gap beneath a door at the far end. Closing the door behind her, Lacey made her way down the corridor, checking back over her shoulder every few steps.

She opened the second door with some effort, it was far thicker and heavier than the one before. Lacey found with no surprise that the Mayor's study was cold and colourless. Here, like his bedroom, the expense and decadence of the rest of the house had been discarded in favour of bare stone walls. A low, sucking whistle came from within an empty fireplace. Lacey stepped inside and closed the door behind her. The sound of it shutting suddenly increasing the unnerving feeling of trespassing. But she didn't know how long Sebastian would take in the bath, and she guessed that Nanny would check on her at least once again before his arrival, so she must hurry. With speed, she crossed to a wide, dark wood desk that stretched before the fireplace, there was only one chair tucked neatly beneath it, no others in the room. Evidently this was Mayor Abner's private study, and not for the holding of meetings or entertaining of guests.

Lacey sat in the chair and pulled open the drawer in front of her. A few pencils and quills rolled into the light, she pushed it shut. She began opening the smaller drawers that ran down the side of the desk to her left. Scrolls of parchment, sticks of wax, pots of ink. On the right, she found much the same, except for the bottom drawer. Lying alone was a small rounded frame, she picked it up and smeared the dust from the glass with her thumb. The name *Venetia Abner* was written in tiny neat letters along the bottom ledge. It was a small painted portrait, the figure wearing a thick fur wrapped around her shoulders and a thin red ribbon at her throat. But her face was strangely distorted. A small, but furious, flurry of scratch marks had obliterated her features.

This was the Mayor's wife, Ma had spoken of her before. She had left when Sebastian was still a baby in the cot. Half ruining the Mayor and earning her reputation for being a wild spirited woman. Lacey stared down at the portrait of the faceless figure.

Suddenly there was a noise outside the door. Footsteps growing louder. Panic bore a hole inside Lacey's stomach. She dropped the portrait and pushed the drawer shut. Her eyes cast desperately around the room, no curtains only shutters, no wardrobes or anterooms. Just the desk, and the chair. The footsteps, echoing on the stone floor, grew louder. Lacey stood up, pushing the chair back, her heart thumping, panic running through her veins. The handle of the door turned with a whine.

Nanny stepped into the apparently empty room, her eyes moving from left to right like the pendulum of a clock. She moved slowly, each step considered, her tread delicate on such hallowed ground. One fingertip reached out and touched the edge of the desk, running along the woodwork. Nanny held herself like a hunter, every movement measured and necessary. A clock on the desk, its second hand previously unheard by Lacey, ticked as loud as a woodpecker against a tree, its tap incessant and unending. Nanny pulled the chair back, the wooden legs scraping deafeningly. Then with an explosive movement, swift and unrecognisable, she bent down beneath the desk.

An empty space stared back at her. She exhaled, and straightened herself, she looked around, an unsatisfied frown on her face. Then, with the palm of her hand ironing the creases in her apron, she marched towards the door, closing it with a firm click behind her.

Lacey listened to her retreating footsteps, though all she could hear was her own heart beating within her ears. Finally, she opened her eyes. What she saw was almost as black as that behind her lids, though looking down at her feet, she could see light coming in from the bottom of the fireplace.

Once or twice as a child, on the rare occasion she would be invited over to a neighbour's house to play, Lacey had quickly found the most successful place to secrete herself during a game of hide and go seek. She would scrabble up the inside of the chimney, using the uneven bricks as footholds. Then wait there while the children searched in vain, her breathing as quiet as possible in darkness so thick it felt like black wool wrapped around her head. She would listen to the frantic searching footsteps on the floorboards above her. Sometimes suppressing her own giggles by biting into her hand. Then in forfeit they would call for her to show herself. The blackened, burnt smelling creature that lowered itself down the chimney was frightening enough to make the other little children cry in fear. She hadn't been asked to play often after that.

Cautiously, trying not to dirty her dress, Lacey began to step down, reaching for the opposite side with only her fingertips to steady herself. A brick moved loosely against her touch, Lacey paused, feeling blindly at the edges of it. Curiously, unlike the others this one seemed only to be resting in its place, not secured to any of those around it. Slowly, and gently, she pulled it entirely away. Lacey felt inside the gap, blindly feeling along the dusty base of it, then stopping suddenly when she felt something. Her eyes widened in the darkness. It was the dry, chalky texture of a rolled piece of parchment, she pulled it out. Then, stooping low, extracted herself from the fireplace.

The sides were stained the colour of burnt sienna, the edges uneven and ragged. It had a layer of dust upon it, the colour of the grey bricks, some falling to the floor as Lacey unfurled it. She stared down at the paper. Her pupils, in the sudden light, expanded, the inky black almost eclipsing her grey iris. She recognised the symbol immediately. It had been emblazoned in a gold stitch, on the back of the hooded figure outside the tavern, carved onto the leg of a dead child and tattooed upon the hands of the owner of this house. The ink was old and faded, below it in a different, newer pen was written the words *35 steps from the base of the 3rd peak.* Lacey felt a tightness in her breast as though a cold hand had her heart within its fist and was slowly squeezing. The three jagged peaks of The Island floated behind the lids of her eyes.

CHAPTER THIRTEEN

Lacey stood in the main room of the manor, staring out at the lake beyond the windows, beneath the stare of the painted birds and stuffed wolves.

'Good morning Miss Lacey,' said Sebastian, she turned her head, lost in her own thoughts, she hadn't heard him arrive. He bowed slightly, and she in turn nodded to him. His hair, pulled into a tight knot atop his head, was smooth and still a little wet.

'Good morning Master Abner,' she said formally.

'Did you think you could trick me?' He asked quietly. Lacey blinked, looking searchingly at him, his face blank. 'Your dress.' Lacey followed his eyes down, to a long black scar of soot running along the side of her skirts, in her haste to return the parchment she must have rubbed against the side of the chimney. Fear twitched inside her but she returned his gaze, the seconds stretched between them, until she managed to pull her voice to her lips.

'I don't- '

'Will you admit yourself then to be a Forest Beast in disguise?' His words coming through a snarling smile, 'will you confess you have taken the body of this young woman as she walked through the woods this morning, pounced on her, muddying her dress, and possessed her body? Be sure not to move too quickly, or else risk a shot to the head.' He raised his hands then, as though he were holding an invisible rifle, one stretched forward cradling the barrel, the other raised at the elbow, its index finger hooked around an imaginary trigger. He lowered his head slightly and closing one eye, squinted with the other. They stood that way for a moment in silence staring at one another.

'I confess.' She said, and held her hands either side of her head in mock surrender, before dropping them once more. 'I can see why you have the reputation of a such a gracious host.'

'And I can see why you have the reputation of a woman a man might like to shoot.' Sebastian said, holding the pose a few moments longer, before relaxing his arms, his invisible weapon falling to the ground. The side of his mouth twitching ever so slightly, as though resisting the itch of a smile. 'I imagine the only dress you will ever wear that is without a mark of dirt will be your wedding dress.' He said sarcastically. But the word, said in such a casual manner, had the feel of a wasp sting to Lacey.

'Wedding dress?' she repeated, alarmed.

'This way' he said, ignoring her and turning on his heels. Opening a door beneath the stairs, he disappeared. Lacey reluctantly followed, walking down a few lantern lit steps. 'I want to show you my favourite room,' said Sebastian, his hands proudly on his hips.

The weapons were laid out with precision in neat lines. Wooden handled muskets, long necked pistols, rifles with thick glass sights, and knives too. Some long and thin with such a shine she could see her own reflection. Others short with a serrated edge, for cutting thick animal skins. Some, in a cruel irony, had the hooves of baby deer as their handles, the soft downy fur in incongruous marriage to the metal blade.

He began to talk at length about the merits of each gun. Lacey concentrated on not rolling her eyes too much. 'This is a blunderbuss,' he said picking up the polished weapon. 'Even a girl can shoot one of these.'

It was with a quick foot that Lacey hurried up the stairs when he was finally done, grateful to be turning her back on his sordid private collection. She followed Sebastian outside onto a wide, flat, manicured lawn. The grass greener and more evenly cut than she had ever seen before. Not one leaf or fallen twig dared to trespass here, it was as clear and smooth as the water beyond it.

The lake, recovering from the brutality of the rainstorm, was calmer today than on many days in recent memory, not a ripple disturbed the clear surface. It was like a sheet of poured glass, mirroring the cool, grey sky. So calm, you might be able to walk upon it as though it were frozen. It stretched out towards a horizon of low fog far in the distance. It was beautiful, especially as from here you couldn't see the village, only the water, the forest and the sky above.

A wooden deck stretched out from the shore and tied to the end, resting gently on the water, was a little boat. Sebastian smiled, pulling at the mooring, causing it to bump up alongside the jetty. It was a beautiful polished rowboat, coated in a rich cherry red, Lacey read the name *Aqua* painted in scrawling golden letters along the side. Ignoring Sebastian's proffered hand, she stepped in and sat down on one of two cushioned seats. The boat rocked gently in welcome beneath her.

'Do you catch many trout in this?' She asked, feeling at the piping on the pristine leather seats, her eyes casting along the spotlessly clean hull.

Untying the rope Sebastian stepped in and pushed off in one elegant kick. 'This vessel has an entirely different purpose to catching fish.'

Sitting down, he smoothed his hair with the palm of his hand and took hold of the oars. He flexed his broad shoulders and the boat lurched into movement, Lacey resisting the urge to hold the side for stability.

'You seem comfortable on a boat, Miss Lacey. Have you much experience?' he asked.

'In sitting and watching? Yes, many years,' she said tightly. He stayed silent, pulling at the oars and looking out to the lake. She wondered if she had been too rude and inwardly chastised herself. She suddenly felt childlike, with a frown on her face and a bow in her hair. She was on the verge of apologizing, when he spoke.

'You have a quick mind, for a baker's daughter.'

He had rowed fast and before long they were far out, far enough that the village, its finer details lost, looked like a child's drawing. But she could just make out Mateo's house, amongst his neighbours. She hoped he could not see them. Turning to the other side of the boat Lacey leant and rested her hand over the edge so that her fingertips drew light, rippling feathers in the still water.

'Why did you name it Aqua?' She asked eventually.

'It is my father's boat, he named it.' He looked up then at the shore, as though checking they were far enough out to not be heard. 'I wanted to call it Venetia, after my mother, but he wouldn't let me.' He scowled.

'Oh?' Lacey raised one eyebrow slightly.

'Hers isn't a popular name in our household.'

Lacey thought of her own Father. Of his total unwillingness to utter her mother's name. She couldn't remember now when it had become an unspoken rule, only that she had implicitly understood it as such. Sebastian frowned as though debating his next move, then finally leant forward lifting the cushion. 'A little childhood rebellion.' He said. Beneath, scratched into the wood of the seat in a childish scrawl was the word *Venetia*. Lacey imagined him as a young boy sneaking down to the boat alone and by the light of a lantern carving out his mother's name. She felt an uncomfortable surge of sympathy for him. 'I've never shown anyone that' he exclaimed in surprise, as though only realising it as he said the words aloud. Then quickly he dropped the cushion and pulled hard again on the oars, the boat jerking forward, a muscle in his jaw twitching slightly.

She looked at him, his face suddenly forlorn and lost. It is his turn to feel like a child, she thought.

'We have that in common.' He said.

'What?'

'Our mothers are both dead.' He said it so casually, in such a matter of fact way, it stunned her.

'I didn't think your mother was dead' she said, in a half whisper.

'As good as' he responded coldly. Then a moment later his manner changed, his back straightening, chest swelling, the seams on his coat tightening. When he spoke again his voice had the usual deep, male tone. 'My father took me to visit Upper Lynch last month. They haven't been burdened by a shortage of fish like us. They export great barrels full of them to other villages, the taste is poor but it will be the poor eating it so there is little worry.' He laughed at his own joke, then, glancing at Lacey, looked quizzically at her unamused face as though he couldn't understand the offence.

'Where else have you travelled?' She asked.

'Many places, most are like this.'

'Oh,' she said, a note of disappointment in her voice. 'I had read of travellers who have ventured out to sea-'

'Well,' he interrupted, 'I meant only of the towns this side of the Hooked Forest. You would have to be mad to go far out to sea. Who knows what the ocean holds. It would be insanity.' His voice had a sharper edge of irritation now. His travels diminished in comparison to the explorers who crossed the sea.

'Do you fear the Sea Gods?' She asked, her eyebrow arching slightly.

He scoffed 'I don't believe in them.'

'Do you fear the Forest Beasts?'

'I don't believe in them either. I'm not a child.'

'Do you fear the God who lives in the church on Main Street?'

He stopped rowing, resting his arms a moment but still holding the handles of the oars, and looked at her right in the eye. 'Do you?'

'Not as much as I fear his parishioners.' She held his stare, the boat drifted gently, still propelled a little by his last pull.

'Don't say that to anyone else again.' His voice was serious and deep, his eyes a watery, concentrated blue beneath his white brows.

'Don't ask me to marry you.' She said in return, in a moment of honest desperation.

Sebastian released his hold on the oars. They slid down into the water before stopping with a thud in their holders. He took a breath, exhaling loudly through his nostrils. She continued, 'if you take me as a wife, Sebastian I promise I will bring you little happiness. Whatever contentment you are looking for, I'm sure I will be unable to provide it.'

'Stop.' He said, his hand coming up and resting in the air between them, his palm as smooth and soft as a baby's. 'You can stop now Lacey.'

She frowned at him. 'You won't ask for my hand?'

'No,' he said, sighing, 'I am going to ask you, and you will say yes. So you should stop your protestations now. You will only embarrass yourself.' Lacey opened her mouth to interrupt, but he talked over her. 'Surely we talked enough about the situation when last we spoke in your garden. I didn't think I needed to make it any clearer to you. Your bakery loses customers every year, it is an achievement alone that an establishment run by a family with a history such as yours has any customers at all.'

'The bakery is surviving.' She answered almost pleadingly.

'Only because my father hasn't allowed the price of flour to rise. He has made his decision for us to be wed. It would not be wise to go against his wishes.'

'Why are you so afraid of him?'

'Because I know him.' He answered simply, then changing tack, he said, 'surely you must be tired of having a black mark against your name. I know your sister and father are.' He leaned forward, staring at her, 'you have the chance to clear your family's name. You can save their business.'

'You could have any girl in town. What do you want from me?' She whispered.

'All I want from you Lacey is to do as you are told. We aren't always the masters of our own destiny.' He sighed, the words harsh and heavy. Then his tone softening, as though imparting a secret he said, 'and in truth you are the first person I have said my mother's name to in twenty years. We may make a better match than you think.' He looked away and busied himself with the lighting of his pipe. Lacey watched his actions blindly. Finally tipping his head back and exhaling a thick plume of smoke he said 'please don't continue to protest Lacey, you have no choice in the matter. You, I and our fathers will make the blood vow, and we shall be wed.'

Lacey inhaled shakily, as though her heartbeat were rippling her breaths. Inside she felt a strange, uncomfortable tightening.

Like a string being pulled too taut. She stared at the reflection of her face in the water. From the centre the mirror began to ripple. She clenched her teeth and held her breath. *Do as you are told Lacey.* The lake suddenly surged up, the boat tilting violently from side to side. In astonishment Sebastian dropped his pipe and grabbed the sides. The water spilling over and soaking his feet, he raised them to save the leather of his boots. Lacey closed her eyes. Sebastian's words repeated in her mind, *you have no choice Lacey.* She felt the pressure expand inside her chest, the boat jerked perilously, almost capsizing. Sebastian cried out in fear. Suddenly behind her closed lids she saw Bella and her father at the bakery. Bella standing at the counter with her apron on, kneading dough, her father sitting rubbing sore knees with sore hands. She felt the tension inside her snap. The water flattened immediately. The boat righted itself resuming its gentle bobbing on the surface. The waves that had surrounded them disappeared.

Lacey blinked as though resurfacing from a daydream. She turned her head to look out at the furthest part of the lake, where the water met the fog and no land or horizon could be seen. Then she looked back to the coast, she could no longer see Mateo's house. Sebastian, rearranging his feet to rest on the side of the hull, remarked in surprise about how quickly the winds picked up out here, but she wasn't listening. She just stared blindly out, feeling again the strange sense of slipping away, like a pebble being pulled out by the tide.

*

That night, once Sebastian had escorted her back to her house, once her father and Bella had been told, once all the talking had stopped and the candles had been blown out, Lacey began to cry.

Not as a child does, but noiselessly, with her back to her door. The tears rolling silently down her cheeks and soaking into her pillow. Occasionally one would run over her lips, and licking them, she tasted the sea and felt that she was again upon Deception Bay.

The ring sat snugly on her finger. With its presence, she felt there were a traitor in the room. Every time she looked at it, the gold winked at her as though in collusion with him. Watching her on his behalf. A shining gold band, like the collar of a dog, on which he could hang his leash. It weighed down her arm as though she were tied to an anchor.

After rowing in silence back to the dock, Sebastian with his eyes set resolutely ahead of him, Lacey staring at the water slipping beneath the boat, he had produced the ring. He had stood on the front lawn and patted at the pockets of his waistcoat. She had thought him to be looking for his pipe but when his hand appeared again it held the small, gold circle, lying flat in his open palm. She leant forward and peered at it suspiciously. He didn't drop a knee, nor place it upon her finger, he didn't even hold it out for her. He just kept his hand open and when she made no move he waited, until eventually, with a crestfallen face, she picked the small ring up and pushed it onto her finger. Then he had nodded.

'We must go and tell your father.'

'And yours?' She asked.

'He already knows,' he said simply. It was then that she saw them, washed out from beneath the seat, floating on the water in the bottom of the boat. Red leaves, like none she had seen before. A bright berry red. Blood red. She heard Ma's words in her ears: *The trees on The Island grow red with blood.*

Lost in her thoughts, she had not noticed him step towards her. He took her jaw between his thumb and fore finger and tilted her head up to his. She hadn't closed her eyes. As he leant down to her she smelt the lavender on his hair, and saw up close how smooth and soft his pale face was. She could see every bleached white hair that grew on his brows. He stamped the kiss on her as though sealing a letter, he might have poured wax on her lips, they might bear his crest. She felt at them in the darkness of her room later that night, her fingers running softly over them. The seal might read *Wife*, she thought, it was, after all, her new name. Now he, just as her parents had done before him, had picked a name for her. Perhaps he would carve it along the side of her body as he had done on his boat, in sharp, deep scratches.

CHAPTER FOURTEEN

The next morning Lacey couldn't get out of bed. She had dreamt that night that the bakery was on fire. She stood in her bare feet and nightdress on the street outside, staring at the burning building. Long tongues of red flames whipped wildly from the windows. She could hear her father and Bella screaming from inside as the door handle rattled but did not open. The thatched roof was a blazing white, sparks danced in the night sky above it as if even the air was burning. Orange shadows spread across the street and reflected in the diamond windows of the house opposite, where the fire burnt a hundred times over. Lacey gazed in numb disbelief, the strength of the fire drawing stinging tears from her unblinking eyes. Slowly she looked down at her clenched fist. Unfurling her fingers she saw the front door key lying in her hand. There was a deep cracking sound and a sudden explosion of flames as the floors caved in. She raised her arm against the searing heat.

Her eyes had snapped open. She lay panting in her bed. Black and white hairs stuck to the side of her brow, the smell of burning still in her nose. Her pale knuckled hands, clammy with sweat, tightly gripping the blanket. Wiping her hand across her face she screwed up her eyes until her eyelids danced with stars. '*Just a dream,*' she whispered to herself. Outside soft grey clouds slid across the window, the noise of Bella working downstairs floated up through the floorboards. Lacey stayed in the same position a while, breathing deeply, collecting herself. Only when she sat up did she see them.

The blanket, still bearing the creases caused by her fists, was burnt. A spiders web of black scorch marks stretched across the white linen. Smatterings of small holes had appeared at points, where the fabric had been burnt through. Open mouthed Lacey touched the singed sheet, then inspected her own palms, pale and flawless. The odour in the room was now distinctly that of burning. The smell of something on fire that should not be on fire is unmistakable to a baker and set a bell of panic tolling inside her mind. I am going mad, she said to herself. Fear clouded her thoughts, and in defeat Lacey closed her eyes and pulled the ruined blankets over her head.

When she awoke again, she found she hadn't even the energy to sit up. Telling Bella behind the door that she had a headache, she remained in bed, staring at the ceiling. Even her stack of books, with their pages of temporary escape, could not help her. Through the floor she could hear Bella and her father chatting happily. They talked of hymns, wedding dresses, morning suits, and cake. Lacey held a pillow over her head until their words lost their meanings and became a foreign language of indecipherable sound.

After noon she heard the door slam and the house grow quiet. She rose with a mix of guilt at having slept so late, and anger at having to wake up at all, and dragging herself downstairs set about doing her work. A scrawled note on the counter from Bella told her that she was in town obtaining a rabbit from Mr Tibbs, to put in a pie as celebration. Lacey, almost grateful to be presented with a task, set about making the pastry. She prepared the worktop, shoving her hand into the flour jar and retrieving a fistful, then spreading it over every inch of the wood. In a bowl she mixed flour, butter, lard and a pinch of salt. She used her hands, crumbling the mixture between her fingers. Then, tipping it out onto the counter, she squeezed until it held together. She rolled it for a moment, using the palm of her hand, shaping it into a smooth ball. Then, not wanting to handle it too much, placed it back in the bowl and into the cupboard.

She stood a moment, her sleeves rolled up above her elbow, her hands on her hips, unsure of what to do with herself. Having appreciated that moment of distraction she looked around the room. After a minute or two, digging her hand deep in the flour jar once more, she set about starting another dough.

Before long Bella arrived home to the house in the throes of much activity. There were three pots upon the fire, all in different stages of cooking. Two pie cases baked in the oven and Lacey worked on an enriched dough at the counter. Flour had spread, like a light snow, over every surface in the kitchen. But Bella for once, didn't seem to mind. She sat down and pulled a jar of honey from the bottom of her basket. Holding it up to the light coming through the window and tipping it, so the golden liquid sunk lazily from one side to the other. 'Is it not too beautiful?' She exclaimed, marvelling at it. 'I can't imagine why we shouldn't have a hive of our own now, it's no great expense apparently.' She placed it, with care, on the table, unbuttoning the clasp on her gloves. 'Mrs White says apparently her husband gets stung quite rarely, if you aren't counting his hands of course. Besides, Mr White is not the most intelligent of men, I'm sure at least half of that is his own wrongdoing. I believe we should, we could make honey based sweet treats, it might be quite a draw to the shop window.'

Lacey, only half listening, stood with her back to her sister, grinding the dough into the tabletop. Bella shone as someone who had woken to a world where the possibilities were endless. A world where they might have the money in order to buy a beehive, and those bees might provide them with honey, they might make more sweet treats and bring in more custom to the shop. And then what? Perhaps they could expand, build out so that they could have another room and father wouldn't have to sleep on the floor. She looked around the room as though imagining it wholly new, her eyes painting in a new oven, a new, wider shop window, a working bell above the door. Bella's imagination unravelled like a spool of thread, with each idea leading to the next, the world opening exponentially.

Whereas Lacey's world seemed to have closed like the quiet shutting of a door. One of the pots began to bubble over, the red liquid spilling out and hissing at the flames below, she crossed to stir it.

'Father abhors bees' Lacey said simply, bringing a steaming spoonful to her lips to taste, before snapping the lid back in place, and lifting it from the fire.

'Oh,' said Bella, crestfallen, 'oh, yes, I remember now. He was stung as a child, on the knee, was it?'

'Ankle.'

'Yes, that's right. Oh well, not in the good Lord's plans for us I suppose.' She said, recovering a little of her cheer at the comforting reminder that all of life was part of God's plan. 'Perhaps we could invest in a few apple trees then, our apple cake is always very popular, we could do a whole range, with different spices.' The beehive in Bella's mind was replaced with an orchard. 'I don't imagine Father to find apples abhorrent! Still it was very kind of Mrs White to have gifted the honey to us. And look at this,' she said in excitement, pulling from her basket a small round fruit. She held it with the tips of her fingers as though it were made of glass. 'It's called a peach.' She turned it slowly in the light. 'Apparently it is very sweet, we are to leave it a few days to fully ripen. Everyone in the choir was quite jealous when they heard. So kind of Mrs White, she had it ordered from across the Lake as a gift.' Bella placed it gently on a dish on the table.

'She gifted it to you?' Asked Lacey, the word catching her attention.

'Yes, upon hearing the good news. She sent her congratulations along with it. Half the town have said they will call upon us this week for bread.'

'So you have told people.' She said, not looking up from her dough, only pounding it harder into the wood.

Bella, arching her back so she could see over the countertop, said 'you have over kneaded that Lacey, it won't be fit for a dog to eat.' Lacey continued to pummel the dough, the flat, smacking sound of her fists against it, bouncing off the walls. 'What's wrong Lacey?' Receiving no answer, Bella stood up and began walking towards the back room, shaking her head. 'I don't understand you.'

'What?!' Lacey snapped, looking up, her voice loud and harsh, 'what don't you understand of me?'

Bella stopped walking and turned to her, 'I don't understand why, upon the day after your engagement, you would prefer to be locked away, elbow deep in grain and flour with a frown upon your face, rather than in town receiving good wishes. *That* is what I don't understand.'

'Good wishes?!' Lacey scoffed.

'Yes sister, good wishes. Is it not nice that the town finally has something nice to celebrate rather than mourn?'

'You mean the girls.'

'Yes,' said Bella hesitantly 'we are tired of mourning girls.'

'But instead of considering why so many are disappearing it is easier to plan a wedding?'

'We know why the girls are disappearing.'

'Tell me.'

'You know.'

'I want you to tell me,' Lacey pressed her sister.

'They are disappearing because they are disobedient. Because they will not take caution. Because they will not listen to their fathers. Talking of which, your father has been accepting compliments all day on your behalf.'

'By which you mean drinking at the tavern since noon. And the Mayor too no doubt. Making plans for the bakery.'

'No, they met last week to discuss the bakery.'

'But I have had the ring on my finger less than a day.' Then scowling she shook her head and muttered 'you and Father have sold me for the bakery.'

'Don't be so dramatic.'

'You have sold my future. Why? So that you may walk through the town with your head held a little higher? So that the church women won't gossip about you once your back is turned? So that you won't hear the word "witch" in their whispering?'

Bella flinched at that, then closing her eyes to calm her annoyance she said 'Father only wants the best for you and in return you insult us and lock yourself away. Skulking in the shadow of this house as though a prisoner awaiting their death sentence.'

'It feels like a death sentence.'

'Oh Lacey! Would you prefer no engagement, no ring, no wedding? Do you wish to sleep in the attic forever? Do you wish to be a baker's daughter your whole life?'

'No of course not. But neither did I wish to be just some man's wife.'

Bella, holding her arms by her side flexed her fingers, the skin of her knuckles turning white. She opened her mouth to speak, then shut it again, gathering herself. Then, in a quiet, steady voice she said, 'you should be grateful for the option, not all of us have that.' She turned and walked into her bedroom. Lacey leant her elbows against the bench and buried her face in her floured hands.

*

A week passed with Lacey not stepping foot outside the bakery. Though she missed him she had a dread of bumping into Mateo on Main Street. So instead she spent her days in the kitchen. It seemed to her every time she crossed to look out of the front window Lek or Bran Barrick stood there, leaning against the house opposite, watching the bakery. Like jailers. Causing her to shrink even further back inside the house.

It wasn't so bad; for the most part she was alone, for although she avoided the village, her father and Bella spent almost all their time there. For Bella there seemed to be some urgent need to visit Main Street every hour or so. She would forget a colour of thread she needed, or else would suddenly feel the urge for beef that evening, or some other excuse. And pulling on her cap, gloves and coat, she would leave with an excited, springing step. Before returning sometime later with the item, or without, but always with a host of compliments and congratulations from the villagers. Her cheeks flushed with pride and enjoyment at the telling of it and though Lacey felt she might scream at the sound of one more, she stayed silent, allowing Bella the satisfaction.

Upon news of the engagement, Frank had firmly set up residence at the window seat of the Inn, where his peers lined the bar, eager to shake his hand and purchase him flagon upon flagon of ale. The celebrations slowly became more boisterous as the hours wore on, inevitably a fiddle was produced, and though not a particularly confident man, buoyed on by the cheers of the villagers, he sang along with vigour. He too would return with a merry attitude to the house, his cheeks flushed with the rosy warmth of too much drink. He would sit at the kitchen table and discuss his plans for the future. The Mayor had suggested that he might be inclined to invest a little in the running of the bakery, and Frank Emerson, in his excitement and relief, could think of little else.

The following Monday, Lacey finally went outside. She hadn't wanted to leave the sanctuary of her home, and now as she walked through town her stomach flitted nervously. The previous evening her Father had questioned why she was spending so much time inside; she answered only that she was suffering from headaches. He had observed her sceptically through half closed eyes. 'No man wants a sickly wife,' he had said to her.

After looking to check the Barrick brothers weren't outside, she walked quickly, with her head down, towards Main Street. The package of laundry under her arm had sat by the bakery door for two days. The Miller children's clothes had needed patching. A rip to the boy's jacket and one to the girl's skirt, along the hem line. It was easy work and took Bella only a matter of minutes, but the distraction of the engagement had delayed their return.

She knocked at the Miller's door. The grey paint peeling slightly at the bottom, thanks to years of rain. It swung open to reveal no one. Lacey looked down. The surly face of the five year old Eva looked up at her. Her hair hung messily down to the base of her back, her bow hanging perilously loose.

'Hello. Is your mother home?' Eva did not reply, only stared up at her blankly. 'I'm Lacey, I work at the bakery.' She gestured to the parcel, 'I am returning your mother's mending.'

'I know you. You're the lady who talked to Jessica down by the Old Oak Tree.'

Lacey remembered the red haired girl, and nodding, said, 'I am.'

The little girl turned and running on bare feet, disappeared into the house. Lacey stood awkwardly on the doorstep a moment, before following her inside. The house was dim, with no candles lit, and the shutters drawn. On the floor, by the ash filled fireplace lay an assortment of children's toys. A board marked with scribbles lay beside a few thumbs of white chalk.

'Mrs Miller?' Lacey called tentatively. She walked through an empty kitchen, avoiding a pale, half full of rainwater, dripping lazily from the roof above.

The back door stood open. Lacey froze beneath it, she blinked, as to reassure herself she was not dreaming. The yard was strewn with bloodied feathers. A carpet of red and white. Like a hunter had dragged his kill across fresh snow. They fluttered beneath Eva's feet as she skipped through them to the fence. She nimbly climbed the rungs before perching atop the post like an owl.

'Foxes,' a voice came, making Lacey jump. Mrs Miller appeared from the side of the house, with her dress sleeves rolled high and an empty hessian sack in each hand. She had a smear of dry blood across her forehead. The woman nodded towards an empty chicken house. Lacey regarded the little wooden structure. There was a frenzy of bloodied scratch marks against the inside walls.

'My husband says he locked it last night,' she said, rolling her eyes. Then bending down, her skirts stretching across her knees she began to scoop feathers into a sack. Lacey turned and placing the package of laundry on the bench, reached for the other sack.

'You don't have to.'

'It's no problem.' Lacey said, grabbing soft handfuls and tossing them inside, feeling that some of them were still wet.

Eva kicked her feet against the wooden post. 'But why can't I go mummy?' She whined, evidently continuing a conversation from before Lacey's arrival.

'She wants to play with her friends' Mrs Miller explained to Lacey, tying her full sack, putting it to the side and fetching another.

'Why not mummy?'

'It's too dangerous.'

'Eden still gets to play out,' Eva said indignantly.

'Eden's a boy,' responded her mother, drawing the back of her hand across her cheek, leaving another bloody streak. 'It's different.'

Eva let out a long, frustrated groan.

The two women worked a while, until most of the feathers were stored in sacks resting against the fence. Mrs Miller had not talked much; as though she were too busy for the luxury of frivolous conversation. She was one of the rare women in town who had never been outwardly unkind to Lacey, but it seemed to her that was more because she hadn't the time to be, rather than anything else. After the work was done, she offered Lacey tea. Considering the lonely silence of the bakery waiting for her, Lacey accepted.

'Excuse the mess. My husband has taken on more work at the mill. And with him not wanting Eva to leave the house it means my hours are even busier. The pot began to boil, the steam enveloping a pile of dirty dishes on the counter. She almost tripped as she avoided stepping on two straw dolls, lying on the floor. 'Eva, come and pick these up. I told you not to leave your toys here.'

She set two mugs down on the table and sat heavily opposite Lacey. Closing her eyes for a moment, she exhaled deeply. Her apron, covered in chicken blood, still wrapped around her body. Lacey tried not to look at the red stains.

'Are many parents keeping their daughters' home?'

'More and more,' nodded Mrs Miller, wincing against the hot tea. Her eyes darted across to Eva who had fetched her dolls and was playing with them in the corner of the room. 'We're all frightened. Of course this town has always been dangerous, girls would go missing, every few years or so. But it's been three girls in the last year. No, four now, since Mary. It's getting worse. No one wants it to be their girl who's next. Kinch's curfew is all well and good for the older girls, but the young ones, they got taken in the day.'

'You've warned her of the dangers of Deception Bay?' Lacey asked, looking across at the child.

'Oh she knows well enough. My husband tells her of it nightly, as though it were bedtime story. I've told him I won't make a difference.'

'You don't believe she'll listen?'

'I don't believe in Deception Bay. I mean I don't believe that's what's happening to our girls.'

Lacey shifted uncomfortably in her chair, feeling the familiar pricking in her cheeks. Mrs Miller, noticing, added with a wave of the hand, 'oh I don't believe in witches either.'

'Then what do you believe?'

Mrs. Miller looked again at her daughter playing with the dolls. She had taken the blue bow from her hair and tied it around the waist of one of them. 'I don't know what I believe. I don't believe they are bad listeners or they are disobedient. The men think so. But they don't know the children like we do. I believe something is hunting them.' Lacey glanced at the women, whose eyes never left her daughter. Eva pulled up the ribbon so that it was across the face of the doll, she walked it across the floor, bumping it blindly again and again against the chair leg.

'After your mother was executed and the girls kept disappearing, the Mayor and the council should have apologised. No one will tell you that of course. I think I would probably deny it if you told someone I had, but it's true nonetheless. This town is foolish to think it was witches. I think they're making the same mistake now. When people get frightened, they make mistakes.' Wearily she pushed her hair back from her brow. Then sprung up, remembering something. She walked to the counter and taking a tin from the cupboard tipped a few coins out into her hand. She placed them on the table in front of Lacey who put them in her pocket.

'For the mending.'

'Thank you.'

'You must be glad all this will be behind you soon. I heard of your engagement.' Her eyes moved to Lacey's hand. 'Your father must be looking forward to taking the blood vow too. Especially with such an illustrious a family as the Abners.'

The ring, as though in response, suddenly sparkled in the light. Lacey withdrew her hand and placed it on the lap, twisting the band round and round her finger. She did it so often it was beginning to leave a mark.

Eva approached and began whinging, pulling at her mother's apron. Lacey put down her tea and moved to leave. 'I won't take up any more of your time. Your mending is on the bench. Thank you for the tea.'

'Mummy come and play,' Eva whined.

Mrs Miller allowed herself to be pulled to her daughter's dolls. 'This will be you before long Lacey,' she said half smiling, then the smile faded and looking at her she added sincerely 'I hope you don't have a daughter.'

*

Knock, knock. Lacey awoke. The thin slither of grey coming through her curtain was the only way to tell her eyes were open at all. She lay completely still in her bedroom, save for her heartbeat which thundered urgently beneath the sheet. She had heard something. The muscles in her legs twitched, she stared at the window, her eyes wide and white with fear. She glanced up at the shadow above her, the rafters, old and dark and unmoving stared back at her. She could hear the wind whistle inside the chimney and through the fireplace downstairs. The curtain flickered and she heard the noise again. Perhaps it was her window, knocking against the casement. She had closed it, hadn't she? Before bed, she was sure she had pulled the catch tight. But maybe that was the night before, she couldn't remember, she couldn't trust her mind. She could hear the leaves on the trees in the forest outside rustling and moving like sholes of fish. *Knock, knock* it came again, this time more certain.

'Mateo?' Lacey whispered, but saying it she knew it wasn't him, she could feel it wasn't him.

Carefully, slowly, she pulled her legs from the blankets and noiselessly stood, her bare feet cold on the floor. Tiptoeing she walked towards the window, telling herself she was foolish to feel so afraid. Nevertheless at the window she paused, summoning her courage. Swallowing painfully she pulled back the curtain. A hooded head filled the pane, it's black staring face obscured by shadow, just inches behind the glass. Lacey screamed. The noise in the quiet house was like smashed glass. Her body, forced backwards in fear, fell to the floor. The curtain dropped.

The sound of footsteps came fast on the stairs below, the door flung open. Bella, her face soft with sleep stood in the doorway. Frank, a few steps behind her, small clumps of hair crushed to the side of his head from where he had lain against it.

'What is it?' Panted Bella, peering into the darkness, 'what's the matter?'

Lacey pointed at the window, 'there's someone there' she whimpered, hearing not her own voice, but a child's, weak and thin as grass.

Frank, pushing past his eldest daughter, strode across the room and without hesitation pulled the curtain aside. The pale blue pane was empty, it rattled gently, but all that could be seen was the sky, the field and the tree line beyond.

Frank turned and walked back to the top of the stairs, Bella stepping aside to let him past. 'A dream,' he growled, 'go back to sleep.' Then he was gone, the sound of his uneven footsteps echoing behind him.

Lacey, still on the floor, looked up at Bella. 'I was sure... I thought I saw...' Suddenly she felt as though the last few minutes had been a dream. Her mind melted with fear, unable to verify the reality of anything. Bella, re-treading their father's steps pulled the handle on the window until it clicked. Drawing the curtain fully she whispered 'go back to sleep.' Then, without looking at Lacey she left, closing the door behind her.

Lacey stayed where she was, listening to the wind whipping around the house, waiting for her heartbeat to slow, before crawling back into bed and lying sleeplessly until it was time to start the day.

CHAPTER FIFTEEN

The following afternoon Lacey worked alone in the house. The sun shone through the orange leaves, soothing the cold bite of the autumn wind. The shadows of leaves danced across the table as Lacey cut pears. She remembered when she and Mateo were children how they had cut out shadow puppets from paper. The two of them furiously concentrated in their tasks, tied the figures to twigs, and, using a candle, directed shadow plays. Great sprawling adventures, with Gypsy kings and sea voyages, on the walls of the bakery while her mother worked. Lacey's hands paused above the fruit, still holding the knife, as she sat there deep in the memory.

There came a short, sharp double tap at the door. The kind of brisk, business-like knock that always came before an unenjoyable meeting. She set the knife down and crossing to the door opened it only enough to see through the gap. Mr Lewis stood with his bag bundled beneath one arm, peering up at her through smudged spectacles. A few small crumbs of a hastily eaten lunch still clinging to his waistcoat.

'Miss Lacey?'

'Yes?'

'It is Mr Lewis.'

'So I see,' she said, not moving.

He sniffed and pushed his glasses further up his hooked nose. 'You are expecting me?'

'I'm not.'

'Oh.' He frowned and made a little frustrated clicking sound with his tongue. 'The Mayor's son told me three. I don't like the manner on that boy, quite presumptuous to think I would have an appointment free at such late notice. But he insisted, and luckily I do have a slither of time available today. Just for a preliminary fitting of course.'

'For what?' Asked Lacey, still not opening the door.

'Your wedding boots. He wants white calfskin, so really time is of the essence. Otherwise I won't have time enough for the dyeing. As it is, we will be pushed, but still if the Mayor wishes it then it will be so. I have no desire to bring about a sudden tax on my leather. Even if it does mean that I have to endure his ill-tempered son.' He shifted his small weight between his feet, 'won't you invite me in? I really am quite busy.'

Lacey sighed and opening the door, stepped back, allowing Mr Lewis entry. She didn't offer him tea nor a seat, but she sat on the stool herself, and taking a handkerchief from the pocket of her apron, wiped the pear juice from her hands. As he was in a hurry, he seemed not to mind her lack of manners, and setting his bag down on the table began folding up his shirt sleeves.

'How many inches long are your feet?' He asked, opening the large, leather bag and taking out a sheath of paper and a pencil.

'I don't know,' Lacey answered. Mr Lewis tutted beneath his breath and reaching inside the bag, rummaged around the bottom. 'Ah-ha!' He said, whipping out a length of measuring tape. Lacey sat, running the tips of her fingers along the wide grooves on the tabletop. Years of dirt and food had embedded themselves within the trenches, as children she and Bella would gouge out chunks with their dinner knives and flick them at each other.

Mr Lewis peered short-sightedly around the room, his eyes squinting to shrivelled slits, the thick glass within his spectacles magnifying them in size.

'Have you a foot stool?'

'Yes,' said Lacey, leaning forward and taking hold of one that stood inches from him, 'here.'

'Ah! My eyes aren't quite as they were.'

'Should I place my feet upon it?'

'No, no,' he said, shaking his head at her ignorance and tucking it instead beneath himself. He sat down and with the pencil he tapped his narrow knee, it made a hollow sound. When she didn't move he looked up and said, 'place your foot here Miss.'

'My bare foot?' Lacey asked, suddenly hesitant, feeling the air in the room alter slightly.

'Yes.' He said shortly, leaning to reach for the parchment and pulling it closer to him across the table.

Lacey bent slowly and one after the other pulled off her house slippers, placing them neatly beside her chair. She wriggled here toes against the cold, hard, stone floor. Her feet felt naked and she resisted the urge to hide them inside her skirt. Mr Lewis tilted his head up to look at her, then nodded towards her feet. 'I haven't all day Miss.'

Lacey lifted her leg and placed the ball of her foot on the old man's knee. She felt the angular bone through his trouser. Pulling tight the measuring tape, he held it against her, from toe to heel, the feeling of the tape lightly touching her, tickled slightly. 'Will you resole my plain shoes too?' She asked, nodding to her tired shoes by the door. 'They have worn away.'

Keeping his head down, the man said, 'I'm too busy now, besides you haven't much time left.'

'How do you mean?' She asked in alarm and confusion. Then her brow cleared. 'Oh. I suppose a rich man's wife doesn't wear such shoes.'

The cobbler said nothing, only noted down the inches, then he did the same for the width. Exhaling inwardly, Lacey went to remove her foot. But quick as a whip his right hand shot out and held her ankle in place, softly, but with strength.

'It is for a boot Miss,' he said quietly, his head not moving from his paper, his pencil scratching away. She frowned at him, not understanding. 'I must take your full leg measurements.' Then he looked at her, and his face, it appeared to her, had changed somehow. The line of his jaw seemed, almost imperceptibly, to tremor slightly, as though he were suppressing a tic. His manner too had changed, the busy irritability of his arrival, was gone, now he was calmer, concentrated. Outside the sun still shone, the shadows of the leaves flitted energetically across the floor. She wondered how long Bella might take at the butcher, and if perhaps she had stopped by the Vicarage for a cup of tea. The sun caught the knife, still lying on the kitchen table beside the cut pears, now browning in the bowl.

He took the hem of her skirt between his fingertips and lifted it up her calf. His progress was slow, the material dragging gently on her bare skin. Lacey heard the blood pumping around her ears. He folded the bottom of the skirt over her knee and left it there. The fair, downy hair at the base of her thighs stood on end. Lacey didn't move. With her foot still resting atop his knee, Mr Lewis leaned back ever so slightly on his stool. Ritualistically winding the measuring tape around his fingers. His head tilted to one side in concentration, appraising her. He made no sound. Lacey stared at a particular patch of shifting shadow on the floor, the light moving so peculiarly there. He wrapped the tape around her thigh. She felt the tip of his thumb as it passed under her knee.

Lacey began, in the dark room, to feel as though the walls were getting smaller. With every graze of his hand upon her, she felt her breath catch. Then, slowly he leaned in. His face puckering as he squinted to read the measurement. Lacey's eyes fell to the top of his head, there were a few determined white hairs still growing there. But mostly it was as smooth as a boiled egg. She might crack it open with a spoon and watch his brains run down his shirt like yolk. His fingers inched up her thigh.

'Enough,' she said quietly, whispering it into the silent room, the word dissolving like mist. His progress remained unchanged. The muscles in her chest tensed like a clenched fist. She squeezed her eyes shut, feeling within her a pressure begin to grow. It seemed to push at the edges of her, trying to burst out. She felt his breath on her skin.

'Stop!' Lacey yelled and reaching down, pushed the cobbler's hand away. At the touch of her fingers, the man cried out and jumped back in alarm. The stool he had been sitting on tipped over and skidded back across the floor. Mr Lewis, his face contorted in pain, cradled his hand. When he looked up at her his eyes were alight with fear and a kind of excitement. Lacey stared at him in confusion, he behaved as though her touch had wounded him.

'I am so looking forward to your wedding night.' He snarled, his words strangely threatening.

The front door flew open. Bella, holding two, large parcels wrapped in white cloth, burst through the doorway, the sun shining behind her. The small, bespectacled, old man, had, as quickly and quietly as possible, composed himself. With his back to the door he collected his parchments from the table. Lacey hadn't yet directed her head back from looking at Bella by the time he had sorted his belongings. The tense atmosphere in the room snapped, like a rope pulled too tight. She swiftly tugged her dress skirts back down, smoothing her apron on top.

'Sorry!' Bella exclaimed, 'I was twice as long as I had estimated. Mr Tibbs was very kind and as an engagement present gifted us a whole joint. oh-' Only just then noticing they had a visitor, she stopped suddenly, dropping the parcels with a thud on the counter. 'Mr Lewis, I didn't know we were expecting you.'

'I was asked as a favour to the Mayor. A last-minute arrangement,' Mr Lewis said, hurriedly placing the measuring tape in his bag and fastened it with a click.

'For the wedding?' Asked Bella.

'Indeed. The Mayor's son has asked for a pair of boots to be made especially.'

Bella looked then around the room. Apart from the narrow opening in the back door, where the sunlight shone harshly, the room was dark. No other shutters were open. The cobbler stood with his bag in hand, shifting nervously on his feet. She glanced towards Lacey who didn't return the look, then down at the stool, knocked over on the ground.

'Boots?' Bella asked, her voice colder .

'Yes, as I said. Now really, I must be getting along, I have much work to do.' Mr Lewis nodded a goodbye in Lacey's direction and muttered a clipped good day to Bella, as he walked swiftly to the door. But before he walked through Lacey called out to him.

'You are on the council aren't you Mr Lewis?'

The cobbler paused and stared at her for a long moment. His face less fearful than before, now with an edge of hatred. Without answering he opened the door and walked out. As he turned Lacey saw a small black burn mark on one his hands.

'Boots?' Repeated Bella, once the door was shut, this time addressing her question to her sister. Lacey remained seated and stared expressionless at the gouge marks on the kitchen table.

'I don't want to live in this town anymore,' she said.

'Don't allow men in the house with the shutters drawn.' Responded Bella.

'Do you hear me?'

'If he must come again for a fitting, and I'm sure he will, ensure I'm with you.'

'And will you come to the Professor's with me too?'

'How do you mean?' Bella asked confused.

'Or perhaps walk beside me and hold my hand every time I pass the Inn after eleven in the morning? And where do you go unaccompanied? The butcher's, the Vicarage, into the woods to fetch mushrooms? Must you too be chaperoned? May we never be able to be alone with a man or else risk-' Her voice fell into silence. Bella, taking a knife from the drawer, cut the string tie on the parcels.

'There is no need for over-exaggeration, I'm only preaching caution. I don't much like Mr Lewis's manner.'

Lacey laughed; it was a short, humourless sound. 'How funny, he was just saying exactly that about my fiancé.'

'Quite the coincidence,' said Bella dryly. She took one of two large joints of red, raw beef and dropped it with a slap onto the chopping board. From the hook by the door she pulled down her apron, then she stood before the meat, one hand on her waist, appraising it. The round, metallic smelling joint began to emit a small moat of blood. She stared down at the pooling blood, with each second her enthusiasm waning. Lacey's words still echoing round the room. For some reason Bella couldn't summon the effort. She turned on her heels and faced Lacey, who held her chin in her hands and stared in misery.

'Have you still a taste for spiced milk?'

Lacey breathed a sigh that turned into a small smile, 'always' she said.

Minutes later, they sat at the kitchen table, their hands wrapped around two cups of steaming milk. Lacey wasn't sure exactly what the mixture was, she could definitely taste the sweetness of honey and the warmth of cinnamon, but there was more that she couldn't quite define. A fragrant, exotic aroma. Their mother had made it for them as children, on particularly cold nights. They would sit by the fire and sip at the smooth liquid, feeling it warm their insides. Apparently she had been taught it by her grandmother, and on Bella's tenth birthday she had passed it on to her. Lacey had been jealous, and her mother, lifting her to her knee, had said that she too would learn it once she turned ten, until then she would just have to guess. Her mother was hung a week after Lacey turned seven, so she never did learn.

CHAPTER SIXTEEN

The next day, with the feeling of not being able to let another night pass without seeing him outweighing her trepidation, Lacey left the bakery bound for Mateo. The Mayor had paid for two new girls from the Upper Lakes to come and work for them a few days a week. Their arrival was gratefully anticipated by Bella. Trade in the shop had exponentially increased after word of the engagement had spread through the town like a virus. From her hiding place in her bedroom Lacey could hear the almost constant ding of the bell as customers came in and out. The Mayor had also sent round builders to measure for an extra room to be added to the back of the house. With all the commotion Lacey could find no peace.

The reception from the villagers she passed was disorientating in its pleasantness. Turning onto Main Street Mrs Pye and Mrs Cole, who usually would have crossed the street to avoid her, now greeted her with a cordial 'good afternoon.' Which, though not a lot, was far more than Lacey was accustomed to. She walked on, a few more neighbours smiling politely to her, Lacey nodding at them in mild bemusement. The role of a rich man's betrothed is far easier than that of a witch's daughter, she thought. Even the Watchmen, who seemed over the last weeks to have multiplied, standing silently on every corner, their rifles at their sides, smiled at her respectfully.

A cool autumn wind blew around her ankles, picking up the fallen leaves and scattering them along the ground. Their crisp paper edges made hollow scraping sounds on the cobble stones. She saw a group of boys at the far end of town playing with a bat and ball. Occasionally one would hit it wide and another boy would disappear into the edge of the forest to fetch it, returning ball in hand. They played happily, unobserved. Not a girl in sight.

She was deep in thought as she turned onto Mateo's street, looking up absently, she stopped dead in her tracks. Lek Barrick stood a little way off outside Mateo's front door, leaning against the dock. He picked at his teeth with a matchstick, stopping to spit pieces of it into the water.

Not having the strength to encounter him that afternoon, she turned swiftly on her heel and immediately into the wide chest of a man. Stumbling backwards she lost her footing. His arm, swift and unquestioning in its strength, reached out and grabbed her around the waist. He held her fast, she felt the muscles beneath his jacket at the base of her back, it was like leaning against the thick branch of a tree. Sebastian's cold eyes looked down at her, the raw intensity of his stare forcing her to look away.

'Hello wife,' he said, the words sounding almost accusatory. He had been standing, beneath the shadow of an awning, waiting for her. In the doorway above his head she saw a spider in its web encasing a twitching fly.

'I'm not your wife yet,' she said, manoeuvring herself from his grip. But he didn't move, his arm vice-like stayed locked around her. She wriggled a moment before she stopped and, exhaling, forced herself to look up at him once more. Her tone sober, her stare serious, she said slowly, as though speaking to a dog, 'let me go, Sebastian.' He waited a beat, relishing his power and then released her. She stepped back immediately, trying to mask the relief on her face by busying herself with the smoothing of her skirts.

'Hello Lacey,' Lek whispered into her ear from behind her. She jumped and he snorted, pleased that he had managed to creep up on her.

'Where are you off to?' Sebastian asked, not taking his eyes from her.

'I'm taking a walk. Is that allowed?' She said coolly, her eyes moving between him and Lek, who walked in a slow circle around to Sebastian's side. He moved like a cat, kicked too many times to ever take a step without arching its back. The match still hung from the side of his mouth.

'A walk,' Sebastian echoed, then nodding, 'a fine idea. We will join you.'

Unsure of what to do, Lacey retraced her own steps and walked back in the direction in which she had come. The two men, either side of her, walked as escorts. What a strange pantomime this is, thought Lacey, they knew where I was going, and they laid in wait. The awkward party turned onto Main Street, Lek stopped to untie Sebastian's stallion. 'Your new saddle is ready,' he said, holding the horse by its bridle. Sebastian nodded, and with Lek lagging a little way behind they headed towards the saddlers.

Lacey walked automatically, with the strange child-like detachment of holding a parent's hand, it wasn't she deciding their direction. Passing the boys still playing ball, she paused.

'There are no girls playing out anymore. Their parents won't allow them.'

Sebastian didn't respond. He glanced to his right. His blue eyes slowly moving between the children with a cool disinterest. After a while he said, 'boys can be trusted to do as they are told. They listen when their fathers warn them of the dangers.' He cleared his throat and moved off. 'Besides, it is better for girls to be at home with the mothers, so that they may learn from them.' Lacey watched as one boy hit the ball high in the air with a resounding crack, the others whooping in excitement. 'Lacey.' Sebastian called to her. Reluctantly she followed.

A group of washerwomen passed, linens piled high in their baskets. 'Move!' Lek called angrily from behind Lacey, seeing the women were in Sebastian's path. Like a sea they parted, allowing the wealthy man and his fiancé to walk through. Lacey didn't look up to catch their eyes, her cheeks flushing pink. But she knew they watched her keenly, from behind their linen sheets. And she felt a new shame, a different kind of shame from being a witch's daughter. This guilt felt worse, unearned, even less her own.

'Already the villagers have changed towards you,' said Sebastian, spying her blush. 'I told you. Even those with the darkest of marks against them can be washed clean. These people have the memories of flies, come the wedding day they will hold you to their bosom and christen you as the favourite daughter of Lower Lynch.'

'And you their favourite son?'

'That's different,' he responded, squinting up at the grey sky, 'men don't have to be liked.'

Folding her arms, Lacey aimed her next step slightly away from him. But as though she were magnetised, Sebastian closed the distance in one stride. 'My father wasn't always a popular man as you know.' He continued, 'there were years when the men of this village shunned him, mocked him. His name was the punchline to jokes they told in the Tavern.' His pace slowed, and behind them Lacey felt Lek slow in response. 'They were dark years,' he said quietly, his eyes locked on the path in front. 'The Mansion was a place of infinite loneliness during my childhood. Locked rooms, dark corridors, a father who kept himself hidden away from the world. Hidden even from his son. I remember nights when I would fall asleep, water leaking from his room into mine. Waking to a soaking pillow. The house nearly crumbled without a woman's touch.'

With the tips of his fingers he soothed his pale eyebrows, then tucked an errant lock of hair behind his ear. Looking down at her he said, 'I'm pleased to have someone speak to of this, you are a good listener Lacey. Like your mother.'

'My mother?' Said Lacey, the hairs on the back of her neck pricking. Her eyes darting around the street to see if anyone was in earshot. But no one could hear them.

'She was the only woman in the village who came to us at that time.'

'Why would my mother visit you?' Lacey asked, her tone incredulous.

'Who knows, it certainly wouldn't have done much for her own standing in society. At that time it was our name that had the mark upon it, not hers. I think perhaps she knew I missed my mother. That my father was not,' he considered his words, 'the most understanding of men. She would sit at the end of my bed and listen whilst I...' he paused, changing his mind. 'Anyway, her visits didn't last long.'

'Why?' Pressed Lacey.

'Father didn't like her in the Manor, he thought her nosy. Thought she was snooping around.'

'How so?' Lacey pushed, intrigued. Through all the years and all the insults that had been levelled at her mother, she had never heard this one. Why would the Mayor think her mother was snooping around? And if his accusation was correct, what was she looking for?

Sebastian exhaled, puffing out his cheeks in disinterest, as was his habit when the subject strayed too far from himself. 'I don't know. He said she was always putting her nose into business that was of no concern to her. Father says you and she are alike in that way.' He glanced at her then. She looked away. 'It wasn't too long after that we found that she had been taking the village girls for her witchcraft.' Lacey's eye twitched. 'Anyway,' said Sebastian briskly, clapping his oar-like hands together, 'my point was that redemption of one's reputation is always a possibility. My father gained the strength, God knows from where. But he went into his room when my mother left a hollow shell of a man and came out *powerful*. He worked his way back from nothing to become Mayor.'

You could tell by the satisfied glint in his eye and the way he tilted his chin high when he talked, that Sebastian liked to tell this particular part. The part when the maligned man gained strength and rose to power. Lacey rolled her eyes. They stopped outside the saddler.

'They want you to go in to check the straps.' Lek told Sebastian, who nodded and entered the building. Left alone Lek sidled up beside her. Close enough that she could smell tobacco and stale sweat on his clothes and see bits of wood still stuck between his grey teeth

He glanced once or twice to ensure Sebastian's attention was elsewhere, then when he spoke his voice was hushed and illicit, his face inches from hers. 'Look at the witch's daughter,' he sneered, 'how's it feel to be on the arm of a respected gentleman?'

'You tell me Lek, you've been on his arm far longer than I.'

Lek's nostrils flared an ugly, angry white, 'shame you have the mouth of a scrubber. I'm guessing those ears still work though cos you'd do well to listen to me.' He leant forward. 'No more running around talking to people and asking the children questions Lacey. No more chats with the stranger. Sebastian's right, you are like your mother, a meddling snoop. Keep your nose out of that which don't concern you. Do you hear me?'

From the corner of her vision, through the dark windowpane, Lacey could see Sebastian paying up and walking towards them. 'How do you know about me talking to the stranger, Lek Barrick?' She said, fiercely staring him in the eye. He gave no answer.

A memory rose in Lacey's mind. It sprung up as though buried somewhere deep inside. A ten year old Lek stood above Lacey on the fence around the village green. His face taut and mean, pre-pubescent spots smattering his cheeks. A crowd of children had gathered, Lek beckoned them closer. Bran stood beneath him, his dull cow-like eyes staring at her. Lek was pointing at her. Lacey and Bella had been the attention of every village child since their mother had been executed earlier that year. Where Bella had managed to ingratiate herself back into the favour of her peer group by affecting their mannerisms and holding her tongue, Lacey had not.

In an attempt to shield herself from their attention, she had found, from her mother's drawer, a cap. Though she were far too young to wear a cap, she had thought that perhaps if they did not see her distinct hair, they would think of her less. And she had come out to play that morning with it wrapped around her head, tying the bow twice as it was far too loose for her.

Whatever effect she had hoped for, the opposite had occurred. Lek Barrick had rounded on her at once, like a hunter in the woods, spotting his prey.

'Look what the witch's daughter is wearing. Come here. Look at her!' A few children had gathered, sniggering at her. Lek, jumping up on the fence, called more over. 'We can still see you Lacey,' he sneered. 'You can't hide behind that cap.' Turning away Lacey had found herself encircled by them. Bran reached forward to pull it off her. The cap fell over her face. 'She's wearing a hood like her mother. Fetch the noose,' laughed Bran. Lacey pulled it up. The tears beginning to burn behind her eyes. She looked up at Lek, a mass of hatred rose inside her like a boiled pot. The edges bubbling and spilling over.

Suddenly a wind came down from the hill. A powerful rush of air, causing the leaves to skitter across the green. Lek, perched atop the fence, flew off and landed inelegantly on the ground, his face in the dirt. The crowd gasped and then immediately erupted into laughter. Lek picked himself up, earth staining one side of his face. He stared at Lacey and what she saw beneath the anger and embarrassment on his face was a realisation. As the two looked at each other she felt as though he had discovered something about her that she didn't want him to know. As though he had found out something secret. Lek turned and shoving his fists in his pocket pushed his way through the crowd. The next day the children returned to their usual mocking of Lacey. But Lek from then on no longer lead the taunts, preferring instead to whisper behind her back, turning others against her.

Sebastian came through the shop door, the bell ringing above his head. Lek took a small step back. Over Sebastian's shoulder lay a soft tan saddle. Pristine and flawless, polished brass clasps and buckles shining in the light. Lek, pulling the horse aside, took it from him and laid it atop the old one on the horse's back. 'I'll fit it for you tonight.' He said nodding as they began again to walk, glancing once at Lacey.

Lacey was chaperoned home, like a child who had run away being delivered back to her parents. Upon opening her front door she turned to bid them goodbye, but Sebastian's wide form had already passed through the doorway and into the bakery before she could stop him. Reluctantly she closed the door behind them, leaving Lek out on the street. The house was empty and quiet.

'Sebastian I-' Started Lacey. He held his palm up in the air, halting the words in her mouth. Keeping his manicured hand raised he tilted his head to one side, looking leisurely around the room, his eyes moving as though he had never properly looked at it before. As he walked the heels of his boots left faint floury indents on the floor. He sat down at the kitchen table, and when Lacey did not follow he tapped at the seat of the opposite stool. She glanced quickly at the closed door before reluctantly sitting.

Sebastian laced his hands together, Lacey folded her arms and for a moment the pair sat in silence staring at one another. Finally he broke his gaze, his eyes landing on the peach, still ripening on the dish. Bella had checked on it again today, assessing it to be finally soft enough for them to eat after supper tonight. It sat in the centre the table, the light from the window falling on it so that its fuzz hovered around it like a halo. Sebastian's long forefinger stretched out and rolled it back and forth. Lacey gave an involuntary shake of the head. He picked it up contemplatively, turning the fruit with his fingers. Looking across the table at Lacey he pushed his thumb forcibly against it.

Then suddenly it was at his lips, his teeth ripping into its white flesh. Lacey stiffened. The peach made a lax wet sound. He tore at it until the skin, with its soft shining hairs, was pulled away and swallowed inside his red mouth. Lacey, transfixed, appalled, was unable to release herself from his stare. A glossy drop of juice ran from the side of his lips down the smooth skin of his chin. Sebastian, knowing her eye was upon him did not wipe it away. Instead he sucked at the fruit for an agonizing minute, until the gnarled, lined brown pit was visible. Finally, holding it with the very edges of his fingertips, he dropped it to the ground, where it fell with a hollow knock. Only then did he take his handkerchief from his waistcoat and with his eyes locked to hers, wiped the juice from his lips and chin.

He gave an indecent moan of satisfaction and his glistening lips stretched into a wolfs smile. Standing, he bowed. Then leaving her where she sat, silently at the table, he got up and left the house, closing the door quietly behind him. Lacey stared down at the pit, its stray strands of yellow flesh hanging from it, gently weeping juice onto the floor.

CHAPTER SEVENTEEN

Later that afternoon Bella and Lacey worked alone in the bakery. A loud, angry knock came abruptly at the door, sounding more like someone had thudded at it with the side of their fist rather than their knuckles. Wiping her hands on her apron, Lacey opened it with the same caution as she had done with Mr Lewis the day before. But upon seeing who it was she stepped back, feeling relief, followed by a wave of unease. Mateo stood a few steps off. His back was half-turned, as though between him knocking and her answering he had changed his mind, and was on the verge of walking away.

His satchel hung across his chest and he wore his work boots. They looked at one another, anger swam at the edges of his eyes. Lacey swallowed, waiting for him to speak. In a formal, forced voice he said, 'I have been sent by the foreman to ask what bed frame you would like in your new house. I have oak or pine.' He reached into his bag and pulled out two short planks of wood. He had never spoken to her like this, not once, and if his intention had been to hurt her, he had succeeded. Her happiness at having seen him, ebbing away. She sighed wearily and turned back into the house, leaving the door open.

'I don't care,' she said in a quiet, empty voice. Mateo followed her inside, nodding to Bella, who gave him a curt look.

'Father will be back before long,' she warned.

'He won't be home until dinner,' Lacey corrected her.

Bella picked up two baking trays, and allowing them to clatter noisily against one another, carried them outside to the basin.

Lacey sat down. Mateo laid the planks on the table and placed his hands over both of them. His nails were lined with dirt and there were small flakes of sawdust in his hair. Lacey, slowed by sadness, stretched out her hand across the table and placed her fingertips against one of the planks. She felt the soft grain, sanded smooth, beneath her touch. One light and yellowish, the other mottled with dark rings.

'The pine takes paint well,' he said 'but being a softer wood it is more likely to scratch. The oak is more durable and less likely to warp should the house grows cold in the winter months. Though I'm sure it won't. It is well built.'

'The new house,' she said, realising, 'off Main Street, the one you have been working on?'

'Yes.'

'It is for me?'

'It is.'

Mateo had complained of his back hurting from laying the floor on the site. He had been on his knees building the house she would be sharing with another man, and today he came to discuss the bed he would make for them. She hadn't yet even considered where they might live. Lacey's raised her fist to her mouth, tears stung bitterly at the edges of her eyes and she could feel her face growing red. With horror, she suddenly realized that she was going to cry. Seeing this and softening, the anger and bravado from his entrance disappearing like smoke, Mateo's expression cleared. He scooped the planks up and put them back inside his satchel. Then, looking straight at her, he asked 'would you take a walk with me Lacey?'

Bella, walking in from the back room, began to protest, but before she could, Lacey answered 'yes.'

The light fell dappled through the trees onto the woodland floor. The ground was covered in a thick carpet of auburn leaves, a rich tapestry of orange and brown, crunching satisfyingly underfoot. The mist was beginning to gather in the shadows, wrapping around the trunks of the trees, but whilst the sun was still out and shining down through the gaps in the leaves, it stayed at bay.

When they were children, not long after her mother died, Mateo had built a swing for them to play on, to cheer her. He had waited outside the bakery with it in his bag. And with a thrilling excitement they had raced through the long grass to the top of the field. They had argued over who should climb the tree to tie it, she had won. She had climbed nimbly and quickly up the tree trunk, eager to prove her ability to him. Her little feet catching every nook available, Mateo's bag with the swing inside hanging around her shoulder. She had reached the widest bough and, climbing like a cat across it, tied it on.

On her way back down, she had fallen. A branch giving way beneath her boots, she had felt the startling weightlessness of slipping through the air. Mateo reached to catch her, but he was too late. Lacey's knee was bloodied and bruised, she held it against her chest, wincing at the stinging pain. Mateo, ducking into the undergrowth had returned before too many minutes with a fistful of bitter dock to relieve the pain. Rubbing them between his fingers he had held the leaves to her swollen knee until she was able to stand again. 'See,' he had said, 'now we both have scars.' Then hours had passed, and whole summers even, with the two pushing each other on the swing. Neither wanting to return to their motherless homes.

Lacey followed Mateo up the same hill. One or two of their neighbours, who stood in their backyards bringing in the laundry, stopped and watched as they had passed. She had noticed their glances, but she hadn't the energy nor the inclination to care. Mateo, half angry half sad, walked a little ahead of her, his satchel swinging at his side, both hands stuffed in his trouser pockets. Neither spoke a word until they were deep within the woods, the trees closing protectively behind them.

'Mateo I tried to visit you. To tell you...' Lacey began.

'The wedding flowers have begun to arrive,' he said, not listening, 'a few hang already from the beams in the Manor.'

'Please don't speak to me of them.'

'They are white as snow and some as big as babies' heads.'

'Please don't speak to me of them.' She repeated in the same tone.

'They stink. Like an old women's perfume.' He spoke in a mean, spiteful manner, but the pain in his voice betrayed him. 'And they lay paving in the Manor garden, so that you might not muddy the train of your dress or the heels of your boots.'

At the word boots Lacey felt a chill crawl up from the bottom of her spine to the top of her back, finally it burst from her mouth. 'Lord! I'm surrounded by this marriage even here!' She exclaimed.

'This marriage,' he laughed humourlessly. Then turning to her, scorn in his eyes and on his tongue, a finger pointed at her face. 'If you so despise this proposal why did you pursue it?'

'You think I pursued it?'

'Didn't you?'

'No!' She cried.

'Why then did you go to The Manor? The men at work say he proposed on his boat. That you ate dinner by candlelight, that a musician was brought from across the lake to play violin, that he spelt your name across the water in floating lanterns!'

'None of that is true.'

'None of it? Do I imagine the ring upon your finger too?'

Lacey sighed. Twisting the ring with her thumb. 'He proposed upon the lake, that much is true. But there was no candlelight, nor violin. The man who sells the sugar to Father has more romance in his voice when doing so. He proposed to me in the manner of someone purchasing a cow they don't particularly want to own.' Lacey started to walk, stepping around Mateo, who, spinning on his heel and overtaking her, stood once more in her path. His cheeks flushed pink with love and anger.

'And this is an appealing proposal to you I suppose? Is that what you want?'

'What do you think? You have known me as long as I have known myself, what do you think I want?' She snapped, her voice higher than usual.

'I don't know Lacey!' He yelled. She saw the hurt in his eyes, his lower lip trembling ever so slightly.

'Mateo had I the choice I would run as far and fast as I could,' she said, her voice softer than before.

'Then why don't you?'

She sighed in frustration. 'Why don't you understand all these things Mateo? When I seem to see them so clearly.'

In a step, he closed the gap between them and, his voice in a low, hoarse whisper, said 'because I never needed to understand any of them to love you.'

They stood, faces inches apart, his breath ragged and unstable, the words spreading through the trees. Lacey held his stare until she could do so no longer, and biting her lip turned away. But he caught her and with one movement pulled her into his chest, his arms enveloping her. He buried his face into her neck, squeezing her tightly, and she in response wrapped her arms around him. She closed her eyes, feeling his heart thundering through his coat. They had never held one another like this. 'I wish things weren't the way they are.' She said, her words muffled but audible.

'Me too.' He said simply.

Had the couple not been so consumed in one another and not felt so deeply alone, they may have heard the light tread of hooves in the woodland. But the rider was skilled and knew how to guide the horse in silence between the trees. The two continued to embrace as the figure, hidden in the shadows, watched on. Before pulling the reins of his steed and cantering quietly off, back in the direction of the village.

After a while Lacey relaxed her grip, and stepping away from him, but taking his hand, they walked slowly through the woods, their fingers laced together. They didn't speak, only listened to the sounds of the forest, their entwined hands gently swinging between them. The world beyond the forest slipped away, for now there was only the trees, the light between them, the occasional low twit-twoo of the birds in their nests, and the pressure of his fingers against the back of her hand.

His hands, like his face, had small scattered scars, and points where the skin was a fairer and softer than the rest. Looking down, Lacey smoothed her thumb over a raised lesion that ran across his knuckles.

'Babies' skin is more sensitive than adults,' he said in response to her touch. 'They got me away from the fire, but the heat still burnt me.' His free hand ran over his jaw, where a few, thin, spider web scars traced across his skin. He had never spoken to her about his family, or The Great Fire. She squeezed his hand a little tighter. 'My parents threw me out of the window. My father wrapped me in a blanket and threw me out the window. I don't know who caught me. They said as soon as he threw me, the floor gave in, and they were gone. They weren't able to throw my sister free in time.' He stopped walking. 'Gypsies believe that a soul is never truly dead as long as there is still someone alive who remembers them. I don't remember what they look like, or what their voices sounded like, and I suppose I will never know now. But I'm pleased to have these scars, as a reminder of them.'

Lacey stood in front of him. Slowly, she raised his hand and gently placed a kiss upon his knuckles. A sad smile pulled at the corner of Mateo's lips, and linking their fingers together, he pulled her onwards.

It was a few minutes later that Lacey saw the tree. Although in truth she almost missed it, but something caused her to stop. Something had caught her attention, like a piece of wool snagging on a nail. She stopped, her eyes scanning the woodland, she took one, then two steps back, still staring. Her mother had told her once that it was a part of man's survival instinct. That even at times of relaxation, there is a whole part of your mind that is alert. Assessing the shapes and images and patterns in the world around, filtering through them for threat. Constantly scanning for an attacker, a face, or figure hiding in wait.

As a child, Lacey had woken once, in the middle of the night, and blinking into the darkness, felt a rush of fear when seeing an apron, hanging from the peg in the corner. The creases and shadow falling in such a way that she had thought it the devil, looming through the dark, his skin snow white and wrinkled, a cruel sneer across his pale face. She had screamed, waking the house, and her mother had sat with her all night. She had explained that her mind was trying to make sense of the shape, and assess its threat, and rather than being afraid she should take courage, it was trying to protect her.

Lacey recognized a shape then, in the woods. She saw the eyes first, the dark, grey eyes, deep, hollow holes of despair.

'What is it?' Said Mateo turning back to her.

'Look,' said Lacey pointing, not moving her eyes from the spot, 'come to where I stand and look.'

He did so and after a few moments he saw. About six layers deep, between two other trunks he saw it. A tree, old and cracked and gnarled, resembling a terrible, ghostly face., as though it were a moment of anguish, frozen in time. It was dead, no leaves grew around it, and its branches stuck out sharply as though snapped off.

'It's horrible,' said Mateo feeling a chill run through him. 'I've never seen it before. I never come this way.'

'I've seen it before,' she said.

'You've been here before?' He asked.

'No,' said Lacey, frowning. 'But I've seen it. In a drawing in that book I found at the Proffessor's. It was opposite the page I gave you to translate. The one with the word witch on it. I remember seeing it at the time and finding it so chilling.' The two stared at the haunted face. Then Lacey set off towards it.

'Where are you going?' Asked Mateo nervously. Lacey didn't answer, and with a sigh he followed behind.

Lacey walked tentatively to the tree, circling around it, inspecting it. The bark was ancient and decayed, its ridges deep enough to lose your fingers inside. Thick, plate-sized, mauve coloured mushrooms grew from the base, their fungal scent filling the air. In the woods, the sun set almost an hour before it did in the village, the light around them was already fading.

Lacey's foot caught against a hard edge. She fell, landing painfully. It was not soil beneath her hands. In the half light, where the mist rose in curls on the forest floor, underneath the watchful stare of the haunted tree, she had found something. It was covered in leaves and thick, green moss, that crept over the edges of the stone.

'Lacey! Are you hurt?' Mateo called, rushing over, then suddenly stopping when he saw where she lay. She pushed herself up and sat back on her knees. Beneath her the slab was as wide as a tombstone. Its face blank, save for a round ring handle. Lacey's hand reached out towards it.

'Lacey-' said Mateo, moving to stop her, but before he could, she turned it and pulled. A low clunking sound echoed beneath them. With wide eyes Lacey stood up, her hand still wrapped around the handle. The hinges turned with surprising ease, and with only a little effort she heaved it open. The smell of mould and stale air filled their nostrils, as they leaned tentatively forward to see a set of stone steps leading down and disappearing into the darkness.

CHAPTER EIGHTEEN

'Have you a box of matches?' Lacey asked, looking up at Mateo. 'This isn't a good idea,' he said, turning to look at the darkening sky between the branches, 'besides, the night is almost upon us.'

'Never mind that,' she answered, 'have you a match?' Mateo felt inside the pocket of his coat, and after a moment, reluctantly handed her a small box. Holding the edge of the door as support, she stepped inside the opening, stopping and lighting the first match before going any further. Her face, illuminated by the flame, had such a look of fierce determination upon it, it shocked him for a moment. Then she disappeared below the ground. Mateo, suddenly alone, glanced around the woodland, the shadows seemed to creep a little closer, he shook his head and followed her.

Lacey held the match out in front of her at arm's length, as she slowly descended the stairs. Around her the stone walls flickered and danced in the light of the flame. A layer of green algae had grown around every brick, emitting a wet, earthy smell. Above, the ceiling hung so close she had to lower her head or else risk hitting it. She held to the side of the wall and felt at each step tentatively, with the toe of her boot, before stepping down. The air was thick and stale with darkness and earth, and water seeping through brick. Behind the limited light of the match there was an endless, silent black. The only sound, aside from the steady rhythm of Mateo's breathing behind her, was an occasional drip-drip.

Finally she reached the bottom step, an arched ceiling opened overhead. A lantern hung off a hook at the base of the staircase and, opening the casement, Lacey lit the short candle inside. In the new light she could see, directly next to the lamp, a set of hooks. From one hung a long swath of black cloth. With a tentative hand she reached out, feeling the thick material with the tips of her fingers. Gently pushing aside a fold, she saw the thread lit golden in the candlelight. Embroidered upon it was the three peaks of The Island.

Mateo leaning over her shoulder, watched her. 'Look,' she said, pulling the material so that he could see. He said nothing, but the edge of his eyebrow flickered slightly and in the dull light his dark face paled. Lacey detached the lantern from the wall and continued forward. Each brick pulsed in an orange glow, around a soft clay floor. The light swelled to the edges of the room, then faded into darkness above them. Cobwebs swayed and danced and long, thick centipedes snaked in and out of the crumbling stone. But for them, there was no sign of life, the air was as cold and stale as a grave. On the far wall there was a wide wooden panel, which bore too an engraving of The Island, hanging like the crucifix at the front of a church.

'What is that?' Mateo pointed to the centre of the room at what looked to be a grey stone tomb. Its broad sides were cracked and ancient. So assuredly angular and square in its appearance it looked as though it must have sat there since the beginning of time. Lacey took a step forward.

'A tomb?' She guessed.

'For who?'

'I don't know,' she answered, reaching out to touch it.

'No!' Called Mateo. 'Don't touch anything. This is isn't a good place. I knew we shouldn't come down here. I think we should leave. There is evil here. I can feel it Lacey, I can feel it in my blood.'

'Your magical gypsy blood?' She said, a half smile upon her candle lit face, as she walked past him, slowly inspecting the room.

'You joke, but the blood inside me ran within the veins of my ancestors. They didn't survive so long without adapting a sense for danger, and knowing when to act upon it.'

'You and Ma are the only gypsies left in town.'

'What is your point?'

'That perhaps,' she shot him a playful look, 'your survival skills aren't as advanced as you suggest.'

'You are playing with me, and that is why I will allow you that.' He said, for a moment distracted from his fear, 'but answer me this, is there any other you would prefer by your side in a haunted crypt?'

'I would prefer you more were you to carry a sword.'

Leaning back to try and see further up the stairs Mateo said, 'at this moment in time Miss Lacey I would be inclined to agree with you.' He paused, a breeze ran down the staircase, bringing with it the return of his unease. 'Let's leave now.'

Lacey nodded to appease him but continued walking slowly around, moving over again to the tomb in the middle of the room. She bent and inspected the edges, running her hands over it. There were no joins as you would normally find in a coffin, she peered closer at the top stone, only it wasn't a top stone. The whole piece, all five sides, were one solid block.

'This isn't a tomb.' She said.

Mateo stood anxiously at the base of the stair, waiting for her, 'how do you mean?' He asked, glancing behind himself.

'It isn't hollow, there is nothing inside, only stone. I see no religious markings, nor name or birth date...'

'What is it then?'

Lacey shook her head.

Suddenly a noise came from overhead. The sinister crunch of dry leaves beneath a foot. Mateo spun on his heels and, quick as a flash, ran up the stairs to investigate. The horror of their discovery was immediately replaced with the fear of being trapped. Lacey saw, in her mind's eye, the closed door of the crypt covered in leaves and moss, Mateo and herself locked inside for eternity. They had only just happened upon it by chance. It mightn't ever be discovered again. She waited to hear the bang of the door closing, the metallic clunk of the stone. The seconds ticked by, but all she heard was her own panicked breath. The candle burnt low in the lantern.

Something beneath her caught her eye. She dropped onto her haunches, taking a closer look at the floor. A shallow trench ran around the edge of the great stone, she followed it to the foot, where it disappeared into the ground. A narrow strip of black sludge lined the bottom of it. She touched it, it felt cold and wet against her fingertips. Moisture from the lake perhaps, she thought, glancing up to the domed roof. The water must seep through the sediment and in through the cracks in the brick. It was no wonder the walls were crumbling.

Lacey reached into the wet sludge and between thumb and forefinger she picked up a small piece of cloth. Standing, she held it close to the lantern light. It was a tiny, green hat, with yellow stitching along the rim. It couldn't have been more than three inches wide. She stared at it in amazement, her mouth open, her breath caught in her throat. But it wasn't the only thing that caused her heart to beat like a drum. The tiny hat, as well as the tips of her fingers, were sticky and red with blood.

A surge of fear rushed over her, she picked up the lantern and held it close to the floor. It wasn't mud, the entire gutter had a thin line of black red blood, still wet enough to stain her fingers. Tilting her head back Lacey closed her eyes in dread. When she opened them she spotted something else. From her position on the ground she could see under the panel hanging from the back wall. There was a small catch. With tentative fingers she reached and unclipped it. The whole panel creaked open.

Behind it, hanging from nails was a series of small rectangular plaques. At least thirty. Row upon row, disappearing into darkness at the top. Moving closer and holding the candle high she read the words upon them. With each she felt as though she were sinking further underground. She whispered the names in the darkness. 'Katherine. Eleanor. Lucy. Lizzie. Mary...' The letters shining in the candlelight. Then she paused, there was one last plaque, hanging at the bottom. It was blank, the name yet to be carved.

'Lacey?!' It was Mateo, out of sight above her, closing the panel she turned and rushed to see him. Feeling an immediate release of relief, she saw that he was at the top of the staircase, his upper half standing above ground. 'Come.' he called, looking down to her. 'We must go now.' She hurried up the steps, before stopping and turning back to hang the lantern where they had found it, remembering to blow out the candle. In doing so however she was plunged into darkness, looking up she could just make out the shape of Mateo, silhouetted by a dark blue sky, his figure only slightly darker than the night behind him. Drawing near to the top she couldn't have articulated the immeasurable comfort in finding his hand reaching down to her. He squeezed her fingers firmly and pulled her up through the dark hole, slamming the stone door behind them.

For a few breathless moments, the two sat amongst the dry leaves, either side of the crypt door. The strangeness of their last minutes, the fear they had both felt, already taking on a strange dreamlike quality.

'Who was it?' She asked, her heart beginning to beat normally.

'I don't know. Whoever it was they were gone by the time I reached ground.' He ran his fingers through his hair, shaking his head slightly. 'Maybe it was no one. Maybe it was a fox, or a deer or the wind. Who knows, you cannot trust your own mind in a place like that.'

They stood to leave, dusting the soil and twigs from their clothes. With the same instinct that caused her to return to extinguish the lantern, Lacey scooped up an armful of leaves and scattered them over the crypt door. Before turning and walking away.

She held tight to Mateo as they made their way back through the woods. Their tread was quick, as the dusk snapped at their heels. The forest behind them closing in darkness, expelling all that didn't belong there in the night. It finally squeezed them out at the top of the field. The village below, snug and warm with its fire lit windows and smoke-filled chimneys, gently exhaling into the sapphire sky. Something inside Lacey's chest relaxed, having the woods behind her. The wide, empty, open sky above comforted her, unlike the forest where the branches tapped you on the back as you walked past. Where the tree roots laced around your ankles trying to pull you to the floor. She breathed easy, and gently tugging on the side of his arm, slowed Mateo's pace beside her.

'That was madness. What was that place?' He said, speaking for the first time since walking away from the crypt.

'It is all madness,' she responded, 'something is happening in this village Mateo, something evil. I told you I saw the figure on Deception Bay that day. What is the answer to that? And Mr Warren, the stranger from the Upper Lakes, he spoke of the impossibility of a body washing away on that bay. And I found a note, hidden in the Mayor's office.'

'What!?' Interjected Mateo, 'you were in the Mayor's office?'

'I snuck in when he wasn't there.'

'Oh Lord!' Mateo exclaimed, his hand coming to his head, pushing the hair from his brow.

Ignoring his worry, she continued, 'on this note it read thirty five paces from the base of the third peak.'

'Third peak?' Said Mateo, knowing immediately this could refer to only one place. 'The Island.'

'Exactly. I think the Mayor has something hidden on The Island. He has the shape of it tattooed upon his body. I even saw red leaves in the bottom of his boat. The type that grow there. The Mayor is lying.'

'But what about?' He asked.

'I don't know. But I must find out, do you see? I must find out what has happened to these girls. Why are they disappearing?' She was speaking louder now and Mateo, in fear someone may hear her, pulled her to a stop. She lowered her voice to a sharp whisper, 'I think the truth is on The Island.'

'The Island.' He said again.

'The note, the crypt wall, the hoods, even the Mayors' hands. It is all linked to it. And I dream of it, Mateo, every single night. It haunts my dreams like a song I cannot forget. I feel like it's calling me.' Her voice shook then, she clenched her teeth to steady herself, 'I have to find out. I have to go there.' She paused a moment before adding, 'Ma spoke to us of The Island too.'

He rolled his eyes, 'Oh Ma is an old woman! You know this. Remember I have lived with her, I know something of the working of her mind, it is not tea alone that she brews in her pot. She has spent years in solitary in the Hooked Forest, night after night with only her memories. Loneliness like that has a way of warping a person's thoughts, even last week she talked of the Water Gods.'

'You believe in the Forest Beasts!'

'That isn't at all the same thing! Forest Beasts are real, it was less than two winters ago that I had my hand almost clean off from a Forest Beast, I have the scars to show. It was a baby to be fair, but their teeth are just as sharp.'

He began to unbutton the sleeve of his shirt. Lacey patted his hand away, then grabbed it and holding it tightly to her chest said, 'I trust Ma, I believe her. And I trust myself. I know there is something bad happening in this village. There is evil here, I know it. I just have to figure it out. Girls are in danger, children are in danger.'

'And it is your duty to stop it?'

'Yes,' she said, staring right at him, 'I think it is. I didn't tell you. I didn't want to believe I had seen it. But the day Mary Morgan was buried I saw a mark on her leg, a scar. The shape of-'

'The Island,' he said.

She nodded, grateful at not having to say the words.

Mateo saw again the unstoppable determination in her eyes and knew nothing he could say would sway her decision. His fingers, that had been so tense against her chest, suddenly relaxed, and he nodded in acceptance. 'If you must go, then I will go with you.'

Lacey shook her head, 'I cannot put you in danger Mateo. I don't want you to be drawn into this too.'

Mateo snapped a twig from a low hanging branch and balancing each end between his fingertips, stared down at it intently. 'I have to tell you something. I suppose now is the time to do so. After the fire,' he said slowly, 'after everything happened, and my family...' He swallowed thickly. Sparing him her stares, Lacey looked away into the green gloom of the forest behind them, losing her sight in the shadows. 'When I went to live with Ma, before she left town. I woke up every night with nightmares. Awful nightmares. But it wasn't the fire, or even losing my parents or my sister that was haunting me. That night, the night of the fire, someone was in my room.'

Lacey looked back at him. He peeled pieces of bark from the twig, gently dropping them to the ground, his head so low in the concentration of it she couldn't see his eyes. 'You know I shared a little bed with my sister, in the corner of our parents' room. That night, the night it happened, a sound woke me. I opened my eyes and there was a figure, by the door.' His hand reached forward, as though seeing the scene again, play out before him. 'It was tall, and moving slowly, walking towards us. It wore a cloak. With the hood up.' Lacey felt goose pimples rise on her arms. She remembered how he had screamed as a child when seeing Frank in his hood. 'But it didn't see the candle still lit, burning low on the dresser. The cloak caught fire immediately. Bright yellow, angry flames. It turned and ran. Then the fire was at the curtain and moving up the walls, then it was everywhere, and my parents woke up.' He dropped his hand, snapping the twig, the pieces landing on the leaves below. 'I thought it was a dream. But I remember the symbol on the back of the hood, it was surrounded by flames when last I saw it. But I saw it again tonight. Hanging from the wall of that terrible place.' He cleared his throat and looked up at her, his eyes glassy with tears. 'If you are going, I'm coming with you.'

They walked in silence down the darkening field to Lacey's back garden, where they embraced again. This time for only a moment. Lacey pushed her face into the hollow of his neck, smelling sawdust and earth on his shirt. She didn't know how to respond to what he had told her. But she knew him well enough to know he was done talking about it. She held him tight, before letting him go, both walking in opposite directions. After a few steps, Mateo turned back to her, remembering something, 'the paper you left for me last week.'

'Oh, yes?' Lacey said, after recent events she had all but forgotten it.

'I cannot read that particular dialect, it wasn't the same as my family spoke. There are many types.'

'Oh,' said Lacey, a little crestfallen. 'Thank you anyway,' she turned to leave.

'But I did recognize one word,' he said. Lacey waited for him to answer, the sound of the grasses in the meadow swaying softly. 'Sacrifice.'

CHAPTER NINETEEN

Lacey shut the back door behind her, resting her forehead against it for a moment trying to gather her thoughts, her mind spinning like a top. Taking a deep breath, she turned around. Suddenly in the dark room a tall, white figure loomed out at her. She gasped, a rush of adrenaline pulsing through her body. The ghostly apparition hovered inches from the ground, in the gloom it seemed to tower over her, she felt for a moment she was back inside the darkness of the crypt. Then she saw the lace detail at the breast, the embroidered sleeves, the netted skirts.

'What is the wedding dress doing here?' Lacey demanded, walking through to the main room. Bella sat alone with her back to Lacey, looking out the front window. Her sewing bag rested on her knee.

'It needs adjusting,' she said, over her shoulder, 'don't take it down, the lace will crease.'

'I thought it was a ghost.'

'In three days that ghost will be wrapped around your body.' Lacey sighed loudly and went to walk back into her room. 'Not that you will thank me but I returned your books.' Bella called after her.

'What?' Said Lacey turning round.

'You had so many books beside your bed, I knew you had read them all, so I returned them to the Professor.'

'To the Professor?' Lacey crossed the room. 'Did you go inside?' She pressed.

'No.' Bella turned in her chair. 'Why do you look so upset?'

'You didn't see Arnott?'

'*Professor* Arnott? No, I left them by his door.'

Lacey sighed in relief and sat on the stool by the fire. 'Oh, that is well.'

'You are a strange girl.' Bella said. 'Where have you been?'

'Around the village.'

'So you've heard.'

'Heard what?'

'About the girl Jessica?'

An image of the red haired freckled girl dancing in the village came to her. *Don't go down to Deception Bay or your children will wash away.* 'What of her?' Said Lacey sharply, leaning forward, her stomach tightening.

'She's missing,' said Bella, turning from the window, 'no one has seen her since this morning. The village men are out looking. I'm surprised you didn't see them.' Her eyes, narrowed slightly, then lowered, taking in her sister's muddy boots and the dirt beneath her fingernails. 'Oh Lacey! Your boots have left red clay all over the floor, I just mopped.'

'They've searched the whole town?' Lacey asked. *Don't go down to Deception Bay or the water will take your daughter.*

'Yes.' Bella shook her head, 'I don't know what is wrong with the girls in this town, there has never been two disappearances so close together. Perhaps if she had the influence of a mother to warn her. But the family she was fostered with the last few years say she is a good, obedient girl.' Bella subconsciously touched her cross, before returning to her sewing. 'Fetch me your lace handkerchief will you, I might check if it needs any neatening before the wedding.'

Lacey, in silence, her mind on Jessica, walked slowly up to her room, then a moment later walked back down again. 'It isn't there' she said frowning.

'Isn't where?'

'In the box where I keep it, it isn't there. The box on my table, I keep it in there always.'

'Did you return it there after the engagement?'

'After the engagement?' Lacey echoed, her face pinched at one side in confusion.

'Yes,' said Bella, still concentrating on the slow drawing of the needle, 'I put it in your dress pocket the morning of the engagement, in case you should need it. I had an inkling you were to be asked.'

The night time curfew bell rung in the distance. A cold sheet of panic fell around Lacey's shoulders. She stood in silence, her eyes seeing the grey slate of the Mayor's study floor. She must have dropped it there, it was the only possibility. Elsewhere in the house and Sebastian would have returned it to her, and both on her walk there and her walk back home she had her coat on. Bella, finally noticing her silence, looked up.

'What is it?'

'It has my initials on it.' Lacey said, staring numbly into the distance. She remembered how Mayor Abner had picked it up for her outside the church, the night Mary Morgan disappeared. She remembered how he had whispered her name to himself. She imagined him spotting the little linen white square in his study and scooping to pick it up. 'It has my initials on it' she repeated.

'Yes, as does mine. You haven't lost it, have you?'

'Yes.' She said in half whisper, feeling the blood drain from her, 'I do believe I have.'

'Oh Lacey!' Bella exclaimed, 'you are too forgetful.'

Lacey stood quite still and stared bleakly at the fire, considering the consequences of the discovery. The Mayor knows, she thought to herself, he knows I suspect his involvement in the disappearances of the children. Why else would I be snooping around his private study alone? The ideas floated past her like mist outside the window, she couldn't force herself from the feeling of dread.

She thought of the Mayor's drawn, grey face beneath the shadow of his wide brimmed hat, staring down at her. In her helplessness at that moment, the image of Professor Arnott came to her, his acidic breath, the feel of his stomach pressing against the small of her back. She thought then of the precise Mr Lewis, and the touch of his thumb against her bare thigh. And finally, she thought of Sebastian, his cold, pale eyes. Suddenly and violently she kicked out at the little wooden stool beside her, it skittered across the floor.

'What's wrong with you?' Bella demanded.

'Nothing!' Lacey snapped.

'You are in another foul mood. And to think I believed you would change once he asked you.' Bella said bitterly, thrusting her mending aside, and stooping to right the stool. 'Once you had the ring on your finger and you could see what life might be like with the past no longer hanging over our heads. I thought you might be less angry, stop fighting. But you will never change will you?'

'Did you want me to change into you?' Lacey scoffed.

Bella absorbed the offence without flinching. When she responded it was with a coolness to her tone. 'I know you think me stern and without happiness. But that isn't true. Or at least if it is true it is only because I had to be. There would have been winters that we wouldn't have survived had I not been prudent. You have the character you were born with, but some of us have had to put all of that away. After,' she paused, 'after Mother died I could no longer be that same child that I was. This is what life has made me.' She raised her hands, gesturing in exasperation to herself. 'I didn't dream of becoming this woman. You will leave here one day. One day very soon. But I cannot, I will be like a wife to our father until he dies. I know you don't feel it, but you are free Lacey. And that, as all things do, comes at a price. I am that price. You believe we have decided your life for you, well you decided mine for me.'

Lacey looked at her then, at this young woman with tired eyes. She did look very tired, though she wasn't even five years older than herself. She had been sewing something white, glancing down Lacey could see that it was her wedding veil. Bella was right, she would most probably never be married. Any ladies still single by her age were all but promised a life of spinsterhood. Bella hadn't been married because she already had a man to cook for and clean up after. She hadn't considered how painful Sebastian's proposal must have been for her older sister, and Lacey had been so ungrateful in her response. She felt a painful stab of guilt.

Lacey opened her mouth to speak but the threat of a sob forced it closed. She swallowed hard and looked at her sister through watery eyes.

Seeing them Bella said earnestly 'what's wrong Lacey? Please tell me.'

Lacey felt the fear and tension growing like a knot in her chest, each strand its own particular strain of worry, pulling increasingly taut. Suddenly she felt so tired, tired of it weighing down on her, tired of having to carry it around. When she spoke, the words came emotionless, automatic.

'I'm afraid that the men in the village are going to kill me.'

Bella stared at her in shock, 'what on earth do you mean?'

'Kill me, or otherwise lay with me, I don't know. I'm not sure they themselves know. I think had they the chance they would slit my throat as soon as put a ring round my finger. And in truth I know which I would prefer.' She did not feel like crying now. Now she felt angry, walking to the window, she looked out of it and asked, 'aren't you tired of living at the grace of men?'

'We aren't here at the grace of men, we are here at the grace of-'

'God?' Lacey interrupted, 'another man! Another man I'm supposed to pray to and thank on bended knee. Well I'm tired of kneeling. Aren't you?' The fear she had felt over the past few minutes seemed to crumble like a log on a fire and erupt into a blaze of anger.

'Oh, Lacey, what talk is this? Is it that you have fears for your wedding night?'

'I have fears for *every* night!' Lacey yelled, not in full control of her voice. Bella groaned in frustration and shook her head, Lacey crossed the room and stood in front of her. 'Don't you see them? They stand just outside the window, they sleep in the houses next door. We sell them bread, they sell us fish, or medicine, or calf skin boots. They walk around with the thinnest facades, the thinnest of masks upon their faces. But beneath...' Lacey felt a surge of rage in her chest, 'beneath they are beasts!'

All of a sudden the fire in the grate abruptly swelled. The bright light illuminating the girl's faces, casting dark shadows against the back wall. Both sisters winced their eyes at the ferocity of the blaze. Lacey holding her arm up at the burning explosion of heat. Then in the next moment it extinguished completely. With a *whumpf* the two were plunged into darkness. Lacey and Bella stood in silent shock, only the sound of their shaking breaths could be heard. The now dark fireplace a heap of smoking ash. By the dim light of the candle they stared in astonishment at each other. Bella looked up to check the drawn shutters, not even a draft flowed through the little house. Lacey opened her mouth to speak.

The front door swung open and Frank stepped inside the small room. Removing his hat, he shook the cold off him, his nose and cheeks flushed. He rubbed his sore hands together and sitting on the edge of his chair, got to work unlacing his boots, he seemed completely unaware of the atmosphere in the house. His numb, warped fingers struggling with the laces. Lacey and Bella stood unmoving, Lacey's jaw still hanging open. Eventually, she closed it and crossed to kneeled beside Frank, helping him with his boots.

'Why isn't the fire lit?' He asked scowling. Bella, in silence, bent to reassemble the kindling and spark a match.

'Is there news of Jessica?' Lacey inquired hopefully.

Frank shook his wide head. 'No one's seen her.'

Lacey had the sudden urge to rest her head upon Frank's knee and sob. She had never done anything remotely like that before to her father, and she didn't do so today. But, with the smoke of the suddenly extinguished fire, still curling in ribbons behind her, she did allow a single tear to fall. It was bitter, and stung her cheek before dropping to the floor.

'Are you unwell?' He asked, the red of his cheeks gently thawing.

'No,' she mumbled.

'You have a tear.' He said, not looking directly at her, but instead addressing his comment to the table. Bella, in silence, lay a fresh log upon the new fire.

Lacey, quickly smearing her cheek on her shoulder, answered 'I'm worried for the girl Jessica.'

'Oh.' He said simply.

'Or perhaps it is the stress of the wedding.'

Frank visibly relaxed, he exhaled and nodded in approval at her answer. 'Yes, the stress. I'm sure that is it. Many young brides feel the same way.' Lacey nodded, feeling her heart sink a little deeper. 'He is a well to do man, Sebastian, and he will keep you well enough.' Bella came forward to take Frank's boots. 'What have we in the pot Bella?'

'Chowder' she answered quietly, bringing their bowls down from the cupboard. 'Mr Turner brought round a gift of haddock this morning.'

'Good man,' said Frank. 'Perhaps I will bring us back a fish.' A smile spread across his face, both daughters looked at him.

'How do you mean?' Asked Lacey.

'Your betrothed has invited a few of us on a fishing trip on the lake, in celebration of the wedding. After all it is not just you and Sebastian taking the blood vow but the Mayor and I too, as the heads of each of our families.' He said proudly, sitting a little straighter. 'There will be a group of us, we will camp for a few nights on Driftwood bay. We leave before dawn.'

'A few nights?' Bella asked with worry as she scooped the stew into a bowl and set it before him with still shaking hands, a little liquid spilling over the rim.

'A few nights,' repeated Lacey, talking to herself. An idea twitched to life inside her mind.

'Depending on whether we catch anything,' he took the spoon up and tipped a heaped serving into his mouth. 'Mr Collins says he heard a fisherman from across the Lake pulled a ten pound trout from the water by Crescent Bay just last week. Perhaps the fish are returning.'

'And what of your legs and hands?' Bella asked.

'He has hands enough to hold a spoon' said Lacey.

'Holding a spoon is not at all like threading a hook' she answered with annoyance in her voice. 'Besides the doctor said I should rub them every night or else the cramps would get worse.'

Lacey went to speak but her father held up his spoon in the air and said 'enough. Mr Tibbs will thread my hooks for me and the doctor has given me some more medicine. So, should I feel the pain too fully I will be sure to take it.' Bella muttered something about the hem of the wedding dress and with her sewing bag in hand, retired to her bedroom.

Lacey sat for a while and listened to her father talk of his trip. Her eyes flitting every minute or so to the clock above the mantel. Only occasionally did she glance uneasily towards the fire. The wind outside whistled through the gap beneath the door and pushed insistently at the windows in their panes, as though it were trying to get in. *Please don't be a storm* Lacey thought to herself. After a while Frank yawned and she could see his eyes had drooped in tiredness. With relief Lacey bade him goodnight.

In her bedroom Bella perched on the bed in her nightdress, plaiting her hair. Lacey grabbed two bowls sat by the back door, ready for washing tomorrow.

'I will just wash these in the yard.'

'Now?' asked Bella incredulously, 'it's dark.'

'It will only take a minute' said Lacey, slipping out before she could argue more.

Outside the wind had thankfully died down a little. Lacey tossed the bowls at the foot of the rose bush and pulling from her pocket the paper and pencil she had stashed there, wrote the words HAMMER BAY. MIDNIGHT. Then, folding the paper, she ran round the corner of the house.

She looked up and down the dark street. A cat wandered across the cobblestones, stopping to look at her a moment before continuing its nighttime pursuits. Lacey waited in silence, her eyes scanning the shadows. Less than a minute later the figure of a black haired boy emerged round the corner. He walked with a casual, relaxed gait, dragging a stick behind him. Lacey waited as he approached, the fold of paper gripped tight between her two fingers.

'Kieran,' she called, recognising him as he came closer, 'come here.'

Kieran Alden stopped a little way off and frowned at her. 'You shouldn't be out miss, there's Watchmen everywhere. Kinch has set a curfew' he said. 'Another girl's gone missing.'

'I know,' she whispered, 'come here.'

Kieran glanced up and down the street, then tossing his stick in the gutter, tentatively approached her.

'Do you know Mateo Fulmar, the carpenter, he lives down on the water.'

'The gypsy?' He asked. Lacey looked at his face, his eyes still childlike, but around his jaw, the lines of a man were beginning to grow.

She sighed, 'yes, you know which house is his?' The boy nodded. 'Good,' she said thrusting the note towards him, 'take this there.'

The boy was promised two free spiced buns and a slice of apple cake before he agreed. Lacey watched him retreat down the street before she turned away. It was a risk, but it was her only choice. If Father was to be gone for two nights, now was the only time. She turned and ran back to the bakery.

Lacey remembered her talk with Jessica. How certain the girl was of the dangers. She felt a sharp gnawing fear for her. She knew she would never have gone to Deception Bay. And if someone had taken her, she had only one idea where she might be.

Closing the back door quietly, Lacey was grateful to see Bella already in bed with her back to her. She didn't want to talk about the fire, she didn't want to talk about anything. The ghost still hung from a hook in the corner of her room, it swayed slightly as she walked past and headed up to her own bed. Lacey sat on the edge of her mattress, the straw poking into her thighs. The room was dark, but the moon came through a gap in the curtain and fell in a broad strip across the floor.

In silence, she pushed her hand into the pocket of her skirt and pulling it out again, uncurled her fingers to reveal the tiny hat. It sat limp and lifeless in her palm. The green stained a dark red at one edge, the sight caused her stomach to lurch. She had realized immediately in the crypt who the little hat had belonged to. Only a week previous had she held the doll in her hand as she stood outside the Morgans' house. She could see it now, its bare head, its plaits blowing in the wind, the dress the same green with yellow stitching. Lacey's hand closed around it and she secreted it back inside her pocket. Then standing, she looked around the room for a bag.

CHAPTER TWENTY

Lacey pulled the old cloth bag from beneath the bed and set about filling it with supplies. She tiptoed silently downstairs, the stone cold on her bare feet. She crept around the front room, moving painfully slowly so as not to make a sound. Her father snored from his bed on the floor, Lacey felt traitorous being in the room as he slept. She hurried to the cupboard, from which she took a loaf of bread and two apples. They lay now at the bottom of the bag, on top of them she placed a change of clothes and a flask of water. Then, finally, a knife from the drawer, wrapped in a dish cloth.

Rain had begun to tap at the roof a few minutes ago, but it didn't sound too strong and Lacey guessed it would pass before long. Returning to her bed she lay down and staring at the ceiling above her, she waited.

One spring, when she was a child, when the flowers had blossomed and the bluebells carpeted the forest floor, a late frost had come. It was vicious and merciless. Most of the flowers had died after the first few mornings, wilting in the freezing cold. The village, which always celebrated the arrival of spring with joy and relief, lamented the passing of the flowers. Lacey and Bella had been especially sad as they had spent the whole winter excited about making a bluebell crown, like the ones worn by the fairy queen in the stories their mother told them. One morning as they slept in their bed, she came in to wake them. Two small, sleeping heads, their minds and eyes still full of their dreams. Their hair a tangle of Lacey's black and white and Bella's brown, as they slept in one another's arms. Their breathing slow and silent, like hibernating bear cubs. Their mother gently shook them awake, placing a finger on their lips to keep them silent.

She dressed them in their winter hats and gloves, pulling on their warm coats over their nightdresses. Two sets of thin, bare legs dangling off the bed as she laced their boots. They crept out silently so not to wake their still sleeping father and slipped out of the back of the house. Their breath rose from their lips in misty puffs, as they felt an intoxicating excitement at being awake at such an early hour. The white frozen land glistened and twinkled in the sunrise. The mist slid and curled at the edge of the forest, but the field was as clear and sparkling as cut crystal. Standing either side of their mother, holding a hand each, they walked in silence towards the woods, their feet crunching on the fresh frost. The further away they were from the village the bolder they became, and soon the three were laughing and chasing one another amongst the tree trunks.

The sound of their giggling and cries threaded through the trees and up into the branches above, causing the waking birds to leap into the sky. Before long they came to a clearing where their mother stopped and knelt on the frosted floor. Around them were patches of wildflowers, which had been brave enough to poke their heads out of the earth, but were now wilting and bowing under the harsh frost. A set of branches, looking a little out of place, had been arranged against the side of a tree, their mother moved them aside. Beneath was a glass dome. A little bigger than a man's hat. It looked to Lacey like the ones they used at the bakery during the summer, to keep the flies off the cream cakes.

Their mother held out her hand, gesturing to them to join her, the two children came closer. Inside the glass was a small crop of bright bluebells. Their petals perfect, and unblemished, unmarked by the frost. She pulled the jar away and they nodded lightly in the breeze. The sisters opened their mouths in disbelief, then grinned in delight. Their mother scooped her daughters up in her arms, and smiling, she buried her face in the warmth of their necks as the girls picked the flowers one by one. They danced and sang fairy songs as she plaited the little buds into two small, delicate crowns.

Lacey stared at the cracks in the sloped ceiling. The rain had stopped, she sat up and noiselessly pulled herself to stand. At the windowsill, she took pencil and paper and hastily scribbled a note. *'Bella, I will be back before nightfall. Don't worry. Don't tell anyone I'm gone. Lacey.'* She left it there, knowing Bella would see it in the morning when she came to wake her.

She pulled on her coat and boots and swung the bag across her chest. Her heart beat thickly as she climbed out of her bedroom window and down the side of the house. The rain had stopped, only a few small puddles had gathered in the back yard. The cold night air pinched at her face. She hesitated at the gate, looking back once at the sleeping bakery before pulling her hood over her head and walking out into the darkness.

The moon was out and that had helped Lacey in the field, but in the woods it did no good. The Hooked Forest seemed, in the darkness, to come alive. It writhed up in front of her. The branches, with their wooden fingered hands, pulled at her shawl and at the bag on her back. The toads sung in chorus to one another, betraying her whereabouts. Every step she took she felt as though someone, or something, was right behind her, ready to pounce, closer than her shadow.

She walked with her eyes to the ground, in one hand she clasped the handle of a spade, stolen from her own back garden.

She held it now more as a weapon than a tool, its weight comforted her. She looked up occasionally to check her direction, and behind her once or twice, when she heard the rustle of leaves or hoot of an owl in the darkness. The Forest Beasts howled she heard. Apparently during The Great Fire that killed Mateo's family, many had run into the woods for safety, only to be eaten by the Forest Beasts. As much of Lower Lynch burned to the ground, the beasts howled in the trees as they feasted on the villagers.

Suddenly she jerked backwards, something had a hold of her, she stumbled and heard a tearing sound. The contents of her bag fell to the floor beneath her. She had snagged it on a low branch. She got to her knees, feeling blindly with her hands for the knife. All she really needed was the knife, she could do without the rest. Her fingers fell upon the smooth, shiny skin of the apple, a small, sharp set of teeth bit at her and she cried out, whipping her hand away and squeezing the wound. After a few seconds, she plunged her hand back into the dirt, bracing for the sting of another bite. But thankfully none came and soon she found the handle of the knife. Leaving the rest of her belongings lost in the dirt, along with the torn bag, she continued on.

The trees moved about her like shadows floating in the mist, her eyes, adjusting as well as they could in the dark, were still unable to warn her when a branch would seem to appear out of nowhere. At one time, she realized she had lost the path, and with a dizzying panic, retraced her steps until she found her way again. She wondered if they had taken her mother's body this way. She imagined the barrow struggling against the tree roots.

Time fell away and she was unable to say, when finally seeing the edge of the forest, whether she had been two hours or only half of one. But still she was grateful to be clear of it as she walked out onto Hammer Bay. The sea spread before her, beneath the light of a silver moon, it shimmered, blue, black and milky white. She walked down, the shingle falling in a smooth crunch beneath her feet, her hand clasped around the knife. At the far side of the bay, which was narrower than Deception Bay, the boats were moored on planks of wood that entered the water at an angle. The tide lapped peacefully at them, making a soft slapping sound, and leaning against one of the boats, with his bag slung around his shoulders, was Mateo.

For the first time since sending him the note, it occurred to her they would be spending the night together. Alone. Her stomach instinctively fluttered at the idea and her cheeks pricked hot against the night air. She remembered him holding her that afternoon in the woods, how his fingers felt entwined with hers.

Deep in her thoughts Lacey lost her footing and skidded down the bank of shingle. Mateo, reaching out, caught her in his arms. For a moment she looked up, catching his stare. His eyes shining in the moonlight. Her chest seized with nerves. Looking away she quickly righted herself and dusted down her skirts.

'Thank you,' she muttered, looking out at the black sea.

'You're welcome,' he answered sincerely. Then swinging his bag into the back of a boat he said 'another girl is missing.'

'Jessica' Lacey nodded. 'I feel as though it's my fault.'

'What do you mean?'

'She spoke to me, I asked her questions. I think someone may have found out.'

'That doesn't mean it's your fault,' said Mateo, then squinting out in the direction of The Island, he added 'She might not even be there you know.'

'Perhaps not, but it's worth looking. Besides,' she said pulling out her knife, 'I want to know what is buried thirty five paces from the third peak.'

Lacey set about cutting the boat free. The thick rope was slimy beneath a coating of dark green seaweed, which wrapped around it like hair. She sawed back and forth, soon feeling the line begin to weaken. Moments later it gave in. Immediately the boat began to slide down the planks and into the water. Mateo hopped inside, then Lacey, throwing the cut rope behind her. The small, wooden skiff lifted slightly, swaying as the sea beneath it took hold. Had anyone been looking, which they weren't, they would have seen a small boat, with two silent passengers, set out to an empty sea, under the gaze of a shining moon.

Mateo rowed first. An unfamiliar awkward tension had grown between them, to avoid catching his eye Lacey turned in her seat to face the bay. She watched how, with each pull, it shrank further from them. The forest, a low jagged line of black, sat above it. The trees seemed so small, compared to when they towered over her, now the only thing overhead was the boundless sky, studded with tiny stars. She thought of her father sleeping on his thin mattress on the kitchen floor, and of Bella asleep amongst the proving drawers. The villagers of Lower Lynch lay still and silent in their beds. Each house was locked shut to the night outside, the rooms filling with dreams. But in at least one of those homes, evil lurked. It moved beneath the gaps in the doorways like a draft.

Before long they were out of the cove, Lacey watched Deception Bay stretch out to the right of her. She turned her head, knowing what she would now be able to see sitting on the horizon. Sure enough, in the distance, the black mark of The Island sat below the moon, it was blacker than the sky could ever be. It's spiked, crown-like facade more visible tonight than usual, as though it were revealing itself to her, inviting her in.

'I meant what I said.' He said, between pulls. 'None of this is your fault.'

'Perhaps I am being paranoid,' she answered. 'I feel as though I'm being watched all the time. I can hardly leave my house without Lek or Bran appearing. The night of Mary Morgan's wake someone was watching me. He wore a hood too. But besides you, who can I tell? No one would listen to me. I know that. Things seem to be happening and I can't do anything about it. It's the girls disappearing,' she said, 'but it's not just that. It's Father and the bakery and the wedding and..' she stopped herself. Thinking of the fire distinguishing itself earlier that evening. 'Things are happening and I have no power to stop them.'

'Well,' said Mateo, holding the oars a little tighter and pulling a little stronger, 'we are doing something now.'

The two rowed on, but their journey wasn't to be simple. Just as Lacey took the oars, the clouds, as though set pieces in a tragedy, rolled in and began to slowly gather above their heads. The stars hid behind them as if a thick curtain had been pulled across the sky. She kept her mind on rowing, back and forth, back and forth. The oars chaffing her hands, her arms already beginning to throb with fatigue. Once the cloud crossed the moon she was shocked at how truly dark it was. Spilt ink dark, eyes squeezed shut beneath the blanket dark, no candle crypt dark. But she wasn't afraid, she kept on rowing.

A current picked up, and as though rocking a baby in a crib, it began to sway the boat side to side, the rhythm steadily increasing with each swing. Before too long the wind was whistling in her ears. Her fingers gripped the oars, the water whipping at the boat, her hair thrashing around her. She tucked it out of her eyes but it was no good, flying loose immediately. Reaching into her pocket, she found a ribbon and tied it back. Mateo, pulled up the collar of his coat, lowering his neck to shelter behind it. Minutes later Lacey felt beneath her seat where she had seen a hessian sack. She shook it, emptying the contents into the hull, a few spools of rope and some weights. Then she pulled it around her shoulders, over her coat, for now the rain had come.

It fell in sheets, sideways as though being shot from the horizon. Lacey bit her teeth and squinted her eyes as it pelted and soaked her face. The sea, in response began to swell. Water lapping and spraying over the side, so now she was unsure of whether it was the rain or the sea that soaked her so. She thought wildly for a moment that she would ask Mateo to speak the Lost Language, to try and appease the Water Gods. But only Ma knew the old spells, and besides, Lacey didn't believe in the Water Gods.

She turned, squinting, to see The Island, she could no longer find it, it was lost in the rain and the darkness. She looked behind herself and saw, with a sinking feeling, that the mainland too had disappeared. The storm around them had grown so fierce, all she could see in any direction was the blurry haze of black and grey. Mateo caught her eye, but she looked away quickly, not wanting him to see fear there.

The boat moved atop the water as though it were riding the back of a whale. Lifting then tilting, then smashing over the waves. An oar snapped, Lacey scrabbled forward to try and retrieve it, just in time to see it swallowed into the water beneath. Then turning, she saw the other one pulled loose from its hold and disappear before Mateo could reach it.

Suddenly The Island was there, looming ahead of them, out of the darkness. Lacey's eyes swept up the side of it, her mouth wide open. It was higher and blacker than she had imagined. It rose out of the water in anger. Its flat, cruel, grey face, impenetrable. The waves crashed against it in a furious crescendo of white foam. Over and over they beat at the side of the unflinching black mass. There were birds here after all. Blackened seagulls, like crows, cried and flew overhead. They swooped in wide circles, sometimes darting down to fly right beside her, then climbing again into the clouds above.

The boat tilted violently. 'Lacey! Get down!' cried Mateo, grabbing her by the shoulder and pulling her violently into the hull. She felt the freezing water soaking through her clothes as she huddled under the seat, both arms clasping the side of the boat. Mateo, with an arm across her back, tucked his head into the space between them. His cheek wet against hers. Through the howling wind and rain, she sensed him hold his breath, felt his heartbeat thunder against her back. She braced her body for the impact of hitting the cliff. The boat, she knew, would splinter into a hundred different pieces. She whimpered like a child. Soaking wet and huddled in fear, she held on for dear life. In that moment, she had never felt so small. The birds flew in loops, screaming above them, although in the rain she could hardly see them. Neither did she see the wave rise up in front of her, but she felt it. Felt her body being pulled forward as it sucked them in, the front of the boat lifting perilously high. The world tilted back on its axis.

Lacey squeezed her eyes shut, the noise of the storm died away. She felt her skin begin to prick. Instead of the roar of the wind she heard her own breath. It was suddenly so quiet. So peaceful. She inhaled then exhaled in a soft whistle and time seemed to slow. Automatically Lacey's arm came up, she held her palm open, facing the jagged rocks. The boat, on its course to collide with them, swerved unnaturally to the side, narrowly avoiding it. A scraping sound coming from the hull as it scratched along the rock. Lacey opened her eyes, and in doing so the storm came full upon her once more, the noise deafening. Her vision awash with rain and seawater. The boat, safe for the moment from the rock face, tilted violently upon another rolling wave. Instinctually Lacey closed her eyes, but she was too late.

A crate, tucked in at the other end of the skiff was lifted into the air. For a moment it hovered, like one of the birds, suspended in time, but then, like the falling of an axe it sped towards her. Flying past her, its corner glanced off her forehead. The noise fell away, the rain fell away, the cold fell away. And so, the world, to Lacey, was stopped. Suddenly, like the slamming of a door. Shut with a final, black, bang.

CHAPTER TWENTY ONE

Lacey sat on the bakery countertop swinging her legs back and forth, the heels of her little leather boots knocking against the cupboard below. Honey coloured sunlight drifted through the back windows. She saw her mother coming in from the garden, holding a bunch of wildflowers. Bella had been at the lake that day. Lacey was still too young to play near the water on her own, so she stayed home with her parents. She would sit on the counter holding the sieve and when her father asked, she would sift flour onto the thick pale knot of dough in his hands. Her mother rifled through the drawer, finally pulling from it a length of purple ribbon, tying it in a neat bow around the posy. She held them to Lacey's face and she sniffed, the delicate petals tickled her nose, making her giggle.

Her mother lifted her up under her arms and hand-in-hand they walked to the church to place them in the window there. Her father had protested, saying he needed her to assist with the bake, but her mother had appeased him with a few soft words and a kiss on his cheek. She had turned away and he had pulled her quickly back to him, she smiled in surprise as he had kissed her on the lips.

Lacey's black and white plaits swung around her shoulders as she skipped along beside her mother, the small bouquet in her hands. Occasionally one or two petals fell to the ground, the pollen falling too and staining her fingers. She would remember that later that night. Seeing the shockingly bright yellow of her fingertips as she cried herself to sleep.

The church was cool, empty, full of echoes. The sound of the door closing resonated around them. Her mother knelt down beside her and told her she would be back before long, then she disappeared into an anteroom. Lacey played amongst the pews, ducking and crawling along the cold stone floor and up and along the wooden benches. She didn't notice the door of the church creak open, but the noise of it banging shut made her jump out of her skin. She looked around, no one was there. But a noise was coming now from the antechamber, she walked slowly towards it. Her small hand trailed along the backs of the pews. Then came the sound of raised voices and the sudden clattering of copper on the hard ground. Lacey poked her head round the corner of the door. The lid of a metal jug still spun from its collision with the floor, the sound seemed deafening in the little room. The wide, cloaked back of a man, towered in front of her. Then Lacey saw her mother opposite. She was sprawled on the floor beneath him, fury and terror ripped across her face.

Suddenly her mother saw her. Her eyes grew wide with fear. She screamed to Lacey to run! To get her father! Just as the cloak of the man began to pivot towards her Lacey sprung back and ran to the church door. She was young and quick as a cat. She did not know if he was chasing her; she didn't want to look to find out. She fled through the streets, her head down, plaits flying behind her, tears threatening to burst from her eyes. She came upon her own door and pushed it open, calling for her father. He stood, looking at her confused, his hands deep in a soapy basin. She screamed at him, a jumbled mix of words spilling from her lips. With an agonizing speed, he undid his apron and pulled on his coat.

When they rounded the corner of the church a small crowd had already gathered. Lacey and her father pushed their way through. They got to the bottom of the steps, where they were greeted by Mayor Abner, who said they shouldn't be there, that it wasn't a sight for young eyes. Her father had pressed him, but he had snapped angrily that she had already confessed to being a witch. Lacey could remember seeing the cruel purse of his lips as he spat the word, she had never heard it before then. The church doors opened, just for a moment, as someone slipped inside, and between the crush of legs Lacey saw her mother. She was being held by two men, her head slumped to one side, her eyes closed. Her pale blue dress stained a deep, dark red, with soft white feathers stuck all about her. Then the door swung shut and the black trousered legs of the crowd came together, blocking her view.

Lacey's eyes shot open. Pulled from unconsciousness by a sharp pain. The sound of a fire crackled and hissed from somewhere nearby, the smoke filling her nostrils and her lungs. She coughed and turned on her side. Wheezing and spluttering, unable to catch her breath, she tasted salt and smoke at the back of her throat. Eventually she sat up, rubbing her eyes. Opening them slightly, she realized she was no longer outside. Aside from the dim light of a fire, she was in a soft darkness. There was a light tapping of water coming from somewhere and she could smell damp. She became aware of a heavy, throbbing pressure in her head. Her hand came up to feel at it, she winced in pain, finding a gash at the side of her temple.

'Don't touch it,' said Mateo, laying a pile of driftwood down and kneeling at her side. 'Here.' Gently moving her hand aside, he placed a damp handkerchief against the wound. Lacey flinched and gasped in pain. 'It's sea water. It will help,' he said soothingly, leaning his face close to hers, squinting to inspect the damage. Clearing her throat, she asked, 'how bad is it?'

'You'll live,' he said, rocking back onto his heels and standing.

Looking around, Lacey could see now she was inside a cave, the rugged walls waving and flickering in firelight. It was no larger than the main room of her house. Mateo laid driftwood onto the fire which flamed white in response, illuminating the ceiling, where long stalactites hung like daggers above their heads.

'Where are we Mateo?'

'We're here. The other side of The Island. There's a bay,' he gestured to the opening of the cave.

'How long have we been here?'

'It looks to be about noon. The storm has cleared.'

'You carried me in from the boat?' She said frowning, feeling an ache in her shoulders, flexing them slightly.

Hanging his socks at the end of a stick and holding them close to the flames Mateo nodded. 'We almost drowned,' he said soberly, 'you saved us.' She saw an image of herself from the night before, eyes closed, arms out towards the rock face as though she were pushing it away. 'You moved the boat,' Mateo whispered, staring at her, his dark eyes glistening in the light. 'You moved it with your mind.'

'I don't want to talk about it,' Lacey said.

'Lacey, you are a-'

'Stop!' She snapped loudly, her voice echoing around the cave, the wound in her head throbbing in response. She lay back and closed her eyes once more. Using a flask in his bag Mateo retrieved a little water from a trickling stream that ran down the side of the wall and fed it to her in silence. Then retreating from the pain and confusion she allowed herself to slip away once more into sleep.

A few hours later Lacey woke again, alone in the cave. She lay blinking at the ashy remains of the fire, her mind still blank. Slowly, as though they were candles being lit, one by one her memories came back to her. She sat up, arching her spine, after hours on the hard floor, she could already feel a stiffness in her neck. She gently rolled her head back and forth, then raising her hand she touched the wound on her head. The gash had dried into a scab, and the swelling had subsided. She peered around the cave, blinking her sleep away. She was about to call Mateo's name when she heard footsteps approaching and his head appeared round the entrance of the cave. 'Can you walk?' He asked breathlessly.

'What is it?'

'Come' he said, then disappeared.

Lacey, still slightly unsteady on her feet, walked out of the cave for the first time. It was good to feel the cool, fresh air in her lungs and against her skin. She took deep breaths of it, as though drinking after a great thirst. The cave opened up directly onto a crescent shaped beach, and, not seeing Mateo, she walked the short way to the shore. Upon touching the icy cold water all of her sleepiness vanished. She wriggled her toes down into the smooth blue shingle. The tide gently lapped at her ankles, and she stood a while, squinting slightly at the bright grey sky stretched over the endless ocean. Their boat lay a little way up the beach. One side had a jagged hole, where it must have hit the rocks. Considering the storm, it wasn't too bad.

She turned on the spot to face the cave, it stared open mouthed back at her. Around it the rock rose steep and high into the air. She wondered how long The Island was, and from where she was, if she would be able to climb round to the North side, the side that faced the mainland. At the far edge of the beach grew a tree, so bent and warped by the ocean's winds it lay almost parallel to the horizon. The trunk bowed low over the water, its bare branches poking defiantly towards the sea. Still not seeing any sign of Mateo, she sat on it for a while, her legs dangling in the air, her feet skimming the surface. She could feel, at the edge of her mind, the muddled swell of fear. Fear of the storm, of what she had done, of being here at all, but she turned away from it, unwilling, for the moment, to face her emotions. Let me ignore it, she thought, just a few moments longer. A bird crowed above her, a sharp, insistent cry. Its head pivoting sideways, it stared at her with its marble black eyes. She raised her hand and reached out towards it.

Mateo appeared, jumping down from the rock face. The bird, startled, took off into the air, a few feathers falling and floating into the water below. 'It's gone!' He called, walking towards her, looking back over his shoulder to the rock. 'Disappeared.'

'What?'

'It was there just a moment ago I swear, but it's gone.' He spoke through laboured breaths, a few brown hairs sticking to sweat on his forehead.

'What?' She pressed, standing to meet him. As he got closer she saw that he was afraid.

'I... I don't know. A figure, looking down at me. It was there, at the top of the cliffs there, I swear it. But then it was gone. I ran up after it, and there's nothing there.'

Lacey glanced up at the rock face, the dark, rain stained slate jagged and unmoving. 'A person,' she echoed, 'Jessica?' Her eyes widening with hope.

Mateo sighed, and vigorously rubbed his face with his open palms, pulling his hair away from his forehead. 'I don't know,' he said, deflated. 'Maybe it was nothing. Perhaps I am seeing things. The light on the rock casts such strange shadows.'

Lacey blinked and looked up, trying to find the sun behind the clouds. 'Bella will be worried for me,' she said after a moment.

'I have collected some wood for oars and some reeds. I think we can patch the boat and go home.' He started off towards the broken skiff.

'No!' She said suddenly, reaching out to grab him by the arm. 'Not until we have finished what we came here for. I want to look for Jessica, I want to know what is on the third peak. I'm not leaving yet Mateo.'

'This is a bad place, Lacey.' He said flatly.

'Then we had better hurry,' she said, and turning from him, she headed towards the cave to fetch the spade.

Mateo and Lacey set off up the steep rock face. The climbing was tough and occasionally the slate would crumble and they would lose their footing. The rock was hard and unforgiving and by the time they were at the top both had cuts and grazes on their hands. Once the terrain flattened the three peaks loomed ahead, like three knives growing out of the land. Through the gaps between them, the mainland could be seen, though a fog drifted slowly from the South seeping towards the shore, obscuring it in parts. Lacey could still hear the waves thrashing at the rocks below, however when she peered over the edge, all she could see was the mist. It whipped up at the edges by the wind, which howled as though in complaint, around each side of The Island.

Mateo, pointing to each peak in turn, counted from the lowest to the highest. 'One, two, three.' He kept his hand high, aimed directly at the tallest peak, in the middle. With her head down, and her lips silently counting, Lacey paced out thirty five steps from the base of it. Her feet moving between small, weathered shrubs that stuck like thorns from the earth, their bare branches growing in resentment of their surroundings. There were only a few places between the hard rock where a spade could possibly penetrate. They began to dig, taking it in turns.

When one was resting the other would sit and watch their surroundings, nervously. After an hour, four holes lay abandoned beside small piles of fresh earth. Finally, at the fifth hole, the spade in Mateo's hand made a hollow metal *thunk*. Lacey stood up immediately and rushed to him. Mateo brushed the soil aside and carefully, with the tenderness of a midwife retrieving a newborn, pulled a cast iron box from the ground. It was red with rust at the corners and upon touching the latch part of it came away in her hand. Holding her breath, Lacey prized the lid open.

She stayed very still, her hands still clutching the sides of the box. Inside lay a book. Black leather, faded to grey at the edges, with a small, silver clasp. Lacey swallowed, reaching for it.

'It's locked,' Mateo said, pointing to the clasp. He had only just a moment to move away, before the spade, swung by Lacey, shattered it to pieces. Retrieving it from its tomb, she opened it. The pages were as soft and thin as pressed dust, and turning the first one Lacey saw a similar illegible scrawl, as she had done that day in the Proffessor's. She closed it immediately. 'Not here,' she said.

In silence the two turned and began their walk back to the cave, leaving the spade and the open box where they lay. Lacey cradled the book carefully in her arms. After a few minutes Mateo, who walked a little closer to the edge, suddenly stopped.

'There's something down there.' He said. Lacey, her mind on the book, looked up distracted. 'An opening in the rock.' He continued, peering over the side.

Joining him, Lacey said 'I can't see anything.'

'It might be another cave, I will take a look.' Upon saying the words he suddenly looked less certain of the plan.

'We'll go together.' She said, placing the book gently inside his satchel.

Mateo lowered himself down with Lacey following after him. The slate was serrated like a bread knife against Lacey's fingers and crumbled beneath the toes of her boots. Ignoring the dizzying swoon of seeing the sea below crashing against the rock, Lacey turned her head and looked. Beneath her she saw the top of Mateo's head, then she saw it, a crevasse between two rocks. Dark and deep enough to see nothing inside. Beside it a tree grew up out of the rock, its determined branches barely shaking in the wind. Lacey looked at its red leaves a moment, then nodded and continued to climb down towards the opening.

Standing on two rocks either side of the crevasse, the pair peered over the edge. The hole swallowed all the light around it. Even the rocks they stood on curved towards it as though some invisible forced pulled them in.

'Can you see the bottom?' Mateo raised his voice to shout over the wind.

Lacey opened her mouth to respond then shut it again, looking down in alarm at the rock below her feet. Her whole body tensed. She had felt it move. She looked up at him. For a split second they looked at one another. Then it gave way. Mateo hadn't even the time to reach out before she had disappeared into the darkness.

CHAPTER TWENTY TWO

Lacey landed on her back. The blow knocked the wind out of her lungs. She lay completely still. Above her, from what seemed like very far away, she could hear Mateo call her name, it echoed infinitely off the walls of the crevasse. The space reverberated with the sound of the waves thrashing against the other side of the rocks. She sat up tentatively, assessing the damage. She was sore but unharmed. Her hand rubbed at what was sure to be a deep bruise along the back of her ribs.

She looked about, her eyes not yet adjusting to the darkness. With blind fingers she felt at the ground around her. It seemed not fully solid, as though she were atop a pile of kindling. The smell of salty seaweed thickened the air. But there was something else, something that made Lacey instinctually afraid. A whisper of decay. Reaching into the pocket of her dress she pulled out a matchbox. She struck a match and immediately wished she hadn't.

It was not logs that she lay on. Though they looked a little like driftwood, smooth and bleached by the waves. She saw porcelain fingers, leg bones, the curved arch of vertebrae. The instantly recognisable slope of hollow eye sockets staring blankly up at her. They still wore their dresses. Lacey screamed and kicked back against them. They made dry scraping sounds. She felt them snap and shatter as she moved. They were all around her. Standing, she could not feel the floor for them.

'Mateo!' She howled, screaming his name over and over in panic. Her fear ripping through her lungs and into her throat. She grabbed a hold of the rock, trying in desperation to scramble up. The slate snapping and cutting her fingers. Her feet desperate for a foot hold 'Mateo! Help me!'

Mateo's arm reached down from above. His other holding the root of the tree, anchoring his body. 'Take my hand!' He yelled. She jumped up, their fingertips grazing against one another's. Agonisingly close. She cried out in frustration as she fell back down. Feeling the repulsive crunch and crumble beneath her body. Attempting to stand her hand became tangled in the tattered shreds of material. Tearing herself free she realised in terror it was the lace of a skirt.

Mateo lowered himself further down, his face wincing at the effort of it. Lacey tried again, crying out in pain at the rock slicing into her hand as she pulled herself up towards him. Finally her fingertips found his and she felt him grip her wrist and pull.

*

The book sat closed on the cave floor, its cover lit by the light of a newly built fire. Lacey had finally stopped shaking. Mateo had not been able to elicit a response from her during the climb back down to the beach. But he had seen her face as he had pulled her from the darkness, and had looked down at what she had been lying on.

Lacey held her arms out to the flames, her bloodied fingers crying out against the heat. But she couldn't seem to shake the cold of the crevasse from her bones. In her ears she could still hear the hollow crunching sound. The image of the flour white bones behind every blink.

'Mateo.' She said abruptly.

Startled he looked up at her, 'yes?'

'I'm hungry.'

Mateo taken slightly aback, nodded and reached into his satchel.

'I found them earlier,' he said, pulling a small collection of roots from inside. 'I don't know the name, but I have seen them in Ma's cabin. They are all we have.'

Lacey took one thumb-sized piece, inspecting it sceptically before placing it between her teeth and chewing. The flavour was strong, woody and fungal. She wasn't sure she liked it, but continued to eat nonetheless. Mateo, taking one, threw another branch on the fire, which crackled in gratitude.

Once the sun had begun to set below the horizon, and a deep orange hue rippled across the sea, Lacey picked up the book and pushed it into Mateo's hands.

'Even if I know this dialect I'm not fluent Lacey,' he argued, 'and,' he eyed her nervously, 'you've had a horrible shock, maybe this isn't the time.'

'We have to. I have to keep going,' she said, then added, 'please.'

With a look of reluctance, Mateo opened the front cover. He swallowed, sighed, and finally began to read aloud. 'My name is Abiah. As I write, I'm at the age of one hundred and thirty.' Mateo paused, frowning he looked up at Lacey, 'that can't be right.'

'Just read it,' she said with encouragement, leaning back against the cave wall. The strong taste of the root, filling her senses, she felt a strange, but not unpleasant, relaxing of her muscles.

Sighing again, he continued, 'I want to tell my story before I die.' His words, stumbling and hesitant, faltering slightly with the translation. Lacey sat rapt, staring at the fire, her mind focused on his voice. 'I'm a First Settler to these lands.' As he spoke, she felt a strange loosening of her vision, the cave walls, began to dim and blur around the waving fire. She could taste the root inside her mouth, feel the juices still pooling around her tongue. She swallowed, and her eyelids felt heavy, though the rest of her body unnaturally light, as though she were unfastening each one of her limbs. Lacey blinked slowly, before her eyes the flames seemed to move unnaturally.

Mateo continued, 'I travelled here by boat as a young man.' As he said this the most peculiar thing happened. Strange shadows began to grow on the cave wall, projected by the light of the fire. Lacey, her head resting on the rock behind her, could not be sure if they were real or in her imagination. The shadows started to take a form. Then the image of a figure arose in silhouette, as though grown from the flames. Lacey's mouth hung open, the black figure was now unmistakable as a man. Beneath him the shadows seemed to leak into the shape of a boat, rocking atop rolling waves.

Lacey looked slowly from the fire to the wall in wide eyed astonishment. 'I journeyed many days on the boat with my wealthy cousin Grace, whom I had married before leaving our homeland.' The flickering shape of a girl appeared.

'I didn't know then what a witch was. They walk amongst us, women with the ability to harness the power of the nature around them. Wind, fire, water even the trees in the ground, they can control them. When young, the powers only come forward when a witch is threatened. And that is when I first saw them. During a terrible storm I saw her controlling the sea on our voyage.' The figure of Grace held out her arms, and the sea below her calmed to a single flat line. 'She told me after we had taken our blood vows, her power was now shared between the two of us. Well... I did not want to share. I knew if I killed her, I would inherit all of it.'

The shadow man crept up behind his wife with his sword drawn. 'But she wasn't willing to let that happen.' The figure of Grace turned and dragged her nails across her husband's face, the fire flared up in rage, leaving an uneven line above his jaw. The scar glowing golden in the firelight. Abiah recovering, grabbed for her, but he was too late. Grace stepped silently from the edge of the ship. Her hair and dress whipping around her, until she was swallowed up by the black shadowy water.

'She refused to let me take all her power. We docked the next day and began making camp. My powers were still new from the blood vow, but I could feel them growing.' The silhouette of the boat pulled up to a shoreline and its passengers filed out slowly. One, Abiah, walking a little distance from the rest.

'You cannot choose which element you can control. I gained the power of fire.' Abiah's shadow bending to scoop a flame from the fire below and holding it in his hands as it grew. 'But I always knew I had only half the power I desired. I knew from Grace there would be other witches, I began sacrificing more young girls, hoping to find some, hoping they would fulfil me. I wrote spells to read at the point of their death that transferred their powers to me.' The shadows grew up to be tall trees sprouting black branches that reached like fingers to the top of the cave wall. Amongst the trees appeared Abiah, a little taller now, holding the hand of a little girl. 'I marked them, as Grace had marked me.' Passing his hand over her arm the same scarred line appeared, the girls head thrown back in pain. Then turning to her and wrapping his arms around her, her little form was consumed by his shadow.

Mateo paused, swallowing hard, obviously struggling, his voice tense with anxiety. 'With each sacrifice my powers grew. Not all were witches, but all were innocent, and I found their innocence fed me.' Little girls appeared from between the trees and Abiah's figure engulfed each one, growing taller each time. 'Soon I was in control of the whole village. They were afraid of me, the men believed me immortal. I built a crypt for the sacrifices. But no sacrifice ever gave me the power Grace had. She was special.'

Mateo stopped, looking up at Lacey. 'I don't know what this word means. It looks like many, or maybe a lot. Grace is a many witch, but that doesn't make any sense.'

Lacey, looked at him through misty eyes, 'keep reading.'

'I believed for years I might be able to find a girl to sacrifice to complete me, for I have been living on breadcrumbs for decades. But now I'm an old man, and death is close, I have failed.'

Mateo turned the page. To find only the torn edges of the rest of the book. 'It's missing,' he said, 'there's no more pages.'

'What's that?' Lacey asked, leaning towards the book and pointing at an inscription on the back cover.

'Buried in the town of New Lynch, with the body of Abiah the witch, the killer of girls.'

Lacey remained sitting, staring at the fire, which had now receded back to its usual form, the flames innocently licking up the back wall.

'My God.' Sighed Mateo.

They sat in silence, absorbing what they had heard. Lacey frowned, 'if it was buried in town, why is the book here?'

'You found the map in the Mayor's office, he must have found it and hidden it here. Where no living person goes.'

'Abiah,' whispered Lacey.

'A mad man,' Mateo replied, shaking his head.

'The Mayor found the book, and is doing the same to our girls,' Lacey said, her thoughts forming like shadows in her mind. Loose and shapeless, but dark nonetheless.

'He must believe this nonsense. This absurdity about witches, the ramblings of a mad man.' Something in Lacey's mind caught and she looked away from the fire. Her eyes resting on the soft twilight outside the cave. Mateo continued, 'it's all a lie, Deception Bay, the girls drowning, he made it all up. He's been taking them, sacrificing them. For what? So he may become a witch? He's mad.'

Lacey stayed still for a long time, then finally said, 'my mother must have suspected him. Sebastian told me that the Mayor thought her nosy. She must have been investigating him, and when she got too close to the truth he framed her.' Lacey's eyes welled with thick tears. 'She wasn't a witch, she never hurt anybody.' Her voice broke, the words forming painfully at the back of her throat, she struggled to bring them forward. 'All these years.' She gasped, holding her hand to her chest, her body curling around it, the tears falling freely down her face, 'all these years I have hated her and been so ashamed.' Lacey whispered, her face crumpling, 'Mother,' she breathed, 'my Mother.'

Mateo placed his brow against the side of her head, she leant back against him and cried. He was silent but his empathy was limitless, and she fell into it. Her stifled cries echoing around the dark cave. When finally her tears subsided, she looked up at him and said only a single word.

'Jessica.'

'She... she wasn't in the crevasse?' asked Mateo, his words faltering.

'No. There's still hope. We must go back to the mainland,' Lacey said urgently, 'we must confront him, the village must know the truth, Mateo.'

He nodded, glancing out at the opening, 'we will go at first light, once I have patched the boat.' Lacey opened her mouth to protest, but he spoke over her. 'There will be no truth to tell if we drown on our way home.'

Lacey nodded once in acceptance. 'Before we go, I don't want to leave their remains here without...' She trailed off

'Without what?'

'I don't know. My mother might be down there, Mateo. Can we not at least give them some peace?'

Mateo nodded. His young mind knew better than most the relationship between the living and the dead.

In the cool twilight, the two looked down once more into the crevasse. Lacey held a bunch of wild grasses and red leaves they had picked in lieu of flowers. Mateo spoke the gypsy death prayer loudly so that it might be heard over the noise of the waves. When he was done Lacey released the leaves. They twirled and scattered in the air. Some carried off by the wind into the sea below. But a few fell silently down into the darkness of the ravine.

Back at the beach, Mateo went inside the cave to weave the patch of reeds for the hole in the boat. Lacey stayed outside. It was dark now, but the moon had grown in the sky, turning each piece of shingle a cool silver. Only the edge of the sea, where it softly came to meet the land, was visible, the rest sat in a deep blackness. Somehow, though it was a cold, dark night, The Island seemed suddenly a less malevolent place. She'd been to Hell here, and she had returned. The peace she had hoped for the remains, she felt herself now. Closing her eyes, feeling the thin sea air on her cheeks, she thought of her mother. And for the first time in ten years, she felt no contempt, no anger, only love.

Feeling a little lighter Lacey walked back into the cave, Mateo looked up at her, the length of woven reeds in his hands. 'It should hold,' he said. 'I will check it against the hull in the morning, but it should hold.' She nodded, sitting down beside him. Her shoulders just touching the side of his arm. Mateo exhaled, placing the patch to one side. He pushed his hair out of his eyes and ran his palm across the side of his scarred face. Not looking at her he said, 'so the wedding..?' He left the word hanging in the air.

She shook her head gently, watching his profile, 'no, no wedding. How can I now?'

*

Mateo nodded slowly, purposefully, preserving his emotions. Lacey looked at him, he, under her stare, looked only at the fire. She felt suddenly so grateful to have him there, beside her. Leaning towards him she placed a kiss gently on his cheek. It could have been mistaken for a kiss of thanks, but then she didn't move away. The seconds stretched in silence. Mateo turned his head so that they were finally face to face. His scars glistened gold in the fire light. Slowly he leaned forward and pressed his lips against hers.

Though his kiss was soft, Lacey felt it as an explosion of heat. Her hands, in reflex, came up and held either side of his face, his arms wrapped tight around her body. He squeezed so hard she felt the breath escape her. Her body felt weightless as though she could float away were it not for his hold. All the pain and pressure of the last few hours, the last few weeks, melted as they kissed. Wiped away like a wave against sand. She leaned into the warm, soft scent of him. All the mornings she had laid in his bed, waiting for him to wake up, all the times they had walked together in the woods, laughing and playing, they came to her now. Moving through her mind like clouds, shaping and reshaping. How many times had she dreamt of him, how many times had she watched his lips as he had talked and now she felt them against her own. They were strangely familiar in their newness.

Out of the corner of her eye Lacey saw something move. A flicker of white. Pulling away she looked around herself in mute astonishment. Mateo too, mirrored her open-mouthed expression as he stared at the cave floor. Where a minute before there had been bare stone, now there was a meadow of tiny white-headed flowers. Stretching from wall to wall, blanketing every inch. Before their eyes they continued to grow through the rock, their papery petals gently unfolding.

'My God,' said Mateo.

'Do you see it too?' Asked Lacey, every tortured hour she had spent questioning her own sanity causing her voice to shake.

His eyes gleaming, he whispered 'I always knew you were magic.'

For the first time after one of these strange occurrences had happened, Lacey smiled. The knot of fear and shame inside her had loosened. She reached out, stroking the flowers gently with both hands, the petals velvety soft against her palms. Glancing up she saw Mateo beaming at her, and though she did not try, she could not stop herself from pulling him towards her. She leaned back against the flowers, her legs folded around him. Their fingers entwined then released, constantly reforming, feeling at the skin of one another. She marvelled not only at his softness but at her own. As though a layer of skin had been removed from her body and she could finally feel. Feel the crisp prickling sea air around her, the hot pressure of the fire and him, his fingertips as smooth as the flowers petals.

She was at once aware and unaware of him. She seemed to slide in and out of her own mind. At some points totally present, able to feel every inch of her own skin and other times she was miles away, a disembodied mass of nerves floating in darkness, belonging to no body at all. He kissed her. A deafeningly soft kiss, arresting in it's tenderness. The world beneath her eyelids flashing bright pink, a startling, burning rose. She remembered how it felt when he would watch her lips when she talked, how it made them prickle at the edges.

The movements and the seconds seemed to topple on top of one another, she began to feel at the base of her the whisper of the river, a tiny rippling stream. She felt him sink into her, and she in turn sunk deeper into the ground. So that she and he and the earth were one. And she understood now what her body had changed for, felt the joy of being a woman, the joy of being able to feel at all. Until finally her body, after years of being tired and corseted in grief and pain and fear, collapsed in pleasure. An acute unbearable pleasure, rolling in like waves on the tide. Whilst all around them the little flowers grew, nodding their delicate heads in celebration, swaying gently in the firelight.

CHAPTER TWENTY THREE

The next morning the sun rose cold and pale behind a sheet of clouds, but thankfully there was no wind. With his trousers pulled up around his knees Mateo waded out into the water, testing the little skiff. It floated happily, bobbing gently in the tide, only a few small trickles finding their way around the patch. He nodded in approval. Lacey felt less optimistic than she had done the night before. The task ahead felt so much more daunting in the daylight. She checked and rechecked the sea, nervous at returning home.

'Don't worry, if there is a storm you can save us with your powers,' Mateo teased, closing his eyes, holding his arms out and wiggling his fingers.

Rolling her eyes at him and suppressing a smile, she hauled the bag into the boat. 'It's not like that.' She said. That morning, when she had awoken amongst the white flowers she had found that they had grown as a crown around her head. Their stems weaving in amongst one another, their roots still embedded in the ground.

Lacey watched the little island shrink in size as the boat pulled away. Then she turned, and did not look back again. The sea was calm, the boat sliced through the surface like a knife. As the mainland came closer, Lacey's anxiety increased. She both wished the boat would move faster so that they may be able to unmask the Mayor sooner, as well as wanting desperately to turn it around and sail away. Mateo, whose eyes flitted between her and the coast rowed steadily, his satchel tucked beneath his seat, the book hidden inside.

They had made good time, but rather than docking on Hammer Bay they steered to the right, finding a smaller cove and coming in there instead, to hide their theft a little longer. They walked through the forest together quickly, purposefully. When they arrived on the edge of town Lacey said 'before we do anything I need to go to the tavern. I must warn Mr Warren. If the Mayor is truly this evil, then he is in danger.'

Mateo nodded. 'I will ask around if there is any word on Jessica. Will you speak to your father?'

'Yes,' said Lacey sombrely, 'he is still expecting to see his daughter wed tomorrow.' They shared a chaste kiss before separating.

Half an hour later Lacey threw open the door of the Golden Tavern, it banged loudly against the wall. Mr Carter stood behind the bar, drying cups with a dirty looking piece of cloth.

'Oh,' he said, 'there you are.'

'Has Jessica been found?' Lacey asked urgently.

The innkeeper shook his head, genuine sadness creeping into the corner of his eyes.

Lacey exhaled, in frustration and fear, and headed towards the back stairs. Then she stopped and looked back towards the man. 'Why did you say oh there you are?'

'Him upstairs,' said Mr Carter, nodding towards the ceiling, 'he were down here last night asking for you.'

'Asking for me?' Lacey repeated.

'That's right. Demanding you be sent for, sayin' he had to speak to you on an urgent matter. I told him it weren't proper to be requesting a young lady like that. I don't know how they do it in Rumford but down here we have such a thing as decency.'

Lacey held her breath, inwardly imploring the man to get to the point. 'Anyway,' he kept on demanding. 'So we sent someone for you, but your sister said you were ill and wasn't to be disturbed.' Mr Carter paused, holding a glass to his eye checking it.

'And Mr Warren?' Lacey prompted impatiently.

The innkeeper shrugged. 'He went back upstairs.' Lacey moved towards the door, 'He weren't looking too well to be honest. Looked sickly pale, must be a bad flu.'

Lacey took the stairs two at a time, the pit of her stomach already telling her what her mind feared. The door was no longer locked, it sighed open as she pushed it tentatively with the tips of her fingers.

'Mr Warren?' She said in a shaking whisper.

She took a step inside. A shirt had been hung across the window in lieu of a curtain, and it painted the room in a dim orange hue. The man had only brought one small sack with him, it lay neatly on a chair beside the bed. His boots unlaced, sat beside one another beneath, both toes pointing towards her. The walls had been painted once, but were peeling now, revealing the sandy, loose brick beneath. And the gaps between the floorboards so thick, she imagined in the evening you could see the tops of the heads of those who sat at the bar below.

She needn't have walked any further, she could see from the doorway that he was dead. The odour was obscene. Sweet and fungal, like decaying flowers but with a metallic twist of meat left in the sun. She held her trembling fingers to her lips in an effort to stop the churning of her stomach.

The covers had been pulled up to his chin, as you do when tucking a child in at night. His head almost lilac in its pallor, except around the eyes where he was quite green. A scattering of dark blisters marked his mouth and a thin line of dried blood ran down to his unshaven chin. And, although his muscles were relaxed in death, Lacey thought his face still held pain. A faint but final echo of agony.

If only she had come back sooner, she could have warned him. She could have saved him. The room tilted suddenly, Lacey took two unsteady steps backwards, her hands reaching out to the walls to steady herself. Then, keeping her eyes from the corpse, she turned and ran.

Lacey rapped her fists so hard against Commander Kinch's front door the sound echoed down the streets. Fearfully she looked over her shoulder twice before hearing the word 'enter,' and opening the door. Every shutter was fastened but a candle burnt on a table where he sat, head down, polishing a rifle. His shirt sleeves rolled high revealing arm hair, as thick as a bear's which stopped at neither the wrist nor the knuckles. Save for the table and two stools, there was no other furniture in this room and the only thing that hung from the walls was a rack of weapons.

'Commander, you must come quick, something terrible has happened.' Lacey exclaimed, her heart beating rapidly.

'Shut the door,' said Kinch, without looking up.

'It's an emergency,' Lacey said in desperation.

'Miss Emerson, shut it or leave.' He said plainly.

Still breathless, Lacey pulled the door to behind her.

'Come here.' He said, his voice a low growl, as close as it could be to a whisper. Lacey took a small, tentative step forward, instinctively wanting to be closer to the door than to him. He continued the slow, methodical cleaning of his gun before speaking again. 'I am a private man. Not many know much about me. But there is something everyone who meets me should know, I'd do anything to protect this town. You women, you don't know how hard this land is. You spend every day in your pretty dresses sipping tea. You don't know how close we are to chaos.' Lacey frowned in frustration, but the man continued. 'Floods, draughts, gypsies, flu, beasts, witchcraft. Even the land itself wants us dead.'

'It is an emergency.' Interrupted Lacey.

From his pocket Kinch pulled a small white piece of fabric, and not looking up slid it across the table towards her. Lacey looked down to see her initials *L.E* on her own handkerchief. The innocent looping embroidered letters jarring so violently with a smattering of poppy red blood stains. Automatically she reached for it, but the Commander's wide hand covered it and returned it to his pocket.

He methodically ran a thin brush inside the muzzle and speaking in such a natural calm manner said 'if you are not stood beside the Mayor's son at the alter tomorrow, this handkerchief will be found by the corpse of the stranger Mr Warren.'

'You killed him.' Realised Lacey.

Finally Kinch looked up, 'I will do anything to protect this town.'

'Even work for an evil man?' She seethed.

'This village needs strength; I don't care which form it takes.'

'We'll see if your fellow villagers agree once they see the proof I have of the Mayor's ill deeds.'

Standing Kinch clicked the barrel in place, the noise resonating around the bare room. Lacey automatically took a step back towards the door, but the man only turned to place the gun onto the rack. 'The problem with proof is, it very much depends on who is holding it. It's a commodity, the value of which is only judged by who the seller is. How much value do you think your words hold in this town Miss Emerson? A witch's daughter, running her mouth, making up lies about the Mayor?'

'They aren't lies.'

'No one is going to believe you, and that makes them lies. No one believed your mother. She couldn't keep her nose out of that which didn't concern her.'

'Like the murders of children?' She said, her voice as quiet and soft as cotton wool. She slid the words across the wooden floor between them. But he heard them well enough, his lips twitched into a snarl.

'You were seen whispering to the unknown man in the alleyway outside the tavern. Then witnessed calling on him, and every other man in town knows he sent for you last night. It is no great stretch to paint some clandestine relationship between you two. The Mayor will call the council to his room and they will see your blood-stained handkerchief and convict you as a murderous witch. You have spent too long reading books girl, it is time to face reality and the reality is, this town is only too ready to condemn you. The fire is set around you, it only needs one spark. Just one little spark.'

'Light it,' said Lacey raising her head, 'I don't care. I won't live with these lies any longer.'

Sighing as he pulled down his sleeves, fiddling with the cuffs, Kinch replied 'the Mayor thought you might say that.' Raising his wrist to the candlelight and squinting at the buttons he asked softly 'how much medicine does your father take for his arthritis? One bottle a day? Two? It would be a shame were the ingredients not correctly measured by the Doctor. Such a fine member of the council Doctor Prior.' Lacey's body began to tighten with anger. 'And if you imagined you would be able to find comfort in the arms of your gypsy boy' continued Kinch, 'you would be wrong. He is not beyond our reach, I would welcome an excuse to finally remove his kind from this town.'

Lacey, who had not eaten properly for a few days, suddenly felt her legs shake beneath her. Her rage slipping into fear. A desperate, child-like fear. It felt as though the ground she were standing on might fall away at any moment. She opened her mouth, but the Commander's final words shut it, 'I will see you tomorrow at the wedding.'

*

It was twilight when Lacey opened her eyes to the faint sound of tapping. She lay on her bed, still wearing the clothes she had worn on The Island. The skin on her face was tight with dried tears. Bella, though frustrated at her unanswered questions, was relieved to have her home, checking on her twice while she slept. Thankfully Frank was still on the lake. The tapping sound continued and glancing up at the window Lacey saw Mateo's face behind it.

'Any news of Jessica?' She asked leaning against the window sill, collecting her thoughts. The dimming sky above him had begun to reveal a few early stars.

'Good news.'

'Tell me,' she said, feeling the small ignition of hope inside her.

'I ran into Mr Corby, the foreman, who told me he knew the girl to be with an aunt in the Upper Lakes. Apparently she stowed away on one of the fishing boats, she has been known to do so before.'

Lacey exhaled in relief. 'Oh, thank God.'

'The search has been called off,' said Mateo, 'all is well.' Reaching out he went to stroke a lock of black hair from her cheek. Lacey stopped him, her hand gently pushing his arm away. The air around them altered.

'What's wrong?' He asked. Lacey only shook her head, looking away from him. She could feel tears begin to again rise inside her. 'Come,' he said, fear already bending his words, he reached for her once more. Again she pushed him away, this time he took a shocked step backwards. 'What's wrong?' He repeated.

'Mr Warren is dead. Poisoned. His body lies in the room above the Golden Tavern.' Mateo stared at her in silence. 'It's my fault.' She said.

'The Mayor has killed many people.' Mateo whispered.

'They weren't my fault,' she responded in dismissal. 'Mr Warren sent for me, he asked for me and I wasn't here. I was with you.' The memory of their embrace on the floor of the cave, filled the silence between them. 'And if we continue, more people will die. Innocent people. How can we be together Mateo when all of this has happened?'

'No.' He said sternly, 'that is exactly why we must be together. There is so much darkness, what we have is the only light.'

She shook her head, tears welling, she smeared them roughly away with the back of her hand. 'You are wrong.' She sniffed, 'I want to look after my family, I need to protect them. I cannot be with you Mateo at the cost of them.'

'So you will marry a man you hate? The son of your mother's killer!'

'It is the only thing I can do now. I have to.' She answered calmly, still unable to look at him.

Mateo nodded and swallowed sourly, pressing his lips together. His face concentrated into a look of wounded fury. He glanced up at the dress, now hanging against the wall behind her, staring at it through dark brows. Then, closing the distance between them he pushed his forehead against hers. She closed her eyes, a tear streaked down her cheek and over her lips. She could hear his breath shaking, then a moment later she felt the pressure lift. She didn't open her eyes but heard him leave. Then all that she heard was the wind between the leaves in the wood and the birds cooing in their nests. When she opened her eyes again she saw that she was alone.

CHAPTER TWENTY FOUR

On the morning of Lacey's wedding day the sun shone. It set fire to the last of the leaves on the trees, turning the wood an angry orange. Lacey spent the morning, in her still dirty dress, with her back against the garden wall, feeling it warm her face. Bella appeared at the back door with a cup of tea for her.

'It's your last day.'

'My last day?' Lacey echoed in whisper.

'As a single woman,' smiled Bella, placing the cup on the step beside two identical full teacups, now cold. Bella, in her inability to get through to Lacey, had resorted to her default of making tea. Lacey nodded once in gratitude and Bella, hesitating a moment, worriedly chewing on her lower lip, finally withdrew inside. Lacey was yet to see Frank but had gleaned from Bella that he had not realized her absence and was in the village, running errands for that night. Indeed, it seemed everyone in town was busying themselves with wedding arrangements. Only the bride sat alone, with nothing to do but watch the sun make its progress across the sky.

Throughout the night, and the early hours, her mind had torn itself apart like a trapped rat, trying desperately to find a way out. Some solution, some salvation, a way to save her family, Mateo, herself. Occasionally the strange, detached thought would float into her mind. *Am I going to die tonight?* But the concept seemed almost inconsequential now. By the time dawn had arrived she had exhausted every option. She could see no escape, no way out. She had awoken to defeat. Behind each blink of her tired eyes she saw Mateo's face, the hurt etched into every line of it, and all she could do was cry.

With her head in her arms she sobbed against the back wall. Something floated down onto her shoulder and looking up she saw the rose bush, leaning low above her. She remembered that night, when Sebastian had first visited, how a thorn had caught in her hair. But the bush didn't look as it had done then. As her tears fell so did the flower's petals. They drifted around her like snowflakes. Each bud shriveling before her eyes, twisting, drying, turning brown at the edges. She held a hand out and they collected in her palm, she stared at them with muted surprise. They twitched and turned over in the breeze, almost translucent in the sunlight. After less than a minute the entire bush was bare, the flowers shed, the branches stripped. The dead petals in her hands, her hair, the ground around her. A few even floated in her untouched tea. She looked at them a moment before wiping them off her and walking numbly inside.

It was well past four by the time Lacey had bathed. The stool was pulled in front of the fire and Bella sat, with Lacey on the floor between her knees, whilst she pulled a comb through her long hair. The black and white splitting and running in strict formation down her back. The water causing it to cling together in thick, monochrome lines. Bella dipped her fingertips in a jar of rose water, then ran them through Lacey's hair, from root to tip. The perfume filled the room in a flowery cloud as Bella set about weaving her plaits. They wrapped prettily around her head in two braids, not too tight, a few locks flowing free and falling around her shoulders.

'Wait a moment,' said Bella before disappearing out of the back door. She appeared a minute later with a small fist of forget-me-nots.

'Stolen for Mrs Andrew's garden,' she winked, 'she won't miss them I'm sure.' She threaded them throughout Lacey's plaits, the bright blue in beautiful contrast with the black and white.

The dress, that had all this time hung in the corner of the room, watching them, was pulled down. Lying limp in Bella's arms it lost all of its menace. It was just a cut of material, thought Lacey, it could perhaps be a pillowcase, or a tablecloth. She held her arms over her head and Bella, carefully, so not to tear it, let the material fall around her. It was many layers of laced silk, the colour of creamed milk. Each sheet individually transparent, but layered as it was, one upon the other, you couldn't see her body beneath. It hung well, close to her frame, then falling loose at the base into a rippling skirt. The sleeves, which came all the way down to her wrists, were tight. At the end she wore thin, white gloves, fastened with a silk bow. She looked down at her hands, encased in lace, feeling at the cloth between her thumb and forefinger.

'I'm wrapped for the grave,' she said quietly.

'Not quite.' Bella gestured for her to sit and tapped on Lacey's bare foot, guiding it to the opening of the white boot. They slipped on like a second skin, Bella laboriously buttoning up each fastening, her practiced hands working quickly. Lacey thought of the cobbler, Mr Lewis, with his long, bony fingers.

'There,' said Bella eventually, lifting herself up from her knees, dusting off her hands and taking a few steps back to get a proper view on her sister. She smiled proudly at her, a small, shining tear forming in the corner of her eye. 'You are beautiful.'

Something about her show of emotion turned Lacey's stomach, and for the first time since yesterday afternoon, the world came into sharp focus. The moment seized her. The words rising from her throat, she was unable to stop herself from speaking them. She stood up, the dress falling around the white boots. 'They don't really swim on Deception Bay.'

Bella, not understanding said, 'what?'

'The girls,' said Lacey, her voice shaking as she inhaled, 'they don't really swim there. None of the children do. They were telling the truth. They are more afraid of it than we are.'

'Why are you talking about this?'

'Because the Mayor has been killing them.'

The words in the quiet moment were electrifying and Bella stepped back as though shocked, her smile instantly gone. 'Why would you say something like that?'

'Because it's true.'

'No it's not.' She shook her head. 'No it's not.'

'I promise it is true. I have proof. That is where I was those two nights. I was finding proof. It is the Mayor who is the cause of it. It is he who is responsible for the girls vanishing. It is all him,' her hands came to her face, she closed her eyes and pressed her fingers against her temples, desperate to stay focused. 'He murdered our mother Bella.'

'He carried out the law. Our mother was a witch. A convicted witch.'

'No. He discovered Mother suspected him and he framed her. He framed her for his own crimes. I speak the truth. Please look at me.'

'How could you say these things? These are mad thoughts, Lacey.'

Lacey breathed unsteadily. 'There is witchcraft here but not our mother's. The Mayor, he found an evil book, and he follows its commands.'

'Is it the wedding? You don't want to get married, is that why you say this? You don't love Sebastian so your mind has invented these things.'

'Of course I don't love Sebastian!' Lacey screamed. The words rung like a bell around the house. 'But it isn't that.'

'Then you are mad.'

'Things are happening to me, but I swear I'm not mad.'

'What things?'

'I know you can see it.' She pointed a white gloved finger at her. 'You saw it that night with me, right here. We were standing right here and I got angry and the fire went out.'

'A draft,' said Bella.

'There was no draft. The book speaks of these unnatural things, and Ma told me-'

'Ma!' Bella interjected, laughing cruelly, 'is that who fills your head with this? Ma Fulmer! A senile old woman.'

'Never mind about what is happening to me. The Mayor is behind the disappearances of the girls.'

'Then prove it,' said Bella, crossing her arms.

'Well,' sighed Lacey in exasperation, 'I haven't the book now. But it documents the sacrifice of innocent girls in order to obtain the powers of a witch. Written by a terrible man from the First Settlers, and his actions are alive still today.' Bella groaned and turned her back to her sister. Lacey continued, 'I have been followed by a figure in a hood, upon which was embroidered a symbol of The Island. The Mayor has it tattooed upon his hands. I found a secret crypt in the woods with the names of each missing girl hanging inside. In the hull of the mayor's own boat were red leaves, the type that only grow on The Island. It is all connected.'

'Red leaves,' echoed Bella.

'It is him Bella, you have to believe me.' Lacey took a deep breath, then stepped towards Bella's back, resting her head against it. She could feel every one of her sister's muscles tense. 'It's not for love or hate or anything other than the truth that I say these things. This is what has been happening in our town, there is evil around us. This is the truth.'

Holding Bella by the shoulders she turned her around. Bella had tears running down her cheeks. A mix of confusion and fear and anger on her face.

'You have to believe me,' repeated Lacey.

There was a long silence. Finally, through her tears, Bella said, 'I cannot.'

Lacey felt as though she were standing at the edge of a tall cliff, and with those words someone had pushed her gently, but firmly, back.

'Lacey!' Her father called. Dressed in his grey suit and tie, Frank stood in the doorway. His hat sat tired and somewhat crumpled to the side of his head. It showed clearly the years of sitting inside a cupboard forgotten and unused. A new black ribbon had been sewn round the brim, no doubt an effort of Bella's to smarten it up. But the contrast between the new, shiny material and the grubby article it was tied around, did nothing but make the hat look even older.

'You look quite fine.' He walked towards her, a little unsteady on his feet and reached out to her. She held his fingers and turned awkwardly, so that he might see the dress, her eyes still upon Bella's face. 'Very good Annabella,' he said, nodding to his daughter. Bella brushed her hair from her face and gave him a courteous smile, her tears already wiped away. The corner of her right eye flickered ever so slightly.

'How are you Father?' Lacey asked.

'I am well.'

'Did you catch many?' Bella added.

'Sadly less than we would have liked.' Then turning to Lacey, 'but today is about celebration. There has been much activity in town, everyone is looking forward to the ceremony. Now, could a daughter be persuaded to help her Father with his tie? A last act before leaving him.' He said, in mock sadness. His behaviour uncharacteristically energised.

Lacey took hold of the ends of the tie and began knotting them into bow, 'I'm not leaving you' she said quietly, whispering it to his breast pocket.

His crooked fingers came to her chin tilting it slightly so she looked at him. 'All girls leave their fathers. Not necessarily on their wedding day, sometimes long before that. You are ours, then you aren't. You are young, then you grow and change. You have your own secrets, your own secret worlds where there is no room for fathers. But that is alright, it is the way. Girls need fathers, women need only their husbands.'

Lacey's mouth opened and closed, without forming any words.

'Besides,' he said, 'I have Bella to keep me company.' Lacey didn't turn to look at Bella, but couldn't imagine that she was smiling. 'Now daughters, I believe we have somewhere to be.' He offered her his arm, and Lacey, in silence, took it.

The three of them walked down the street towards the church, which hummed with light in the twilight. The windows glowing golden against the dark wood. Frank walked proudly, his chest pushed forward, his head held high. He had a daughter on either side, holding an arm each. He did not notice that they did not smile.

White flowers had grown along the edge of the street. Their little heads pushed up between the cobblestones, gently swaying back and forth, their petals flickering in the light. They caught Lacey's eye, she had never seen them there before. In fact she had only ever seen that type of flower one place, growing through hard rock. She remembered Mateo's arms around her. Suddenly Lacey stopped. Her father and sister turning towards her in question.

'I've forgotten something' she said.

'Lacey.' Bella said, in fear, seeing her sister's face. 'No.'

'You go on. I will meet you there.'

Frank reached into his jacket pocket, pulling out his watch. But by the time he had looked up Lacey had already turned and was running in the other direction. She called over her shoulder 'I will meet you there,' as, with one hand holding her hair in place and the other pulling up the skirt of her wedding dress, she sprinted in the direction of Mateo's house.

Breathless, she arrived a few minutes later, a kind of wild excitement pulsing through her veins. Not bothering to knock she pushed through the door calling out 'Mateo!' The house was cool and dark, the only sound the gentle lapping of the water on the stilts below the floor. 'Mateo?' Her heart skipping a beat. The house had been torn apart. Every chair was tipped on its side, shards of smashed plates strewn all over the floor. Mateo's work tools scattered in each corner of the room. Looking down she saw with horror, spots of blood on the floorboards. Then stooping to pick something up, Lacey held between her gloved fingertips, a chewed matchstick.

Fear washed over her. It rose around her like an incoming tide. It filled the air, then wrapped itself about her, slowly crushing her insides. Then she was aware of another feeling, one that would take hold of her for some time. It was a kind of blind, numb calm.

Lacey in mute panic stood a moment, blinking. Fear had turned her mind into mist, she could see no other option before her. Dropping the matchstick, she walked back outside, and in the direction of the church.

CHAPTER TWENTY FIVE

Lacey watched the warped, watery figure of Sebastian through the misty window of the church's antechamber. He swayed slightly from side to side, his figure bending and melting in the glass. The faint scent of mildew hung in the air in the small room. Bibles smelling sweetly of mould piled in the corner, amongst prayer cushions awaiting mending, and a small collection of mismatched vases. She glanced down, looking at the darkness between the floorboards, thinking of her mother. Through the glass she could see guests arranged in neat lines in the pews. Their shirt collars stiff and starched white. Lacey imagined the hands of the local washerwomen to be red raw as they had kneeled by the washing mill, scrubbing and rinsing and scrubbing again. Making sure there wasn't one spot of dirt on the collars or cuffs. Then later pressing them into sharp white edges, sweat pricking their foreheads beside the fire. The same shirts were sure to be stained red with wine before the evening was done.

She could see her neighbours, the women with their caps tied tight, blush pressed upon their cheeks. The men reserved and clean, their beards and hair neatened in the presence of God. Mrs Turner the fishmonger's wife, sat on a pew close to the back, beside her husband. Their neighbours either side left a conspicuous gap. Rose water, after all was only so strong.

Like a dressmaker's doll, Lacey was placed at the end of the aisle. She felt the world move past with a strange, sluggish speed, as though she were underwater. Bella stood next to her and pulled the veil over her head, the lace so thick and heavy all the congregation became faceless shapes, looming out of the pews, watching her descent. The organ sounded, the guests stood, and her father tugged her into motion. The chaos of anger and fear raged inside her, but a heavy, white veil lay on top of it, smothering the panic below. She walked down towards the altar like a coffin being lowered into a grave. The mourners, in their finest clothes, leant forward to get one last look.

Beneath a bough of hundreds of white flowers, Sebastian stood tall in his ancestral robes. They hung about him, blood red and heavy as bear skin. Badges and buttons and unknown symbols of men pinned to his chest, his sword hung stiff and shining at his side. Even behind the veil she could smell his sticky, sweet perfume, and something else, vinegar perhaps, used to polish his sword. Lacey squeezed her bouquet between her gloved fingers. Her father pushed a small neat kiss into the side of her jaw and docked her, like a boat, beside her betrothed. The couple stood together beneath the church window, the sun, finally surrendering, set in shame behind the stained glass.

The Vicar, who looked even shorter than usual in his loose, green robes, cleared his throat and raised his hands - his demeanour a little lighter than when Lacey had last seen him, standing above the grave of Mary Morgan. 'Dearly beloved, we are gathered together here in the sight of God, and in the face of this company to join together this man and this woman in a blood vow.' As he talked his head moved side to side, as though he were reciting the lyrics to a song. His eyes in their deep pockets remained closed, his breath smelt of communion wine. Beneath her veil Lacey watched his lips move but didn't recognize the words. He sounded to her ear, to be speaking a language wholly unknown. The words rose and fell like waves but all she heard was noise, it swirled around her ears with the beating of her eardrum.

Once, a few years ago Lacey had become drunk on cider. She had stolen it from Frank's cupboard one summer evening. She and Mateo had drunk it lying on their backs in the back of a hay cart, staring up at the sky. The stars had swum and danced above her as she began to feel reality slipping away. Her words had blurred and her mind became lost in a thick, deep fog. She tried to hold on to herself but still felt the world sliding from her grasp, like water through her fingers. A guilt-ridden Mateo had carried her home, greeted by the disapproving eyes of Bella and her father. She could remember how it felt to be held in his arms, her face tucked against his chest. She sighed deeply and the veil in front of her swayed a little.

Then suddenly the curtain was pulled up and Lacey was face to face with Sebastian. She gasped at the unexpected exposure. The faces of the crowd came into sudden focus, she had half-forgotten they were there. The Vicar was still speaking, Lacey couldn't tell how much time had passed, but the light through the window was blue.

'We are here today, before God, because marriage is one of His most sacred wishes, to witness the joining in marriage of Sebastian and Lacey.' At the sound of her name Lacey blinked awake and turned her head to him. 'Who gives this woman in marriage to this man?'

Frank, hat in hand, half stood and gave a little wave, as though afraid he might not be seen, 'I do,' he said. Lacey closed her eyes. *I have been wrapped like a sacrifice and carried by my owner who gives me now to you*, she thought. She looked at Sebastian, a small vein she had never before seen pulsed along his neck. His jaw clenched, he stared blankly at a space just above her chest. *I'm not so sure my new keeper even welcomes his gift.* The Vicar continued, now turning his small head to Sebastian, but try though he might, he couldn't persuade him to meet his eye. Sebastian stared resolutely ahead of him like a man destined for the gallows.

'Do you, Sebastian, take Lacey to be your wife, to live together after God's ordinance, in the holy estate of matrimony? Will you love her, comfort her, honour and keep her, in sickness and in health, for richer, for poorer, for better, for worse, in sadness and in joy, to cherish and continually bestow upon her your heart's deepest devotion, forsaking all others, keep yourself only unto her as long as you both shall live?'

His voice, in answer, was as cold as the stone upon which they stood, and twice as hard, 'I will'. The Vicar paused a moment, leaving a space for the groom to smile perhaps, or look at his betrothed. The silence was awkward and heavy, when nothing came he turned to Lacey, and repeated his words.

Lacey, unlike Sebastian, couldn't have been persuaded by anyone from staring directly at her fiancé. Look at me as you kill me, she thought. But he was a coward, and she was a woman with no choices left. A figure of a tall, skinny boy, chopping wood in the forest, appeared in her mind. As though in reflex Lacey took a small step back, then another. I'm going run, she thought. The words coming to her mind from nowhere, her body following them on instinct. She took a breath and moved to turn. The hand of the Vicar shot out from within his wide sleeves, like a snake striking a mouse. He gripped her by the forearm, she looked at him. His stare, that of an owner with a disobedient dog, his eyes demanding submission.

She looked down at his hand upon her. His action unseen by the crowd. Then she saw his feet, the toes of his shoes peeking out from beneath the hem of his cassock. The soles were caked in a thick red mud. She had seen that mud before, on the floor of the crypt. She remembered Bella admonishing her for tracking it through the house. Lacey felt her last morsel of hope die. A few seconds later she answered him. 'I will,' she said.

'What you had committed to words you will now commit to blood.' With his free hand the vicar pulled a short dagger from within his robes. One of Lacey's eye lids flickered as he drew it across her palm, but she did not move.

The Vicar then cut Sebastian in the same way and forced their bleeding hands together. Holding them tight he closed his eyes and bowed his head in whispered prayer. Sebastian's hand was bleeding more than Lacey's. Thick red streaks ran drown his wrist and into his shirt sleeves. The feel of his hot blood against her skin made her stomach twist with nausea.

Mayor Abner and Frank were called forward. The Vicar in turn took their hands and drew a thin gash across them. 'Shake' he ordered, they obeyed. Frank withdrawing his hand and turning quickly to shake Sebastian's. The Mayor spread his bloody palm towards Lacey, his fingers puckered and peeling. The skin lined in slivers of white flesh. He kept his tattoo out of sight, facing the floor. She observed her own coming up to shake his, as though she had no control over it, as though it were not connected to her body. His hand, unlike his son's, was freezing cold. It felt like plunging your arm into the lake in winter. The chill ran all the way up to her shoulder. She pulled away, but his fingers gripped hers like a python, squeezing tightly, not wanting to let her go. She looked up at his face to see his eyes closed, his lips parted grotesquely. Lacey twisted her hand out of his grip. A few flecks of blood landed on her dress.

Lacey let her bleeding hand fall to her side, not accepting an usher's offer of a handkerchief. The Vicar intoned another prayer. Lacey heard not a word. The ceremony was over. Beneath the thick, heavy arch of a hundred white orchids, to the ringing of the church bells, the pair left the building. The villagers lined the streets throwing rose petals and rice at the couple. Neither bride nor groom smiled.

The party walked the short distance, holding lanterns upon sticks, to the Mayor's manor. The lights a glowing serpent that wended its way along Main Street and up the hill. Sebastian held her hand like a vice, marching ahead of the villagers. Even when her feet faltered on the uneven ground he persisted, pulling her along like a child. His walk was so quick and determined a few guests joked behind them that the groom was keen to see his new wife home, perhaps to acquaint her with his bed chamber. Their laughter rippling along the procession.

The Manor looked as though each inch of brickwork had been polished. A lamp had been lit behind every window and fresh blooms planted in the flower boxes. Staff, dressed in pressed, white aprons, hurried back and forth from the side entrance to the garden, carrying jugs of wine. A great fire had been set in the middle of the lawn and it burned fiercely as the guests arrived. Long arms of flames reached up and waved in the darkness. Tall candles were stuck into the ground and between some, at the edge of the woods, a rope was hung like a boundary line, heavy with garlands of more white flowers. They lay in vases on tables, and along the backs of the benches, where the partygoers now sat to enjoy their first glasses of wine. The smell in the air so dense with flowers it stuck in Lacey's throat.

Beyond the light of the fire and the candles, the forest loomed in the darkness. Though the sky wasn't yet black but still a deep, rich blue, a few eager stars already twinkled. The woods however, where there was no light at all, cut a jagged, black line into the sky. The deep mass of trees throbbed with darkness. But the fire, and the candles, and the merriment of the evening was distraction enough for the guests not to feel any unease. The lake was lit with the reflection of the party, and the many-candled windows of the Manor behind. Some unknown manor worker had carefully folded small paper flowers and inside each one placed a candle. They floated out now across the black water, mirroring the stars above.

The wine poured; the band began to play, striking up the first few tentative chords to the sound of cheers. The fiddle player tapped his foot merrily on the flag stones and the villagers began to sway in time. Lacey was stuck to Sebastian's side, as though her dress were sewn to his coat, as he pulled her to and fro to receive the compliments and good wishes of the guests. Each took a kiss from the new bride, Lacey portioned them out as though she were carving pieces of flesh from her own body and feeding it to them. They consumed her greedily. She met them with hollow, glassy eyes, wishing she could pull the veil back over her head and hide from them all.

The party drank and laughed and danced. The revellers applauded as a hog was brought out. It spat and hissed as it turned on the spit, the acrid smoke of burning fat mixing with the perfumed flowers. The two smells merged to create a rich, nauseating odour, and Lacey felt an ominous reflux at the back of her throat. She held her fingers to her lips and took a deep breath, trying to take no air in through her nose. The other guests didn't seem to mind.

Sebastian began to drink his wine as though it were water, throwing his head back and swallowing great gulps. Then he would lick his lips, his eyes full and wet from the alcohol, and hold his cup out for more. Each time Lacey made a move to pull away from him, for she hadn't yet seen her father or sister, his arm would grip her tighter, the corset of her dress digging painfully into her waist. She scanned the party, searching in vain for Bella, but try though she might she couldn't find her. The faces of the villagers swam in front of her, moving in and out of focus. Their speech and manners diminishing with each poured cup. Their movements clumsier and laughs louder, their cheeks flushed a deep crimson. All strange blurred figures in her nightmare.

Sebastian emptied the last dregs of wine into his mouth. Lacey watched his Adam's apple bobbing inside his wide throat as he swallowed. Then, wiping his mouth with the cuff of his jacket, he turned to her. 'Come' he said, tightening his grip on her waist and pulling her towards the Manor. The crowd around seemed not to notice their departure, but through the gathering Lacey saw the men of the council standing either side of the doorway. The eyes of Professor Arnott, Mr Lewis, Doctor Prior, the Vicar and Commander Kinch too, watched as she passed them. The sight caused Lacey a new, deeper fear. Each of their faces taut with an eager anticipation, their necks twisting as she went. Lacey returned their looks with horror.

As they stepped through the French windows the noises of the party immediately fell away. Taking her by the hand he pulled her up the wide staircase that wrapped around the wall to their left. 'Wait Sebastian, wait.' She said, leaning away from him, 'my sister, I haven't yet seen my sister.' He ignored her, his hold unflinching as he continued up the stairs. His determination scaring her. 'Where is Mateo?' She cried out, 'I have married you Sebastian. I'm yours now, tell me where he is.' She tried to pull her hand away, but he only squeezed harder, his stride unwavering.

He grunted, more in frustration than in the effort and said under his breath 'you are not mine quite yet.'

The top of the stairs met a long corridor. Ancestral portraits, hanging from the walls, glared down at them in gloomy distain. Sour faced men peered out irritably. One perched atop a horse looking angry, one posed with his sword in hand looking angry, another sat in a library looking angry, his bony fingers clasped around a thick, dusty book.

At the end of the corridor the couple came to a door, turning the ornate polished handle, Sebastian pulled his wife inside. The room was dark and, blinking to make out her surroundings, she felt him push her shoulder, she stumbled forward. Suddenly with a dry rasp a match was lit at the other end of the room. Nanny's figure stood by the window. Even in the golden light of the match her face was grey. She leaned forward, igniting a candle on the table. Lacey wondered how long she had been sitting alone in the dark room. She picked up the candle and walked towards them.

'Go wash your hands and face Sebastian, give us a moment so that I might make your bride pretty for you.' With a huff, Sebastian did as he was told, leaving to room.

'Sit.' Nanny ordered as, turning from Lacey, she walked to the dressing table taking a small vial from the drawer. Sitting on the edge of the bed Lacey watched her, her own breath shaking in her chest. Using the tip of her finger the old woman dabbed the ointment onto her skin then held her finger to Lacey's throat. Lacey flinched away.

'It is only perfume' she said, holding her eye. Lacey leaned tentatively forward, offering her neck to her, allowing her to smear a little of the potent mixture on either side. Lacey's eyes stinging at the strength of it.

'Nanny?' Said Lacey slowly, 'do you know?'

Nanny pulled a comb from the pocket of her dress and began to brush the stray hairs from Lacey's plait. She didn't answer, it was as if Lacey hadn't spoken. Lacey began to shake, her lip quivering, Nanny's hand still brushing her hair. A sob broke from Lacey's mouth.

'No tears,' Nanny said curtly. 'You don't want to ruin your makeup.'

Sebastian re-entered the room. 'She's ready,' said Nanny, standing and picking up the candle. 'I will take the light, you will be wanting a little darkness.' Not catching Lacey's eye she pulled the door gently closed behind her.

As Lacey's vision adjusted to the little light there was that fell from the window she felt her throat tighten. Sebastian sat heavily in a chair in the corner, reaching down and fumbling with the buckle on his boots, she heard the metal clinking between his clumsy fingers, he swore beneath his breath.

'Where is Mateo?' She repeated once more, trying not to let him hear the shaking in her voice.

Sebastian in his frustration sighed and dropped the boot, 'what is it about the carpenter that thrills you? Please, answer me honestly. I have spoken to him many times and I simply cannot fathom what he has that enthrals you. He is a half destitute gypsy orphan with a house that stinks of piss and fish guts. I simply cannot understand, it is surely not his wit.'

'He is my friend. You wouldn't understand.'

'So you would marry him? If you had the liberty to choose.'

'I...' Lacey thought, unable to concentrate, 'I don't know.'

'Then that is your answer. Had you the option you still wouldn't choose him.'

'I cannot even imagine having the freedom to choose. That is why I don't know, because I cannot even begin to fathom it.

When you have all your choice taken from you, you cannot even imagine what you would do if it was given back.'

'Choice is just an illusion.' Sebastian spat, 'who really has the command of their own destiny? None of them out there,' he gestured angrily at the window, through which the noise of the party could be faintly heard.

'They are free,' she said.

'They are *sheep!*' He yelled furiously, the vain in his neck now red and pulsating. 'If they have a choice then look what they are doing with it! Getting pissed every night at The Golden Tavern, waking every morning to work for pennies only to spend it in the pub the following night, just to get pissed again. They are born penniless, they build a few houses, catch some fish, or bring corn in from the field, then they die penniless. It goes round and round forever. That is not freedom.' He stopped, his breathing heavy and uneven from his outburst.

Lacey spoke slowly and softly, 'I don't think you know what freedom is either Sebastian.' Then with a realisation she said, 'I don't think you really know what is happening here. Do you?' His face was covered in shadow and he bent it now to rest in his hands. She continued, 'I know sometimes it seems as though you have no choice-'

He cut her off abruptly, his voice tight and cruel, 'there is no choice!'

'Do you even know why he has taken Mateo? Do you even know what your father has done? He is an evil man!' She shouted, panic spiking her voice.

Immediately Sebastian stood and kicked back off the chair, which fell onto the carpet behind him, in one stride he crossed the space between them. He reached for her shoulders. Throwing her arms in front of her she smacked him away. For a moment they fought in the semi darkness, her arms flailing, trying to fight him off. She was like a cornered cat, her hands desperately trying in vain to land a strike.

When the blow to her face came, the power of it astonished her. Her head snapped to the side, stunned, she could no longer hear anything. She blinked in shock then the world tipped onto its side. A rushing, white pain spread across her face as she fell onto the bed with inevitable heaviness. Blinking like a dying fish, she lay still. Her eyes on the window where the firelight from the party downstairs came through the gap in the curtains. She could no longer hear the noises from outside, only the throbbing charge of blood in her ears. The pressure on one side of her face was so strong she wondered if perhaps he still had his hand on her and was pushing her head against the bed. But, moving her eyes upward, she saw he didn't, both his hands were busy fumbling with his fastenings in the darkness. A slow sheet of blind, numbing dread drew over Lacey as she lay with her cheek pressed against the soft linen, her still booted feet hanging inches off the carpet.

A glass tumbler sitting on a side table across the room began to shake. The water inside rippling. Eventually it tipped, landing noiselessly on the padded carpet. The water pooling unnaturally, beginning to snake across the room towards where she lay on the bed. The ivy growing on the wall outside pushed through the window, causing a narrow splinter on the glass in the top right pane. The sound of it cracking muffled by the thick velvet curtains. Sebastian leaned in close to her, his breath smelled sweet and foul, like mouldy fruit.

She wanted to tell him his breath smelt. She wanted to tell him that, if she could have, she would have married Mateo. She wanted to tell him that really she was just a girl. A girl who wanted more than anything to be at home, safe with her family.

She wanted to tell him that though she had tried for years to suppress the memory, she could remember being held in her mother's arms. She could remember the feeling of her mother's hair falling down onto her face. She could see the sunlight now, through those strands of hair. She could feel them stick to the tears on her face when she would hold her after a fall. She wanted to tell him that even though they had come far down a road neither of them wanted to be on, she was still that girl.

But she had no words, and no mouth with which to speak them. Between slow blinks she saw the light through the gap in the curtain and imagined it was sunlight falling between the trees in the woods. She imagined herself lying there, watching the leaves swaying gently on the branches. When the wind blew they sounded just like the sea. She closed her eyes and the small part of Lacey that couldn't escape to the woods, the part of her that was still in the bedroom, braced itself.

CHAPTER TWENTY SIX

If Lacey hadn't had her eyes squeezed so tightly shut, she might have seen the door open and a figure appear in the light. Its shadow fell long and clear across the back of the man in the bed. For a moment, the silhouette took in the scene. The limp bodied woman in the white dress, lying across the mattress, the arched backed man above her, fiddling with his trousers. The figure grabbed a candlestick from the table to its right and crossed the room. Then, without hesitation, it raised its arm and swung the object down in an unflinching blow.

A hard crack sounded out in the dark room. Then with a low, animalistic grunt, Sebastian collapsed on top of Lacey. Beneath him, she held every muscle in her body tight and kept her eyes clamped shut. The only thing moving was her heart, which beat so incessantly inside her chest it hurt. She lay suspended in terror, unable to move her body or even open her eyes. Then, in the black, she heard a voice. Like a match being lit in the darkness.

'Lacey!?' It said urgently in a hushed whisper.

Lacey's eyes shot open. On top of her lay Sebastian, heavy as a sack of earth. She stayed frozen beneath him. Then something dropped into her eye. Sebastian's blonde locks had fallen across her cheek, and something else, something wet and warm, was dripping from them and falling onto her face. She blinked.

'Lacey?' the voice came again, its owner stood somewhere nearby, but somehow it sounded so far away. She half thought she was imagining it. Besides, whoever it was, Lacey still had no voice with which to answer them. She couldn't yet manage to form words. Whatever was dripping into her eyes was filling her field of vision and blinding her. She attempted to blink it away but with no success, she freed an arm and began to wipe at her face. She pulled her hand away, she could see a little now. The light from the door fell in a golden strip and it illuminated her white gloved hand. Turning it slowly, she gently rubbed her thumb against the tips of her fingers. They were covered in something shiny and black. She stared in puzzlement. She suddenly had the intense feeling of déjà vu, which slipped quickly and uncontrollably into dread. Where before had she seen blood on her fingertips?

Then a sound came again. Lay - see, Lay - see. Something in the room moved and Lacey's eyes transferred focus from her fingers to the figure in front of her. 'Bella?' She whispered. Bella's face, suddenly visible, was bathed in the light of the hallway. She looked intensely afraid. Lacey stared at her blank-faced, her eyes travelled down Bella's arm, at the end of which she was holding a gold candlestick dripping in red black blood. It fell in small taps on the plush carpet.

Then, finally, Lacey looked down at the man lying limp on top of her. Suddenly the situation came into a sharp plunging focus. A rush of panic rose in her chest and with both her hands she moved to push Sebastian off, her legs kicking and flailing against him. She wriggled and squirmed but he was a large man and she struggled beneath his dead weight. The two bodies entwined, fell clumsily off the bed. Bella reached and pulled Lacey free. But, half stumbling, her legs gave way and she fell on the floor once more.

Her breath came in short, painful bursts, and the pressure in her head caused her vision to swim. She reached out for Bella one moment, then back at her own face the next. Feeling, in horror, the wet blood still on her, she rubbed violently at it, picking up the skirts of her dress and wiping them across herself. Bella, sensing her sister slipping into a frenzied panic, wrapped her arms around her, and Lacey began to cry. Her body shook as though she were freezing. Between choking sobs, she tried to speak, but the words were washed away in the tears.

'Be calm, be calm,' Bella whispered.

Eventually Lacey managed to wrestle herself from the brink of shock. Her breathing calmed and, sniffing back a few tears, she wiped her eyes and looked around. Sebastian lay dead on the ground beside her. His head was cracked open and, if the girls had doubted his mortality, the sight of his brains had lain those doubts to rest. She stared at him in a mute surprise.

'I overheard the Barrick Brothers talking downstairs,' said Bella. 'They said they had kidnapped Mateo at Sebastian's orders. Held him hostage. Then they said that you were to be,' she paused, her voice shaking 'sacrificed.' Lacey closed her eyes again. 'I came up to check on you, then I saw what he was doing.' Bella's words stuck in her throat.

'So, he is dead,' Lacey whispered, her voice now flat and emotionless.

'Yes,' said Bella, unable to look at the body.

Lacey sniffed, then reopening her eyes, stared down at him. Her face set in blank detachment. The strangeness of having him standing above her yelling and hitting, alive with anger one moment, and then watching his insides soaking into the carpet the next. His eyes as dead as the wolves downstairs. Like a flame he had been so quickly and so finally snuffed out. She felt bile rise in her throat and with an effort forced it down. She looked at Bella, her mind focused, 'there is much I must tell you.'

'Then speak quick, for we haven't a lot of time.'

Then as though untying a corset, pulling the lace from each eyelet in time, Lacey picked the whole thing apart for Bella. She talked sparingly, but unlike at the bakery she was able to lay out the facts methodically. To the softened sound of the fiddle and laughter from the party below, Lacey revealed the full story to her sister; emptying it out in front of her, until she was finally done. The feeling of having unloaded herself of all these secrets made her feel suddenly weak. Bella stood and crossed the floor, peering out of the window, her face pressed close to the curtain.

'The Mayor will be up here before long I'm sure. We must be gone before he is.'

At the thought of him downstairs a feeling of dread returned to Lacey and she held her head in her hands. She was able to smell Sebastian's blood now. Metallic and repulsive, as though he had already begun to rot. 'They will come up,' she said shakily, 'they will come up, we will be discovered and they will hang me for it.' She felt the fingers of hysteria tighten around her once more. She pursed her lips, her breath whistling. At once she was a child again. She saw her mother's feet suspended in the air, the rope taut. She pushed her palms against her eyeballs. 'I don't think I can do what needs to be done.'

'Yes, you can.'

'No, Bella I need to finish this, and I can't.' She bit her lip, holding back the tears, 'I can't.'

'Nonsense.' Said Bella, her matter of fact tone sounding strangely incongruous in the situation, 'they haven't won yet sister. You are strong.' She said, pointing a finger at her. 'Stronger than any man, stronger than anyone. I know it seems a hard thing to do to be brave right now, well that is because it is hard. I won't say it isn't. But most things worth doing are hard.' She reached out and putting her hand on the back of Lacey's head, drew her forehead to hers. 'You must take all the courage you have left, gather it from every corner of yourself and hold it tight now.'

Lacey's breathing slowed. 'Yes' she said.

'I'm sorry,' whispered Bella, 'I'm so sorry. I'm sorry I refused to see there was something terribly wrong. I didn't listen to you, I wouldn't let myself.' Now was her turn for her voice to shake, it trembled as though it may crack.

'I didn't tell you,' said Lacey.

'You told me every day, I just wasn't listening. I wouldn't open my eyes. Well,' she said taking a deep breath and patting her palms on her knees, 'they are open now.'

Lacey felt a surge of courage, for the first time all night she felt something close to being herself. She wrapped her arms around Bella's neck and squeezed, kissing the side of her cheek.

'Lacey, you will strangle me!'

'Sorry,' she said, releasing her.

'Now, tell me, what is the plan?'

Lacey took a deep breath. 'They have Mateo,' she said, 'they have him captured and I don't know where he is.'

'Good thing that I do then isn't it?' said Bella.

'What? Where? Tell me!'

'Well when I heard Lek and Bran talking downstairs I could hardly believe what I was hearing. So, I stood a little closer to them so that I might hear better. I suppose eavesdropping is wrong really but-'

'Bella! Where is he?' Lacey asked urgently.

'In the woods. In a crypt, they said. I don't know what it means, that's all I could make out.'

Lacey didn't hear the second half of what her sister said, a feeling like falling into cold water came upon her. She closed her eyes, the image of the crypt came to her. Dead cold and silent in the woods at night. She could feel the stone beneath her fingertips. She could imagine no worse place in the world. And he was there, held captive there, beneath the earth. She opened her eyes. 'I know what to do.'

The two sisters stood at the top of the wide staircase. After the darkness of the room Lacey felt acutely exposed in the well-lit corridor. They waited a moment until no footsteps could be heard below. They crept down a few steps. A group of servants cluttered past below them, carrying trays of food and wine. The two girls pressed themselves tight to the wall and stood very still. If any had cared to look up they would have been discovered immediately, but none did, and they continued on. At the bottom of the stairs they paused, behind them the staff worked noisily in the kitchens, ahead the party continued in full swing. The bodies of the villagers flickered and waved behind the glass.

'Don't let anyone go in the room.' Lacey whispered.

Bella nodded, 'please be careful.'

'I will, I won't be long. I know the way, even at night.'

'I think-' A loud roar of celebration came from outside, Bella shot a nervous look over her shoulder at the party. 'The way they spoke, the Barrick brothers, it sounded like they would return to check on him soon. They may already be there.'

'I understand. Go now, I will return before long.' They exchanged a brief look, then Bella, smoothing her neat bun and standing up straight, walked out into the party. Lacey watched her a moment, before turning to leave by the side door. She stopped suddenly, a thought crossing her mind and she darted back towards the entrance to the cellar.

A few minutes later Lacey walked through the darkness of the woods. Her bloodied wedding dress blowing in the wind, a long, grey blunderbuss at her side. The moon had slipped out from behind the clouds and the light lay in silvery slivers across her path. She breathed heavily, not bothering to stop at any of the forest sounds that usually struck fear in her heart, they didn't trouble her now. She concentrated, wary of losing her way in the dark.

Her pace was quick, and her direction was good, before too long she came upon her marker. The haunted tree loomed out of the gloom ahead of her. Its face desperate and fearful in the darkness, she gave it only a sideways glance as she passed. Suddenly, in the black, came a small flash of yellow light. Lacey immediately dropped to her knees, crouching behind a tree. Slowly leaning out she could see the face of Bran Barrick, lit by the match held against the pipe in his mouth. He blew it out quickly. But each time he took a puff, his wide, dumb face was illuminated by the burning embers. His eyes looked tired and Lacey wondered if he hadn't already had much to drink at the wedding. Between draws on his pipe he stroked his hands across his jaw, feeling at the stubble. His fingertips occasionally picked a scab where he had cut himself shaving.

He sat unsteadily on a tree stump and blew the smoke out in long, lazy breaths. The more Lacey watched him, the surer she was he was intoxicated. The way he swayed as he stared up at the stars through the trees, below his breath she thought she could hear him humming a tune, one the fiddler had played earlier in the night. He stood up and walked with a staggering gait a little way from the crypt door. He was fumbling with the belt of his trousers. The clink of the buckle sounded with horrible familiarity in Lacey's mind, but she pushed the thought down.

Bran stood with his back to her, the noise of his stream hitting the leaves below. Slowly Lacey crept out towards him. She held the Blunderbuss by her side like a bat, her hands gripping the barrel. Her feet softly tiptoed through the undergrowth, taking care not to make a sound. Her white boots moved gently through the leaves, doing her best not to disturb them. She was almost upon him now. She could see his tufts of unruly hair poking out of his bent head, and in the air, she could smell the thick scent of wine on his breath, mingling with his piss. Lacey swallowed and pulled her arm far back behind her shoulder, ready to swing down.

Suddenly two things happened at exactly the same time. The crypt door opened to her left, light spilled out into the darkness and a loud, deep voice yelled 'HEY!' Every inch of Lacey was electrified with panic, she shot back like a frightened cat. Her heart threatened to leap from her throat. Bran turned his head towards the voice as his brother, Lek pulled himself up from the open door. Then, as though sensing her more than hearing her, Bran began to turn the other way to look behind his shoulder, exactly where Lacey was. As quickly and noiselessly as she could she sprang back into the darkness and ducked down behind a tree.

'What was tha- Arghh!' He cried out feeling the warm liquid soak into his trouser. The shock had distracted him, he buttoned himself up and shook the leg to try and rid himself of some of the moisture.

'Hey!' Lek repeated, 'I'm talking to you!' And crossing to his brother, he hit him hard with an open hand on the back of the head.

'Stop!' Bran barked, drunkenly raising an arm in defence. 'I were just havin' a smoke.'

'Get back in there,' Lek said leaning down so his face was so close to his brother's that their noses almost touched. Though skinnier and shorter than his brother, Lek had a nimbleness that was more than a match for Bran's dog-like strength. 'The Mayor wanted it done before the end of the night.'

'I don't wanna go back down there,' said Bran, sitting down again and fumbling with his matches and pipe. 'I don't wanna be out here at all. It ain't right out here.' He peered into the darkness, 'I thought I heard something. Something ain't holy about these woods.'

'The most unholy thing in these woods is us Bran' said Lek, looking up at him. 'Besides there is far more to fear if we don't follow the Mayor's direction. I would take a Forest Beast over the Mayor any day.'

Bran laughed at that, a low, barking laugh. Lek snatched the pipe and matches from his hand and lit it himself.

Less than a few yards from them Lacey crouched against a tree. She concentrated on breathing as slowly and quietly as possible, though her lungs burnt with fear. She gripped the gun in both her hands and tried desperately to think of her next move.

'Come, I have the words the Mayor uses,' said Lek after a few minutes, tucking the pipe into his coat pocket. 'I wanna see if they work.'

'I'm not wearing the robe Lek. I don't care what you say I'm not wearing the bloody robe.'

Lek put an arm around his brother, then half pushed him down back towards the crypt, 'Yes you bloody are,' he said, and the two disappeared beneath the ground.

CHAPTER TWENTY SEVEN

Lacey waited a few moments in the silence to be sure she was alone, before standing up and walking out towards the crypt. Slowly she opened the door, wincing as its hinges creaked. Then, by the light that shone from within, she crouched down and loaded the blunderbuss. She pulled the hammer to half cock and poured a little of the gunpowder into the pan. Though her father preferred a rod to a gun in matters of hunting, you didn't grow up in the Lakelands without knowing a little of the workings of a firearm. The remaining gunpowder she poured carefully down the barrel.

She slipped through the crypt door, as quiet as the night, and climbed down the stairs. With every step she took the light grew, drawing up the shadows around her. She began to hear the brothers' voices again, but though she was quite close she couldn't make out their words. One hand on the gun, and the other feeling at the brick on the wall, she made her descent. With only a few steps remaining, she stopped. Their voices were clearer now, they were less than a few feet from where she stood. Crouching low and holding her breath, Lacey poked her head round the corner of the low-ceilinged crypt. As quick as a whip, she retrieved it again, leaning back against the cold brick and swallowing hard. The scene was still emblazoned behind her closed eyes.

Mateo lay on his back, his arms and legs bound, on the stone slab. His eyes were closed and around his mouth a cut of material had been tied as a gag. He was shirtless and the shadows around his ribs were deep in the candlelight. Lacey squeezed her eyes tight, trying to remember if she could see him breathing. But she hadn't looked long enough. Standing at both end of him were two hooded figures. Their black cloaks hung loose around them. One, she thought it might be Lek, stood, with his back to her, above Mateo's feet. He held a scrap of paper in his hand, from which he was reciting, in a low, quiet voice. All of this struck a deep horror inside Lacey, but none as much as the long dagger, clasped between Bran's hands.

Lek continued to read, only now his voice rose, and he began to pick up speed. Looking out again, Lacey could see Bran raise his arms above his head, the dagger glinting in the candlelight. Lacey fully pulled back the hammer on the gun. It made a sharp click, but Lek's voice was too loud now for it to be heard. She breathed deeply, once, twice, then she spun round into the room and raised the gun.

'Stop!' she cried, pointing the weapon at the men, who stared at her in astonishment. Lacey kept the gun raised high. Neither man moved. On the table Mateo's eyes shot open and he began kicking and wriggling against the stone, his voice desperately moaning behind the gag. Lacey kept her eyes on the two brothers. 'Stop,' she said again, this time quieter. But there was something in her voice, a fault line of weakness. She was asking, not telling, and the two men could smell the fear on her. Bran's cow eyes looked across at his brother.

'She doesn't know how to shoot a gun.' Lek said, then quickly returning his brother's gaze, he spat the words, 'kill him.'

Bran stiffened and braced to swing the dagger down, Mateo's eyes widened in silent terror as his feet squirmed desperately against his bindings. Lacey pulled the trigger. The shot was like an explosion in the small room. Bran flew back into the wall behind him, then sunk to the ground. Smoke, and the strong, acrid stench of gunpowder, filled the crypt. Lacey had staggered backwards from the recoil but had still managed to stay standing. The impact of the gun's barrel against her chest had felt like a punch. She stood for a moment, dazed, the shot ringing painfully in her ears in an endless, incessant loop. The smoke settled slightly and, slumped against the opposite wall, she saw Bran. His arms lay limp at his sides, his head lolled lifeless against his chest. A wide, red circular stain spread across his stomach.

Suddenly, out of the smoke, came Lek's figure, running at Lacey, she raised the gun once more and turned it to him. Though she knew a little about firearms, in her panic, her knowledge abandoned her, one piece of information in particular. Notably, that once fired, the blunderbuss would have to be reloaded. She pulled the trigger, bracing herself for the recoil, but this time no explosion. No bullets came, only a small, dead click. She pulled it again, and again and again. But nothing happened. Lek roared and threw himself at her, his eyes red from the smoke and wild with anger. Just as he was upon her, she sidestepped, narrowly avoiding him. He hit the brick badly, there was a dull, crunching sound and he spun round, blood pouring thickly from his nose. He swung his arms, trying to hit Lacey, who, having abandoned the gun, was running towards Mateo. But Lek's long reach caught her, his bony fist clasped her hair, pulling it loose from its plaits, tugging her painfully backwards.

'You witch!' He snarled, 'you dirty little witch!'

Lacey kicked and struggled against him. He pulled her down, her knees dropping with a bruising thud onto the floor. He wrapped his fist within her hair, tightening it, she could feel the strands tearing from the roots. 'Damn you!' He cursed at her, his blood and spit peppering her face. Lacey leant her neck back, then with all her might, brought her head crashing forward, hitting him square on the nose. He recoiled, but there was enough time, and she did it again, hearing once more the grinding crunch of bone in his face. Lek cried out in terrible pain, like the howl of a wounded animal. Releasing her, he stumbled backwards, both hands held over his nose. He sat heavily on the floor, leaning his head back, crimson blood flowing copiously between his fingers and onto his thin goatee.

Lacey seized the opportunity and scrambled across the floor towards the stone slab. Mateo, meanwhile, was straining like a mad man against his ties, trying in vain to release himself, his wrists purple and swollen from where he pulled. Lacey ran to him, but in her panic, didn't even know where to start. She reached for his hands, then seeing how tightly bound they were, went to his feet. Her fingers desperately trying to loosen them. Behind her she could feel Lek was starting to recover, she could hear him pulling himself up.

Mateo began jerking and shaking with an increased vigour. He was whining and mumbling behind the gag, his head nodding violently in one direction. Lacey stopped and looked in his eyes, he looked at her, then across at the corner of the room. She followed his gaze to the lifeless body of Bran, lying lame on the floor. The dagger, gold in the candlelight, lay beside him. At exactly that moment Mateo made another muted cry, Lacey turned and Lek was upon her again. He tackled her to the floor, she fell painfully on her side. He pulled himself up above her and with a tightly clenched fist, aimed a punch at her stomach. It didn't land, his robe hindering him with all the loose material.

'I'm going to kill you.' He hissed as he struggled to free his arm.

Lacey, beneath him, began to wriggle towards the knife. She wasn't much more than a few inches from it now. Close enough to smell the stain on Bran's trouser leg. She stretched, her fingertips whispered past the hilt. But it was too late. Lek, having freed his right arm from his robe, managed to land a hit right on her stomach. It was a forceful blow, she could feel every one of his bony knuckles smashing into her. All the breath was knocked out of Lacey and like a rag doll she doubled over. She lay beneath him, sucking at the air, unable to breath, she felt for a second that somehow she might drown. Her lips opened and closed silently as she squirmed in pain, her arms wrapped around her waist protectively. Lek sat back on his heels and pinched the bridge of his nose. He breathed heavily, and on each exhale sighed 'damn you.' Then slowly, reaching for help from the brick wall, he pulled himself up.

With his free hand he untied his robes, the folds of loose material falling like a curtain, at his feet. Mateo continued to writhe and silently scream in the corner.

'Be patient gypsy boy, you'll get your turn. Just got to deal with the witch first,' said Lek as he spat a glob of blood on the ground. He drew back his leg and kicked Lacey in the stomach. She made a small, deflated, wheezing sound. Half cry, half sigh.

'I've always hated you Lacey. You and your sister, you think you are too good for us by half. Lord knows where you get it from. The daughter of a witch! Bran and I almost died in shock when Sebastian said he was to marry you. Poor Bran, what an idiot.' He snorted and spat once again, a spray of red mist. 'Our mammy always did say he'd catch a bullet. Still, she'd turn in her grave if she knew it was at the hand of the uppity Miss Lacey. Always with her nose in a book, always looking down on others. Oh well, look at you now. You will die like a dog on the floor. It is a shame, because to be fair you ain't too bad to look at.'

'You are a murderer Lek Barrick,' wheezed Lacey, 'don't stand above me when it is you with blood on your hands.'

'It is because of you I have blood on my hands! Because of your filthy meddling. Talking to the stranger. The boat taking the Morgan girl's body to the Island was seen by him. They had to throw her overboard, she was never meant to wash up. He might have seen it, we couldn't have him talking. But you couldn't help yourself. That's why I was involved. I was never part of the rest of this.' He yelled, gesturing around the crypt. 'That was the Mayor and his men.'

'What men?' She asked, feebly pulling herself onto her elbows. 'Tell me Lek. If you are to kill me you might as well tell me. Do you mean the councilmen?'

He stood a moment, contemplating, running the back of his thumb against his jaw until finally he said 'Yes.' From the corner of her eye Lacey felt Mateo look at her, but she wouldn't take her eyes off Lek. 'All of them. They're under his command, he's powerful.'

'Is that why they obey him? Fear?'

'He came to them when he found a book, years ago. He had obtained some mystical powers. Power over water. I don't know now whether it was fear or greed or both that compelled them to follow him. He promised them money, protection of their businesses. He has a plan. The next step will bring powers far beyond what he has now.'

'So you all murdered for him.'

'The doc poisons the brats, gives them sweets with a sleeping draft inside. There's no coming back from that. Then they bring them here and the Mayor says a prayer as they go. That's how he gets their power see. They pray and chant and cut them with a knife. Not me though. We,' he stopped himself, casting a glance a Brans lifeless body, 'I do other things, useful things.'

'Like what?'

'The Mayor let me pick one.' He said this with a kind of sneering pride. 'I picked the girl.'

'What girl?'

'The girl. The orphan.'

'No.' Whispered Lacey whispered, 'no, Jessica's in the Upper Lakes, with her aunt.'

Lek chuckled, 'I knew you and your gypsy would be snooping around after her, so I told the foreman, and a couple of others to say that. Cost me a round in the Inn.' His foot kicked out one last time, hitting her temple. Making the crypt explode with stars.

'No,' breathed Lacey, the room spinning, the corners twisting in on themselves. Looking up through the pain she saw again on the wall the row of plaques, the panel having broken open when Bran hit it. Each engraved with a girl's name. The last, blank one, she had seen on her first visit, had been filled. Her vision dimmed, her eyes closing. As she read her own name Lacey's body stopped moving and she fell back against the ground.

Lacey lay still and silent, the gap between her half-opened eye lids showing only white. He crouched over her then, and with his hands wrapped around her neck, pulled her body up so that her face was close to his. She had known he thought her pretty. Before he had hated her he had liked her. But she had shown no signs of sharing his feelings and he had turned cruel. He seemed almost grateful when her mother was executed so he could pour his rejection into that hatred. He squeezed her throat, watching her lips part at the pressure. His own lips pulling back from his teeth in a snarl. Mateo's feet kicked wildly at the stone slab. His desperate cries muffled.

But knowing that Lek thought her pretty, Lacey had guessed he wouldn't kill her by kicking her to death. He wasn't the type of man to kick a woman to death. Much more likely he would want to hold her in his hands, to squeeze the life from her. To be able to watch her closely, so he might see how prettily her lips swelled when he wrung her neck. Lacey knew all of this, so while he talked and spat and called her a witch, she had slowly reached for the knife behind her back.

Lek's snake like fingers tightened on her throat. Quick as a flash her hand came up and hit him hard at the top of his spine. The look on his face was one of pure shock, almost amazement. He immediately released her and sat back, landing heavily on the stone. The dagger remained inside him, sticking out at the top of his spine. His hands came up in wonder to feel at it. This foreign invasion into his body, the strange incongruity of hard steel and soft flesh. Then his whole torso stiffened painfully, as if in cramp. His shoulders arched like an old man, he tried to bat the knife away as if it were a wasp. But the blood poured out of him and his hands, with every movement, grew weak. His movements slow and clumsy. After a moment or two his arms fell to his lap. Then he looked Lacey right in the eye.

'Witch.' He said plainly. As though it were her name.

She held his stare, this time unafraid. 'Yes.' She answered. And with that he fell back against the stone floor, and didn't move again.

The crypt fell silent. Lacey looked from Lek, whose blood was slowly spreading in a puddle across the floor, to Bran, whose dead cow eyes stared lifelessly at his own shoes. Her pain was suddenly so acute she thought she might be sick, she grasped her side, beneath the bloodied wedding dress a bruise the colour of blackberry juice blossomed across her stomach. Perhaps, she thought, she could lie down, just for a moment. She could curl up in the corner and be as still and quiet as the Barrick brothers. She looked up and saw Mateo's wide, brown, tear filled eyes staring down at her, and she knew she couldn't. With an effort, she stood and hauled herself towards him, then stopping halfway, her hand raised slowly in the air as though remembering something, she turned and walked back. It took a moment to retrieve the knife from Lek, but with the toe of her boot on the side of his head, she managed.

The gag around Mateo's mouth gave the strangest impression of a smile, she tilted his face towards her, and with the knife, cut it off. His face hollow, and paler than she had ever seen it, shone in the candlelight, his skin cold to the touch. Brown hair stuck with sweat around his clammy forehead. With her fingertips, she felt at the skin around his mouth, which was rubbed red raw and sore. He stared at her with fearful, shadowy eyes.

'How badly are you hurt?' He asked weakly as she set about cutting the binding on his hands and feet.

'I will live,' she said.

Mateo made a sound then like a whimper and she thought he might cry, but instead it turned into a yell. A great, guttural, animal scream, like nothing she had ever heard him make. A painful mix of frustration and love and fear at watching her fight for her life. It filled every corner of the room, and only stopped when his breath finished in a hoarse rasp. Lacey looked at him, her eyes filling with tears. His gaze fell to her dress, where across her chest a wide flower of blood had bloomed, and further down on her skirts the frenzy of bloodied finger marks, where she had desperately tried to wipe her hands and face. Mateo sat up, taking her by the shoulders.

'Whose blood is this?' He demanded. She didn't understand the question at first. He shook her gently 'Lacey! Whose blood is this? Is it yours?'

Dazed, Lacey looked down and remembered. 'Sebastian's,' she said, 'it is Sebastian's blood.'

Mateo swallowed and in a cold, quiet voice asked, 'did he hurt you?'

'He tried.'

'Is he dead?'

She nodded.

'Quite dead Lacey? You are sure of it?' He bent then, to catch her eye.

'Yes,' she whispered, 'he is dead.'

Mateo stayed silent for a moment, his brow furrowed, trying to organise his thoughts. He was, to her, transparent, she could see them pass across his mind like clouds in the sky. So when a particular one came to him, she knew what he was going to ask even before he voiced it. Her heart thumped inside her chest. 'Have you taken the blood vow?' Beneath his dark, fearful, gypsy brows, his eyes shone in the lantern light. 'Are you married?' She said nothing. She could tell by his face that he knew. Her silence was answer enough. Without thinking she bent down and kissed him.

Not tenderly or sentimentally but forcefully. As though wanting to make certain he were really there. Wanting to feel his face against her own so desperately she would be grateful for it to bruise her. She leant against him, holding his head in her hands. He reached out and held her arm. The softness of his touch seemed almost as arresting to her as the violence of the blow's she had endured that night. She inhaled deeply and in the dark, damp, dusty crypt he smelt like pinecones, and chopped wood and rainwater in glass jars.

'Can you walk?' she asked.

Mateo nodded.

With effort she helped him down off the stone slab and together they made their way up the stairs. At the top Lacey glanced up at the closed door then stopped and turned to him. He seemed grateful for the rest, leaning against the wall. 'Mateo, if one of us is caught, the other one must run for help. Not try and fight, just run.' She held his stare forcing him to look at her, 'you promise?'

'I do.' He whispered. Lacey began to move, but stopping her Mateo said, 'If I am killed-'

'You won't be,' interrupted Lacey, walking on. His hand on her wrist stopped her.

'If I am killed' he continued 'please bury me with my parents and my sister. I want to rest beside them. Do you promise?' He managed a weak, shaking smile.

Lacey tried to look at him but found that she couldn't. Feeling the prick of tears behind her eyes she said, 'I do,' and kissing him swiftly on the lips, turned and pushed the crypt door open.

CHAPTER TWENTY EIGHT

The black hood had been waiting for Lacey. She had only hallway emerged from the crypt door when it was thrown over her face. It was yanked so violently backward she was pulled to the ground. Her neck still bruised from Lek's fingers, exploded in pain. Immediately she kicked and writhed like an animal in a trap.

'Run Mateo!' She screamed. Her words cut short with one swift blow to the head.

Minutes later Lacey's eyes flickered open. The hood was so dark there was as much light behind her own eyelids. She could feel the heat of a fire behind her. As she became more conscious she was aware of a pulling ache in both her arms. She moaned in pain. Then, from the dark, there came a low whistle in response. It snaked through the air around her, the tune immediately recognisable, turning her blood to ice. The notes rising and falling.

Don't step foot on Deception Bay
Or your sisters will wash away
Don't step foot on Deception Bay
Or the water will take your daughter

Her head darted pointlessly from left to right, trying to locate the whistler. Then it stopped, the silence grew deafening. She braced herself for another blow.

Without warning the hood was pulled clean from Lacey's head. She saw the forest all around her. The trees flickering in the orange firelight, stretched up into the night sky. Looking up she saw that she was hanging by her arms. They were spread wide, a thick rope tied each hand to the branches of a tree. Her torn, bloody wedding dress hung limply, her feet a few inches from the ground. Lacey pulled against the ropes, but her wrists screamed in agony. Her fingers an unnatural purple, the tips already numb.

Finally Lacey looked around herself, what she saw frightened her even more than the ropes around her wrists had. Five silent figures stood around her in a circle. Their heads hidden beneath large black hoods, their hands clasped before them, each with his fingers wrapped around the stem of a bronze goblet. They made no noise. A violent shiver ran from the base of her spine to the top of her neck.

Mayor Abner stepped forward into her line of sight. He walked slowly, with his back to her. 'Commander,' he said, stopping beside one of the figures.

Kinch stepped forward, taking his hood off. 'Yes sir?' His Watchmen badge just visible below his collar.

'Kill the gypsy boy.' Said the mayor. With the tone of a man ordering a drink.

'No!' Lacey screamed. Both men behaved as if she hadn't made a sound. Kinch gave a nod to the Mayor, then pulling his hood back up, he vanished into the darkness. 'Mayor!' Lacey called.

He turned to her then, his manner soft, almost pleasant. He was happy. His happiness sat badly upon his face. As though his features were not used to it. 'Not yet Lacey' he whispered, as though they shared a secret.

Then addressing the circle, he picked up a pewter jug. 'Now gentlemen, after all our hard work, after all our years of planning, after all our great efforts we have reached the night. We have fought tirelessly and without thanks, well now we shall reap our rewards. Will you join me in a toast?' One by one he filled each figure's glass. Raising his own he declared 'to the councilmen of Lower Lynch.' The men lifted their goblets to the shadow of their hoods and drank.

Whatever poison the Mayor had put in the wine worked almost instantaneously. Sounds of coughing filled the forest. The first hood was ripped off to reveal the tortured fat face of Professor Abbot. His glasses fell from his nose and were immediately crushed beneath one of his stumbling feet. His eyes swelled inside their sockets threatening to burst out. His cheeks flushed purple and red. Beside him Mr Lewis wheezed and spluttered, gasping for air, wearing a look of such horror Lacey physically winced. There was an acrid, burning smell in the air. Where the drink had fallen on the council's robes, it singed the material. The Vicar, having torn his hood from his head, dropped to his knees as if in prayer, his fingers desperately clawing at his throat. The Mayor stood back, appraising his work.

Only one councilman had not removed his hood. He stood watching his peers dying before him. The goblet, still raised to his lips, though not a drop drunk. Slowly drawing the hood from his head Doctor Prior stared at the Mayor.

'How could you?'

Calmly the Mayor answered 'after tonight Doctor I will have no need for any of your help. As a man of logic surely you understand. After this,' he said with a nod towards Lacey, 'I will be all powerful.' There were no more noises coming now from the councilmen. The Vicar finally keeled over in a slump. His eyes stared hopelessly up at an empty sky.

'You devil!' Doctor Prior cried, and with one swift throw he dashed the drink into the air towards the face of the Mayor. With a calm and simple movement, he raised his right hand. Through the pain and the fear, Lacey's mouth fell open in astonishment. The poisoned wine had stopped mid-air. It was suspended a few inches from the Mayor's hand, rippling as though it had hit an invisible pane of glass. Prior, knowing he had lost, lowered his head.

The Mayor extended his arm towards the doctor. The liquid lengthened as though it were a snake. Directing it, he pushed it into Prior's face. The poison went first up his nostrils, forcing him to open his mouth. It rushed into his mouth and filled his throat. His face contorted into an appalling expression of agony. Tears streamed down his cheeks as, still standing, he vibrated in pain. Until finally he dropped dead beside his fellow councilmen.

The only sound left was the soft crackling of the fire behind Lacey. The Mayor smoothed the sleeves of his coat as though brushing the last few minutes off himself and turned on his heels to face her.

'Well Lacey, here we are. Alone at last.' He exhaled, pulling a dagger from his coat. 'I will say you are full of surprises. You made light work of the Barrick brothers. I wonder what Sebastian will say when he learns you killed his favourite drinking partner.' A sneering smile itched at the corner of his mouth. 'There really is no doubt who is the crueller sex.'

'I know,' he spoke, as he walked slowly between the corpses, 'that you like to pretend you are afraid of us. Well I will let you into a little secret, really it is men who are afraid of women. I don't think I have ever said that out loud. There is a kind of freedom in speaking to someone you are about to kill, a kind of privacy you can find nowhere else. Yes, we are terrified of you. It is a little like having a wild dog on a lead. Of course you are the one holding it, controlling it, but you cannot help wondering, occasionally, what it might do, were it to get loose of its collar. Sometimes you think, it might not be a dog after all, it might be a wolf.'

Lacey was only half listening. One side of her mind was fully focused on the fire behind her. She could feel it in a way she had never been able to before. Feel each slither of flame dancing in the air. Each whisper of burning heat. She willed it closer, willed it to the rope around her wrists.

'You don't remember that I took you, do you Lacey?'

Lacey's concentration snapped back from the fire. She stared at him, not allowing him the satisfaction of seeing her surprised. The Mayor continued, 'I always wondered if it was somewhere inside of you, an echo of that day. I'd taken a lot of girls already. A good many years had passed before I moved on to you. You parents were kindly and simple and didn't heed the warnings. Everybody thought it was Forest Beasts. They had left you in the garden on a rug, you sat there like a little lamb. One moment you were there, then you were in my arms within the darkness of the forest. I hadn't yet enlisted the councilmen to help. Nowadays I merely arrive to make the sacrifice of whichever girl they have picked for me. Back then it was more,' he paused, 'intimate. Just you and me walking alone amongst the trees.' His tone was soft, almost wistful. 'We were maybe halfway to the crypt when it happened. You were screaming for your mother, but they all do that. I was carrying you so tightly and you were screaming and I looked down and a spark flew from your eye. I could hardly believe it. Fire Lacey. Fire.' He whispered the last word. A tear welled at the edge of his one persistently watery eye.

'I stopped, but you didn't stop crying; another spark then another. And I looked up and the leaves on their branches bent towards you. I laid you down beside a puddle on the ground and the water swelled and vibrated, it pulled itself from the ditch and ran in your direction. It was... beautiful. I knew then Lacey that I had finally found you. I had finally found what Abiah had sought all those years. I almost cried. It was the simplest and easiest thing to return you home. I held you to my chest and walked back through the woods. I had in mind to say you had crawled from the garden and that I had rescued you in the field. But there was no one to answer to, your parents were already out in the village searching for you. So, as if nothing had happened, I placed you back on your little mat and left you there. But that was foolish of me. Of course your mother had already looked there, she knew something was wrong. She was immediately suspicious. Her instincts about me were too good, and I was never able to shake her off from that day. Still it was worth it, because I had found you.'

'Why didn't you just kill me?' Lacey hissed through clenched teeth, the fire was closer now, the heat pricking at her arms.

'Because you aren't a dog Lacey; you are a wolf. I couldn't have killed you if I tried. Only those who are bound by blood to a multi-elemental witch may kill her and absorb her magic.'

'The blood vow' murmured Lacey, thinking aloud.

The Mayor nodded. 'I wanted to feel the power Abiah so desperately craved. You are a very special witch, the blood of Grace runs inside of you. You can control all elements, the earth, the wind, the water, and the fire. Don't you know this yet?'

The sound of the ivy pushing through the glass in Sebastian's room came to Lacey; she remembered the fire extinguishing itself in the bakery, the boat swerving in the storm, the flowers growing before her eyes through the rock of the cave.

'In order to kill you I had to make you my kin and that is where Sebastian came in. He knew little of my plan, only that it was important to me. I raised him to follow orders and I'm grateful he wasn't born with a curious mind. Besides, fear is a great antidote to curiosity.' Lacey's mind spun, she thought of the meetings the Mayor had held with her father. She thought of Sebastian's obvious reluctance to marry her. Even his words to her that very evening, *Fates greater than yours hang in the balance Lacey.* That is why he had proposed to a baker's daughter, and not one of the girls in the village, who wore silk and perfume and tied their hair with ribbons. He had dragged her down the aisle just as the Mayor had dragged him.

'I've been watching you all these years. I planned it from the first moment I knew.'

He looked up at her, his face shone like a ghoul in the darkness. A sharp, tight grin sliced into his jaw. Beneath the brim of his hat his yellow eyes glowed with madness, his eyelids pulled right back. 'It was all for you. All the girls over the last few years. I had to take more than before, so that I may be strong enough to kill you tonight. It was all for you.'

Suddenly from the woods came the sound of a gunshot. 'Mateo,' Lacey cried desperately, instinctually. Her head twisting in the direction of the noise.

'Kinch always finds his mark' said the Mayor. Satisfaction filling his eyes.

The darkness of the forest around her closed in and she felt something collapse inside her chest, like crumbling stone. A flood of grief forced her head down as she opened her mouth to scream a silent cry. Her eyes clamped tightly shut, her mouth wide in rage and sorrow, like the face of the haunted tree. Her grief pulsated in her head.

Then, from the forest, came another sound. Lacey looked up. Through watery, half closed eyes she saw lights between the trees. In her grief she closed them again, what did any of it matter anymore if she never saw Mateo again? But something inside her forced her eyes open. Golden torch light bobbed and swayed amongst the branches. She could hear the calls and shouts of the men as they got closer. She turned her tear-stained face to the Mayor. He snarled in almost painful frustration, his fists clenching in anger as he cursed beneath his breath. Then looking up to her, his annoyance cleared. 'I'd do anything for you Lacey.' He whispered. With a blank determined look, he raised the knife and unflinching dragged the point across his cheek. His face opened and the wound began gushing blood, which ran down his neck, disappearing into the fabric of his cloak. He tossed the dagger into the darkness. Lacey stared in mute bewilderment. Just as the first people began to break through the trees he cried out.

'Come! Come quick, I have restrained her.' The Mayor called, his voice high in false panic, as he beckoned the villagers. Who, one by one, as they emerged from the treeline, stopped in surprise at the sight of the dead councilmen and Lacey Emerson tied up before the fire. The ladies clutched their crucifixes in fear, the men halted in their tracks, absorbing the scene. 'I got here too late, she had already killed them. She almost killed me, but I managed to overpower her witchcraft,' the Mayor panted, pulling a handkerchief from his pocket and holding it to his face. Realising what he was doing Lacey closed her eyes and concentrated once more on the fire. *Please* Lacey pleaded internally, *please help me now.*

Pushing her wide body through the circle of villagers Nanny emerged into the clearing. 'Nanny, I'm glad you are here.' the Mayor lied. 'How did you find me?' His question fell away at the sight of her. Her cap had fallen from her head and like Lacey she had blood stains across her dress. They shone a silvery red in the fire light, a blurry smear where she had held a bloody head in her lap. She half stumbled forward towards the Mayor. Her face was a twisted grimace of grief, it shone with pain. In her agony, her features became almost unrecognizable, her mouth distorted, her eyes, two round disks of despair.

'Bella Emerson said you were in the woods sir, then we saw the firelight. Something terrible has happened. She,' she nodded a shaking head at Lacey, 'she's killed him. She took a candlestick to his lovely head,' her words crumbling into a sob.

The Mayors face clenched like a fist, not a muscle moved. 'Speak plainly woman.'

'Master Sebastian sir. He's dead.'

The Mayor dropped his hand from his face. The wound sparkled red like a jewel. He closed his eyes, then whispered the word 'Witch.' None but Lacey heard it, he looked up at her. His pupils eclipsing any white at the edges of his eyes. It was like staring into the opening of the crevasse. The darkness seemed to pull her in. Then addressing the whole crowd and pointing a bony finger at her he cried 'Witch!' The villagers drew their breath in a hiss, like the sound of water poured onto fire. Lacey looked amongst the scornful faces where she finally saw her father. He stared into the fire, his face drawn and sad, his shoulders sagging, his hand's twisted and limp at his sides. Her stomach lurched.

'Murderer!' the Mayor accused, 'child killer!' The crowd, in response to his words, began to jeer and shout. He raised his voice, wet spittle gathered at the side of his mouth. 'Did you design your devilish plans as you baked our bread? Just as your mother did. Sitting beside your sister perhaps. One wonders why she hasn't yet married, maybe the answer is now clear. Is she too a witch?!'

Lacey had stayed silent all this time. Only her eyes moved in their sockets, watching, tracking the Mayor's movement. But now her lips twitched in fury and her nostrils flared white at the mention of Bella. 'It isn't me who is the murderer, but you!' Her voice came out louder than she had expected and all looked at her in shock. The words fell like a stone in water, rippling out through the crowd. They murmured to each other and a few faces turning to the Mayor to see his reaction. She continued, 'it is the Mayor and the men of the council who have crept within the shadows of the village and snatched your daughters from you.' Lacey swallowed, shaking her head. 'There is no danger on Deception Bay, there never has been. He has been taking girls and sacrificing them so that he may obtain the powers of a witch. It is he who is the devil, not my mother, and not I. For years he has spilt the blood of innocents for his own gain. I have been beaten, shot at, bled, bled upon, married and widowed in one night. I'm tired,' she yelled. 'But I was tired before tonight. Tired of living alongside this evil, feeling it move amongst us, invisible as the wind. Burn me upon this fire, tie me by my neck from the Old Oak Tree, send my body to The Island. I no longer care: any fate would be preferable to that which we live in now.'

A strange quiet fell. The noise of the party shifting on their feet and the crackle of the logs burning in the fire, grew louder, expanding to fill the void. The firelit faces of the crowd looked nervous and confused as they absorbed Lacey's accusations. The Mayor stood frozen to the spot, staring at her. Then, with one word, he undid all Lacey had said. 'Witch!' He cried, shattering the silence. The eyes around her seemed to narrow in understanding. The crowd, as though relieved to be presented with a word in which to pour their anger and confusion, began to yell again. It was all too easy for them. In her untamed passion hadn't she revealed herself as a witch? She indeed looked the part, her hair fallen loose, hung wildly around her, her eyes red with tears and fear, her dress stained in her husband's blood.

The word caught like a flame and it spread throughout the villagers. Others cried 'liar,' 'murderer!' And 'string her up!' Some just screamed in hatred, shaking their fists in the air.

'Stop! Please!' She cried, but her voice sounded like a pleading child, 'you are being deceived!' It drowned in the chorus of screams. Then through the crowd came Bella, she stepped free of the jostling throng and made her way to the centre of the clearing. Treading neatly around the corpses. She walked with her back straight and head high, coming to a stop she raised her hand in the manner of a school mistress.

'Enough!' She yelled. And whether it was the shock of her raised voice, or the strangeness of her matronly finger in the air, the crowd obeyed. An unsteady hush fell, once again. Across the clearing her father took a step forward, but then, suddenly hesitant, retreated, returning to stand shoulder to shoulder with the other villagers. Bella's voice rung out clearly.

'I'm a God fearing woman. I know my bible better than most of you,' she said glancing at the Vicar's corpse, 'so I know enough about evil. And I can tell you Lacey speaks the truth. There is an evil in this village, one that has rotted away at the roots of Mayor Abner. A corruption so deep and unholy, I myself could hardly fathom it. But now, I don't know how I could ever have mistaken it. There are, it seems, some people, true of heart, who can spot evil, even when it is most cunningly hidden. That is my sister and I will bear witness to what she is saying.'

Bella paused, smoothing down her skirts before lacing her fingers neatly together. 'But I have lived long enough in this world to understand the weight of a woman's word. Were it gold it would not be enough to buy a cup of flour. I know it isn't the word of two girls alone that will convince you, and I know too there are those among us that have held the truth hidden for years. So, will no man speak for us?' The crowd stayed frozen in silence. Bella slowly turned on her heels, facing behind her, 'will you not speak Father?'

CHAPTER TWENTY NINE

Every eye in the crowd turned to look at Frank Emerson, whose face was a pale mask. His brow glistened white with sweat, his mouth twisted into a pout as he chewed the inside of his cheek. He stared resolutely into the fire. Bella took a step forward.

'Father?' She prompted.

Frank swallowed hard, then slowly shook his head.

'You must be tired,' he said. 'Both of you. The stress is too much for you.' His words quiet and sober. His tone still holding his usual authority. But at his side he rubbed his handkerchief furiously between his fingers, then holding it in both hands he tugged at it, pulling the material taut.

Bella, her voice even and calm, said simply, 'I found red leaves in the folds of your coat.' The words, in the circumstance, seemed so strange and unexpected. Lacey pulled her eyes from Bella for the first time and looked across at her father. Frank frowned at first, then a moment later his expression cleared, and his eyes closed in resignation. 'You should have done your own laundry,' Bella said quietly. 'I didn't think much of them, until Lacey told me those leaves only grow in one place. The Island.'

A small, strangled whimper came from Frank's mouth then, and he held the handkerchief to his lips as though suppressing nausea. Lacey felt the world around her tilt on its axis. She closed her eyes and concentrated on breathing, focusing on each breath. Then, somehow feeling worse, she opened them again.

Bella exhaled, clenching her fists, trying to calm her shaking breaths, 'It isn't for grief but for guilt that we have not been able to speak our mother's name inside our own home for all these years. She was about to expose the truth, and unmask the Mayor wasn't she? And you warned him. Sending her to her death. And now your daughter stands before you to do the same, to expose the ill doings of the same man, in order to prevent the slaughter of more girls. And you stay silent. You have blood under your fingernails Father. Will you not speak?!'

With the handkerchief still clutched tight, Frank's hands dropped to his side, he breathed deeply, and when he spoke again, he didn't stutter. He was calm in his confession. 'I'm sorry,' he said a little above a whisper, his voice hoarse and tight, his mouth dry. He looked at Bella, 'I never ever meant for any of it. I was only trying to protect you two.' Lacey's body began to tremor at hearing his words. 'The Mayor found out your mother was investigating him and he came to me. He told me if I didn't stop her, he would kill you both. He enlisted my help in order to ensure my silence.'

'What help?' Bella demanded. The Mayor, his face rigid with anger, took a step toward Frank, but stopped when he felt the villagers' eyes on him.

Any colour that was left in Frank's face drained away. 'He needed a way to dispose of the bodies. I knew no one would go to The Island. I took his boat out from Deception Bay, we spread rumours about there being danger there so that I wouldn't be seen. I did it to save you two, I had no idea he was planning this.' From the corner of her vision Lacey saw the firelit figures of the villagers recoil in shock. A few with their hands coming up to make the sign if the cross. Some started to cry, soft muted sobs.

'What about mother?' Bella asked. Speaking each word separately as though it caused her pain.

'She could see that the Mayor was corrupt and ill of mind. I begged her not to do anything, but she couldn't be convinced otherwise. She was like you girls, a strong headed woman,' Lacey clenched her teeth so hard her jaw ached. 'When the Mayor discovered she suspected him there was nothing I could do. I knew she was going to unmask him, and God forgive me, I told him. It was only a day later that he confronted her in the church.'

Bella closed her eyes then and spoke with them shut, her voice calm. 'You have aided in the murder of children and allowed your own daughters to live in pain and abject shame. Because of you we thought our own mother a witch. You have wasted Lacey's life marrying her to a scoundrel, and I have wasted mine in service to you.'

The man who stood before her looked much older than his years and achingly tired. The skin around his eyes and mouth hung as though it no longer fit him. The secret that he had held so tightly, had escaped through his lips and left him a hollow shell. He turned for the first time and looked at Lacey, who still hadn't spoken. She hung limply from the ropes, for in her shock she had lost all her strength. Seeing her, his eyes grew wet with tears, he blinked at her.

From very far away she managed the words, 'it was you.' Lacey's mind was back to that day, sitting on Deception Bay. The hooded figure, his awkward gait, the furtive movement of his head. She knew now it was her father, carrying the body of Mary Morgan. The realization cut through her like a knife. Her father stared hopelessly back at her.

Finally, the Mayor spoke. Pulling his gloves off to reveal his white puckered hands. The flesh so pale it shone in the darkness.

'Well, now you know,' he said casually, 'I suppose I can speak plainly. After my wife left you all laughed at me.' His eyes moving around the crowd. 'You won't laugh now. I will be more powerful than you can imagine. Soon, should I wish, I will be able to bring the lake up around you and drown you all. You pathetic, fat, lazy men, who sit perfectly content in your weakness. Never trying, never striving for more.' The crowd stared in horror, without moving, like an army of statues. Their disbelief immobilizing them. 'Whilst your women run wild making a mockery of you. If the girls had been truly faithful, true daughters of God they would have been safe, they would have listened to their parent's warnings. But they never did. They never obey our words. My wife wouldn't obey, this witch wouldn't obey,' he said, pointing at Lacey. 'And neither would her mother. Look at the blood that has been shed because of it. Because of them. I had great plans, my power was to bring true riches to this town. All I have done is for the betterment of the village, but they in their selfishness have caused so much harm.'

'No!' a voice rang out. Lacey looked up. Her father was shaking his head, his eyes red. 'No, you are wrong. This is wrong. I only went along with your plan to protect my daughters. If I had ever suspected you would do this, I would never have stayed quiet. If I had thought you would hurt Lacey, I wouldn't have...' He stopped, his eyes filling with tears. Looking directly at Lacey, he said, 'I'm so sorry.' She stared back at him, unable to focus, his face suddenly unrecognisable. Turning to the Mayor, Frank said, 'your unstoppable pursuit of power has caused this. Don't listen to him,' addressing the crowd, 'it isn't the fault of the women, but his own.'

It was then that the Mayor, in the most natural manner, slowly lowered his hand to rest it upon the hilt of his sword. No one saw him do it, the whole party was watching Frank. Mayor Abner wrapped his fingers around the sword's handle. Looking at him, Frank said honestly 'you were always weak.'

'Enough of this!' the Mayor spat. Turning to face Lacey and whispering an indecipherable prayer, he unsheathed his sword. With horror she saw the glint of the blade as it caught the fire light, it seemed to wink at her. She pulled wildly against her restraints. The Mayor's arm arched high across his body. His yellow eyes stared with a venomous hatred at her, his lined lips reciting the spell. The sword swung down.

With a small, noiseless step to her left, Bella had changed her position. The sword finished its arch with a silent finality. Not one person in the woods moved, their breath halted within their lungs.

Bella stood with a look of stunned realisation on her face, her eyes slowly widening. She blinked twice, as though finally understanding something. And then the blood came. Like a pump it came gushing forth from a yawning opening in her neck. Her hands came up instinctively to her throat. For a moment, in vain, she tried to hold the wound, patting pointlessly at the blood. Within a second it covered every inch of her arms. Someone shrieked and as though moving as one singular form, the crowd shrank back. Bella dropped to her knees and began to keel over.

'No!' Lacey screamed. The fire in response erupted behind her, burning the rope from her wrists, releasing her. Rushing forward, she caught her sister and they both fell to the floor. Bella lay on her back against the cold earth, Lacey cried out as she held her hands over hers. 'No, no Bella. Please!'

Looking up, Bella's eyes were already half glazed, slipping in and out of focus. Her lips parted, then came together again, soundlessly, a small, clear bubble forming between them. She couldn't speak. The ground around her was already soaked. She placed her hand on top of Lacey's. Lacey looked down at her. Their eyes met. 'Please,' Lacey whispered to her helplessly. With her last morsel of energy Bella gave Lacey's hand the gentlest of squeezes. A second later both her arms fell limply to her sides.

Lacey snatched her sister's hands back up and placed them on her chest. She couldn't bear to seem them so lifeless against the cold earth. She shook her head violently and in confusion began to pat at the side of Bella's face, frowning at her in shock. 'Bella? No, no. Bella come back. Bella please come back. Please don't leave me. Please don't leave me alone.' Bella's mouth fell slackly open. Her eyes stared into nothingness. The wound no longer rushed with urgency, instead it pooled lazily around her head. Lacey pulled her up by the back of her neck, into an unnatural sitting position. Bella's body slumped like a child's doll. Lacey couldn't breathe, she gasped, open mouthed, her throat turning to stone. When she was able to pull any air into her lungs, she exhaled it in a scream. The howl ripped through her lungs and tore into the air around her.

Lacey stood up and turned to the Mayor, who stood in shock, a few metres off. The sword still in his hand, blood running freely from it. From deep within her Lacey felt a strange power. The world seemed to slow down and clarify. She breathed deeply as though she was drawing the air from the space around her. Through her feet she could feel the throb and life of the earth below her. It flowed up through her legs. She could feel every drop of water in the clouds above, and the movement of every current on the wind. She could feel the burning intense heat of the fire, and beyond it, the cool wide expanse of the lake. She began, as though she were inhaling, to draw them in to herself. The water, the fire, the earth, the air. Refocusing their energy, until she could feel it pulsating through her. The trees surrounding her leaned a little closer. Their branches creaking.

Lacey, with the movement of pushing him away, threw her arms out towards the Mayor. There was a flash of white, like lightning, which tore through the space between them, rippling the air. Lacey, her face squeezed tight in pain and anger, screamed - the cry erupting from deep within her. Mayor Abner flew violently backwards, his body skidding and finally coming to a stop, crumpled on the floor. Lacey opened her eyes and dropped her hands to her side, panting as though she had been sprinting. Then, in exhaustion, she fell to her knees once more and pulled herself back to Bella, collapsing on her chest.

Frank Emerson who, along with the crowd, had watched with a strange detachment, as though he were in a dream, was, all of a sudden, awake. As though suddenly electrified, he leapt at the Mayor, grabbing him and pulling him to the fire. He fastened his large hands around the man's neck, the ache of the arthritis forgotten in his rage, pushing through the pain he tightened his grip. In one swift movement, he pushed Mayor Abner back into the fire, his wide brimmed hat falling off and skittering away. The Mayor yelled out. Frank, with his arms still fastened around his throat, leant his full weight onto him. Beyond the forest, out of sight, the lake rippled against the shore.

The Mayor's hair caught fire first. Beneath the hat his hair was black, and fine as a child's, combed into a greasy middle parting and tucked behind his ears. It burnt like tissue paper. The golden blaze of light cast shadows of the stunned crowd across the trees. The smell in the air was immediate in its offence. Acrid and poisonous. Then he began to scream at the scorching agony of the flames. His heeled boots kicked at the muddy ground, his fingers scratched and tore at the baker's face, leaving long, angry red marks. But Frank's hold was unflinching. As the Mayor's face burnt and melted away, the shrieks became a different sound altogether, a kind of burbling squeal. Until eventually with a small, wet gasp he stopped fighting and made no sound at all.

Frank released his grip and leant back onto his heels to sit beside the fire. His hands hung beside him, blistered and bloodied, his fingers, from the knuckle down, charred black and without their nails. His look of violent, vengeful anger slipped into empty grief as he turned and on all fours crawled to the body of his daughter. Lacey lay half on top of her still, her arms clasped around Bella's neck. She hadn't bothered to look, even as the Mayor had shrieked and cried, she hadn't lifted her head. But hearing her Frank beside her, she stiffened and sat up. She looked down at her sister's corpse, then up at her father.

'She's dead.' Lacey said in a flat, passionless voice and she watched the words break across his face. Then, with an effort, she stood and limped away. The crowd parted in shocked silence. Her wrists were burnt, her elbow throbbed, her torso thrummed with pain and the heat of a punch could still be felt across her jaw, but she kept walking. She could feel her understanding of the night slip away. The unreality of it. The betrayal of her father. The sudden, jarring, incomprehensible loss of Bella and Mateo. That surely made no sense, she had just seen them, spoken to them, touched them, it was wholly impossible they had stepped so quickly and so brutally to the other side. As she walked away, someone from the crowd kicked something and it skittered into the fire. The wide brimmed, black hat caught alight and was consumed in a moment, the metal buckle glowing golden amongst the flames.

Suddenly from behind her there was a noise. A commotion, men yelling, the sound of their feet upon the ground. She didn't stop to look behind her. There was nothing left for her. The noise grew louder, but she was further from it with every step. Until one voice, above the rest, cut through the others, speaking directly to her.

'Lacey!' It cried. She stopped. She knew that voice. Knew that soft, sing song tone. She turned slowly, her tattered, bloodied wedding dress dragging on the ground beneath her. The crowd staring back and forth at the two of them.

Mateo stood, with one arm slung around young Eli, his body black with mud. In his hair leaves and twigs hung freely amongst the locks. His wide, wet eyes staring at her.

'Lacey.' He whispered.

EPILOGUE

The weak winter sun shone down through the bare trees as Lacey came upon Ma's house. The forest had exchanged its bounty of berries and rich orange leaves, for naked branches. The green and brown foliage had degraded and been consumed by the earth. Now all her feet trod upon was the bare ground and an occasional puddle on the point of freezing over. The air too had changed. Once the wedding had passed the world had slipped quickly into winter and now, only a few months later, Lacey could taste snow on the wind.

She walked slowly, she was tired still. Her grief was exhausting. Though she often slept late in the day and retired sometimes even before the sun had set, she couldn't shake this dull, aching, all-consuming tiredness. It wrapped around her like a thick blanket, muffling her from the rest of the world. She remembered little of the first few days after the wedding. She had hardly left Mateo's bed. She couldn't even remember how she had arrived at his house that night. Someone had carried her, cradling her limp body. Not Mateo; he could hardly stand. Kinch had never found him. The villagers thought he had run away, but a few days later the remains of the commander's body had been discovered. What little the wolves had left of it.

It was in fact Mr Morgan who carried her home. Having seen Lacey swaying at the sight of Mateo, he had stepped forward from the crowd of astonished onlookers and caught her in his arms.

Lacey was plagued by memories of her wedding night. When closing her eyes all she saw was Bella's shocked expression, a scarf of blood hanging from her neck. But her body was healing slowly. Across her stomach the bruising had turned a sickly mustard yellow, with a faint purple, brown centre. She felt a strange fear of it fading altogether and in the madness, that falls in the darkest hours of the night, she would lie in bed and press against the bruises. Pushing her thumb against her tender skin until tears sprouted from her eyes and fell down her cheeks.

She did not eat for the first few weeks. She was rarely awake, and when she was she did not speak. Mateo never once left her side. Time passed and the pain, though unrelenting, lost its initial sting. The grief didn't lessen, merely settled in, and like unhappy bedfellows, they learned to get used to one another. One day when it had been raining for hours and showed no signs of stopping, she lay in Mateo's bed, absentmindedly touching the window. Her fingertips tracing the raindrops on the other side. The water began to gather itself at her touch, forming a line behind her finger. Following her every movement it snaked after her as she moved her hand back and forth. Beside her she felt Mateo stir, and looking back she saw him smile. And as though remembering something she had long forgotten, Lacey smiled weakly back. The next day when she woke, she did not cry straight away.

A month later Lacey returned to the bakery. She had tentatively pushed the door open, nervous of what pain her return might conjure. Then she had stopped in the doorway in surprise. She could not see the countertop for gifts. Sacks of sugar, jars of honey, boxes of tea. Bunches of cut yellow roses, dried now but still bright, tied with black bows. Lacey turned to Mateo confused.

'They're from the villagers.' He said, smiling, taking her gently by the hand and leading her in. She walked forward reaching out to touch them. 'A gesture I think, of good will. Or apology perhaps.' She had stared at them in disbelief. On the kitchen table lay a slip of paper reading *'The first meeting of the New Council of Lower Lynch. Town Hall Wednesday evening at 8.'*

Lacey had sat at the back of the town hall beside Mateo. She wore black, but no cap. And indeed, a few of the council women wore no cap either. It was the strangest sight to see the ladies, some far older than her, capless in public. There were seven new councillors, four of whom were women. One of whom was Mrs Miller, who nodded to Lacey as she sat. The meeting concerned mainly the division of the harvest and talk of investing in new fishing boats. But at the end, the head of the council, a middle-aged woman called Mrs Lockhart stood and addressed the crowd. 'We are grateful for all those who have volunteered for the New Council. What has happened in our village will have repercussions for years to come. There has been great injustice done here, injustice that needs to be addressed. And a lot we still don't understand. Word of what happened has spread far. There are questions still to be asked by wider bodies from further afield. We will have to deal with those in time. But rest assured we will do so together.' There was a long silence, until the lady spoke again. Taking off her spectacles and placing them on the desk. 'And as a last point, commemorative graves have been erected in the churchyard, for each murdered girl. As well as one for the falsely accused Alice Emerson.' Mrs Lockhart then turned and looked at Lacey, the rest of the room turning too. Lacey swiftly averted her eyes to her boots, but not before seeing that many of them had smiled.

The winter wind blew through the woods, tossing a few dried leaves across Ma's porch. Lacey raised her fist to knock on the crooked, wooden door, expecting to hear Ma speak before she reached it, instead she heard a loud crack from the back of the house. Walking slowly round she found, to her astonishment, Ma, standing beside a pile of freshly cut wood, axe in hand. With a heaving effort, she pulled the weapon above her head, the shawl falling about her shoulders, revealing arms the size and look of chicken legs. The upswing threatened to topple the old woman over, and Lacey instinctively stepped towards her, but knowing better, she stopped herself. Gripping the handle tightly Ma hauled it down where, with momentum, it fell in a heavy crack, breaking the wood. She stood a moment, axe in place and sighed with satisfaction, before levering it out and leaning it against the stump.

Pulling a handkerchief from somewhere within her tattered robes, and without looking up, she said, 'hello there Lacey.'

'Hello Ma.'

'It has been a while,' said the old women, patting the cloth along her brow. 'You have been a little scared to see me I think.' She leant backwards and perched her tiny self on the tree stump.

'Yes,' said Lacey sitting on a fallen log, 'I have been.'

'I understand.'

The two sat across from one another, Ma with her eyes closed, feeling the wind cool her face, Lacey, her head down, digging her fingers into the rotten wood beneath her.

'Today was the last day of Frank's trial. News came on a boat across the lakes,' said Lacey.

She pushed her thumb through the soft bark, a family of wood lice scuttled out and hurried away. 'He has admitted to using the Mayor's boat to take the remains out from Deception Bay, to The Island. He confessed that they invented the rumour of the beach being dangerous in order to prevent his being discovered. Even allowing a few of the girls to wash up in order to support their lie. He will spend the rest of his life behind the walls of Faulks Prison. The judge won't sentence him to death, he says that too much blood had already been spilt.'

'That is true. Did you not want to go to see him sentenced?'

'He called for me, sent me letters, but I cannot see him. I don't think I could bear it. Besides with managing the bakery alone I'm too busy. I haven't the money nor the time to go across the lakes on a whim.'

'Aren't you the wealthiest woman in all the Lakelands? Aren't you the sole recipient to the Abner fortune?'

'All that man had is soaked in blood.' Lacey sighed deeply, 'I cannot touch a piece of it. It sits in the bank behind bars, like Frank.'

'Very well my girl, you will know what is best. And, how are you?'

For a moment Lacey nodded and attempted a smiling reply, but her face quickly creased in sadness, her hands coming up, covering her eyes. 'I miss her, Ma. I miss her every minute.' Wiping a tear away she continued, 'sometimes I can go a little while thinking of other things, then suddenly I cannot breathe for missing her. I can feel her absence within me, as though she were carved away. It feels... I feel, empty.'

Ma's head bobbed up and down in understanding.

'I'm afraid there will never be happiness again Ma.'

'There will be, but don't worry about that now. If I were your doctor I would say to you, my dear, you have a broken heart. You are right, she is gone, your heart will never be the same again. But it will heal, not in the same shape as it was before, a little crooked, a few more scars perhaps. But it will heal. It isn't a broken ankle or a cut finger, or even a bullet wound. This is deeper than all of those. So, give yourself time. It isn't easy, I know. But the sun rises every morning and one day, when you aren't even expecting it, happiness will rise with it.'

Lacey sniffed and stared at the ground with watery eyes, 'I'm proud of her, she was so brave.'

Ma nodded and pulling herself to standing answered, 'oh yes, she was brave that one. A very brave girl, you are both brave girls.' Then, as though correcting herself, Ma said, 'You are a brave woman.' Her eyebrow raised slightly, 'I hear some villagers are talking of something you did. A flash, or a blast of energy? Others say they only saw you push him.'

'I don't know. It's like a dream now, a terrible dream. I did feel something, and things have been happening to me recently. I have... changed. I feel something new, something powerful.' She looked down at her hands, then sighed. 'But what does it matter? Whatever this power is, I didn't summon it when it counted, when Bella needed me. I'm not brave. I wasn't even brave enough to let her die peacefully. She died in my arms whilst I screamed her name and pleaded her not to leave me.' Tears swam in her eyes at the memory of it, 'I'm not strong Ma. I'm not this powerful witch.'

Ma shrugged, 'Perhaps not. Perhaps none of it is true. Perhaps it was just writing in a book, we have seen what happens when man takes too seriously that which has been written in a book hundreds of years before. You know your mother wasn't a witch Lacey. She was just a woman. A woman who refused to stay silent when she saw evil. Maybe you aren't a great witch, maybe you are just a girl.' Ma narrowed her eyes and squeezed her little hand into a fist. 'Then if so my dear, be proud, for you have shown more strength and courage than any book could prophesy. It is because of you that there is no evil left in the village. Take pride Lacey. There is nothing so brave as being yourself.'

The wind blew and the branches overhead creaked in response. Pulling herself up with the handle of the axe Ma said, 'and you will need to be brave, for word has spread far. Now is when the real danger comes. We have a lot of work to do.'

'What do you mean?' Lacey was confused. Ma walked towards the hut. 'Ma?' Lacey called after her.

The old woman absent-mindedly waved a thin hand at Lacey, as though patting her away. 'Be calm now child. It is only the beginning.' Lacey stared at her, wide eye. Ma hobbled towards the door, 'come Lacey, I have tea in the pot, and it needs drinking.'

Lacey stood a moment looking out at the forest, then followed the old woman into the little wooden hut as the crooked, crumbling door swung gently closed. A cold wind, come in from the coast, whistled through the trees, causing their bare branches to shake. Behind them, though it was only early afternoon, the winter sun, in a haze of milky yellow, began slowly to set.

The End

Printed in Great Britain
by Amazon

34754207R00195